About the Author

CHARLIE SMITH is the author of six novels and seven books of poetry. Five of his works have been named *New York Times* Notable Books. His numerous awards, grants, and fellowships include the Aga Khan Prize, the Levinson Prize, the J. Howard and Barbara M. J. Wood Prize, a Guggenheim Fellowship, and a grant from the National Endowment for the Arts. His writing has appeared in numerous magazines and journals, including *The New Yorker, The Paris Review, Harper's, The New Republic,* the *New York Times,* and *The Nation.* He lives in New York City and Key West.

Three Delays

Also by Charlie Smith

Word Comix

Women of America

Heroin and Other Poems

Cheap Ticket to Heaven

Before and After

Chimney Rock

The Palms

Crystal River (Storyville, Crystal River, Tinian)

Indistinguishable from the Darkness

The Lives of the Dead

Shine Hawk

Red Roads

Canaan

Three Delays

A Novel

Charlie Smith

HARPER PERENNIAL

NEW YORK • LONDON • TORONTO • SYDNEY • NEW DELHI • AUCKLAND

HARPER PERENNIAL

No person, place, or exact situation in this book ever existed on earth before, including (despite their names) all states, cities, towns, tribes, oceans, parks, and general zones.

HarperCollins books may be purchased for educational, business, or sales promotional use. For information please write: Special Markets Department, HarperCollins Publishers, 10 East 53rd Street, New York, NY 10022.

FIRST HARPER PERENNIAL EDITION PUBLISHED 2010.

Designed by Justin Dodd

Library of Congress Cataloging-in-Publication Data is available upon request.

ISBN 978-0-06-185945-8

10 11 12 13 14 OV/RRD 10 9 8 7 6 5 4 3 2 1

To Daniela

Acknowledgments

Portions of this book have appeared in earlier versions in *Five Points, The Georgia Review, Narrative,* and *Northwest Review.* Thanks to the editors.

Part I

NAPOLEON OF THE CAMPAGNA

I'd returned from Indonesia the year before, sunburned, with a slight drug habit, sporting a fungus under my fingernails, and after receiving my draft classification as an undesirable, I spent six months wandering around Europe with my high school friend Henry Devine, an ex–Green Beret medic who'd been shipped loco out of Vietnam. One night, stoned in Istanbul, shortly after his hair caught fire and I put it out with my own tender hands—as we lay out on our hotel balcony looking east toward the smoky lights of the Bazeen district—Henry put his head on my shoulder—I could smell his scorched hair, a smell like burned peacock feathers—and said, "Are you ever getting back together with Alice?"

I was taken slightly off guard. Her name hadn't come up in a while. "No," I lied, "I think I'd rather poach in my own spit." Alice and I had been childhood sweethearts, lovers at a young age, but we had broken up—exploded, convulsed, detonated, kaboomed up, was more like it—due to our scorpion death fight tendencies and some ugly business in which she and her sister had me arrested for malfeasance both general and specific. I say broken up, but that wasn't the name for it. Both of us had gone right on being together, at a distance. Together in our minds. Sometimes she was in the back of my mind, sometimes she was in the front. She was always in there somewhere, circulating. "She's living on a music farm, isn't she?"

"That's what they call it, yeah."

"Rock and Roll Ranch—that one, right?"

"With her husband."

"We know him, don't we?"

"He was in high school."

"I remember. I don't think he's ready to give up."

"Oh, he'll be tired of her soon."

"What about *her*?"

He gave me a big smile, one of the ones filled with the knowledge of oncoming delights, and said nothing.

"Come on."

"Don't worry."

"You mean there's such a powerful charge between us that no mere human complication can keep us apart. Some nonsense such as that?"

"You two are bound."

"Bound?"

"Sure. Meant for each other. It's a matter of the spirit."

"Ah me."

But I liked the whole fate thing, or thought I did. Destiny—the idea of having one took away responsibility, even accountability, which I wanted in a deep and desperate way. According to this philosophy, it didn't matter what you did, how you screwed up—things worked out the way they were supposed to. It was because I believed so completely in the opposite of this that I was attracted to it as a philosophy. What I actually believed was that every little thing I did had meaning and the meaning was sinister. I saw myself as a fuck-up beyond belief. So I liked to hear that I was in some way off the hook, which is what Henry's appraisal seemed to mean.

We took a cab down to the American Express office and I called Alice again. She was home this time. But it was the middle of the night—maybe not the middle, but after her bedtime. I got her sleepy voice. "Alice," I said breathlessly, "how are you?"

"Billy," she said. Then a pause. Then: "What sordid place are you calling from now?"

"The nose of the Orient. And what do you mean now? I haven't called you."

"Yes you have. You call all the time. Where are you?"

"I'm in Istanbul, at the American Express office. I'm here with Henry."

"In Istanbul you decided to beg my forgiveness?"

"Yeah. How about it?"

"I'm asleep."

"What time is it?"

She told me, but I didn't catch it. Then she said, "I'm married—did you know that?"

"Henry told me."

"You probably figured that makes it safe to call me. You probably think marriage has quieted me down and made my thoughts of you generous and sweet-minded. You probably think I'm calm now."

"Not that calm."

"I wish you were standing in the doorway right this minute. I'd shoot you and claim I thought it was a burglar."

"What about if it's an emergency?"

"Is it?"

"Somewhat."

"I expect they've caught on to you. You can't even fool a bunch of Turks."

"I'm not trying to fool anybody."

"That's good because you sure aren't fooling me."

"I have a troubled spirit."

"You do not."

"I do too. Henry and I were just talking about it. My spirit is wan and troubled. I am one of the poor in spirit, naturally and chronically."

"You are actually a puerile liar who's been reduced by unfettered drug use to an infantile state. That's not the same as being poor in spirit."

"Actually I've perked up. I bought a couple of yellow finches."

"Are you just spouting whatever comes into your head?"

"Yes. I am a desperate case, troubled and in love with a mean woman."

"Well, you should put her behind you."

"I would if I could."

"Billy, don't start all that again. You can't come around here with that business."

"I'm not, I'm not. I've come around with some other business."

"Which is what?"

"I want to marry you."

"Oh come on. You do not. You want to stop feeling bad, that's what you want."

"I don't feel bad. I feel better than I ever did. Henry and I are having a wonderful time. It's out of the joy of our adventure that I'm calling you. I thought of you, Alice."

7

These desperate acts were like playing the slot machine—sometimes you hit. It was never personal. A pause appeared then, both of us taking a little break. It was during this pause that something in her shifted, something I had nothing to do with. "I'm not so mean," she said.

I waited a beat, waited for the distant drum to strike, for the fires on the hill to be lit. "No, you're not. Not always."

"I took David out duck hunting last week."

"David your husband? "

"Yes."

"It's not duck season."

"We went up to that preserve you took me to that time."

"The one where it's all rigged."

"Yes. He wanted to go so I took him. I felt so sad."

"Did they still have that kid at the top of the chute throwing the ducks?"

"It was terrible. But David loved it. He shot twenty ducks."

"A real Daniel Boone."

"You sound a little spazzy. Are you drunk?"

"No—just coming down from the hash—that's why we're here—to get some drugs—but not really drunk. It's 4:30 in the afternoon. Henry and I just had breakfast."

"I miss Henry."

"You want to talk to him?"

"Yes, I do."

I called him over and handed the receiver to him, presenting it like a gift. "You're a mess," he said to me. "Hey, sweetheart," he said into the receiver.

Then I went outside and hung around in the street, feeling appeased. I couldn't help it, simply talking to her, getting her attention, made me feel better. I knew I was an idiot, knew I was hapless and hopeless, all that, but it didn't matter. She was still in it too, I could tell; I could hear it in her voice. I knew right then, standing on the low curb of a Turkish street, that there would be another round, and I knew everything that was to come in the stupid way you think you do and later say to someone that you did, but it's only what you are telling yourself. "Right here," I said to myself, "on this street, I see it all." The street ran straight as a wire into a dusty distance. You could follow this street right into the heart of Asia. Eventually it would dwindle to nothing, an erasure, a fade into the stony grass of a continent. And what then? The end? The miracle of my experience with Alice was that her street, the Alice street in the Alice town, never played out. And what a poignant, interesting street it was, saucy little street with its flags in the sycamores and its taffy shops, its abattoir and munitions factory. Its sad-eyed clerks taking a smoke out front. Three times now, as I remembered it, her street had almost disappeared. But here it was, as each time before, revivified, lively. Maybe she had a bunch of streets. Maybe the supply was endless. Or maybe this was the way of true love. And here I was, on it again, set upright, this Istanbul West Asia reality avenue nothing to Alice's boulevard, the short man switching flies off a blood-streaked white side of lamb with a beech sprig, the old woman tapping the fount of a solid gold coffee urn the size of a coffin, soldiers scratching—none of it of real significance, set against the open avenue, the Alice avenue, appearing before me now.

"What a pathetic way to look at things," Henry said later, shaking his head.

"You miss the deep resolving power of the image."

"Not really."

"You're the one promoting it."

"Yes."

"It is one of those storybook romances."

"*Tales of the Darkside*, yes, exactly."

This was just like Henry. Wither when the facts drew nigh.

"You're the one made me think of it," I said.

"Nah. I just caught the wave."

He was lying, but it didn't matter. We were on a ferry crossing the Bosphorus. From a loudspeaker a heavily accented voice droned in English, constantly referring to "the sights." Sites or sights, I wasn't sure which he meant. I thought of a Turkish novelist I wanted to read, but I couldn't remember his name. Morty Wietz, my AID doctor friend in Indonesia, had read one of his books, a complex story of many levels, disaster run through heartrending adventures and transmogrified eventually into a sadder, wiser life—a story like my own, I thought at the time, my future story. The harbor was filled with treasure, the guide voice said, Persian galleys and Roman triremes and Russian battleships. "They ought to drain this cesspool," Henry said. "I don't believe a word of this crap!" he shouted. The night had unnerved him. He hated himself for loving boys so. "The hell with this," he said loudly. A soldier in a tan and black leather uniform swung a machine gun against his hip, jiggling it like an insect he had control of, and ignored him. Henry had forced me into coming on the boat with him. He wanted to veer off the line of travel. Compose himself out on the open water. "Unkink," he said.

"A tour boat?" I wanted to head home, right now.

"She's not getting out of her marriage."

"Sure she is."

"No. She said for me to tell you."

"Yeah? Tell me what exactly?" I felt defensive, which was one of my oldest feelings in matters concerning Alice.

"She said, 'Tell Billy that I am not leaving my marriage. So don't come around.' "

" 'Don't come around'—she said that?"

"Yes, she did. Those exact words."

"The smirk too?"

"No, I added that myself. I think it goes well with it, though, don't you?"

"I thought you said she belonged to me."

"You occupy a permanent place in her heart."

"You were the one who said we were bound to each other. That's your word—bound."

"You are."

"Then what part does her husband play? Scorekeeper? Extra dick?"

"He's on the way out—I'm telling you. But she's an honorable woman—she can't offer anything until he goes."

"She's not an honorable woman. Neither of us is honorable."

Henry grinned, his face splitting like a melon. "That's the charm of you two."

We were thinkers, Alice and I, ruminators, obsessors, people who brooded. You could see her out in somebody's backyard sitting Indian-legged on a wall with a cup of tea cooling beside her, thinking about something. Everybody had that picture of her. Some vengeance or pilferage she was conjuring up probably. Everybody knew that too. And me out on the lawn pacing. Both of us—you could tell this simply by looking at us—were nervous about life. Something, our faces said, was about to get us, something powerful. This was an overwhelming fact, to us. So we sat off to the side pondering, trying to figure out what to do. Like the operators of some internal star shield defense system, we endlessly processed data, sorting through the incoming material, searching the sky for the missile aimed at our hearts. We always expected it. We were afraid it was already in flight and locked onto us. And we were each other's (only) relief from such a difficult, never-ending job.

"I got to get out of here," I said.

"You'll have to wait until we dock."

"Then I'm getting out of here."

"Home?"

"Yeah."

But it didn't work out that way. We got diverted, doubly. Fifty kilometers west of Istanbul, at the end of a night we spent sleeping in a barn off the highway to Greece, we were robbed. I waked in the earliest light, in light the color of the pale blue sea, to see other men standing up out of the hay straw. I hadn't noticed them during the night. As I lay there, thinking of Alice a little but thinking mostly of the calmness of the morning and of a Turkish family I'd seen standing by a river, of the way the father swung the little boy in his arms, I saw a man crossing the barnyard carrying Henry's black and white-striped satchel. The man jumped into a small flatbed truck and sped away up a dirt track between some bare gray hills.

I waked Henry and we got in the car and followed him. The

Citroen could take the road, which was stubbed with rocks and barely a lane wide, but it had to take it slow. The man lost us in the distance. We caught a glimpse of him once as the road climbed on a switchback toward the top of a naked hill, but then he was gone down the other side and we didn't see him again. We stopped at the hilltop and looked about us at a cracked and forlorn landscape. The gaps between distant hills seemed places where the land had sagged, and the fields, washed halfway up their sides, were stony and depleted, roughed up as if the people who farmed them hated them and had done what they could to strip them of their dignity. Here and there small stone houses were scattered about like clots of refuse. We could see a road, maybe it was the road the robber had fled on, and a couple other tracks branching off from it. I felt a strange desolate exhilaration, like some strung-out romantic poet or wasted individual. I asked Henry what he thought. "Maybe give up?"

"Shit no," Henry said. "My passport's in the bag, and the money."

To me it all seemed replaceable. Maybe because the gear was Henry's and not mine, but I think more likely because it had nothing to do with Alice. I had called her again, and though this time she wouldn't talk to me, I felt in my gut a sense of her complicity, her willingness to re-fire the old furnaces. I was active again—so was she—we knew it. So what, getting burglated?

Henry got out of the car. He walked a couple steps down the road, dragging his leg as if this episode had hurt him physically, and stood looking across the landscape. Some late flowering bushes drooped beside the road, asters or fleabane, some kind of roseate flower, pale, maybe slightly purple. He plucked a sprig and switched it against his leg. I gave him time to be by himself, to get over it. "You get over it, Henry," I said softly, speaking to the steering wheel. He turned then and looked at me with a sad and forsaken expression on his face, the motherless child look that only Americans give each other, and only when they have realized once again that it is a hostile world after all.

We never caught up with the robber. The two days we chased him were futile, we wound up exhausted, arguing, sitting sadly in the car in a village square drinking acidic yellow wine, arguing about who was quicker on his feet mentally, our eyes flashing, hating each other and hating the world, and for a while it looked so bad I thought we would break apart for good, end the friendship, and gladly.

In Venice not long after this Henry got sick and we had to get up in the middle of the night to find a doctor. The hotel manager directed us and we went up some smelly stairs by a canal and waked a little man in a New York Knicks T-shirt who was angry and sharp in manner, but who told us to come in. Henry lay on a couch in his office while the man probed him. He had a pain in his side that turned out to be appendicitis. The doctor took him to the hospital by boat. I rode with him, and despite Henry's pain and distress, I found it lovely to be riding at night through the canals of Venice.

It was very quiet and the wind picked at the surface of the water and lifted my hair. I smelled the sea, which seemed like some dark and kindly companion traveling along with us. The first floors of the buildings were dark, but in upper stories lights burned and I wondered what the people up at this hour might be doing, and wondered if they were men thinking about women they loved and couldn't get to, or women thinking about their marriages, about whether or not they would stay with their husbands or leave to return to their old true loves, and then I took Henry's hand, which was hot from the fever, and I held it while the boat ran smoothly on along the canal to the hospital and the troubles in Turkey seemed far behind us. I felt a deep tenderness for him, as if we had been married many years.

The appendix came out smartly—scooped out like a melon ball, Henry said later—but an old East Asian fever caught up with him and he nearly died. They kept him in the hospital for two weeks, then he was moved to a recovery house over on the bayside in back of the barrier islands. It was a pretty, monolithic pale blue brick place, his part of it a room on the second floor looking out over a paved courtyard toward one of the islands, maybe the Lido, or was it the cemetery island? Henry thought he was looking at the cemetery. His fever lingered for three months.

I moved into a small apartment I sublet from a man I met at the American Express office. He was pinning the rental notice to the bulletin board when I came up to him. The place was a studio that overlooked a small canal the color of daiquiris. A narrow stone sidewalk ran along one side of the canal, and shops were set back from a pint-sized, cluttered street on the other. A trattoria served fish dishes and made sandwiches that I took with me to the hospital every day. A diesel mechanic in the nearby boatyard told me where to get drugs—from some Pakistani men who were studying architecture at the university. Or from friends of theirs. I'd go over to their apartment and get stoned and lie on the floor listening to Armed Forces radio, polka hour, and a strange western swing program that occasionally seemed to be offering subliminal messages to me. Time was a small boy playing with stones at the edge of the sea, as they say.

Fall gave up and handed itself in to winter. I began to write poems, which is what I always wanted to do. I started calling Alice every day, but she wouldn't speak to me. "I can't talk to you," she'd say, and we'd sit there in silence a couple of minutes listening to the space wind blow through the lines. Then I'd hang up. She waited for me to hang up. I sent her Henry's number at the hospice and she called him; she didn't have any trouble talking to him. I could tell every time I came into his room if he had talked to her, it was like that. She told him things to tell me. They were simple adventures-in-her-garden type things which strung me out but half satisfied me too. She said the zinnias were as tall as her head. Said hail broke the stalks down and she had to pick all the flowers in one day. "Her sister came over and set up a card table out on the paved road and sold them for a dollar a bunch," Henry said. "That's nice isn't it?"

Yes, I said, it was.

She said they were eating hot cucumber pickles she'd put up in the summer. And the tomatoes and the gleaming beans, eating those too. Every day a feast, she said, West Miami backcountry style. I pictured her offering a bean to her husband, then changed that and pictured her sister getting the bean, but I couldn't hold it and went back to her husband. It wrenched my insides to imagine this, but I couldn't help it. I could see her husband grinning at her, his embouchure gleaming like a licked spot. It was just life, I knew that, mixed up and confusing as it always is, and he was probably wondering if he'd done the right thing by marrying her—how could he not wonder this, married to such a woman, this woman—but he had been willing to stand up for her before God and man, which I had been unprepared to do, and now he was the one getting up glumly or with a heart filled with joy from the breakfast table, leaning across the oatmeal dregs to give her a kiss. I cringed a little. It wasn't guilt exactly, the cringe—I don't believe I felt much guilt—it was a kind of existential shudder, a slight allergic reaction to pain and truth, to the helplessness all of us feel before our desires, as sad and ridiculous as those desires so often are, an acknowledgment of fallibility and general human dumbness, and for once, for a moment, a clear sight, a glance I mean into the irrepressible and terrifying future awaiting us all, that made me wince.

I saw this for a second. Did the horn player, her hubby, see anything? Probably not. Or if he did he was not disheartened. He was a man without pathology—as I understood him—which is what I aspired to be. This aspiration was what drew Alice and me together—one thing: we both wished to be normal, in this sense, and raged because we weren't. We had plenty of pathology. But the jazz player? What would happen to him? He would live, he would go on to fame and the earthly version of happiness, you could tell. In Venice I thought about this and drank the hard-skinned north Italian wine and sat in an osteria watching soccer games on a television that was set on a wine crate at the end of the bar. She said she had a freezer full of black-eyed peas packed in plastic sacks. The tomatoes, whole, peeled, and red as paint, looked naked and helpless sitting on a white plate. Like little skinned heads, she said. Henry said her husband was often away.

"Away where?"

"Don't worry," Henry said, "the collapse is on schedule."

Henry's fever was actually a disease, a malaria-like compilation he'd picked up in Indochina that made him often stuporous and ignorant, like a man coming off drugs. I'd arrive at eleven in the a.m. to find him snoozing, dribble on his chin, the window open to the Venetian winter which was cold and ice-strewn and muttered miserably in the naked wisteria vines covering the nailed-back shutters. I'd sit with him, try to talk, but he'd be half deranged, lassitudinous with thoughts of mischances back home—he'd flunked out of college and wound up in the army; he wanted to get married; he wanted to be a doctor, not an ex-medic—and I'd fall asleep over my book and dream he was dying.

It was my season of failing to save the dying in my dreams. Henry, my father, Mother occasionally, often Alice—I dreamed of and couldn't save them—and someone like myself too, some substitute character dream central came up with, a skinny boy whom I discovered crying into his hands in the bus station, a pox riddled boy who shrank at my touch. I couldn't do anything for any of them and this scared me. It was too much like life. I waked up crying sometimes, sweaty in the torn armchair. I'd talk at Henry's laid out form—*You can never tell, can you, Henry, what might happen?*—and he'd lie there feigning death, which I appreciated, letting that be his answer, his face white, sweat like a fuzz on him. I'd lift his hand to my lips and kiss his fingers one by one. He'd look up at me, turn onto his back with a sigh and look at me, an extremity of tenderness filling his face, and say, "I want to live a life filled with regret." I thought it was a beautiful thing for a twenty-two-year-old man to say.

Then I'd dial Alice's number and listen to the phone ring. When she answered I'd hang up—after a minute of silence—and then sit in the cold room, dumb like some breakdown case, stunned by the power of my longing, gasping, trembling with emotion, her voice having done it to me—the telephone ringing in her house near the monastery—her voice helloing over the ocean, stronger than the winter and the cold sea breeze, stronger—more powerful, more alive, carrying more Billy-referential life, that is—than anything else I could possibly find in this world outside my own fucked up family. It would knock me out. I'd go down on my knees beside the bed and dial her number again and crouch there with the phone cupped like a conch against my ear and listen. Three rings, four rings, sometimes five rings, and then her voice. She wouldn't talk to me; I tried to get her to but she wouldn't.

"You're nuts," Henry said. "You have to do something about yourself."

I thought so too.

In the courtyard there were withered orange trees in big cloisonne pots. Spindly, neglected trees. The ungathered oranges were shriveled, apricot brown like eclipsed moons. I was drawn to them and went down there, passing the padrone's office, where an old man sat watching TV variety shows laughing a menacing and totally insane laugh, and picked the oranges. Alice and I had once driven up to some groves near Kissimmee and picked bushels for gifts. It was something we came up with to keep from driving each other insane, a way of taking a break from fighting. But out in the country—a wilderness, Bessarabia, to us—we'd fought on and told each other we hated each other, spitting words as if we were excoriating a despicable enemy. She'd bitten into a orange then mashed it hard against my chest, against my white shirt, and laughed hatefully with a coldness in her eyes as if she wished it was a dagger, and I had slapped her and pushed her out of the car and we'd rolled on the dusty, grassy ground until, looking up to noise that had been going on for a while, we saw (we were stopped on a farm road by some mango trees) a truck full of farmworkers right ahead of us blocked by our car and honking the horn to get by, and all of them glowering at me, the woman-beater, as if I should be dragged out and hanged. Later we made exhausted, famished love in a ditch that smelled of oil and mud and sun-burned grass. We pulled the heavy grass stalks up over us like a blanket and supped on each other's bodies, lingering like thirsty beasts in the low, damp places. And slept a while like babies and waked to the sound of bees buzzing around the oranges. I thought of this as I picked the fruit. Little wizened, eyeless heads. I split one with my thumb, and the smell, a bit of it, was still there, the sweet homey citrus smell; it was so emotionally powerful tears came to my eyes. I was only twenty-two and already I wanted to live my whole life over, exactly as it was, not change a thing. For one second there, holding an orange in Venice, I felt so happy to be alive, to be myself, to have done what I had done that I wanted to replay all of it, same style, same gas, over and over. I never had a feeling like that before, and I haven't had one exactly like it since. Who knows why the sweet moment comes or when it will arrive?

Upstairs, Henry, roused to his feet, stood in the window, a bright blue scarf around his neck, talking into the phone. Talking to Alice. The connection ran unbroken for three thousand seven hundred thirty-two miles, as I figured it, across the Atlantic Ocean, over the plains of Portugal, across Spain, including the Catalan desert and the Pyrenees, over the Alps and the Riviera, by Milan and Genoa and the industrial smokestacks of northern Italy, through the marshes and canals, down the Adriatic littoral, to Venice—where it snapped off, fell forty feet short. No wire available to string between me and the last relay post. It wasn't that she didn't want to speak to me, she said that. It was that she was married. She wanted to be honorable. "She doesn't want to have to lie to her husband," Henry said. "You can understand that."

"Yeah I can," I said, "but I don't care."

I did care, but I couldn't help it.

"That's what all you guys say," Henry said.

"All you guys who?"

"All you junkies and liars."

You're misrepresenting me, I told him, but he wasn't. I went out into the town and picked up a woman in a bar. She had a boy's haircut, slender hands, and an Australian accent. We went back to her hotel and made love. There was something undistinguished about the lovemaking, something stupid and careless and unresolved, as if the whole thing was a query lost in a post office. The two of us were like crippled people. When it was over I went out in my naked body onto the balcony and stood in the cold rain thinking about Alice.

Those days in conversation Henry would stop, he'd drift off, lose the thread and then he'd be staring past me out the window, a sad look on his face as if just outside they were saying something terrible about him, people he trusted were, and there was nothing he could do about it. His father was dead and his mother was an island of corpulence uprisen in a bed on Moraine Street in West Miami—there was no one to come see about him. The doctor told me he was getting worse, which was an unhappy surprise even though I could see for myself he wasn't getting better. I expected him to get better no matter how he looked and he looked like a man who had been shut up too long in a damp place. His eyelids sagged and his face was puffy and the color of oatmeal. He talked sometimes about Vietnam, but it was always stories about the Montagnards, whom he said were arrogant people without hope for the future, people who would be swept away and crushed by time. He was very bitter about it, as if they had done him great harm. He'd say something cruel—"They were always mocking their children," for example—"Bastards," he'd say, and then he'd look surprised, as if he'd shocked himself by thinking this way, and then his face would change, it would seem to fall apart, and a sad expression would appear and he would look away. He was a man who had never wanted to think a bad thought about anyone, and now he thought badly about everyone.

I went out and sent a telegram to Alice. They didn't drive out to the house bringing the little yellow sheets with strips of typing pasted to them, they didn't do that anymore; they called you on the telephone. I figured she would take a call from a stranger. I wrote, "Henry grave. Come immediately." The operator understood the word grave, but only as a place, not as a situation. There was really no need to explain it to him other than humanness—that we both were human and it was always a good idea to get a connection going—but I tried, and was able to get it across with the help of one of the Pakistani architects, who spoke Italian. The architect had become friendly and visited Henry sometimes in the hospice. He was a big help, not only with drugs. He explained the difference to the operator, who when he got it smiled happily. "O-*kay*," he said, and went off to send the wire.

I walked out into the street ahead of the architect—Hanif was his name—and leaned over a stone parapet looking at the canal. Out in the big canals the lagoon, the sea, washed up into the buildings. You could look into the first floors of houses and palaces and see the tide surging across, slapping softly against stucco walls. It was just the sort of thing I hated, cold water coming in—as a child I'd dreamed of cold floods, the bedroom filling slowly, no place to escape to, drowned vermin floating—and it reminded me of TV pictures of Mississippi floods, not the crowd-pleasers of houses drifting in the current, but the others, the photos that showed some sad farm-town fellow looking at the yard of mud the river had deposited in his living room, the way you felt sorry and aggravated at the guy, sorry for his loss and aggravated because he didn't know any better than to put his house so close to such an untrustworthy body of water.

I felt this way about Henry—as if he had put his house next to untrustworthy water, meaning me—and I meant to own up to this, and offer to recede, but when I got back to the hospice he appeared to be dead. He lay shut-eyed on his back with the gold coverlet pulled up to his chin, tucked under the jowls as if it had been gently stuffed there. His face was smooth and cleaned of sweat, impeccable in the way dead faces are, and I thought, as a large area inside my chest I didn't know I had access to gave way—*He's gone.* The mansion of childhood was swept suddenly away, that's how it felt. Tears started in my eyes and I stumbled toward the bed. I may have said something, I don't remember, some evocation or his name, whatever the drug-addled say at what they think is a time like this. There was a harsh and accelerating jolt inside, like a car hitting the gas, and then loneliness and desolation boiled in the space that was opening behind whatever was leaving and I was terribly angry. The wallpaper and then the wall, the house, all of it was going. The place, the era. Something clutched really hard and let go. I sensed my own faith—ex-preacher boy son of a preacher faith—hiss and let go. It was that dramatic. Henry's face was a human face, a finer, leftover, untroubled version of himself, but what had slipped away from his body was not a soul, not some immaculate wisp, but animal, feral, the bestial truth of our nature—that's how it looked to me. I wanted a drug in my system. Ah. I stopped, halfway to the bed, turned around and went out into the hall. The architect, Hanif, was out there. "Do you have any opiates?"

He didn't, but he knew where some could be acquired.

"Good. Let's go there."

What about Henry?

"He's passed," I said.

"Oh no. I am so sorry."

"Yeah sure."

"Don't you want to stay?"

"No, I don't."

We went out and caught a water taxi over to the San Polo district, where stubby apartment buildings were piled one on top of the other like stacked and crooked cardboard boxes on a little street near a motionless canal. The apartments were also the color of cardboard boxes, boxes slathered with colorful stickers. The stickers were posters, mostly for rock concerts. The taxi let us out at some steps that were wet with green algae, slick as if they had just been hauled up from the sea bed. In Venice the lagoon was constantly sending up evidence of things unseen, bubblings, roiled patches, whirlpools, streaks of gassy current. Intimations of the dead world. Tip-offs and clues. At the bottom of the steps a dead cat bobbed against the stone abutment, gently nudging the stone as if he would like to get out. Hanif pointed at the cat and began to cry. We hadn't talked on the way over. Hanif respected my grief and didn't intrude. "Ah, Henry," he said now and sighed heavily. He was a handsome man who planned to reorganize the building codes in Pakistan. One really good earthquake, he told me once, and the whole country would be returned to dust. The ride over—the restlessness of the water, the boat that could sink, maybe even the moon, which was up early, a thin sizzle in the late afternoon sky, giving up on itself—had given me a sensation of slippage, of unchecked movement, hints not of escape, but of vacuity. All my thoughts seemed farewell speeches. The ride was the first without Henry in the world. He couldn't, no matter how memorable it was or how unimportant, know a thing about it. The thought was as stark as a shaved head. I wanted amelioration, distance, false comfort, a mediating effusion that would make life livable.

Now my extremities tingled and there was a lightness in my mind, a drift and displacement that made me feel half drunk. I followed behind Hanif. For a moment, at the corner where a trattoria was just now turning on its lights, where a young woman in a yellow apron reached up onto a shelf and drew down a basket of oranges that gleamed under the coppery lamps like balls of gold, I thought

I had lost him, and then, which was exactly why I needed drugs, I thought I had lost everything I was connected to so that it seemed I was turning a corner into oblivion. The cut stone curb looked like a line I was following to the brink. Ahead, some camellia bushes in big pots stood a morbid green watch. Hanif, who may have had a limp, came back into view, swinging left behind the camellias. The bushes formed a corridor that led to the steps of an apartment building. Hanif was waiting inside the lobby. "I think it's going to rain," he said. "I hate to get wet. That's why I was hurrying."

"Hurry's good." I was winded from panic, sweating as if I had run all the way from the hospice.

"You need more exercise."

I thought of the telegram, of the wording, and was suddenly sure I hadn't made it clear to Alice whether Henry was in grave *condition* or *in* the grave. It didn't matter now. "Hold on a sec." I leaned against the wall, which was root beer colored and interrupted about halfway down the corridor by glass. Beyond the glass was an elevator with a gold door. I had been working on a poem about gold metal doors, what they opened onto. You always expected to find something important behind big gold doors. Behind these was a wizened fellow in a pink doorman tunic and plumber pants. He punched the button as if he hated it.

Upstairs some feckless people—stupefied Air Force personnel, diarists, professors on the lam, drifting doxies—provided us with drugs. The flyboys had some hospital morphine, which they let Hanif onto fairly cheaply. It was in little clear ampules with needle attached, military issue. A girl with a large wen above her right eye insisted on handling the insertion. "Thank you, Doctor," I said. I hadn't had any opium derivatives since Indonesia, where I habitually smoked reefer with a paregoric soak even though in that area it was a capital crime to do so. Occasionally we'd come across some heroin, yellow potent material from the inscrutable East, or North as it was in our case. We shot up out in the boat colonies, in rickety plywood and palm frond sampans drifting among the floating cities, boats that had crumbled off the island kingdom like bits of cracker. I'd lie on the deck feeling the low roll of swells passing through the Strait of Malacca on their way to join their sisters in the South China Sea. No one ever came to roust us, but if they had we could've shoved the drugs down the fish well and let them dissolve into the ocean. I thought of my poem, little handcrafted piece Henry would never see, thought of a gold door opening onto a sea drug supper. I thought of the island women who wore coral bracelets on their arms and legs, clanking around like armored knights, of Esel, who was one of them, of her glistening brown skin under the bracelets, of Esel who would stop to talk to me as she passed down the walkway, out of pity. The only way I knew I was high was that I wasn't worried. Henry, I thought, was in the place he belonged, the one we would all soon repair to. And Alice, she too was fine, just as she was, married to another trumpet player, playing piano and raising vegetables among the alligators and swamp rats. I turned to Hanif. "Once," I said, "I was, briefly I mean, a boy preacher."

"How is that?"

"I was a preacher, an imam."

"You? Never happen."

"It's true."

"A child?"

“Yeah. I used to preach sermons at my father’s church in Miami. Sometimes at the big service Sunday morning, but mostly on Sunday night.”

“But not a priest.”

“I carried the word of God to the people.”

“This is unusual—or not unusual, depending on how you look at it.” His face, which he turned to look out the chalky window, bore an expression of self-satisfied sadness, as if what I told him only confirmed the unsightly, indefatigable truths he already had to live with.

“My favorite sermon was on the Eucharist,” I said, and leaned back onto the faintly dog-smelling floor, trying to remember what I had said about the bread and the wine. Like the Catholics, I maintained the host was actually the body and blood of Christ. Maybe I didn’t believe it, but I liked the idea. At first I had been hesitant about it, but toward the end of my career I began to come right down on it. “Give me a chunk of that red ripe meat,” I’d shout, “give me a swig of the blood.” This was either just before or in the middle of my breakdown. It was the breakdown that removed me from the pulpit. The doctor said the agitation that sent me shivering through the house would subside if I let off with the preaching, which made sense to me. Jesus and his cohorts had become wild uncontrollable Hell’s Angels style thugs. “What’s the biggest lie since the founding of mankind?” I’d yell. “Redemption!” I screamed. They took me off the scene like James Brown led away under a cape.

“I hate religion,” Hanif said without looking at me. “All religion in every form. I hate substitutes for religion and quasi-religious movements and all forms of faith. Life is a blueprint, it is clearly an orderly compilation of laws and rules and we need no religious interference to live it."

"What do you guys think?" I said, addressing the gathering in a generalized way. Everyone else seemed stoned, but maybe this was just me. The light was cloudy and in it faces were indistinct, barely there. "The whole thing's about erasure," I said. "Don't you know that?" A woman near me did look half erased. She'd obviously come to Venice looking for the grand scheme that would change everything back where she came from. As if change would help in the slightest. A man leaned out of the dimness and began to sing in huge oracular phrases. The air smelled of fried fish and of a sweet archival perfume, something some old woman years ago leaned over me to float whiffs of into my face. I thought of my aunts, my father's sisters, who had died together in a car wreck in Florida, on the beach causeway in Miami, our hometown, and this, as it had at the time, seemed impossible to live with. My eyes filled with tears. I got up and went looking for a phone, to call Alice.

"You too?" I said into the receiver. "You too?"

"You too what?" the man's voice said, her husband I assumed.

"You are in on it too, aren't you?"

"Is this a crank call?"

"Yes," I said. "It is."

"Well, that's that then," he said and hung up.

I was in a little phone room down the hall. I had a feeling of urgency, but an urgency from within a complacency. That's good, I thought, getting this set up in my mind: urgent but complacent. This figure seemed to express much about my life. Incorrigible was another word I used about myself, or that had been used about me.

I dialed the number again. I had the procedure memorized, the strings of numbers, the codes, none of which had unlocked her voice box. "Listen, this is Billy Brent."

"Oh, Billy," he said, "I didn't realize it was you."

"I probably didn't make that clear."

"No, I don't guess you did. Are you all right?"

"Yes. Could I speak to Alice?"

"She's on the way to the airport."

"Fleeing the scene?"

"She got your telegram."

"And she's gone?"

"Lit right out of here." Something inside sped up—love, the base accelerant. "I'm so sorry about Henry. It's such a sad thing with all the way he'd come."

"He hadn't come that far."

"From the war, I mean—you know."

Had hours passed? Had I been lying around in a Venetian hog heaven for days? Like Wild Bill Hickock on a drunk? I felt capable and calm. Urgent yet definitely complacent. "I didn't even realize there were any flights from Miami to Venice."

"There're not. She had to go by way of Rome."

"She's a caring person."

"Is she? I don't know. Listen, I don't think I can talk to you now."

"Why not?"

"Are you brain damaged?"

"Brain damaged?"

"Is that what makes you so reptilian?"

"Reptilian? What—like a snake?"

"No, like a fucking turtle, that just hangs on until sundown."

"Until sundown?"

"Stop repeating me."

"You think I'm like a turtle? A reptile?"

"Sundown is coming for you a lot sooner than you expect."

"I'm not even thinking about sundown. My day is just dawning."

"That's the light from your ass on fire, buddy—that ain't the sun."

"I didn't call up to be insulted."

"How could you expect not to be? And that's another thing. How could you just keep on calling my house like you've been? Your daddy's a Christian minister—didn't he ever teach you any manners?"

"You think manners are important at a time like this?"

"Yes, I do. Manners—courtesy and respect. They pay off."

"What do they have to do with the fact that Alice loves me?"

He sighed. "Nothing, I guess. There was nothing at all I could do about that fact."

"You knew about it?"

"I knew it when we married."

"And you went ahead with the marriage? What are you, some kind of masochist?"

"We all have these childhood tokens we carry around."

"I'm no token, bub."

"I'm sorry—that's right, you're not." He paused. Through the phone I could hear the ocean washing everything away. "You know," he said, "she was almost happy."

Charlie Smith

"Don't start with that false nostalgia. She wasn't happy."

"How could you know? How . . . could you . . . know?"

"Reptile instinct."

"She's going to make you just as jittery as she's made me."

"I like jittery."

"That's good for you."

I thought of Henry lying under his gold coverlet, his evacuated face turned up. "Ah, God." Yet, like a lamp thrown into the ocean, I saw a light descending toward me. "Do you know when her plane's arriving?"

"7:30 a.m. your time. That's in Rome. She has to catch another to Venice. She gets in at 10."

I understood an exchange was being affected. "Everything will be okay," I said. "I'll take care of her."

"No you won't, sport. You'll misinform her and give her nose bleeds and take away her dignity. You won't take care of her."

There were tears in his voice.

I hung up.

Some time ago I had carefully explained to myself the necessity of being kind, of offering help and sweet feeling to others, I had talked to myself until I thought I understood—as Jesus said, I prefer mercy to sacrifice—but whenever I got the chance to be generous I started grabbing instead, I turned nasty. I couldn't understand how someone with such tender feelings as I had could be so hard. It was something I wanted to talk to Alice about.

I drifted among cobblers and boat builders. I was in the Dorsoduro, a dim district of artisans, of men who attached bumper stickers to the carts they pushed around. Tinkers and specialists in gravestone rubbings, clerks taking courses in library science, artists' wives who had fled their morganatic stateside marriages, Evinrude mechanics, this was their place. I was in a church. I don't know exactly how I got there. Probably, as I usually did, I had decided to go for a walk. I had a habit of impulsively walking off. In Venice I had stood beside a canal in the rain, crying—I remember now. There was a church nearby, holding some kind of fellowship service. I entered and passed through the sanctuary where people milled about and entered a large hall where food was being served. There were dozens of people and no one seemed to mind that I was there. I helped myself to slices of prosciutto and some cheese, got a glass of wine. A couple of people acknowledged me with little head bows. "You know," I said to one of them, "I am a living anomaly."

"How so?" someone said kindly, perhaps an assistant priest.

"Usually poets wind up in Venice at the end of their careers, when, washed out and corrupt, they come here to recharge themselves among the painted palaces. But me, I am here at the beginning."

"Everyone comes to Venice," a voice, that seemed to be interrupting, said.

"That's not exactly what I am saying."

"What are you saying?"

"I'm saying it's an anomaly."

"Hardly that."

"No? I see it as a kind of reverse ordination."

"Into—or out of—the priesthood of art."

I could make out the person now, a tall man. They were all tall. I was inside the arc of an interlocutory half circle, like a star inside the arms of the moon. My mind began to wander, but not far. It brushed against Henry and came back.

"One never trusts a stranger's claims to poetry," the voice—or another voice like the first, now become bitter—said.

"I'm not making any claims."

Off to the side conversing priests in black vestments gesticulated wildly. They seemed, despite the arm movements, to be watching us. Probably they recognized a fellow cleric. I turned back and now I could focus: three couples, tall, bug-eyed men, slender, mean-looking, cranky women. I was in a trap, but how I had gotten there I didn't know. Had Hanif set me up, given me drugs and then led me into a social situation in which I would be shamed, then maybe arrested? But no, Hanif was kind, I was sure of that. He had cried over Henry. I had brought myself here, or fate had. "I may be here meeting someone," I said.

"Another Canadian?"

"Another? No. She's from Miami."

"Ah. A German? They all go to Miami, isn't that right?"

"She may be Jewish," another voice said.

"Actually she's both."

Off to the side a man moved slowly in place, weaving, as if he was dancing or charming a snake. He had a nervous, Henry-like manner, and short hair brushed forward like Henry's, though it was much lighter. I went over and joined him. I caught the rhythm easily and leaned into the dance. He stopped. "I don't like being mimicked."

"Is that what it looked like?"

He was short and willowy, and looked as if he could bend his knees backwards. "You were mocking me."

"Well, that's a different thing. That's past mimicry."

"Why would you mock a stranger? Someone who wished you no harm, but only wants to be left alone to exercise his grief."

"I was looking for company. My friend just died."

He winced, turned half away and turned back, his eyes burning with tears. "I too lost someone dear."

"A friend?"

"My wife."

"I'm sorry."

I experienced a doubtful exhilaration. Alice was, if I remembered correctly, on her way. By this time tomorrow we would possibly be in a vicious argument. I could well be cowering in a Venetian alley with my hands over my head begging her to stop hitting me. Or maybe desperately wrestling with her, two lunatics rolling on the cracked pavement of the Riva Grande. Yet, on the other side of love's battlements, was a paradise.

The dancing gent and I drifted apart. Shortly afterwards I was explaining to a priest how I had gone from a boy preacher to a smart-ass. "It was the next logical step," I said. He looked at me with a cruel and irrepressible disdain. I couldn't get a grip on myself, on anything. The world, not just Venice, seemed to be floating. I was slightly seasick. I had come up in the era of boy preachers, maybe I mentioned this to the priest. There was a slew of us, all around the South. South Florida was no exception. I knew a dozen by name. We were like spelling bee champs or local tennis wizzes, clarinet prodigies. The spirit had descended upon us and given us voice. We called people to the altar in the name of the Lord. At ten I had been a phenom. By twelve I was washed up, a broken boy. At fifteen, for reasons that continued to elude me, I had tried a comeback and was laughed out of the pulpit. Just after that Alice took full precedent.

I was in the open air by now, sucking in a sea breeze. I had left the church revels in a water taxi. "Take me to the Rome airport," I had said to the captain. I don't know what he said and when re-queried, I lost track of myself. I had waked—in Indonesia often waked—in strange houses, a man sleeping on a plastic couch, roused by sunrise from spurious, complicated dreams. Big men wearing batik sarongs, open Dutch-door style, fed me breakfast, led me by the hand to the bus stop, and left me there, a spindly, dazed character swaying by a dirt road in the East Indies. That was the way I felt now. Accompanying this feeling was a thin sensation of panic. As if something I thought I'd put behind me, something scary, wasn't. Maybe Alice, maybe Florida, maybe love itself, maybe a branch of hopefulness, maybe Henry; there was a selection. Henry—he was primo now—lying dead in a yellow bed in a cold sea town: I saw him, and began to weep. The drugs were wearing off, which was always a sad time for me. Sometimes I suffered vast, Icarusian, seaward plunging headaches, but mostly I just slid down off them like a boy sliding tiredly off his bicycle. It was after that that the mournful agitations began.

I had actually had more conversation with the willowy dancing man that I forgot to relate. Bent like a bow, he told me of his troubles. "It's my wife," he said.

"Isn't it always."

"No. We were so happy before."

"Before what?"

"Before I discovered her true nature."

"What was that?"

"Greed."

"Disruptive?"

"I mean . . ." An anguished look, that seemed oddly practiced, passed over his face, and then another look, the one that asked if I was carrying the reprieve, came and went, went into blankness. "But no," he said, "I was wrong—you're right—even before that, all the way back to the wedding—I knew."

"Knew what?"

"Her parents rented a sleigh to drag us from the church to the reception hall. Can you imagine that? A sleigh, like we were children. It was Wyoming, winter, twenty below, killing weather, way up in the Rockies. It was so obvious what they were after, the assassins. You would have seen right through the whole thing if you'd been there."

"Seen through what?"

"There we were, under a buffalo robe sliding across the snowfields in a big sleigh like some Wild West version, or some Russian version, of a gangster death ride, and we were supposed to pretend we didn't know what these killers had been up to by sending us out into the Arctic that way. We huddled up under that robe like cubs, freezing. There was frost in her eyebrows, the poor thing. We were just holding on for dear life. It came to me all at once that I didn't know a thing about this woman or her people. I've never been so unhappy."

"I'm sorry to hear it."

"She must have sensed it. I squirmed under that blanket. In every one of the wedding photographs I'm grimacing with pain. I look like a man with a corncob up his ass."

"Weddings are like that, aren't they, sometimes, for the guy?"

"How would I know?" he said sharply. "I've only had the one."

We had moved away from the venerate revelries—I had wanted to make confession, it came to me now: that's why I'd entered the church—in fact we were by now outside the building, drifting toward the iron railing above a canal. We reached this railing and leaned against it, our hands out before us, dangling over the shiny water. He continued to speak of his marriage, his sad experience now come to its incommodious end in old Venezia. Then we seemed to be on a boat, a ferry maybe, or a water taxi, traveling north into a cold wind.

"We tried to have a family," he said abruptly—each thing he said seemed abrupt—"as compensation. But we were unable to."

"They say that doesn't really work."

"Who says that? You mean babies? Or compensation? They're wrong, and you, Ned, of all people, should know better. Ninety-eight percent of life is compensation."

The water was lit in colors, trails, streaks of red and blue lights, white patches, wakes and slight sea rolls, disturbances, shimmers. He had been calling me Ned all along.

"I love it here," I said, "some of the moments."

"Sure you do. But then they present the bill. Just like my wife." He spit harshly into the water. "I can't believe I just stepped up and went on with it. But what was I going to do? I had married her. I'll tell you, Ned, once you marry them it's not so easy to change your mind."

We pondered this.

"At any point, before the cuffs were on, I could have stopped it," he said. "That's what I tortured myself with, but the truth is, when I consider it closely, I don't think I could have done a thing about it. I don't mean exactly that it was fate, but, and here's where folks get confused—thinking everything's fate, I mean—there might have been some way to stop, some point I mean, when I could have said *basta,* but it was so early in the game, and so only peripheral, or seemed so only peripherally a part of the confabulation, that I would have had to have been a genius to see it. Should I have simply not answered her that time after the book club meeting? Simply turned around when she asked me what I thought of Hermann Broch and gone home? She had a lovely, rabbity smile and her teeth were two shades of white. You know what I mean—that two tone white business?—you used to see kids with teeth like that when I was a boy. What do you think caused that?"

"Calcium deficiency?"

"Yeah. It knocked me out, that little detail. And the way her mouth moved when she spoke, like she was chewing the words out—I had never noticed that before. I loved it. She had a wonderful angularity about her, a list."

"A lisp?"

"List. She leaned. I loved it. Ah, but you know, it's always like that, isn't it, Ned?"

"Sure."

I wanted to get in a few words about Alice, but I couldn't. We were in the boat now. I leaned back on the cushions, looking up into the night that was blank and cloudy, like the bottom of an empty milk glass. Up there Alice was flying along. My friend whose name was Percy continued with his explanation. I tried to listen a little, but it was just as easy to let my mind drift. How irrepressibly I wanted to return to the thoughts in my own head. Alice, fly yourself to me, dear. Just then we bumped over something and the taxi slowed. We weren't going very fast to begin with, but the bump was large and continued as if what we hit was banging along the side.

The captain exclaimed softly and expelled breath. "What is it?" Percy interrupted himself to look over the side. "Jesus Christ," he said. "It looks like a person."

This was the beginning of my period of tribulation. It was like that Buddhist story in which the guru sends a young student for a glass of water, and the student gets in adventures, rises and falls, and years later wakes back where he started with a glass of water in his hand. *What kept you?* the guru says, grinning. Such was my night in Venice. The bump was in fact a body. A body we at first thought was a woman's—it was wearing a dress—but that turned out to be a man's. Just before this bit of confab I had administered another of the morphine ampules. This one made me vomit, which I did—drug nausea's like a sneeze, it whips right by—releasing my snack into the canal. Percy had begun for some reason to mock me bitterly. I think the grief was turning on him in this way. I wrenched around to explain myself, good-naturedly to defend myself, rose, lurched and fell into the water. The body washed against me, bump, bump, in a hard and insistent way. I shoved it off and it seemed to me I was burning in a fire. At that moment lights hit the scene: a police boat. I was hauled out of the water and subjected to questioning, just before which the ampules of morphine were found on my person. Where Hanif had gotten off to, I didn't know. They put me in a cell. I wasn't allowed to use the telephone. They didn't say what I was charged with, but I understood it was more than the drugs. Across the corridor a man in a pale blue suit wept into his hands. Down the way shouts and curses—I took them for curses—swelled like a tide. All the lights had beautiful purple haloes around them.

It was here, in Italy, I kicked the first time, here I found myself on my knees speaking of important things. Like Napoleon, I remained in the Veneto for two and a half years. It took that long for me to get out of prison. Alice came by the jail, angrily remonstrated with me, and left. Henry did not die, he was only sleeping. My father, a frail man, and my mother, a woman of many sorrows, entered the picture briefly and vanished. An AID friend who had spent a year in Venice on exchange got me a good lawyer. The lawyer worked on my case and after a while made progress. I was transferred after trial to the Fillionnia con Minesetre Prison back in the marshes. In the evenings I watched the wood ducks return to their nests in the ponds. We ate polenta every day and drank a light acidic wine, a failed soave, with meals. I wrote poems and studied the history of the region. By the time I was twenty-five I was back in the States, working as a reporter for the *Miami Herald*.

What kept you? I imagined her saying, but she was long gone.

Part II

BIGAMY

Sometimes I'd leave the newsroom and go out to one of the little parks by the bay and sit with the Cuban gentlemen who were quietly taking the afternoon apart, drinking rum. There was a year when I especially liked to do this. It was the year of the Laughing Boy Spree Killer, so named because he once wrote the words HA HA—or somebody did—on the bathroom mirror after one of his killings. Everybody was afraid that year of getting killed in their beds. Of getting killed in the dark, of being roused out of sleep to meet an unruly end. Homeowners bought guns and formed clubs and vigilante associations and went out on patrols in station wagons. The Laughing Boy—killer of seven—was supposed to operate out of the Everglades, but this was really only speculation, not fact. The police figured if *they* were spree killers that's where they'd hide out. Alice was living with her second husband in a big mansion out in the western Glades and when I went down to the park to do a little crystal and drink some rum with the Cuban gents I'd think about her out there in the wide prairie sitting on the gallery of her big house. I'd wonder what she was doing. I hoped for the Laughing Boy's sake he didn't run into her.

I was often mortified in those days, as a general condition, stung by my own ability to botch things, and coming into the newsroom made me tremble with apprehension. I was an erratic and undependable reporter. The news, which for others appeared straightforward and comprehensible, for me seemed filled with wandering lines of mystery, of asides and shady cul-de-sacs, and I could not find my way through. I had some gifts, maybe they were gifts, as a feature writer, sent out to shackland and into the colorful dubious world of dicey behavior, to some family fight over lobstering rights in which the matriarch had put a bullet into her favorite son, or some squatter's camp out in the cane fields where some boy, some cross-grained child with buggy eyes, had begun at age eight to do calculus, to some girl who thought she was connected to the Virgin Mary and manifested this by shaving the flesh off her arms—these children of God were my beat, what they came up with at the paper for me to attend to. I was all right at this. I caught the air of things, the mood, I sensed and described the tone. The sounds of pleading, the excuses, the regrets expressed haltingly, the ineffective vows of renewed love or revenge, these interested me. Facts confused me, and seemed oddly threatening; the addresses of victims haunted me, and the correct spelling of their names slipped by me in the fog. Did Connie—or was it Consuela, Gillespie, or Garcia—take three or was it five bullets in the back and buttocks, or did she take six in the sides and feet and one in the breast, and did she name the killer with her last breath or was that only another name for the Lord that she either did or did not utter as she lay dying in a bed or in marigolds or daisies outside the Lucious Lady Hair Parlor over on Fifth or was it 45th Street last night? I could not tell. The real reporters looked on me as an amateur, a rookie who could never get out of his rookiness. I often came in slightly buzzed, sliding along on rum punch and Quaaludes, sometimes a meth topper if the coasting had gotten too severe, and though this smoothed out the mortification it often opened me up for a more intense ridicule.

Out in the park, across the bay from the foam and bubble-gum-colored structures on the islands, I'd sit with the Cuban gents, these men who were going nowhere, and let the afternoon get huge around us. Each afternoon the sky put on another of its theatrical productions, promoting the idea that amassing then clearing everything away was the solution to all ills. We watched and commented, always taking the side of the little guy. If we got tired of the cloud play, we could shift to the foreground, to the sandy embankment where hermit crabs in their party hats poked into the darker places under driftwood. Small, unusual items got washed up. Roots stuck out of the bank and hung naked, reaching idiotically toward the water. Gulls expressed themselves badly. Plumeria blossoms drooped. Many of the Cubanos had the faraway look of sea captains lost on land. They had ideas about how to hem the Laughing Boy up and they spent hours going over the details of the operations they'd like to run in this regard. The Laughing Boy didn't scare them, some crazy character with a gun was nothing to these men. You could see that the dark had already climbed up onto their backs. In their open mouths you could glimpse small pieces of the darkness lodged, and these pieces they chewed down and swallowed with a swig of rum. They didn't go for drugs. Once or twice I shot some heroin into a vein, but they heartily disapproved of this and in fact said they would turn me in if I did it again. Like many who had been overrun, it was important to them to know where to draw the line.

I told them about Alice, about her strange and barbarous beauty, and they too, as far as I could tell, were charmed. "I myself would go get her, *companero,*" my friend Suezo said. "I would not delay." In the stillness of a tropic afternoon this seemed good advice. But Alice's heart, like old Pharoah's, had grown hard. "It's a savage love," I told Suezo, and at this information he would nod his head sagaciously and look off into the scintillations of distance, musing about barbarous women. We all had stories about such women. Every one of us had loved a woman who, as if the devil had sneaked into the house, was one day transformed from a sweet-tongued beauty to a screeching murderess. "Ah, I could show you my scars," another friend, Alberto, liked to say. He meant, so I understood, his literal scars, streaks of tallowy flesh across his back that his wife had raised with a coconut rope. Constantine was missing the last two fingers of his left hand, fingers his wife had whacked off with a machete. "She would have thrown those fingers to the dog if I hadn't snatched them off the floor," he said. Unfortunately the doctors at Dade General were unable to reattach the digits.

Alice, I informed them, was a dispenser of scar tissue, but she was also a bearer of scars. Half her back was a sheet of muddled flesh where as a child of three she had fallen into a fire. Fallen or been thrown, it was not clear. She was a living illustration of one of philosophy's most exciting and hotly debated topics: Is what we bear inside expressed externally? We all believed it was. Out of her own flesh Alice had produced the Fata Morgana of sin and horror that tattoo artists the world over would have given their working finger to be able to reproduce, not to mention a few priests and many saints. She should have been stripped naked on the altar for all to see and learn from. This was how I saw it at the time, and how my friends saw it, these men who in their own faces enunciated their bitter internal lives. This I know now is the perception of ignorance, but then I was on the lookout for easy interpretation. I spoke of Alice's scars to my friend Suezo and he nodded wisely and whistled softly through his teeth. "It was the devil's kiss," he said, quick to put a canonical interpretation on human experience. I agreed.

Miami was a young city, founded in 1896, once only a string of huts along the brackish Miami River. My great-grandfather as a young man lived in one of those huts. Alice's great-grandfather lived in another. They were not friends, but they worked together. Alice's grandsire operated a small way station on the riverbank and mine supplied vegetables and game for the table. Both of them missed the orange blossom redemption that Julia Tuttle grasped, and Flagler's railroad skipped them. Their sons, our grandfathers, sank back into the foliage. Her father was a lawyer, a mercurial man, a charming conniver and a hothead, who committed suicide by throwing himself off a hotel balcony in Miami Beach, hitting the parking lot face first on a hot February day. My father, after an impressive start in the preaching profession, had settled into a job running one of the downtown ministries for the unfortunate. Once in a while the mission van would pull up at the park and a couple of his crucifixiated minions would circulate among *los borrachos*, passing out leaflets and offering aid, God style. When these goons appeared I tended to drift off toward the shadows. I affected scorn for my father, but really in those days I was ashamed of myself and did not want reports of me as a layabout getting back to him.

Truth was, my thoughts didn't dwell on family matters. Alice was my study. I mused and speculated on Alice Stephens, on the knotty fact of her, on her life, on her thoughts and interpretations of difficult matters, on her loping stride, and especially on the sharpness of her gaze.

"Look," I said from a phone booth in Bayside, "you came all the way to Venice, Italy, to plight me your troth. Why won't you see me now?"

"Because I might wind up making a similar mistake."

"That's because you love me so much, isn't it?"

"Yes, I love you. So what?"

"So, love's the baseline; it's the universal fertilizer. If there's love everything else will grow."

"Are you having some kind of mental attack? You expect me to go for this nonsense?"

"I'm working on a way of putting it that will close the deal."

"You have a ways to go."

"I know. It troubles me. I seem to have lost my touch."

"I was listening to one of your sermons."

"Oh yeah? The tapes?"

"Yes. It's the one where you're damning this and damning that, sending everyone to hell. You start in about how even grandmothers will burn, and then all of sudden you stop, there's a big pause, and then in this sweet twelve-year-old voice you say, 'Ah, it won't be so bad.' Do you remember that?"

"Sure. I caught sight of Grandmama."

"It's the best, the most lovable part. Of any of your sermons. Of you. You ought to listen to it."

"I should. You're right. I didn't even know what the good part was."

"That's probably why you had to give it up."

"Not probably—it was why."

"Have you been out to the snake ranch?"

Distraction, I thought, she was distracted by something. "Not since I was little. I went with you."

"I remember. You were so scared. You were afraid the snakes were going to get loose."

"I don't like to remember that occasion. I was not myself."

"You were yourself all over. Oh, that reminds me" (I could see her standing at the kitchen sink looking out over the back precincts of her Everglades domain at the slowly circling hawks and buzzards and water turkeys and such—I could see her standing there with a chilled glass of tomato juice in her hand, gripping the glass so hard that if she didn't come back to herself in a second she might crush it), "I heard from your mother."

"What did Mama want?"

"She wanted to know if I'd heard from you. She sits out there in that house by the interstate, thinking about you. She's like me, in that way."

"I mean to go see her."

"No, you don't. You mean to suffer because you don't go see her."

"It's the same thing. Why did you leave me?"

"Leave you? Did I? I thought I did, but I don't believe I actually did. I think leaving you was just a dream."

"What I understand is you came over to Italy to be with me and then you left."

"I didn't leave. I stayed to take care of Henry. There was no need to look in on you anymore."

"Because I was the same old Billy."

"No, you were worse than that. You were the same old Billy plus hatred."

"Hatred? You're the one gives lessons in hatred."

"Is that what it is?"

"Are you on dope?"

"No, just sad. Hearing your voice makes me sad."

The sound of her crying came over the wire in faint, hushed snatches, as if in code, broken by distance and discretion. When we were children, I'd panic when she cried. I was so used to her rage, maybe, but no, it was that her crying would open up in me—I don't know what it was, empty Sunday streets of sadness, the dog loneliness, I don't know—it scared me, and I'd run around trying to get her to stop. I'd do anything. But I'd found other ways now to avoid those venues, and I had come to accept, if not be indifferent, to her tears, over time I had, and now I simply waited. I didn't even try to soothe her.

"Are you still there?" she said finally.

"I was just listening. You cry the most private tears of anybody I ever knew."

"I used not to cry around you at all. Do you remember when you told my father that? That, 'unlike every other girl in Miami,' you said, I didn't cry. It was like you were turning me in, to immigration."

"You *didn't* cry. There were five years when I never saw you cry. You raged. You did that. But no crying."

"I just didn't cry around you."

"Why?"

"Because you made me so mad. I never got to the crying part."

"You did eventually. After I ratted you out to your dad, you cried."

"Um. It was like a job."

"That's a cruel thing to say."

"I mean one to please *him*. So he wasn't scared. If he thought I wasn't a normal girl it'd scare him. He'd feel guilty."

"You're a responsible child. To a point."

"Then I get angry."

"And rude."

"I rip flesh." A silence then. "Ah, Billy." Then a rustling, scraping sound, like a glass door sliding open. Now she would let the buggy day right into the house, torture herself with mosquitoes and horseflies, make herself pay for having talked to me. "Billy."

"Yes?"

"Let me tell you something."

"Okay."

Her voice flowing like the breezy tops of grasses. "You twitch along over there in Miami, wandering around the city stoned and telling everyone you meet—mostly the drunk and deranged—that this woman, this Alice Stephens, whom you are only too willing to name, has roughed up and abandoned you, and you expect this information to get back to this woman, this Alice Stephens, who upon receiving this news flash will somehow appreciate that you are a heartbroken soul, a noble sufferer in the vales of romance, who should be taken under the wing of said Alice and comforted. Come on, Billy. You think girls go for that? You think something like that is going to work?"

"Why not?"

"Don't you know that girls—and it's not just girls—don't you know people want to be brought a gift, not presented with a problem?"

"But it is a gift. My love is a gift."

"You are so far from being a compliment to my life."

"Aw, you're just sad. Don't you think I know how sad and mournful you really are?"

"No, you don't know how sad and mournful I am."

She'd left her first husband to be with me and then I proved, once more, to be a bad bet. She never pitied herself for this, though, not in my hearing. There was a difference between grief and pity. I could hear the sadness in her voice, hear it moving, like something shifting places out in the dark.

"I do love you," she said.

"I know."

"You're my river blindness. My sleeping sickness. My break-bone fever."

By then I would be all turned around in the booth, corkscrewed, standing on my knees with my face pressed against the Plexiglas, wishing with all my shameful heart that I could somehow, some way, squeeze this whole matter like coal in my fist, squeeze so hard I made a diamond. Tension pounded my body like surf, and the fearful nuttiness of my thoughts poked my brain, alarming me. I'd grit my teeth. Then, God forgive me, I'd begin to insult her. I couldn't stand the rage and terror and the squalid sense that I had ruined everything. "Your mean, angry, cuntiferous way of loving," I'd say. "Your ruined—" And she'd hang up the phone.

I'd sway there on my knees, trembling, watching the sea breeze dance in the coconut palms along Biscayne Bay, and the whole world, the city and environs, would seem charged with duplicity and error, all of it, hurtling toward fiery disaster. The world was an emergency on Saturday night, everything shot in the head and screaming. I'd get on a bus—I wouldn't even bother to pick up my car—and ride out to the beach, where in some lounge, some crumbling, spray-painted place below Fifth Street, among sullen and craven individuals, I would attempt to mash my perturbations out like roaches against the bar. Slowly the need to preach would rise in me, like a spring boil coming up through sand. The need, as it had once agitated in me, all those years ago, when as a boy I would find myself out by the bay speaking of the Lord, reappeared, redirected. Now Alice had replaced the deity. It was Alice I worshipped, like some small-time King David, drunk and nudging a chippie, some Oral Roberts on a spree, evangelizing for the Church of My Sweetie. In that place, that barroom, late, after those who wished to dance their troubles away had danced and given it up as a bad job, after the fighters had bottle-whipped each other, after the insults and the surliness had subsided, after the pleas had faded into whimpers and sighs, after this, I would rise to speak my sermon.

"Love—right?" I'd loudly begin, and often the taunts would rise in accompaniment; the curses and the threats.

If there was a cleared area, a small stage or an opening near the bus table, a little DMZ just mopped clean of blood, I would approach this, in a rush, like a man throwing himself over a barricade. There

I'd draw myself up, pause for breath, giving the spirit time to rise to its feet inside me.

"You want me to tell you what love is?" Sometimes, for a moment, no one would answer. Through that silence, that second or two, a dark world rushed by, shedding the faint cries of the damned.

"Sure, you tell us, A-hole," somebody would offer, finally, someone in the shadows.

"Love's a bucket on your head," I'd say. "Banged by a bully. You all know that."

"You tell 'em, ace."

"Love's a daylight robbery, right? It's your chest ripped open and the sanitation department dumping rotted fruit baskets in there and love letters and those beautiful trinkets you gave her, marked Return to Sender. It's a guy on his knees in the Holiness Church begging God to give him one more day with her. And it's that voice on the other side of the wall, that voice calling for Vickie."

"Vickie's in Chicago, pussyface."

"Yeah," I said, "calling for Vickie. And then you remember: it's not on the other side of the wall, that voice—it's in the room. It's you calling. Right?"

"Not me, bud."

"Yeah. And it's that sad, sick, deranged feeling you get, love. The one that makes you drive over to her house and sit in the car honking the horn until the cops come and make you stop."

"That wasn't me."

"And love's sticking with it no matter how they beat on you with their nightsticks and other implements of false witnessing."

"That's my mama's house you're talking about."

There was the summer we ran away to this beach, to South Beach, when we were sixteen, and lived a month in a hotel on Ocean Drive before they found us. It was here among the oldsters and the derelicts and the drunks that I first used drugs. She'd sit on the bed watching me shoot heroin into the vein inside my elbow, her hazel eyes wide and shining, like a child fascinated in the temple. "Friends, I had her cornered. I had her hemmed up, but she slipped out."

"I know that noodgie," the voice came back.

"I had no wisdom in my ways. I had no surety in my hands. I did not understand the nature of love."

"That bitch'll teach you," a voice, a female voice, suggested.

"The truth is, none of what I just said is love. You know that. It's not this ignorant thrashing about. It's not maneuvers and ploys. Love doesn't struggle, it doesn't carp or pine. Love knows no loss, no lack of faith. Love does not contend or dispute with fools. It doesn't sue. Love sways in place like yellow poppies along the highway. It's a sweetness in the middle of disaster, and it's the disaster." My mind by then had begun to sputter and skip. I snagged, and stumbled. Images fluttered up, of broken-backed people, of somebody crying at the end of a dock, of Alice shrieking that she hated me—and, just as when I was in the pulpit, I began to grope for some way of putting things that would get me to safety. "Love's the circus," I'd say, something like this. "Yeah, and the heart's the big top it operates in." I'd turn about then, lifting my arms to catch the breeze of certainty. "I tell you, friends, the elephants of love are marching through our town. The clowns are tumbling down the midway of our passion." And then I'd stop. *Nothing*, a voice said, *will ever work*. I'd look about me, at the stupefied or reckless or totally bamboozled forever lost expressions on the faces of my congregation; I'd see the scars of desolation and loneliness, the spots where the terror continued like an oil seep to ooze. And I'd see what it was going to be like, later, after the bedside lamp went off. I could hear the whimper, so small, and the tap tap tap on love's wall. "Oh you, you cuntified and prick-ridden souls," I'd cry. "Oh you luckless and defeated, you ought to be locked up."

Later, thrown down into the street, I would struggle to my feet and walk to the beach, where under the sea-grape trees I would stand in the lee of a dune wondering how in the world I would ever get this woman—this Alice—to go along with me. Far out there, an unseen hand reeled the big tankers along the horizon.

Henry didn't want to talk about any of this. "You need to do something about your life," he'd say. "Forget about Alice. Alice can take care of herself."

"That's what I'm afraid of."

Yet all was not lost. I was fit, still young, I looked good in summer clothes, and I could write. An editor from New York, passing through on his way to the Keys, stopped in to talk to me. I was writing a series of articles for the local arts paper about my misshapen love of Alice—articles that deeply offended her—and he'd read them, or someone had and told him about them; he came by to see what was up and if I had anything else. "There're certainly more where those came from," I said.

We got drunk together and he offered to give me a blow job, which I said yes to. His large mouth worked on me earnestly and with I thought a kind of irrepressible tenderness. I leaned back in the rental car and looked out over the Glades. We were in West Miami following the track of a missing author, a cracker heiress who had written a manuscript that excited them at the main office in New York. The book was about a celebrity interviewer who came to know secrets about famous people, secrets that tortured her. She tried to expunge these secrets in confession, but the priest, a sleazy fellow, revealed the material to the media. The celebrities formed a cabal and sent operatives out to kill her. It was a chase book; the dashing interviewer, a slim cracker blonde, on the run from the celebrity financed assassins. The editor loved it.

"I sense something with this power and energy in your material," he said.

"I know it's there," I said.

In a lame and unbecoming way I daydreamed about celebrity. At my desk at the paper, a green metal desk piled with farm catalogs and instruction manuals, I dreamed of tooling down the Overseas Highway in a red Jaguar, singing out loud, waving avuncularly at filling station attendants, Alice beside me spitting orange seeds. My dreams—which Alice said were not my *real* dreams—were a pill I could take, or a pill I could take after I had already taken a pill. An enhancer. What I wanted from drugs, and for that matter from life—and dreams—was for an accelerant to be applied, then something else added, embellishment. It's the topping up that's the key, I told my friends, in life and drugs. The overtopping. I didn't want just to get there, I wanted to be spun wildly once I was there. This, I knew, association with Alice—my main fixer upper—could accomplish. She herself was a maniac for the extra spin, and a provider. No need for fantasy with Alice around.

The stories I'd written for the arts paper were half true, some of them, and some were almost all the way true; others were made up. I described, for example, the time I drove out to the western Glades and peeked in her windows. I watched her make love to herself, watched her, her fingers gleaming with Oil of Olay, touch herself intimately. She'd caught me and run me off the property with a shotgun, so I said. Stories such as this were the ones she objected to most strongly. There was no shotgun, she pointed out. She had gotten me to leave by out-arguing me. By arguing me, that is, to a point in which I was humiliated by my actions. "You have no love security here," she had said, "and sneaking around spying on me won't provide it for you." What she said was true. The next week I wrote a retraction and told the real story in which I stood at the bottom of the steps, caught misdemeanoring for love, shamed. To the editor, Minx Averroes, I mentioned my insight, about the need for hyper reality—this was the stuff I wanted to push—but he wanted to read more about the humiliations, the moments when I got caught. "I like the way she wagged the stalk of celery at you," he said. "And the other story where you told the truth—that was hair-raising. And the time you phoned from Italy and talked to her husband—good stuff. The story where she called the cops on you for smashing all the plants in her garden. Yeah. Veggicide, you called it."

"She called it."

"Sure. That was hilarious. And the time you were put in jail, up in, where was it . . ."

"I don't know—Kissimmee?"

"Sure, and she and your friend—Henry?"

"Yeah—"

"They broke in—broke *into* the jail. That's good material. You have a gift for expressing what's behind the—I don't know, the sorrowful countenance. The failed gesture—that's your speciality. And that business about being a boy preacher. That's good too. You were a couple then, weren't you? Didn't you have some kind of children's wedding?"

"Yes. In a manner of speaking."

At age six, during a Tom Thumb wedding ceremony I was conducting, I had attacked Alice's seven-year-old bridegroom. We both had. Out in West Miami, out where the city faded into cropland and beyond that into the swamp, among the crackers and their kin, in those communities where people still liked to sit out on screen porches and take drives to the store for banana ice cream, out where boys played ball next to irrigation canals and girls practiced majorette moves in the mirror, they thought up the idea of children's weddings, as entertainment. What they wanted out of this was hard to say. Maybe like everyone they just wanted to work some sweetness into their lives, and it was easy to use a child to do it. These mock weddings were the rage for a season or two. They chose brides, chose bridegrooms, from among the kindergarten set, put them into formal clothes, played music, marched them down the aisle and married them one to the other.

Alice and I met through this device. I was the mock minister, and for some reason her bridegroom, Jim Haugh Williams, infuriated us both. He was a nose picker and a surly boy who salivated when he talked, but I don't think it was only this ungainliness that set us off. We'd discussed it since and agreed it was probably that we were simply knocked out to be in each other's company. We'd been starving for a look at each other, without knowing it. I loved her quick hands and her blush and the dark painted rims of her hazel eyes. She loved my pale soft skin and my glossy suit. When Jim Haugh went to wipe his snotty fingers on her dress, I slugged him, as she, at the same moment, swung her bouquet at his face. The ceremony fell apart in a scuffle, Alice's dress flashing like sparks, Jim Haugh sapped.

"The early preaching years," I said to Minx.

He loved this story, Minx, as did some others. It was the sort of story family members liked to tell at reunions. But Alice didn't care for any of it. She didn't want her life, didn't want her life with me, or with anyone else, to be laid out in some crummy paper. I loved the way the stories dived like dolphins into the love and came up grinning. I loved what was behind them, loved the scuffed, sun-drenched world we had lived in so close to each other, out on the grassy edge of the swamp, unaware, like Adam and Eve, that we were being watched. She spoke to a cop entirely in American Sign Language, once when we'd been stopped for speeding. Her blouse was open and her breasts, which were soft and swayed when she moved, were half-exposed. "Would you cover yourself?" the policeman asked. "I can't," she signed, "my hands are filled with words." That was the way it was. My hands were filled with words.

"You want to pay us all back, don't you?" she said once, but I denied it. How could I know the answer to a question like that?

She'd call sometimes after one of the stories came out, and she wouldn't say much, but I'd know the story was why she called. I'd ask what she thought and, in a very quiet way, she'd object to one of the details, a very minor detail. "My fingernails were carmine, not pink," she'd say. It was like she was on her deathbed and in a whispery, I'm-headed-out-of-here fashion, correcting a slight imperfection, just something she wanted to clear up before she left the scene. But the truth, like somebody's bulldog, crouched between us, softly panting. Or not the truth, the fact, the burned out, dilapidated construction site each of us had in his own way sneaked into to do a little work on. We'd sit there, me in my hotel overlooking Washington Avenue in South Beach, and she out in the Glades where the bugs ruled, and a silence would fall, like night falling on the long stretch of road between us. Both of us, as I experienced it, would peer into this silence, out at this highway of dereliction and desire, staring at the rank life tossed down along it, the various hostages and dead pets we'd thrown out. She was married again; it was like she couldn't stop herself.

"You're already two ahead of me," I told her, and she just laughed, a laugh that had an old lady's surprised anger in it. "I'm glad I didn't find out about it before I came back from Italy," I said. "I would have died in prison if I had." She said she didn't want to talk about it. But we could talk about the stories. In them were little flecks and spirules of life, the past life, still pulsing. "You remember—" I'd say, and some rearranged fact would spill out, some twist on the truth that sounded as if the life we lived out in the rural suburbs was a life filled with happiness, a quirky goodness. "You're always looking," she said, "for a new slant on an old slant, and there just isn't enough of one."

"I write about you and the hairs on my arms stand up."

"You liar."

"I write about you and you become this girl without restraints or difficulties. There's nothing off-key between us except what happens in the story."

"There's everything wrong between us, and there always was. What about that?"

"*What's* wrong?"

"You mean besides your telling dishonest and ugly stories about another man's wife?"

"Everything I make up that sounds real gives me extra life with you."

"The one we had was life enough."

"But think of it. We have the one life, the one we've had and will have, and now we have this extra life. We can build it up as big as we like. We can make heaps of extra life, set them around everywhere, like fruit baskets. Piles of us, of—"

"You wrote about shooting up at the Irene Hotel."

"I know. Do you remember that?"

"Yes. I'm the one who remembers everything, accurately. That's what infuriates me. You ate the center out of a loaf of bread and went around wearing it, like a muff."

"And you sat on the bed and the breeze kept blowing the curtain over your face, so you were disappearing and reappearing. I thought how beautiful you were like that, and wanted it to be that way all the time, you going away and coming back. Every time like seeing you for the first time."

"But it's not real, Billy."

"It's more real than you out in the boondocks hugging a contractor."

"Fucking a contractor, you mean?"

"That too."

You glance down some passing street, some summer day when

the dust hangs in the air, some street maybe in the Grove, and for a minute the way the street curves toward the left, under the royal palms, makes it seem there's a grand design to life, it all means something. And then you drive on and the world shrugs back into itself and you forget. Even though I was the one on drugs, I wanted to save her. I hated the troubles in her life, and I wanted to kneel down and fix them, to somehow soothe what burned inside her, even if I never understood it. I'd always thought that was what she wanted too. "It's getting a little desperate out here," she said.

A chill rippled across the back of my neck. "In what way?"

"Bobby's threatening me."

"About what?"

"About you."

"About the stories?"

"About all of it."

"Us?"

"What there is."

"There's not much—did you tell him that?"

"Not really."

"Why don't you tell him?"

"He knows I love you."

"Tell him it's one of those old stagnant pond loves. One of those drainage canals with no outlet to the sea. It's dead water."

"Why are you being bitter?"

"Why do you think?"

"Because I won't make love to you while I'm married to another man?"

"Nah. I got my whores."

"What whores?"

"Mary Clutchdemember and her all girl band. No. It's because you married him in the first place."

"It wasn't the first place, or the second. It was the only place. You had gotten yourself into prison in Italy. You remember?"

"You couldn't wait three years?"

"No. I couldn't."

"That's a mystery to me."

"Is it?" She sighed. "It shouldn't be."

"Is our love only a false lead?"

"I don't know what you mean by that."

"A trail that goes nowhere."

"No. I think the crime is solvable."

"Good."

"So what about Bobby?"

"Are you in danger?"

"I guess so."

"You want me to come get you?"

"I don't think that would do any good."

"How is he threatening you?"

"Studious looks."

"Looks? Those scare you?"

"They are very penetrating. He stares at me. I'm out in the garden picking tomatoes and I look up and he's at the end of the row, staring at me. Senegol says he wants to kill me."

"How is Senegol?"

"She's turning yellow."

"Agh. I thought that went away."

"It doesn't go away, Billy. Or it goes away and comes back. Like you."

"I don't want to talk about that."

"Why don't you write a story about Senegol?"

"Look who's bitter now."

"I'm not bitter, I'm under pressure. My husband is wearing me down with dirty looks."

"So what do you want me to do?"

"I don't know yet."

"Something nuts, huh?"

"Maybe. Do you remember that time at the swimming pool I slapped you? And you climbed up to the top of the diving platform and threw yourself off backwards?"

"I remember it."

"I loved that."

"You want me to make a sacrifice?"

"No. Maybe I want a gesture."

"Honey, you know I'm good at that. The gesture is my specialty. Especially the futile gesture."

"Yes. It's the follow-up that confounds you."

The next day I was at the boat show, standing beside one of the big Hatteras-style cruisers, when a large man in a red spandex shirt and white crinkly running pants came up to me and knocked me down. I fell in under the green crepe skirts surrounding the boat. The man began kicking at me through the crepe. I scrambled to my feet on the other side, ran up the gangplank, through the saloon—where a salesman in a pale blue suit was holding up a picture of the same boat bounding across the main—and out the other side and down the far plank. There was a knot on the side of my head. The man didn't follow me. An assassin, I thought with sudden clarity. I knew the setup. Bobby was a dangerous man, unlike Alice's former husband, who was a pushover, no matter how deeply he felt. This husband, this Bobby Concannon, was a contractor out in the Everglades. He was one of the guys they'd had to throw their arms around to keep him from tearing the Glades up for residential developments. He hated all that black water and grass. The hoot owls and the gators offended his idea of order. I'd seen him lean over a blueprint, salivating like it was a pornographic tract. *Give me some fill*—that was his motto. The dump truck was his weapon of choice. And now he'd sent an assassin after me. At the boat show. He must have been desperate. I went to a phone and called Alice. "How do you know it wasn't the Laughing Boy?" she said.

"I'll be out to get you this afternoon."

I stopped out at the monument yard on the way west to see Henry. He was off in back behind the shop working a stone saw. The funeral statue he was carving loomed like a big woodpecker set on its haunches. "They want a bird on their grave?"

"It's not a bird. It's a heroic figure."

"It looks like a bird to me."

He pushed his goggles back farther on his head. He was going bald and he'd built himself up to compensate; his big forearms were crusted with coral dust. His clear blue eyes set in their circle of red flesh gleamed from the Kabuki-white stone dust his face was powdered with. "You look like you've come up yourself out of the grave to do the job."

"I was just going to say the same thing about you."

"But you didn't."

"Because I am a courteous and generous man, able to hold his tongue."

"That is the dognab truth."

I told him about the attack at the boat show.

"I thought you'd been fired."

"Who told you that?"

"I think it was Ike. He said they kicked you off the paper."

"They kicked me, but not off. I am invaluable for getting the scoop on crazed powerboat captains and such."

I was slightly buzzed, a bit zippy around the edges from a crystal-lude mix. I'd also stopped for drinks at Deeter's on the way out. Deeter, who had been killed the month before in an accident down in the Keys—soared drunk off the Seven Mile Bridge, headlights arcing into the water—Deeter's wife, who now ran the lounge, I mean, had wanted to talk about life after death, and I couldn't get away. She wanted to know if there had been any changes on the ecclesiastical front since she'd last checked. None I knew of, I told her. "Mrs. Deeter sends her love."

"Shirley? How is she?"

"Looking for a loophole."

"What makes you think the guy who hit you was sent from Concannon?"

"It fits."

"That, pissed about your articles, he'd send a goon to the boat show to level you?"

"If it's not that, then it was random, and who could accept such a state of affairs? That would mean we live in a chaotic world."

"We do live in a chaotic world."

"Not me. I take drugs. There's nothing chaotic about the drug world. It is very orderly."

"You're being humorous."

"You're being prim."

"So what are you going to do?"

"About the attack? I'm going out to get Alice. She's also being threatened."

"She says okay to this?"

"Yes, my love, yes."

Behind us a canal stretched away, a black line drawn under South Florida to emphasize something to those looking down from space.

"Do you have a plan?"

"No. That's the beauty of it."

"It is?"

"Concannon won't be able to anticipate our next move. Because we ourselves won't know what it is."

"I don't think Alice will go for that."

"She's shook. Concannon's been giving her the evil eye."

"You mean dirty looks?"

"The old menacing stare treatment."

"And that bothers Alice?"

"Hadn't she talked to you about this?"

"Yes, she has. I'm just surprised she mentioned it to you."

"Why? You think you're closer to Alice than I am?"

"No. But she knows you'll just react in some confused way and cause trouble."

"Well—what? You think I ought to just let it lay? That guy who hit me knocked me under a Hatteras Ocean Cruiser. He was trying to kick me."

"It could have been anybody."

"You think I have the type of life where people regularly come up to me and knock me down and kick me?"

"Yes."

I stopped. Out over the prairie an osprey hung. He looked unconfident to me, afraid of life. "Building funeral statues has made you mean. Alice herself said she was desperate."

"You know what it is? You know what's wrong with you?"

"Why don't you tell me?"

"The minute somebody starts to open up to you, you go to pieces. You jump around like a drunk trying to stamp out a ditch fire."

On the other side of the canal, just this side of the swamp prairie, a small woods—a few cabbage palms sticking up out of some Australian pines—looked like a place where lonely men went to sleep. Maybe some of my Cuban friends were over there, barbecuing boondocked chickens and drinking rum. Yesterday in the park I had slept in the sun beside Suezo, until the tide crept up over our feet. "I'm already pretty tired."

"Why don't you go on over to the house and lie down. I'm going to be through here in a little while and we can go up to Scorchy's and get some mullet."

He lived only a few hundred yards from the stone yard (Silvio's House of Monuments), an artist who liked to be close to his work. You could see the green roof of his house upraised among some bushy oleanders out in the marsh. A bone-white crushed shell road led up to it.

So I went over there and fixed myself a drink and sat out on the back porch until a man came along the canal in back in a natty blue motorboat. He was someone I knew, a man named Homer Baker, who owned a worm farm over near Homestead. He had been a friend of my father's, from his youth as a matter of fact. He pulled in at the little cypress dock and came up to the screen porch. Without intro, we conversed awhile, talking of the cracker life, the life, that is, in which the truly oppressed, men such as us, triumphed over the scoundrels in charge. As we chatted I noticed that for some reason his face was changing shape. Like a balloon puffing up, collapsing along one side, then filling again. The skin above his eyes looked stretched and rubbery. "Do you have something wrong with you?"

"What do you mean?"

"Your face is swelling, then unswelling."

"There's nothing wrong with my face."

"I mean your head."

"My head neither."

"Maybe my eyes are fluctuating."

"It could be that."

I asked him if he knew whose house this was and he said yes. He was on his way here. Then he began to haul packages from the boat into the house, groceries and such. "I'm going to make a snack," he said. "You look like you need a snack." A tiny chipmunk-like creature poked up from behind his ear and ducked back. I didn't mention it.

"I think I want to go lie down."

"Good idea."

I went out and lay down on the dock. The old cypress boards were warm from the sunlight that poured its amber dregs over the landscape. "We're on the way to Scorchy's," I said when Homer brought me a cutlet sandwich and a fresh drink.

"That's a good idea."

He sat with his shoes off, his toes dangling into the canal. The water was chocolate colored and sighed lightly, as if pushed by the tide, among the yellow-green grasses. I felt a little jealous, but I didn't want to let on. "My emotions have been getting in the way of my life," I said obliquely.

"That'll happen."

"Has it ever happened to you?"

"I think it's more like they are my life."

"It's like that at the worm farm?"

"It's like that everywhere,"

"I'm on my way to see Alice."

"Into trouble?"

"Not necessarily."

I didn't think I needed to comment about what was obvious here, but it bothered me. I thought it was irresponsible for Henry to be getting romantically involved with someone from our parents' world.

"What was that?" Homer said.

"What was what?"

"You said something—about being irresponsible."

"I didn't realize I was speaking out loud."

He looked at me, studied my face as if there was a price tag on it. "Are you just going through a bad patch, or is this more like a permanent condition?"

"I'm trying to get used to it, whatever it is."

"People probably recommend that you get some rest."

"I do lie down a lot already."

"What do you think makes you like this?"

"I'm jumpy about the Laughing Boy, I think."

"You're never serious, are you? You used to be serious, but you never are anymore."

"I don't think I was that serious."

"Oh, you were. You were the most serious boy in West Miami."

I went into the kitchen and poured myself a glass of rum and then I went into the bathroom and dropped a couple of ludes into my system. In the mirror a gentle soul, an abashed and tender soul, looked back at me. Out the window a bird called, requesting something from life, nothing important, just asking. I had a thought, one of the difficult ones where everything I loved was taken from me and distributed among those who would misuse it. It was so painful I climbed out of the window, went along the side of the house to my car, got in and drove away.

After a while I was on the highway crossing the Glades, driving west into a lowering late spring sun. I pulled the visors down, put on my shades and drove at speed. The swamp off to my left had that lonely aspect that makes you want to kill yourself. Way off and up high, buzzards circled above a fresh corpse. Some species gone under, some special kind of panther or yellow-winged bird dying on a bump of land among the waters. Up ahead somebody hitchhiking, some kid, like me except without a car, looked up. I stopped for him and he swung a duffel bag into the back and got in. He offered his hand and we shook on it. "I'm glad you came by," he said. "I felt very alone and naked out there." I knew immediately—or I got it in my mind—that this was the Laughing Boy.

We were an hour away from Alice's and I used this time to speak to the boy about my life. I brought him up to date on my local activities, my adventures overseas, which I hadn't talked about in some time, including my time in Italy, as well as my period of employment as an all purpose feature writer for the *Herald*. He could tell I was afraid of him, anybody could tell it.

"Is there ever anything else you'd like to do?" he said.

"Instead of take drugs and write for a newspaper?"

"Instead of what you've said so far."

"Sure. I want to live on a bluff and see two kinds of weather at once and I'd like to insert myself head down into the heart of the woman I love."

"That wouldn't do it for me," he said.

"What would?"

"I just want to get them to leave me alone."

"I feel like that too, but then I get alone and the loneliness starts pecking at me like evil chickens."

"I never get lonely. I never been lonely in my life."

He spit out the window.

We were driving without the air conditioner, which was a pleasure of mine in the country. I liked the smells, the hot air rushing by.

"Where're you headed?" I said.

"West."

"We're going to run out of west pretty soon here."

"West or south, maybe north."

"Ah, yeah. I'm familiar with that destination."

He gave me a hard look, and the look, which was just as human as anything else I had seen lately, made me wonder about murder and sociopathism and what it was really like. Just loneliness taken to the extreme was what I figured, despite what the boy said. He was thin and about my height, but he had that stringy backcountry hardness of bone and muscle that made me think he could probably lift twice as much weight as I could. Two of his victims had been found outdoors, stuck up in the crotch of gumbo-limbo trees like the prey of some African leopard. He'd probably simply raised their bodies up there all by himself. He had the physique of a lonely person, one of the physiques.

"Loneliness?" he said. "I don't know what you are talking about. Watch out!"

He grabbed the wheel, jerking us back onto the pavement. "Jesus—are you all right?"

"Just a minute."

I pulled over, got out and vomited into the ditch. There were fish in the ditch, small silver creatures swimming along in black water, happy as could be, fully fishified, the ditch everything to them. What a world, I thought. Life poking up all over it.

"I am terribly stoned," I said when I got back to the car.

"You shouldn't use that shit," the boy said. "You should stay as far away from that shit as possible."

"I wouldn't be myself without it."

"That's a spineless thing to say."

"Well, I think it has a certain poetry myself."

"I don't want you to drive."

"It's no trouble."

"It is for me."

He wouldn't go on if I drove, so I climbed over into the backseat and let him take the wheel. I lay down and took a nap, first telling him how to get to Alice's house. It crossed my mind that it was not the best idea to give a murderer directions to your loved one's house, but my thinking also went like this: I had already lost her through some terrible play of chance, more than one play, and now chance had come again in a spiky and possibly penetrating way and what was I to do? If I shed this buckaroo I might not get to Alice in time. Not only in time to hook up with her, but in time to save her. Lack of drive, that's what they said about me at the office, one of the things they said, and I thought of this as I drifted off zipping through the outback—drive, getting it, employing it, sticking with the plan no matter what happened, all that American crap I used to ridicule, but which now haunted me—the getting something and getting somewhere business—haunted me as if I was guilty in an especially sordid way, which I was and as far as I could tell always had been. "You sure you can get there?" I said.

His answer came back as coos and mutterings, soft animal reassurances that I couldn't follow and didn't worry about.

I waked, shook myself out of a splitting headache, to find the car stopped in Alice's driveway and the boy in a fistfight with her husband. I stuck my head up over the backseat and gazed at the spectacle. The fight was human, not a movie fight, and as such fights are, it was a display of uncertainty. A punch now and then, a half wrestle. Slipperiness and indecision. The men cut a quandaried circle across the oyster shell driveway and the lawn that was constructed of scruffy bahaia grass shorn to stubble, speaking to each other in that abrupt and flabbergasted way men do who fear the crunch of bone.

"You're gon' let me into that house," the boy said.

"I'm going to let you into hell," Bobby Concannon said.

The fight continued for some time, the men leaving pink marks like little blushes on each other's bodies. I was keeping a lookout for Alice. I could tell she wasn't home. The house looked deserted. Even the flowering plants she had set in buckets on the wraparound porch had the abashed air of abandoned things. The rakes and other farm implements propped next to the front door looked left over, as did the stack of books on the cane sofa under the front windows. There were no pets, none that weren't locked up or out of barking range.

I took a swig from my vial of traveling spirits, returned the bottle to my bag and got out of the car.

"You," Concannon said.

The boy took advantage of BC's shift in attention to whack him hard on the ear.

"Ow, damn it," Concannon said, and staggered. He seemed all right and then he wasn't. He turned, groping for a chair, but he couldn't find one. His brain found it perhaps because he turned slowly back and sat down into air, as if the chair was securely behind him.

The boy lurched away, dragged himself in a slant run up the steps, grabbed a shovel and came back with it. He raised the shovel against BC's slumped frame, but I stopped him, "Whoa—hey," then caught him by the shoulder. He wrenched away and lifted the shovel at me, but he didn't strike.

"Wait," I said. "He knows where she is. We don't know."

"I've lost interest in that."

"It's my whole purpose."

"You go find her then." He laid the shovel down in the grass, staggered over to a plumeria bush and dry heaved into it.

I understood there were times when we had to have death and violence—just as we had to have sex, or the bright fair face of a child looking straight into ours, or we had to notice, as we fell a thousand feet, what a beautiful morning it was—and I thought we had now come to one such.

"I ought to introduce you to my friend Henry."

"I know enough people already. I'm trying to forget the ones I do know."

"You're doing fine."

"You 'speck her address is up in the house?"

"Maybe."

"Then let's go check."

Concannon didn't get up to accompany us, which made it breaking and entering, and after the boy helped himself to a handful of blackberry pie from the refrigerator and a long pull on a carton of milk, burglary as well. I went upstairs to the phone in her bedroom—her separate bedroom that I already knew about because she had told me she lived in it alone like Emily Dickinson, looking out at the marshes and writing stories herself that had nothing to do with me.

I called the *Herald* city editor, Ike Hamlin, who was also my cousin, and told him I had come upon the Laughing Boy.

"You were supposed to go talk to a Mrs. Garcia," he said, "of Homestead, Florida, whose only child, a boy with an IQ of genius"—he said it with three syllables: geen-y-us—"was run over by his father's bread truck."

"I was headed over there, but then I had a fit of conscience and stalled out."

"You have had too many fits of conscience lately."

"It seems just the opposite to me."

"That's where we differ. What's this with the Laughing Boy?"

I said I picked him up hitchhiking.

"How did you come to the conclusion he was our LB?"

"Instinct."

"That the same faculty sent you out to the Gables running after that woman you said could tell the future?"

"I had a feeling, yeah."

"She was nobody."

"Not to her family."

"Jesus, Billy."

On my first visit this woman, a Mrs. Mandell in pioneer skirts, had said love was falling like a spring rain on all of Miami. If only we could see it. I wanted to talk to her again about that. "This is more a fact," I said, "than a feeling."

"Has he confessed?"

"By deed rather than speech."

"He has killed somebody in front of you?"

"Almost."

Here I was, bragging.

"If he doesn't confess it doesn't matter who he is. They haven't got any clues about that fellow anyway."

"I thought I ought to call and tell you."

"I am glad you did. I'm always happy to hear from you." He said something to someone nearby then was back. "Your mama called."

"Oh?"

"She said Uncle Louis is not doing well."

"That's what she says to try to get me to come by."

"I'm just passing it on."

I felt the shiver of my errancy.

He said, "What are you going to do about the LB?"

"I think I'll stick with him for a while."

"If he really is the killer, then that might not be such a good idea. I'll call the state patrol. They'll pick you up. You out at Concannon's?"

"Why don't you hold off on that."

"Why?"

"There's something I really want to ask him. I need time to remember what it is."

"I'm going to call them right now."

"Nah, it's okay. But it's nice of you to think of it."

"It'll be bad news for all of us if something happens to you. Especially for me."

"Especially for *me*, you mean."

"Yeah, that too."

Then I called Henry, who was still looking for me.

"I thought you had sneaked out to the bar."

Three Delays

"Hold on." There was banging downstairs, the sound of drawers opening and crashing shut. I went out on the landing. "What're you up to down there?"

"No good," the voice came back, the boy's voice, sounding strong and refreshed, the voice of youth.

"Who was that?" Henry said when I came back.

I told him.

"He *made* you bring him over to Alice's, didn't he?"

"She's not here."

"I wonder what she's doing right now. She said she was coming this way—I don't know when it was—today or tomorrow—sometime. She wants to see the sculpture I'm working on."

"You didn't say anything about that."

"I don't guess I had time to."

"I mean to talk to you about Homer."

"No, you don't. You're not like that at all."

"Like what?"

"Like those who lecture others about the way they live."

"Oh yes I am."

Bang bang bang went the percussion section downstairs.

Henry said, "I'm worried about you out there, with that boy. Why don't you jump out of the window and run away."

"All right."

I went out onto the balcony—a white open porch that looked east toward Miami and my apartment in South Beach—and started down a drainpipe that was clamped to the white clapboard side of the house. Just as I did this, the boy poked his head out the bedroom door. He looked at me with an assessing gaze but didn't say anything. I climbed back up the pipe and onto the porch. Alice had set out lawn furniture, striped plastic chairs, and the kind of chaise lounge you take to the beach. There was a little white plastic table by the lounge and on the table was a glass that had the dregs of some dark cola-like liquid in it. I sat down on the lounge and drank what was in the glass. It was coffee, gone stale. The boy sat down in one of the chairs, crab-legged it over and leaned out above the rail. "It's scary how far you can see in a place like this," he said.

"I can never see quite far enough."

I went back in the house, followed after a while by the boy. Her bedroom looked like something from an outraged millionaire's safari. The expensive furniture was made of canvas and leather strips and it was stained with lipstick and rouge and other colorful unguents. The narrow camp bed was trampled on, stirred up like a whirlpool just after the explorer has sunk into it. On her desk were books with angry titles like FOLLOW YOUR HATE; ARGUE YOUR WAY OUT OF IT; TAKE IT—NO WAY!; and THE FIST OF LOVE. Books with all the letters in their titles capitalized. Paper scurries, manuscript drifts, lay against table legs and under the TV, which had a crown of coiled wires resting on it. Dead coffee in enameled cups. Slack tide, I thought, at the asylum. A trail of shoes led into the dressing room, which looked through its open doorway as if some explicit and terrible fight had occurred in there. She wasn't inside. "What were you looking for downstairs?"

"I don't know," the boy said in a disgusted voice. "There's always something."

"Something what?"

"Some I don't know, some some-which-a-thing that tells what these people's lives were all about."

"Were?"

"What made them tick."

"This guy's a contractor. He wants to bulldoze the swamp."

"What about her?"

"Her who?"

"The woman you came out here to see."

"She's flown."

The phone beside the bed rang. I picked it up and received her voice, attenuated and harassed, coming over the wire.

"Where are you?" I said.

"Everglades City. Is BC there?"

"You want to talk to him?"

"I just want to know if he is there."

"Last we saw of him he was unconscious out in the front yard."

"That her?" the boy said.

I nodded. He ducked, smiled, and tiptoed out of the room, exaggerated in his style, but showing some kind of manners nonetheless.

"I thought you were going to be here," I said, already aggrieved, already regretting the aggrievement.

"Why is Bobby unconscious?"

"This boy I am traveling with beat him in a fistfight."

"A boy? He beat up Bobby? What else can he do?"

"I think he is the Laughing Boy Spree Killer."

"That too?"

"I'm sorry to bring him to your house."

"But not sorry enough not to do it, huh?"

"I don't know why I picked him up. It's one of those things you do that you can't explain."

"Like come bothering me?"

"Hey. You asked me out here. Why are you in Everglades City?"

"I thought we could get a boat. Go to Mexico or New Orleans."

"Either one would be fine with me."

I slid a little packet of powdered mushrooms out of my back pocket, excused myself, went into the bathroom, drew water and took a dose, tapping the powder into my mouth like country people did with their headache remedies. It was horribly bitter, but part I had already accepted of the price you pay for remission. For liftoff. The miracle fell right on top of the Quaaludes, on top of the rum I had been sipping, and shifted me ASAP into another, a more actual and relevant world.

I returned to the bedroom where somebody, maybe me, had already pulled the canvas shades, encapsulating the space in a soft yellow light, a light that would soon turn to gray and then to black, and lay back on the bed. It was hard, ungiving under me. Alice's tiny voice floated up to me from a long way off, but I was by this time thinking of something else. I was remembering, with a deep, rugged sadness, a woman, a friend of my mother's, whom I encountered a year ago. She came to a meeting I attended of the Founders Society, an organization that promoted backwardness in all things and attempted to put the quietus on Miami progress, both social and cultural, a local reactionary group in fact started by members of my own family, among others. I had risen for a question to the current president, a cousin of mine, given a short and desperate rant, and sat down. This woman approached me afterward and for some reason I was kind to her. Kind in the manner of listening to her, and then, with a delicate and completely false motivation, comforting her vis-à-vis the recent death of her son.

Last month she phoned me at the paper to say she had cancer of the breast. She was scared to death; she said so, and I could hear it in her voice. "I need to talk to you again," she said. "Of course," I said, "I'll be right over." But I didn't go. Instead I walked upstairs to the composing room and sat two hours conversing with the layout artists, mostly with a young woman from Idaho who as she knuckled my thigh explained to me how the Mormon Church worked. Then I left the building, drove out to the beach, where I gave a short talk—after a series of shots in a bar on Ocean Drive—to a group of regulars I knew (assembled around me or within shouting distance at the Sea Breeze Tropical Paradise)—ne'er-do-wells, Cuban freedom fighters and representatives of the morally confused—about the necessity of loving our brothers no matter who they were. Then I went home to an early rest because I had to get up at five the next morning to meet the trade boat coming in from the Lower Bahamas. On the boat was a political refugee my cousin the city editor wanted me to interview. During the interview I had to take a break because of an inexpressible sadness, which as soon as I sat back down I attempted to express. This sadness, as far as the refugee could tell—a mild slender man who was leaving a large family to come tell of tribulation in the Caribbean—was generalized, nonspecific, and endemic. The man before me, in short, pithy, heavily accented English phrases, explained to me the necessity of fighting against repression. I sat there marveling and trembling, flooded with shame. I never did go see the woman.

Charlie Smith

Then the boy called me from the yard. An updraft caught me, some thought that had started out this way a thousand years ago, some drifting emotion just released from the dog latitudes found me, and soon I was on my feet and downstairs, out onto the brilliantly sunny lawn where Concannon sat at a picnic table drinking a beer.

"I could have told you she wasn't there," he said.

One half of his face was red and swollen.

"Then where is she?" the boy said.

"Who is this nut?"

I remembered I hadn't hung up the phone, but when I ran back upstairs the line was dead. The room, the family compound, the whole Everglades itself, without her in it, was dead.

Later we were in the car together driving toward Everglades City. Concannon sat in the backseat sullenly drinking beer. He said he didn't want to see her, but he wanted to go to Everglades City anyway, then he repeated this several times in slightly different ways, sounding cracked.

"I don't even know how I feel about her," he said. "I might hate her, I might love her—I can't tell. You could put a gun to my head and I wouldn't be able to say. Do you have any idea what I mean?"

The boy beside me sweetly hummed and leaned his head against the doorpost, looking out on the wide damp prairie. The grass looked as if the sunlight soaked ten feet down into it. Westward leaning, the boy caught the sun in his eyes; it reflected in them, wet eyes like the eyes of a retriever. He stretched his arm along the seat, sank a hand low and patted Concannon on the knee.

"Hey!" BC said, but he didn't do anything. He started telling a story about Wolfie's in South Beach, Wolfie's and the dawn. It was muddled and pathetic, a common tale. I had no idea what had happened to him. Maybe it was simply Alice. She had told him she was leaving. He was known as a rough character, relentless, a disputer, ungovernable really unless you took him in his sleep, but now he was meek, or something like meek. Maybe it was the boy. Maybe the boy had shown him something—knife or kiss—that got to him.

I thought I'd write a series of articles on him, on the boy—face of a nineteen-year-old, body of a sharecropper's son—the Laughing Boy (maybe he only laughed on the job, a professional), and fax them in to the paper. I couldn't remember if I had suggested this to him and now looking at him I was overtaken by a shyness. "You fascinate me," I said silently to the windshield.

"What was that?"

"Ugm." My life (at this time) moved by in a series of cloudscapes, weathers, each isolated from the other, each with its own special climatic system, its drenches and ventilations, its substratospheric variety; it was hard to tell if anything was connected.

"What did you say?"

"Something general."

His face, breaking into a grin, disputing my whole outlook, was a poem. His hair, thrush brown, brown thrasher brown, cut short, jutted from his skull. His face was an interdiction of bone and skin, a wedge, an ax. His grin a V splitting it. It was a grin of such sterling quality, of such sweetness and with such peculiar hints of insight, that I think for a moment I was struck dumb. A poem, I mean, that you catch a snatch of some night while crashing through the furniture. Come and gone.

And this may not have happened.

All of this, dusk to dawn, and round again, may not have happened.

"We're at the end of it?" the boy said, stretching his hand out.

"Florida?"

"Does it go on from here?"

"You haven't ever seen the Keys, have you?" BC said.

"I'm taking the area a little at a time. Small bites."

We passed the motels and the city waterworks with its low white cylindrical tanks, and the electric plant and the truck stop with its salacious silhouettes of girls in short dresses painted onto the side of the building, bumped by the entrances to the brief, thoroughly humiliated residential sections and through the clustered strip of downtown to the water. The Gulf at this point was darkened by the swamp. It lay off from us inside the brushy yellow arms of the peninsulas that formed the harbor. Out from the bay you could see the islands, tousled and bristling, glaring up into the sunlight.

We let Concannon off at one of his construction offices, which was in an aluminum trailer behind the hardware store. A man sat in a folding chair outside the trailer, a derelict looking fellow, suntanned like all the homeless in South Florida, one of those who always made me think of where I was headed. He struggled to his feet as Concannon got out of the car, came forward rubbing the rust off his hands and offered the right one. Concannon, who as I understood him would normally swat someone like this aside, took the man's hand and shook it enthusiastically. "How are, dear?" he said. Then I remembered: Estel Concannon—he was BC's father, Alice's father-in law. The old man beamed at him. Concannon turned back to us, holding in his face a contrite and undistilled sadness—overwashed by happiness. What had happened to him? "I'll be fine now," he said.

"What did you do to him?" I asked the boy.

"Just the usual," he said.

I parked in front of Dowell's Supply Store and used their outdoor phone. From the ground, oyster shells caught sunlight like pearls in their hollows and threw it back into my eyes. Bedazzled, overcome by drugs and light, by a glimpse of some improbable beatitude, swaying, for a second I was lost to myself and to everything else. It was a genuinely beautiful feeling, a feeling like fever coming on in sunlight, as if I could lean back into a gentleness that would let me down, forever, into its ongoing self. From this place I saw my hand reach out and dial Henry's number.

"I'm here," I said.

"Me too."

"Here?"

"There, to you."

I wanted to tell him how much he meant to me, how fine he was as a man and a friend, but I was realistic enough to keep my mouth shut.

"I had such a strong feeling about you just now," he said.

"Me too, about you. It was so sad."

"Sad?"

"Sure. A sentimental, entirely inappropriate sadness, but as real to me as a goat in the road."

"You want to tell me?"

"I do, but Alice has just come into view."

"Where?"

"Down at the end of the street."

This was true. She lay on her back on the bow of a boat resting on its trailer at the marina. Her legs, long and brown as butternut, hung down. Her hand, as if signaled by a director, slipped slowly off the blue ledge of the bow and scratched along her thigh, seemed to pull the leg up and scratched her ankle bone. She held the ankle, half circling it with her long fingers. She was a block and a half away, but I saw all this. A telescopic reality pushed my vision out to her, bringing her closer, a living figurehead, sprawled above the grass. She was twenty-six-years old and I knew everything about her. I could have written her biography without having to look up a single thing. This is not to say I knew anything about her at all. I waved, but she wasn't looking in my direction. "There she is, old boy."

"I miss you two," Henry said.

"Who wouldn't miss two such as we?"

The street was dusty, paved with ashes or with the pulverized bottom of the sea, white like the streets of old Jerusalem. Down it staggered a few tourists carrying booty in straw bags. An Indian, a Miccosukee warrior, stepped from a bar and looked musefully up at the sky. Maybe he was remembering what life had once been before the white man came. He looked toward Alice, who seemed to be drifting in a dream. It amazed me that she was alive, that one such as her walked around on the earth.

"Halloo," I said softly.

"Halloo back," Henry said.

"Have you talked to your mother recently?"

As children we lay in his bed on Saturday mornings while his enormous, unhappy yet soulful mother told us stories about her childhood in Cuba. She was raised there by missionary parents who had not loved her as much as they loved their flock. We were young, barely fledged, and the stories were so sad, so ponderous with their figures of desertion and unrequited love, their mournful breezes blowing through the poincianas, that we wept, the three of us, holding each other in the bed.

"This week," he said. "Has your mother gotten hold of you?"

"She did once, but I wrestled free."

There was the usual brief moment of silence as Henry restrained himself from admonishing me.

"It's medieval," he said.

"What is?"

"Your parents' lives."

I didn't want to hear about it, not the first thing. And said this.

"I know," he said. "How's everything with your spree killer?"

"He's just this moment stepped out of Dowell's wearing a blue straw hat. He looks quite handsome."

"Maybe he'll want to go his own way now."

"I plan to write something about him."

"Did Ike tell you to?"

"It's my idea."

Some freakish, misused young people came out behind him, shaking their long, handsome hair loose. The look of distress in their eyes, the sadness behind the face paint, was familiar, these kited checks of progeny, guys like me. The look, the futile disputatiousness, the barely concealed almost feral sadness—you saw it all over Miami. Like a dress code just before it goes out of style, it circulated among the groups, the Cubans and the Latino vacationers and the quarrelsome Jewish pensioners and the crackers, the conchs, and the old folks rattling their bones inside the dice cups of their ruined bodies. The goggle-eyed looks in the supermarket parking lot, the stuttering rages interrupted by cops on Calle Ocho, the frenzy at the fronton, all were part of and exemplified it; my father, God bless him, had made a life's work of dealing with it, of subverting it, a kindly quack whispering into the microphone attached to the loudspeaker on top of the company car: *Come unto me, all ye crazed and slap-faced folk, and I will give you rest.* What it had come to for him was a cramped and impoverished senescence over on Fifth Street, under the ratty palms and the dying grapefruit trees. I just didn't want to hear about it.

Then it was later and Alice was pointing out to me how I mutilated everything she loved and leaning across the little ship lamp's table light to stroke the boy's wrist in the feral and seductive way she had even in her sleep, looking from him to me, exchanging, in the time it took her eyes to swivel three feet, invitation for disgust and not even acknowledging what was going on. We were eating pounded conch and oysters. The boy was nervous about the shellfish, but he was game.

"Listen," I said. "Are you sure Concannon is a threat to you?"

"He set off an M-80 outside my bedroom."

"A firecracker?"

"He tore up my clothes."

"I thought you said it was just the looks."

"After the looks comes action. That's how it works."

I didn't want to hear any of this. I wanted to talk about cabins in the mountains, some such thing, clicking little streams, pools under the hemlocks, flight into Egypt. Keep it light, settle in, lay back and then go intense, but only in the talk, romantically intense only. Stay away from the rough business, be nice. I say this, but yes that was me too, back in 19—, outside the Shirley Lounge shrieking at her, attempting to crack her skull with a hammer. And that was also me in downtown lockup blues, sitting in the pen, waiting for my name to come up on the court docket, Henry dragging some useless lawyer over to talk to me, nothing for it but to go to jail or leave the state. And it's true I got something out of the rage, some kind of oxygen, or oxygen substitute. Still, I would call myself a tender man.

From the first minute she'd bored right in. Springing off the boat and striding toward me with her ears flattened against her head and her hands balled in fists, her eyes spinning. "Where have you been?"

"On the way since about five years."

"Well, come on, boy."

Roughly she grabbed me, sank her claws into my body, snatched me from air into the fiery substrate she breathed. She shook me, she bounced hard against me, she shoved me, she knocked me off balance so I nearly fell. It was all right. Almost all right, I was so happy to see her, it didn't derail me. Later, as on the dock we fingered some sponges brought in that afternoon from the Sunken Keys, she turned viciously on me when I told her—gasping, suddenly afraid, paralyzed in some way in my will—that I hadn't appreciated the way she spoke to me the week before on the phone, that it was harsh—turned wildly against me cursing, her body shaking, fire in her eyes, the old demonic business, the devil in human form, all that, so familiar to everyone out in West Miami, beauty as banshee, all that, no stopping her if you weren't armed. I shouted at her. Shouted her name once, sharply. She came back to herself as if I'd slapped her. Blinking, in a clump. An old, sweet, left-for-dead consciousness dredged up from a ditch. Not quite abashed, not able even to apologize, but in manner contrite. At least quiet. In me, the same rage, almost, yet encapsulated inside a hollow shell of fear. Something in me shrank, fell back, groped for the exit. And now the boy across the table from her, receiving little pats and strokes. She didn't know what she was doing, I saw that.

"Why don't you take him to the room?" I said.

She looked at me, embarrassed, shy of herself, explicitly focused. Everything inside her was expressed in her face. She was like an infant. It was the same as always. Hurt, fear, chagrin, some wild Arabian nights kind of thing, slyness, the slyness apprehended, misery, an ancient ungovernable sadness, hatred, disgust, a Daffy Duck idiot wiliness, bafflement, lust, blank feral staring, love—they were all there. She was better than jai-alai, better than the movies, better, almost, than drugs, and she always had been. I hadn't been able to take my eyes off her since we were six. She grinned, snatching out such a grin I fell back as from a magician pulling doubloons from the atmosphere.

"What?" I said. "What fourteen hundred things could you want now?"

"Let's go down and look at the fish."

This is what we did, careened down to the end of the public dock to catch a look at the big fish swimming around under the lights. The water was a little milky, but you could see them, sleek torpedo-like wahoos and mackerel, and the big slow fat groupers and jewfish, the mincing redfish, all pumping along, all circled and whipped about by the little baitfish style characters, as in a aquarium, or a dog pack. We dangled our legs over the edge jeering at them, marveling. The boy was as happy, he said, as he'd ever been. He jumped up, skipped back to a stand and bought us ice cream cones, peach for me, banana for Alice, which she wolfed.

"Kiss, kiss," she said, smiling with a smeared and sugary mouth. I gave her one, one of the millions I had backed up. The two drugs—the woman drug and the low fire, slow cat stretch of the Quaaludes—met and mingled. I found her hand, which was as large as mine, longer in the fingers, bony rather than fleshy. The hand, the grip, the kiss, the snug body sliding against me, took me over, like an army in a movie, like a government of children, and began to order me around, to pass new laws. It was okay. I wanted to be subject to some irrevocable tyranny. She grinned at me, only a slip of the madness peaking out from behind her eyes, the distractedness which is what it was, recall from some distant furnace in her brain she tended at all times, some munitions works, bomb factory, demonic engine turning over, just now almost out of view as the love welled up. "Sure, sure," she said, "only this, nothing but this all the time."

"Agh," I said, dumbfounded, speech blown out of me, drugged.

I placed my hand on her chest and it was as if my hand entered her body, as if I touched secrets on the inside of her, equipment and materiel and gadgetry from the interior, local stuff known only to those born in the area. Touched an essential hominess that saved me. I wanted at that moment no more drugs. Then, as if some chill blew in from the Gulf, I did want drugs. She sensed it and pulled back.

"No," she said, "not right now."

"I can't help it," I said.

"Okay."

We got up and went back to the motel, where I shot up. The boy watched me do it, sliding up close so he could see the needle go into the skin.

"It's like your flesh rises up to take it," he said.

I was violently sweating—the taramosalata of pre-rush grabbed me this way—and then I was released from claws I didn't know clutched me and I slipped into a sweet world made for me. A little while later I got to my feet. The two of them were lying on the bed in their underwear talking.

"That looks nice," I said, and it was sweet to me, so kindly I thought, this love that circulates through the universe. You just have to raise your eyes to it. "What are you doing?"

"Talking," she said.

"I just thought that."

"You're speedy that way."

"I would like to go outside."

"We just ordered some refreshments."

"You don't like those."

"I do too. I've come to."

"Really? What a mystery you are. After all this time. I'll never get to the bottom of you. What's up, sport?" I said to the boy, who was studying me.

"Alice was telling me about when you were a preacher."

"A rectifying time it was."

"You didn't say it was when you were so young."

"I started at six."

"Did you have to have a license?"

"All you needed was the call."

"Why did you give it up?"

"I had a nervous breakdown."

"What does that mean? I never know what that term means."

"Life got more serious than it actually is."

"I know times like that."

"You have to make a change then."

"That's when I move on."

"To another park, sure."

"Sometimes a whole other world."

Confused, smelling of fish, hating redemption, I entered the palace. A poem maybe, or the title of a poem, little bits of blood and evacuated air clinging to it.

"I'm having trouble with my thoughts," I said. I wanted to go sweep, clean a house, get into the work of making a place for us.

"Where?" she said.

"What do you mean?"

"The house—where is it?"

"Did I say that?"

"Say it again," Alice said, her face like a 2-D affair that had just gone three dimensional. Nothing special really, it was only heroin, not the hallucinogenics. Maybe some leftover lumps of psilocybin, some undissolved bits kicking in, maybe some herb I didn't recall.

"Could be that," the boy said. "I don't know anything about drugs."

They were laughing then, probably had been for hours. I didn't mind. The laughter—we were outside now—was like a good surf. I picked my wave. Out beyond, in the blackened area, millions of whitecaps like an audience of the alarmed, the wide-awake dead.

She shook me, someone shook me, in my mind it was always her.

"Stop talking like that," she said.

"Look," I said, "I didn't mean it." But I did. Whatever it was, I claimed it.

"You contradict everything. You shouldn't say that if you don't mean it."

"Maybe you can marry the two of you yourself," the boy said. "Maybe, being a preacher, that would work."

We were on the back steps of a bar, possibly a bar, a restaurant maybe, on the lingering edge of the town. Beyond—mangroves, the slim shrieks of black palm trunks. There were others around, boys in white aprons eating crab legs. Inside, Boy Scouts sang camp songs. Their cracked, thoraxic voices wafted from the screen porch. The cooks, no, busboys, splashed beer in on top of the crab legs, looked at us laughing and wanted to know when the wedding was. Alice sat on a lower step looking up at me in a friendly, slightly demented way.

"When did we say?" I asked.

"*Inmediatamente*," one of the boys said, a wide-faced character into which no spirit had ever entered.

"*Falso, mi gusano.*"

"Hey," the LB Spree Killer said, "be calm."

I was calm. I was comatose nearly, laid out by love.

She had heard something, that was obvious. Some promise, some proposal. Some words from the cache of words that rang a bell.

"You're correct," I said, "I have it with me." Gloriously, I did, folded in my wallet, the marriage license. We had taken it out in Miami, one afternoon in the spring when she came to the city, both of us drunk, telling lies to the clerk, offering proof, turning ourselves in. It was a lovely business that day, Henry wandering in and out of the conversation, waving a sprig of bougainvillea, offering us blessing, grinning at us, only slightly terrified, a business that ended with accusations and rancor and a drink thrown in my face. "Yeah, I have it."

"Can you get married suddenly in Florida?" the boy said.

"If you have this."

It was in my hand, creased like a map, still in force.

"What, suddenly?" she said.

The justice of the peace was only slightly older than me, a lawyer actually, recently returned home from FSU, a married man himself who took the phone call and waited for us on the screen porch of his little house on Bethune Street. "I even have a ceremony," he said—"Hey, how are you—it was written out for me by my uncle who is an Episcopal minister up in Clearwater. Would you like to use that?"

He grimaced in a dyspeptic, self-referential way.

"No, it's not really illegal," the boy said in answer to something he thought he heard. "Not under these circumstances."

"Illegal?" the JP said.

"It feels that way," Alice said.

"Yes," I said, "like racketeering. Or vandalism."

"I know," the JP, just a boy, said. His face was colorless as rain, round, wide-eyed, maybe the ceremony a first for him. "Actually," he said, "I've done this by now nearly a dozen times. It's what I like best, really, the JP side. Human detail work."

His wife watched television in the den. Some animal program in which vicious doglike creatures tore the throat out of a little deer.

"Would you excuse me?"

I stumbled into the dark of what I hoped was the bathroom and vomited. Behind me a human shape, then light—the light of justice that falls on us all—revealing a child's bedroom, some goggle-eyed tyke whimpering, and the JP looming up, pronouncing something, Alice cursing colorfully.

"Jesus."

No rugs, so it was easy to clean up, which the boy did—our boy—without complaint.

"The shellfish," I said.

"Allergies," the JP agreed, undaunted, the wife furiously soothing the little muchacho, patting him with blows to the head, something like that, ruining his whole life in this fashion, I was sure of it, and misrepresenting me.

"Don't say a word," Alice said.

"Each new day," I said, "is a memorial to the one just passed."

"Which one?" the boy said.

The JP indicated the place to put the slop bucket. I gave the boy an eye roll, some gesture of the face, that he caught with alarm. I grinned, what I thought was a grin, revealing bloody teeth by the look of him.

"Excuse me," I said.

"Oh no. It's down the hall."

Alice accompanied me. We squeezed into the tiny ship's closet they used for washing up. Her face right up against mine now. Her breath strong of mint and sadness and compacted unresolved rage, bedrock emotional honesty, despair, all the factors that made up her inestimable self. She was about to cry, I could see that. "Billy," she said, "I'm so scared."

"Okay," I said. "Let's call it off."

"No! No, no."

On the walls photographs of fifties rock and rollers, wait, I have that wrong, of the JP dressed up as Elvis, as Little Richard, as Jerry Lee Lewis—the blond wig—as Chuck Berry with low-slung guitar and his wife Patsy Cline.

I let silence speak for me.

What it said she apparently didn't like. Whack. A blow. Or no, I slipped, that was what you always said at the hospital, and cracked my head against the tile wall, dislodging Carl Perkins.

"Do you want to take something?" she said.

"You'd rather me drugged, incompetent?"

"You've always been incompetent."

"I could use a little crystal."

"I don't even know what that is."

"Here," I said, and showed her.

"Do you want me to take some with you?"

"Only if you want to."

The alternate universe—maybe it was the Messiah—smiled at me, and winked.

We introduced the substance into our bodies.

Just after that the JP's wife offered us a selection of dime-store jewelry, from which we picked rings, pewter colored, that fit well enough. They were the same size, I remember that. Then she, the wife, snatching glances at the TV as she did so—sadly, as if a beloved national figure was dying on screen—fired up the tape player and gave us some music, just a snatch of it, a country ballad, followed by voices arguing, hers and her husband's, accusations flung—*You sorry son of a . . .*—and then an astonished silence, a moment of it, preceding the florid and incapacious words, the bejeweled and vacuous entreaties and promises that stood for everything inexpressible, stood, as Alice said later, for total hopelessness and disaster, which we accepted, swaying nervously under the cloud formations of our own thoughts, the drugs kicking in at just this time, so I heard along with the ceremonious diction other bits of imprecation and a few lies repeated in a voice I had come to call my own. And thus we were married.

"When I was seven," the boy said—this was later, at our wedding supper over at O.Z.'s Fish Ranch—"I saw my cousin who at only sixteen years drove a school bus, which was quite a feat, but I'll tell you, I knew, even then, I didn't want to be driving no school bus."

"What did you want to do?" said my nervy young bigamist wife.

"I wanted to be a boxer. We used to watch the Friday night fights—"

"Every Friday night," I said.

"Hey," he cried, "don't." Laughing as the JP's spouse sprayed him with lager. She was drunk, she had been drunk all along. "Actually

I knew I was something different, something that hadn't even been discovered yet."

"Like what?" Alice said.

"Something like a rheostat. Or an insulator. Expediter, I mean."

"That's been discovered."

Her face was red, as if the speed of the marriage had given her windburn, and damp with tears. Now she could cry, she said. She had just returned to us from the telephone, calling her stepmother, or the emergency room, someone out in the darkness who might be interested in us. Through a mist I had watched her approach, the way she moved decisively on long legs the same as it had been since I first saw her, doing the same thing to me, the tilt of her head the same, the righteous carriage of her shoulders, the slightly pointed chin held high as if she was wading in deep water, all the same, all still doing the same thing to me, this wonderful apprehending consistency of her comforting me, a consistency I burrowed into each moment of her presence, that gave me time to deepen and lengthen the space I occupied, setting anchors and root work, laying tile, constructing the little room in which I reclined in a chintz La-Z-Boy, watching the human interest news.

"You're like all the boys," she said to the boy, "wanting some handy dandy call sign that makes you Mr. Peculiarly Special, but every one of you—"

"Now, now, sweetheart," I said.

Her voice was hollow, famished, a desert ocean solo sailor voice.

"I feel *peculiarly* lost," the boy said. "Lost and waiting. Overwaiting. Like I'm in a bus station at three in the morning. Eating supper out of a cup."

"What satisfies you?" I said.

"Nothing for long."

Alice turned her head away and it was as if an empty vista opened, a patch of raw ocean the rain blew over. But I wasn't afraid. She turned back and her face was like a harbor, despite the look in her eyes of devilment.

"That's a strange way of putting it," she said, since I had spoken this last part out loud.

"Tell me things you've never seen."

She went first, an old game. Facial expressions, types of Argentinean lingerie, a photograph of the stretch of beach Columbus landed on, the flowers and fruits he mentioned in the ship's log but didn't name, now lost to time.

"So much lost to time," the boy said.

The night kept coming up, asking what it was we really wanted, the night or some member of its staff. In the false dawn we took a car ride, piled into the vehicle of one of the Cubano busboys. We headed out to the saltwater, to the left, west, to catch whatever part of the sunrise we could. On the way we ran over a possum and got out to look at it, to minister to it, but it was fearfully, anguishedly dead, its little rat teeth bared. Alice began to cry or maybe that was me, sure, I was the one, I began to cry, sobbing for the lost of this earth, ourselves prime examples. "Sucker tears," she said, crying too.

Then we bumped out a county road to some dunes piled against a brushy area where the mangroves drew back skirts off their spindly legs, and got out of the car. The waves, the little finger roll Gulf waves, whispered, per usual, deciding something they told no one about. That was how Alice put it, lying on her back looking at the morning star. A huge fear, bearish and irrepressible, something to do with an emptiness right next to the place I was sitting in, exposed itself to me. I jumped up, ran down the strand and tripped onto my face in some railroad vines. A small hairiness scurried away, ocean rat or goblin. Had we called Henry? Sure, that was the first thing we did. "It was inevitable," he'd said, half a smile in his sleepy voice.

"You promised her to me," I reminded him, "on Hagia Teresa Street in Istanbul."

"Sure I did."

Alice had talked rapidly and happily into the phone, maybe a little frantically.

My bones had begun to hurt, to express themselves badly inside my body. A breeze sighed in off the water, this and wintertime the only thing that kept the bugs off us. We lay down in a hollow among the vines, pulled them over us and slept.

Two days later—still in town due to some exit complications—a man came up to me on the street and told me Concannon was dead. I half fainted, knees reversing; he caught me, a man I thought I knew from newspaper work in the city. Across the street, from an outside second floor balcony, Alice in a yellow and white striped bathing suit languorously waved.

"Naw, buddy, I was just kidding," the man said, laughing, his laugh like a shaken bag of rocks. "I'm a sheriff's deputy and you're under arrest for assault and for bigamy. Or maybe it's your wife," he said in italics, "on the bigamy thing."

So once more to the jail. It was during this time that Minx Averroes, the New York editor, came by to see if I wanted to write some pieces about what had happened, which I did, typing them out in the rec room of the Monroe County Detention Center while I awaited trial on a charges of bigamy and assault. The boy had disappeared, which Minx was sorry to hear since he was happy to believe as I did that he was actually the Laughing Boy Spree Killer. But I wasn't interested anymore in psychopathology and told Minx so.

"You're grieving about the loss of your wife," he said sympathetically.

"She's not really my wife," I said. "Not yet."

"That's the spirit, though," he said.

Some old nolle prossed charges from years ago that Alice and her sister Senegol had brought came back to get me, since Monroe County did not consider it sufficiently adjudicated, a problem Alice herself was only too happy to solve by repudiating the charges, a maneuver however so insulting to the local D.A.—and which would cost the county, as he said, probably in excess of eighteen hundred dollars to run through—that he would not countenance such a strategy, would in fact prosecute Alice too, on the bigamy charge, which though it was antiquated and slightly ridiculous would, he assured her, result in real jail time for her.

"I'll do it anyway," she said when she came to visit. She was wearing clothes very like the ones I had on, that is, a pale yellow jumpsuit minus in her case the appliqué stitching saying Monroe County Jail Auxiliary above the left breast. Her dark hair was held back from her face by a child's blue monkey barrettes.

"I don't think you want to do that," I said. "Then they'd just have us both."

"I'm divorcing the Bob."

"That's good news. For a married man like myself, it is."

I was a little smooth from the pseudo opium I had dropped an hour before, but I could still feel some of what it was to be human in a situation like this. I didn't want to feel much. Always, so it seemed to me, if I experienced the true quality of human life I would begin to scream and not stop. Everyone in the jail agreed with this point of view. I had gotten the drugs from a Cubano accountant who was there for ramming his wife's boyfriend's Lexus with his pickup truck, ramming it actually over the guard rail on the Watson Slough Bridge and into the Gulf Coast Waterway, where the boyfriend all but drowned.

"Here," she said, offering me what looked like a nose on a string.

"Can't pass things," the guard said.

"Careful." She was out on bail, an extravagance I hadn't yet gone for but which would soon, I hoped, come my way if my friend Minx could get funds from New York. "What is that?"

"A nose."

A joke plastic nose on a rubber string it was in fact, put it on change your whole personality. She put it on. It made her look feral, and conniving but not cunning—subhuman.

She showed it to the guard, Ralph.

"You could use that to escape," he said. "Disguise."

"Who would it fool, you figure?"

"I don't recognize you," he said.

She wore it the rest of the session, which saddened me. She was disconnected, scared, making claims about the future that had little to do with reality. The nose, as I saw it, was an emblem of her unexamined outrage. The swell of fury converted to plastic. "Fuck you," she said when I asked her to take it off.

"What happened to the boy?"

"He's gone."

"You look like some really mean carnival employee."

"How dare you."

"What dare?"

"Oh, Billy. You are so spineless."

"Fuck I am."

"That's menacing speech," the guard said.

"What you, fuck—" she cried.

"Shut up, you!"

The fit snapped. She'd slumped in her chair, looking out a window through the one unclouded pane. When she looked back her eyes were wild. Wild and hurt and sad and baffled and held captive—her spirit gleaming way down in chains—by some imperious internal cabal.

Even through the drugs the nervousness reached me, my own that is. I couldn't take my eyes off her. Like a man dying obsessed, I stared into her face, studying twitch and fascia, the gaunt imperiled bone structure, the fey slant of her neck. Her hazel eyes were round and yellowed-out; like a pelican's, I thought, and laughed.

"What, what?"

She laughed too. The laughter like a rescue squad coming over the wall of her melancholy. The sadness not dying out, not converting to anything, simply smoothed over like a water trail as the gator sinks. And me in an orange plastic chair at a Formica covered table thinking how beautifully wide set her eyes were, and dawdling in this, not even wishing to mention it to her, the notation rising barely to consciousness, something about it still connected to a plush and helpless quality extending so far back into my life it seemed as if everything in me I had felt since before I was born, since before anyone was, was part of it.

"Yuk, yuk," she said.

Her hand crossed the table like Patton taking Europe away from the Nazis, and touched my fingers. Not electricity, but a proper fit. Adhesion, as they say.

Once, on a sunny day before she took off, she appeared in the parking lot across the street from the jail and made signals to me with a hand mirror. They came out and made her stop. I wrote about the mirror—"little transmogrified face, white flashing dummy expressing in sparks and flares what couldn't otherwise be said . . ."—and about the nose and her rumbustious talk and her decision to fight the charges. I wrote about the scowling, wide-mouthed monkey look she gave the guard. About how you could see her soul shining like an all-night supermarket in her eyes. Minx said what I wrote was the best thing of its kind he had seen—what else of its kind have you seen? I asked, but he answered only with a bonhomious smile—and sent it off to New York where everyone there liked it too. A contract was drawn up that I was allowed to sign since it had nothing to do, so my lawyer said, with the actual charges, which was not strictly true, but which got by anyway since at that time in the country folks were not as outraged as they later came to be concerning the designated guilty making money in this world.

Part III

SMUGGLERS

Chapter One

Alice was upstairs making shelves for some skulls she'd found in a dig up by the Calusahatchee River, north of Big Cypress, that was what she said. Not found, really, someone had taken her out there and showed them to her. Old Miccosukee skulls from a burial mound which she'd been unable to resist snatching. "I don't know why I'm this way," she said, "but I am. It makes me nervous to be around myself."

Greed, I told her, that's what it was.

That and something else, she assured me.

"I'm about to jump out of my skin," she said. In pink underwear, squinting, she sat at the top of the stairs gripping an ocherous and earth-stained skull by the fontanel, scrutinizing it. Her mouth twitched. "Like death's a big wind he's caught in," she said. "All the flesh and skin blown off him." She bent closer. "What is it the eye cords are anchored to?"

"How many did George give you?"

"Sixteen."

"The whole neighborhood."

"I like to make sure I have enough."

"For what?"

"I don't know. Something uncharacteristic."

"What could that possibly be?"

She cocked her head and stared at me, her gaze focusing three inches deep. "The secret is what a good girl I am. You don't forget that, do you?"

No, I didn't. "You're going to make yourself feel bad."

She shuddered, caught in an undertow. Gesturing, hacking with one hand, she began talking about being scared. She had a way with the terrors of life, they were her hand-raised puppies.

"Henry would be angry I had these skulls," she said.

"He might not say it."

It hurt us terribly to be so close to each other. We couldn't stand it. I knew even now, leaning against the breakfast room doorway, if I advanced one step toward her she'd began to berate me. I'd fight back, and then life for us would become briefly cataclysmic.

"The dirt around the bones," she said, "was made of flesh."

"Bits of it?"

"Now it's dirt, but it used to be flesh. You couldn't tell. It really was dirt, not dirt substitute."

"Dirt helper."

She held the skull up beside her face. "Can you see me under here?"

"Every minute of the day."

I went out to the patio and lay down on the chaise. My notebook was on the little white wrought-iron table she'd bought last week, a revision of something, in her mind. Round about me, flickering among the vines, lizards, like a colorful, reptilian ornamentation, entered the day. Cataracts of greenery roared silently up out of the earth. The bushes looked uncontrollable. My curiosity—about life, about myself, about Alice: what was she doing *right now*?—mixed with languor, and I approached my happiest state. Morning raked streaks of light into the loquat bushes. On the lawn the shadows were long, like tall old men lying around on the grass. Juanita brought out a pot of espresso. I waited a minute before starting on it, let the chill in me warm in the sunlight. Something crouched just outside the gate of consciousness, something mean and overscrutinized. I sat up. The coffee steamed, a full pot of black chemo. I poured a cupful, dashed cream and Sweet'N Low into it and drank.

I began to write about the skulls, little death buckets, life buckets, God, some force of design, bailing our ration of consciousness out of the fathomless dark, all that. Alice lining them up in the bedroom, conducting a little symphonic variation on the silent scream. I was afraid to touch her. Days went by in which I couldn't bring myself to caress her body, even to look at it. If I came close to her, something terrible would happen. She stepped into the shower and I stepped out, scalded by proximity. What was that? What is that? she asked. Same as you, I said. It made us blustery in public, and ashamed, lurkers, lungers from the dark, people who ranted at strangers. The skulls meant nothing, not to her, or to me. She would return them in a cardboard box, guilt-ridden, but unable to apologize. Cranial peaches, by Cezanne, by Chardin. Walking around with this knobby, blood-streaked tabernacle on top of your shoulders. No, not that. It wasn't going anywhere.

So I got up and followed her, as I often did. Out into the world where she went shopping, stopped on Ocean Drive for coffee, walked out to the volleyball net and watched the players, came back, went to the variety store, stopped on 16th to speak to an old woman using a grocery cart as a walker, accompanied this old woman to her apartment a block away, stayed thirty minutes and exited ashy-faced, shuddering, abashed, and sat in her car with the windows down looking up the street, watching a Cubano man stripping fronds off a coconut tree beside the Alhambra Apartments for the hats he wove to sell to tourists. What was up? What life was this to long so for something I already had?

I called Henry. "I'm afraid to look at her naked."

"Me too."

"You're not afraid to look at Homer."

"Sometimes I think I'll pass out. Sometimes it chills me, the amazement, the wild thought of it."

"I don't mean the poetry, Henry. I'm overrun by the fact."

"It's a good sign."

"That's what you always say."

"It is because it is. You wouldn't feel this way if you weren't with the one you really love."

Passing by, she looked at me, wild-eyed, her soul cocked at a rakish angle, spectral curses frothing on her lips.

Back home I listened to her on the other side of the house, mouse approximations of human yearning, squeals and shudders converted into sighs, the languor of an afternoon become cheap songs on the radio, sounds of fake weeping. Disenchantment—for two weeks that had been her subject. It was clear she hated me. I slunk around like a stool pigeon.

In the afternoons I watched her sitting on the white decorated terrace of a beauty shop, of a hair dresser who did not understand her either but who intimidated her briefly. She was extemporizing with a woman about some bitter pill she'd had to swallow. The woman couldn't believe it either. Then she rose from her white wrought-iron chair, from the cockpit of her fighter jet, and began to shout at me, sitting on the steps of the Basel Hotel across the street. I too was in white. And I, a tender man, naturally quiet, shouted back.

Later she wanted to discuss this, my spying on her, but the look in her eyes scared me. I retreated through the house keeping large pieces of furniture between us. She followed, asking in a threateningly affectionate way what the matter was. But I wouldn't say.

"You won't or you can't?"

"Both."

We went out to the kitchen, where I threatened her with a corkscrew, I couldn't stop myself.

"You worthless wife stabber."

I wanted to rake it across her face. Something in me rushed up, rushed to the brink, pirouetted, whirled, slashed across the fog, and—nothing. I didn't stop myself. I simply couldn't move forward.

So I went down to the Keys for a few days, lay drunk on the back porch of Willie J's house, eating shrimp and throwing up into a bucket. Willie and his wife left me alone. A goat came to the screen door and looked at me. It seemed to be a very important goat, able to understand the vagaries of human behavior. I wanted to get something straight, but I forgot to mention it. I ate fudge, had more shrimp, drank rum, went over to Alice's friend Lorraine's house where I sat in the front room listening to her make love in the bedroom to her sailor boyfriend. The two of them came out looking cockeyed and happy. We all knew the happiness would pass. Lorraine ran a dive boat out to the reefs that lay like bruises just under the waterline. I rode with her, sank into the depths and panicked inside my mask, terrified I would never draw breath again. I swam up through a patch of jellyfish that had no stingers. They were iridescent and reflected the sunlight like souls passing by in some inter-universal transmigration. They didn't try to contact me, which hurt emotionally for a brief period that passed into a preachification I extended to Lorraine and her customers concerning the necessity for topping up on the Eucharist at regular intervals.

"That again," Lorraine said.

"Are you a priest?" someone asked.

"Defrockified."

"I love to see priests in frocks," someone else said.

I puked into the ocean, gray misty matter that trailed behind us like a shroud.

"Next year we're going to Rome," he said.

About five one day we drove up to Big Pine to look at the deer. The heat nearly killed us, but by dusk it had cooled off some. Lorraine got stung by a poisonwood tree, but the welts weren't that bad. We treated them with alcohol and hallucinogens. I took some mushrooms in a bottle of lemonade. Something in the mossy, mold-laced, fungal taste suited me. The old man, the retiree who kept the deer count, came out of his shed and told us it was time to leave. We tried to, but we weren't able to make it. Dark found us out on the trail walking through a marsh. Pines had given way to openness, to a vastness almost within reach. We headed for it.

Charlie Smith

"I almost stabbed her," I said.

"You couldn't hurt a fly," Lorraine said.

"She probably deserved it," Sam, her sailor, said.

We stared at him.

Two deer the size of Labrador retrievers appeared at the edge of the woods, caught sight of us and vanished. Sam crashed away after them. The grass islands out in the bay were dark now though the sky was still light. The woods too were dark, darker than we cared for.

Lorraine said, "I hated when we were children how because of the bugs we could never have barbecues outside after dark."

"I was just thinking about the mosquito trucks."

"You remember my sister choked to death on mosquito dust."

"That's right."

"She had a pink bicycle with a bell on it. I can't remember what happened to that bike."

Everything in the universe sang with vivid meaning, exclusively and irreproachably itself. The Gulf gently patted the sand, reassuring it, sad little scared earth, baby brother, sleep well.

"I wish I had a boat with me at all times," L said.

"Me too."

Some conveyance, I thought.

"You never stop thinking about her, do you?"

"No, I don't."

"You're a love devotee."

"We've been over that."

"She's like you and me—just a cracker from West Miami, cleaned-up version."

"It doesn't matter. I couldn't resist her if she just stepped out of a nuclear meltdown."

We waded out into the bay. The sand was firm, slightly ribbed, partially plated with sand dollars that we gouged up with our toes. The underside of the dollars, their bristly stiffness, felt good against my skin. I sailed a couple out into the vastness. They curved into the surface and skipped like stones.

"Love trouble bores people," I said. "Why do you think that is?"

"It's not really love?"

"It's the not really love they like to hear about."

"Actually me too. I actually love to hear about not really love."

Behind us the drugs made the woods seem huge, enfolding, upreared, lurid in an affectionate way, sloping toward us as if the continent was backed up behind them, capacious and soft, a tropic protectorate. Lightning bugs flickered, pinpricks poked into a sheet of darkness, light, brightness, just as I hoped, behind everything. Sam back in there faintly hooted, happy, I guess, to be on land.

"When are you going home?" she said.

"It's all I can do not to leave right now."

"Last week I went out to the woods—near here actually—and sat three hours under a pine tree. Or would have if the bugs hadn't made me move. I just wanted a rest."

"From what?"

"Love. Not-love. I picked some grasses and made a little bundle of them. That was the most I could do all day. I wasn't sick, I just didn't have any motivation. That's what that fool in there running in the dark has done to me. I couldn't even take the boat out."

Somewhere inside me, somewhere close by, I entered a sanctuary. The world came with me, the faded brightness of the Gulf and the darkened woods, the thin strip of sand, all came in, all roofed over by tropical architecture, white board ceiling under which we hovered, the world, and Alice and me walking in.

"I have to be back to go to church with Willie," I said.

"He wants you to preach?"

"He wants me to be a charm, help his magic work."

Images cascaded through my brain, drifting like dandelion cotton, flickering and fading. Then I was in the kitchen brandishing a corkscrew, someone was.

"What's the matter with Willie?"

"Munch's pregnant."

"Oh that. I thought she wasn't going to tell him."

"She tried that last time. I don't think it would work twice."

A man in the kitchen—trapped there—lunged in a rage, reared up like a horse before a ditch. Beyond him a reptilian chorus of fury.

"What?" she said.

"Nothing."

The next afternoon, after the cops let us go, Willie said, "I was reading about these pitcher plants, about how maybe twenty-five different bugs and wasps and spiders all make a living in the deadly digestive juices of the pitcher plant, some Sumatran, Indonesian variation of what we could see right now at any pond around here, all thriving in this tiny death chamber, and I began to wonder at the world, at how crazy it is, and how nuts we all are, all of us doing whatever we have to to survive, making do, wherever you look somebody getting by, somebody doing laundry and putting dinner on the table somewhere you thought nobody could possibly live. Munch and I are like that, and you and Alice are too. Local nutcases, all of us, bug couples living in the throat of a bug eater."

It made sense and I told him so. But then we weren't exactly thriving. There was an unacknowledged element, something that separated us from others.

"So you fight," he said. "You fight and go on and there you are—you come to the end of it."

"Of what?"

"Life. What else?"

He grinned one of his loopy exhumacious vivid hurt-erasing grins, put his hat back on and opened a beer, which he passed to me. Outside the house big flotillas of yellow flowers surged in the breeze, looking like outriders to happiness itself. I was packing to catch the shuttle to Miami. Alice had called. As she listened in silence I'd berated her in a ritualistic manner. Her silence also was ritualistic—and rapt, I thought. Inside it, under the clamor, as in a drug deal in a hurricane, alliances were forged. It was our way. I said I was sorry I picked up a weapon. She didn't even acknowledge this. It wasn't necessary. Infestation, zeal, the arm going into the sleeve—connection, that was the whole thing.

"Get back up here," she said.

As for how we wound up in the hands of the cops, here's what happened. Sam came crashing out of the woods carrying a deer. The deer, dog-deer, night-gray, squirming in his arms, made little sounds I'd never heard from a deer.

"I thought they were mute," he said.

Lorraine told him to let the animal go.

Charlie Smith

"I want to take it back with us."

The deer squirmed, kicked briskly, ran in place, and grew still. Breath blew from the boxy little muzzle. I reached for it, brushed the face, felt the breath on my hand. I wanted to help the creature, but I couldn't figure how to do it, I was at a loss. I squatted on the sand, defenseless myself, unable to assist. Lorraine began to argue with the sailor. Each stubbornly confessed a need for an approach diametrically opposed to the other's.

"You can't make him a pet," Lorraine said.

"He's already human tainted—he can't go back. They won't take him."

"You idiot."

"Don't call me that, you fucking cunt."

She swung at him, caught him a blow to the side of the head that staggered him. They angled off into the water, Sam clutching the deer like his four-footed child, holding him up with Lorraine in pursuit.

"Put that damn deer down."

"You won't make me do a thing, bitch."

He backed deeper and she caught him. Bigger and stronger, more determined, far wiser, she raised her hand to club him, but at that moment the deer thrashed, driving his hooves into Sam, and broke loose, leaping into the water. Little sword-like flashes were going off in the east all this time, but I assumed these were caused by the drugs. Sam lunged, flopping after the deer, which swam away from him, headed out into water that for a mile wouldn't be over any but a deer's head. The sailor thrashed on, dived, came up, started to swim and immediately gave it up, snapping his head back as if jerked by a rope. "Damn," he said. "Anything could be out there." The creature swam expertly, head high, maintaining his dignity. Sam leaned back into a clumsy stroke, stumbled to his feet and with Lorraine and me leading, waded ashore. The sky, vaporous, one light-streaked patch of color high up, lay like sauce on the water. The deer kept to his task.

"We're a sorry bunch," she said.

"Where's he headed?" Sam said. "Mexico?"

"Ah little deer, come back," Lorraine said. She whirled around. "We have to get back from the water. Give him room to turn around."

"He doesn't look like he's coming back," Sam said. "Anchors aweigh, little fellow."

The deer's head was a black chip on the water. Dark bit aimed into the dark. Just then the lights hit us, the flashlights of the rangers come along the trail to look for us. They arrested us—both of them angry and harshly silent beyond the necessary charging sentences—and walked us back through the woods to their truck. We had to ride in the rear, handcuffed. They didn't seem worried about the deer. I called Willie, who came up to bail us out. It wasn't a big crime, and didn't trigger any old warrants on my behalf. I wasn't wanted at that time anywhere in the state, not by policemen. The sailor was turned over to the Shore Patrol who drove up from the base in Key West to get him. He was more scared than Lorraine and me. She was only sad, sad for his trouble. She asked the SP boys not to treat him harshly, begged them really. Women are like that, she said—apologetically, as if I had criticized her—when they love somebody.

* * *

By the time I got home, Alice had all the info. She was still on the phone with Lorraine when I walked in. They had decided, she said, it would be best to keep their distance. Said this, and then she approached me in that sidling half-looking, fey-grinning way she had, a tension that was not really tension in her body, a strength, muscularity of affection was what it was, edging in against me, her arms coming up a fraction later than her body reached me so we bumped, our two electricities, the housing of flesh, the darting looks, the vitality in our eyes all reaching the other at the same moment. She set the phone back in the cradle without saying goodbye.

I nudged her and slid away, crossing the room that in its dimness seemed suited to anything we might want to do. Allie, Allie, incomparable, venomous Allie, let me look at you. We circled each other, snapping glances. Both of us ached. You could see it by the way we bent sideways, clutching ourselves. We gave each other the cramps, love cramps, so astounded, buffaloed, so impressed and in our nutty way honoring each other's inestimable humanity, the beauty we walked in, you name it, we couldn't touch each other. We didn't even kiss.

"You want to go on a walk?" she said.

"A walk. Yeah." Hell, we were surrounded by a paradise. A walk would be great. "Nothing better."

I choked back a sob.

"Let me get a hat."

I followed her like a puppy, watching her prepare herself to enter the world. Soon I would take her in my arms, but not now, not just yet. She changed clothes, her body so blinding in its fructitude I had to turn away. I glimpsed her only, sneaking glances through half-closed lashes, caught flashes of white, of softness, the rim of her shoulder as she dipped down to fresh panties, the ridge of her knuckles, a breast disappearing. It unnerved me, I had to go into the living room and sit down. In there the light filled the area with an expensive yellowness, some orange thrown in, a mango yellow, papaya orange, a simplified ceremonious mix I lay back in watching her through the open door as she passed, transferring the materiel of beauty from one section of her being to another. Every move she made—every gesture—added something, changed something, reset the medley; her hand raised to her dark hair brought forth an unimpeachable aspect, a radiance that made my breath catch, the swivel of her waist, the way she patted the back of one hand with the other, the sidelong glance she gave herself in the mirror, each an opposition and resolution of what came before so I had to duck down like a child watching some scarifying movie, fascinated but aghast.

Outside things were better. The sunshine, the vast and unhinged sky, subdued us. Shadows played like giants along the back wall of the high school. An old lady on the corner, her face as tan as Tarzan's, whacked out a laugh. We spoke of apartments, of flowers, of streets we had played in when we were children. I explained about the deer, making gestures that she without even noticing mimicked. Her face passed through emotions like a tourist passing through a fiesta. She turned away and made a spitting noise. "I hate that man," she said, speaking of Sam.

"He's in the brig."

"Chained, I hope."

But she didn't really care about the deer.

We walked along, bouncing. Up the street a boy with purple

hair reminded me of the clowns I hated in childhood. She held her palm up flat like a shield between her and the boy who laughed as we passed him, delighted to be observed. We strolled to the beach under the mangoes and the heavy kapok trees, past the luggage shops where refugees huddled around suitcases large enough to transport a body, checking the fit, by electronics shops outside of which young men with glazed eyes leaned against the open doorways, swaying and working toothpicks. Music bleated from the record shops. The Dorado Hotel, as flimsy and shining as tinfoil, reared next door to a tattoo parlor. Alice made sweeping motions for the benefit of Angel Montez, the proprietor of a liquor store. He nodded and winked and shook his hand in a slight amaze, grinning at her.

We stopped in at one of the little Cubano restaurants on Collins where as teenagers we had sat around congratulating everyone, astonished at ourselves and our wondrous magic lives alone together at age sixteen in the Irene Hotel on Ocean Drive, a couple of sambaneros, drunk and stoned and capering, flinging silverware and cross-examining the anti-Castroites until we were tossed laughing out the back into the dunes, free for the first time in our public lives to be nutcases. We stopped by for a drink, just a moment, and stood at the bar in the cool gloom of late afternoon sipping rum, letting the moment sag into us like an old-timer giving in to dreams. Through the back door, past the patio and a frieze of bristly palms, a homeless man rested with his back against the low side wall of the hotel swimming pool next door. It was a tough city and you had to rest—that was the way we looked at such things. Children leapt from diving boards and you could see their slim forms rotating in the air as they dropped into the crystalline water. The homeless man, deeply tanned, wearing safari shorts, didn't look up.

"*Un desastre,*" someone said loudly, as if to make a point.

The huge charm of the afternoon, the light scuffing a shine into the glittery sand, the dunes' little pompadour of greenery, was a promise to us. The room was half filled with the deserted and the ruined, afternoon drinkers, the compromised and impotent characters of a beach life gone awry. Everyone, like us, doing his best to avoid a conclusion of any kind. Someone laughed, a reproachful, self-mocking sound, as if at mention of a terrible crime he was trying to live down. A monster in the form of a wasted figure in black sidled up to us and made remarks about Alice's clothes. I hadn't noticed anything amiss, but they provoked something in him.

"What was that you said?" I asked.

"You going to the *baile de circo,* huh?"

She was wearing, I realized, a black diaphanous cape over some flounced crepuscular orange concoction, a costume I had seen parts of before but never paid much mind to. I myself sometimes dressed in riotous garments.

"You having an adjustment problem?" I said.

"No, not me, friend. Here I belong."

The bartender, mired in fat, beamed indifference from squinted eyes. A squad of cowboy hats over in the corner never looked up, not once. I glanced at Alice to see what kind of mood she was in. Her eyes were hard, focused in a dark brilliance. It was the old readiness, the internal assault team poised on the brink. I didn't mind this much, or not always, but just now I was too tired for mayhem. I thought of the deer, the way it swam so resolutely toward the dark other side of the Gulf of Mexico. I said something to the monster, something almost apologetic, and then he began to mock me as well, to mention my large nose and my narrow shoulders and the way I seemed to lean over to the side when I walked. All this had been pointed out before, I was familiar with it. A sadness entered the bar, or so it seemed, some miasmic cloud of failure and desolation stirred up off the floor by someone passing by on his way to the restroom. For this man, as for all of us concoctors and mishabitués, the escape route went through it. I remembered a sermon I had given one sunny morning in May when outside the church in Hollywood I listened to a child crying all the way through my speaking, a little boy with meningitis, they said, whose whole body hurt, and I'd talked about the freakishness of us all. I never could quite explain it, couldn't get to the bottom of it.

"It's okay," I said, but this was not what the man wanted to hear. It wasn't okay, that was obvious. He flashed his teeth and insulted us again, favoring Alice with the harshest points. She cracked him upside the head with her glass, her eyes furious and piercing, and under the fury, distracted. The glass didn't break, but the blow knocked the man off his stool.

He came up like sweepings tossed into the air, a cloud of humiliated pride sporting a blade. The blade flashed and we jumped back. It had barely missed Alice's face.

"Whoa," I said and snatched her to the left.

She staggered, caught herself, and we ran for the door.

The assassin came after us, the blade raised like a comic's idea of murder.

We banged through the back screen door and out onto the patio, where I grabbed a piece of aluminum pole and turned, not knowing exactly what else to do; it didn't seem we'd get free without a little more of this business.

The *acuchillaro* halted panting and moved left, but just a step or two. I saw he wasn't coming on. He insulted us a few more times, timely material but bargain basement, wiped the blade ostentatiously against his sleeve, leered, and went back inside.

Alice headed straight to the phone on the wall of the public bathrooms and called the cops. She had no pity for such characters, just as she had no pity for herself.

"Why don't we let it go," I said. I was angry too, but I knew there was a drug, the old drug, faithful and spiky, that would take care of it.

"I'm too scared to," she said, clicking her teeth. She grinned at me like a dog, like a hyena. I walked into her, just to get the whackery of her body against me. She said something short to the police, put the phone down and grabbed me, clutching at me, wringing my wrist. We kissed hard and then bounced off each other like magnets reversed. We turned away, shy, and walked out onto the wide gray compacted strand. The Atlantic rattled pebbles away down on the far side. Only Europeans and the mentally confused went out on the beach at this time of day. One of them came up to me offering drugs. I made a purchase of some light material and ingested a portion of it with an iced tea I got from Horace Harris at his trailer burger stand. Alice got a burger and wolfed it. Horace, a gentleman, didn't comment on the sweat streaks and panic on our faces. He was, as usual, happy to see us, a kindly soul and a little outlandish himself, always looking for company.

"Wait," he said, "I'll join you," which he did, and watched me sink the drugs, sparing me a lecture but letting me in on his disappointment nonetheless.

"It's all right, Horace," I said.

"You're so gifted," he said, "I don't know why you do it to yourself."

Horace and I had met at a religious affair, a kind of interfaith preach-off, Jews against Christians, when we were in high school. We had spent the time since generally laughing at ourselves.

We were parked at a table under a red and green striped umbrella, looking out at various little umbrella cities cast upon the plain. "All this you're doing," he said now, not able to help himself, "is going to come back on you someday, like a bad loan. Someday when you're old and not even thinking about it anymore."

"Oh, Horace," Alice said, "we just this minute escaped with our lives from a knife fight."

"Assault," I said. "That's not quite the same as a fight."

"You might not even live to get old," Horace said sadly.

"It was the most peculiar fight," Alice said. "His eyes were shining as if he wanted to lick me, but all he did was throw insults. Actually it was kind of familiar." She grinned. "I was about to give him a little peck on the cheek, but then I decided to hit him."

"Stepped right over the common ground," I said.

"I didn't see it."

"You're going to get hurt, Allie," Horace said, "if you keep hitting people."

"It's a vulgarity I have, I know." She reddened slightly. "It springs out of me. I have to work on it."

"Keep banging away at it," Horace said, smiling.

"What are you doing, Horace?" I said.

"No good business. I was sitting in the trailer thinking about my father. You remember him, Allie?"

"Not completely."

"Billy does. He never left the house at all. Just sat at home studying the Talmud and waiting for students who never showed up. That's what I'm doing too, except instead of the Talmud I study food service manuals. He used to annoy and embarrass me and now I am annoying and embarrassing myself."

He plucked at the small nest of hair just above his forehead.

"His father was this crackerjack Talmud scholar. He had a round handsome face and a wispy beard like a Chinese man's."

"You gave him the willies."

"The heebie-jeebies—that's what you said last time."

"It wasn't personal. He didn't want to get that close to a minister."

"Ex."

"Nonetheless."

"I appreciate it that you let him live with you," Alice said. "I've always appreciated that, Horace."

"I've been depressed since he died."

"Haven't we all," she said.

I excused myself, got up and walked down the beach, some notion, sensation, or whatever it was, rotating through me, an idea I would like to change the angle, get a better look at the sunlight striking a line of red lounge chairs, some thought rising over it related to the trip Henry and I took those years ago to the West Coast. It was there he entered the army and there I got the job as apprentice in Collier Adler's private charity and flew to Indonesia. There we waked on the beach in Malibu holding each other's bodies, chilled by a corruption in us, some lie in it, Alice far from me. The thought pressed into my head, but the drugs lifted it off.

A timely dusk had begun to dismantle the sky. The stillness stirred, the late afternoon dead time giving way to a sweetness of aspect, a congeniality in the little clean-up breeze coming along. The lifeguards got down from their stands and swept the sand mounds in front with whisk brooms. The entrepreneurs rolled up their ropes and began to load the jet skis onto the trailers. Tourists, refreshed by naps or by drugs or lovemaking or simple brooding experiments deep in the fastness of their sporty hotels, reappeared wearing fresh, colorful clothes. I walked on a while, vague to myself, but the movement began to unsettle me so I took a seat on a ridge, on a stalled wave of sand, and peered down at the green milky water sighing up. The little waves flopped in with their curious hesitancy. Behind them the calm continued all the way out, the ocean's oily complacency interminate, the tankers in their regimental reds and blues jammed against the horizon, the cruise ships distantly awaiting their signal to enter Government Cut. I stared out until I became stupefied with the abstractness, the holistic qualities of the scene, and lay back drifting into a dream in which I studied maps to find a passage into another world that to my amazement became not a world but a woman in Halloween clothes lying beside me. Alice.

Her hand touched me, the sand grains on the tips of her fingers arousing the molecules on my chest, sending a message to my far off places that called me back into beach time; I looked up and saw her sunny, side-lit face, half light, half dark, her eyes unaffected by sunshine, gleaming with good humor and concupiscence. She bent down and kissed me and it was like the little hiccup of time in the movie where the hero suddenly notices they've substituted another universe for this one. "Let's go underground," she said.

"I love every hour in that world."

She flopped down on top of me, nearly knocking the wind out, but careful too in her way, catching my shoulders on her hands so my head bounced off her knuckles and it hardly hurt.

"Would you have intercourse with me right here?"

"You bet."

I commandeered a yellow umbrella, nodding to the concessionaire, whom we also knew from high school, indicating with a frolicsome gesture I'd return it in a minute, set it as a kind of lean-to, and we lay down. No one was nearby really, it was just us. The unreflective, white and candy-colored hotels floated among their palm trees. The ocean worried its little memories. Far down the beach a group of South Americans played volleyball. To the north, just above the Holiday Inn, a bit of cumulus hung like a blank slate.

She lifted her skirt and climbed on top of me, screwing herself down onto me like a nozzle going onto a hose. It hurt a little and I flinched, but I was also amazed and exhilarated so I didn't stop her. A child's moment of concentration tightened her face and then she looked scared, startled, as always, surprised, as if this was the first time this had ever happened to her—a look that knocked me out, that brought tears to my eyes sometimes—and then, never letting go of me, she seemed to fling herself forward out over me, or into me, fling me into her maybe, crying a little noise like something from the forest, like the deer down at Big Pine before it leapt from the sailor's arms and began to swim for its life in the dark sea. I bucked and jammed, looking for the rhythm that was almost impossible to find, but which we always searched for like drunks fumbling in a closet, knocking our bodies into each other, sweating and sincere and grabbing each other's skin. She grinned down at me, a wild, embarrassed, excruciated, joyous grin, and scared of herself, of me, of what we were doing, swooped down and kissed me on the mouth. It was the kiss that always took us. She made a noise like a small engine failing. But the kiss kept going. It was something we could handle, really get into, the totally heartfelt impress of self on self coupled by mouth; we drained into it and held on, something inside us riding sweetly out as the rest of our bodies, the slash and burn of our congress, the ungainly desperate uncontrollable flesh, thrashed on to resolution.

Right after this we were busted—I had forgotten that Arnold Capisano, the concessionaire, was not a friend from high school but an enemy—but the offense was only an ordinance violation, not a felony. The arrest threw me off anyway. We were remanded not to the jail but to a ticket the officer handed me as I held my pants up and that called for a court appearance one month hence, which we made on time with my lawyer Arcadio, who argued that Alice and I had not seen each other for some time, etc., etc., which did not in any way impress the judge, a man who also knew me well from church pancake suppers out in West Miami, but who since he had come to town made sure none of his former associations interfered with present duties, so gave me a large fine, due to my history as a recidivist ne'er-do-well, etc., and which reduced my bank account to the point I became afraid of what might happen next—it was just like me never to have a fear for money until I got a little—since we owed so much in payments for the house and since the upkeep of our lives had somehow increased to the point we were living as if we really did know how to produce cash, thus I was slightly unmanned, which I guess was why I was open to the proposal made by Jonnie Devane, another acquaintance from the old days now receding, who captained a supply ship running out of the Miami River to rural islands in the Caribe.

For some reason Alice's sister Senegol came to court—I hadn't seen her since before Henry and I went to Europe—which angered Alice until Senegol told her she was married again, which calmed her down, and soon enough they were co-conspirators, happy as could be. Alice got a lesser fine, which seemed unfair to me, but I said nothing. I fired the lawyer before we got out of the courtroom. He laughed and said he'd wait by the phone for me to change my mind.

"Your file's always open, Billy," he said.

Senegol, who looked skinny, and harassed but pert, carried an ugly wormlike scar running from her forearm up into her short-sleeve shirt, which she said she got on a bird hunt up in the plantation country when her horse shied at a snake and ran her through a scrub oak thicket. She had become a horsewoman now, an upright, capable individual, unlike Alice and me, or unlike me, and she wanted to show this off. Alice didn't mind at all. She was like that. She never held anyone's aspirations against her, even when the aspirations were fulfilled. Unlike me and everyone else I knew, she did not fear another's happiness.

When she came up to me, when Senegol did, I went red in the face with shame and began to sweat in such an obvious manner I had to wipe my forehead on my sleeve. Neither of us mentioned anything about it, but Senegol got a mean, happy look in her eyes, a look Alice was also master of, and went right on talking about her new life as a rich woman and about the course she was taking at Miami Dade Community College. Jonnie, who was getting his mate off for something, and who'd had a hangdog crush on Senegol for years, came up and it was then, probably simply because he was energized by seeing her (so I thought), that he proposed I join him on a little island venture he had in mind. He had everything arranged, he said, but he needed company.

"Company for what?" I said.

"To ease my mind, make me feel safe."

"How will I do that?"

"You're an old friend. My regular mate can't leave Miami and I've known you always and you can keep things calm all the way across."

There was good money in it, enough to pay down the house note a little and support ourselves for a while longer out at the beach. The book Minx Averroes had put together of the Alice stories still sold, but already money was fading out of that production. The Hollywood possibilities that generated the option money we put down on the house had sputtered and died.

Alice, who was listening in, said she wanted to come.

"It's fine with me," I said, "but it's Jonnie's job and I don't want us to cause bad feeling."

"None on my side," Jonnie said. "I'd rather Alice went. As long as you two promise not to kill each other."

We raised our hands in mock avowal, not at all concerned for the moment about ruining our lives.

"You come too," he said to Senegol, who curled her long lip in refusal.

"She sure is gorgeous," he said to me a moment later when we stepped aside to firm things up.

"She's a killer," I said.

"You got in trouble with her, didn't you?"

"Yes, I did. My actions with her were the precipitate cause of my getting hauled up in front of the judge the first time."

"Alice did that, didn't she? Had you arrested?"

"I did it to myself."

"What was it she had you accused of?"

"Troubling her sleep."

"No, really."

"Statutory rape and kidnapping."

"Jesus."

"It was nolle prossed."

"But not forgotten."

"Not by the fellows over here."

"Nor by me, if it was me. I don't see how you go on—with the situation."

"No way to explain that."

"Well, how—"

"Those're all the questions I better take," I said.

Under the skylight, the sisters, looking like two beautiful angels, plotted mayhem and disaster. They couldn't help it, I knew, and I couldn't help my part either.

"Now what is it," I said, "we're going to be carrying out to the islands?"

"Just some special material these boys over on St. Cris want to get their hands on."

"What kind of material?"

"Supplies, medical stuff, that kind of thing."

"Drugs? You making a reverse run?"

"No, not that. It's legitimate stuff, antibiotics and sulfa and all that, helpful material. They just can't get it through regular channels."

"What group is this?"

"The Sea Light."

"Oh, man. You're talking about a rebel movement."

"They're actually very conservative, upright people. They're like Methodists."

"I never was that much of a fan of Methodists."

"What denomination was it you preached in?"

"Holiness."

"Aren't they pretty narrow?"

"Until the emotion rises."

"Oh yeah. I get it, yeah." He looked at me earnestly, with expectant eyes. "Well, you want to come? You'll be great. And I promise you we'll get some real money."

There were all kinds of things I could have said, there were all kinds of things I could have instantly realized, but I paid no mind to anything. I was bamboozled by events, it was that, and for a second, which was the second I had brooded on for years, the one when all your lifetime of paying attention to what was happening, the attention you pay no matter what else is going on, no matter how upset or argumentative or even drunk you get—you still in some deep alert place are aware—that attention broke off. What will happen then? I had always wondered. Now I would find out.

As we walked down the front steps, Senegol gave me a look, a triumphant, harpy look, and I remembered how years ago in the meeting in chambers, when all the felonious business had come down to a fuck-up, I had attempted, a weak person of the worst possible kind, to denounce her. I had called her a devil. The judge had looked at me totally disgusted. But Senegol, sitting with a little parsons table between my side and hers, had given me that same look, of triumph and malice. It had been Alice who backed down, who, though she withdrew nothing of what she'd concocted, went mute and refused to speak. They asked her questions, but she wouldn't answer. Wouldn't even when they got angry at her. At the last, she broke down, cracked open in sobs that tore the heart out of the proceedings. She fell on the blue carpet crying like a lost soul. The shame and sadness of it was too much for everyone. Like anybody would who had a life anchored in the real world, the judge, shaken, grim, white in the face, washed his hands of us. It was just after that Senegol gave me the look.

She gestured to the driver waiting for her and her scar flashed, it seemed to flash, in the bright September sunlight. I wanted to run to her and unzip it, rip it open and pull her body out through it. I felt a hatred like some other being inside me stepping forth. It was similar to what I'd felt when in the kitchen I picked up the corkscrew and brandished it at Alice. Some monstrous, volcanic thing, not new—this was the astonishment of it—but old, something from the ancient times, something waiting all along, rose up. I started down the steps to bash her head in, but she slipped through the lunchtime crowd and disappeared into her limousine. Alice, who had followed her down, gave me another kind of look.

"What are you so scared of?"

Was that what it was? Was what I thought of as hatred, experienced as hatred, a mordant fury, was it only fear?

"What do you mean?"

"You have a terrified look on your face, Billy."

"I don't know what it is."

"Probably because of how close we just came." She laughed sheepishly, or maybe it was sadly, humiliated by the courtroom. It made me sad too, for her. We had each other in a chokehold—that was what she said to the judge, stiff with embarrassment. Down the street the palm trees creaked and shuffled their cards and refugees entered South American stores to get a sense of home life and the aged Jewish population went on bickering about something that would never be resolved and the Cubans and the Crackers and the Black Folk went on distressing themselves and each other. The city was like a huge cruise ship with everyone waiting tensely for the all clear to sound. A Latino man lay stretched out on a bench as above his head three yellow butterflies danced. Angels, I thought, willing for a moment to give the world the benefit of the doubt. The big steps, the openness of the street, the heavy limousines angling through, gave me hope. Henry, who had been waiting for us out front, came up and offered me a peanut from a small sack.

"I'm not hungry."

"You looked furious coming down the steps and then your face went blank."

"Probably that's for the best."

Jonnie D slid by, giving me a pat and a wave. "I'll call you to-night," he said and went off with his mate.

"What is it?" Henry said.

There was a thin crust of stone dust on the rim of his left ear.

"Nothing important."

"They threw it out for the frame it was, I hope."

"No, not quite."

Senegol's limo was caught at an intersection filled with traffic. Her head was like a target in back, black and anonymous.

I mentioned her to Henry, who frowned. "I'd stay far away from her."

"I would too."

I made a reference to my love of resolution, and Henry looked at me in a disappointed way. He had heard my evasions before. He wanted me to do more with my life than I was doing, wanted Alice to do more with hers, but he couldn't get us to stay on the subject. A breeze trickled down the street carrying its smells of citrus, grease, garbage, and salt. I wondered how the Cubano gents over at the park were doing. Beside the courthouse the big mango trees looked dark with griefs. Beyond them the bay glistered and baked, shining like a holiness revealed. Clouds to the east, out over the beach, the piled-up cumulus, looked like an entrenched monarchy, never to be deposed. I suddenly wanted to go swimming. Lie back in the water waiting for Alice to paddle up and intercede for me.

"I've been writing some poems," I said. "For the bet."

Henry, in hopes of stimulating me, had bet me a hundred dollars I couldn't write a poem a week for a year. He knew nothing about poetry, other than the poetry of stone he brought to life out at the monument yard, but he thought this would get me involved.

"How many weeks has it been?"

"Thirteen."

"That's good. I'm not worried about losing my money, though."

"We should have made it a thousand dollars."

He snorted a laugh. "A lady came into the yard last week, she wanted me to build a statue of her husband for the grave. She wanted him in a safari outfit."

The day began to resolve itself into a series of cloudscapes, a dimness in the west that obscured the last sunlight. The breeze had turned around and begun to blow off the swamp that seemed to be burning. Later we went out to Scorchy's for mullet and Henry sat out on the deck looking across the marshlands at the moon that had come up like a wet, floury thumbprint beyond the canal.

"Nothing helps," he said. "Not really."

Alice was inside playing the piano with Artesia Bivins, a woman who had once accused her of stealing her boyfriend and hated her until Alice explained this was impossible due to her undying commitment to bringing me into the human family and so was forgiven and embraced. They were playing some cranky jazz tune that had everyone near them irritated.

"There has to be something," I said.

"There's not. What there is is the getting used to this information."

"I try, but I don't seem able to."

I had stepped into the hall and phoned Senegol, whom I caught at a party at her house out on Key Biscayne, and suggested we have a drink together. I have something important to talk to you about, I said, and she had laughed at me, a mean and razory laugh, but said fine she'd meet me. I intended to apologize for the business of long ago.

This will settle things, I said to Henry.

Your hash, he said, is what it'll settle.

He leaned forward now and a look of excitement came into his large round face. "What you have to do is just stay with it."

"With what?"

"With yourself. With what's going on inside you."

"I have no idea what's going on inside me."

"That's the point, Billy. You never stay still long enough to find out."

"Every time I've come close I start to hear this wild shrieking in there and I want none of it."

"It can't be any more than human."

"Maybe so, but it's a kind of human I want nothing to do with."

"It's just you."

"Well then I'm not my type."

"Senegol's not going to fix it."

"It's not her, it's me. It's what I'm going to do."

"Which is what?"

"Repair the historic damage. Go back down into the wreck, pump air into it and float it to the surface."

He gave me a long, searching look, open-faced, scrutinous, like a man gazing out of the window of a submarine—gazing at another submariner passing far down in the dark depths. We could look into each other's eyes for days if we wanted to—we used to do it all the time—finding there a sustenance we got nowhere else. It made me, made me now, want to go out to the monument yard and sit around under the Australian pine trees while he worked, watching him blast a monument out of the dusty stone nothing, listening to him talk about what life was for him now. "I'll come out and see you," I said.

I excused myself, or thought I did, and eased down the deck to get a better look at Alice. Her too I loved watching, up close or from a distance. Sometimes better from a distance. As she played now, bending to the keys as if with a sudden inclination to kiss them, or to kiss the hands of her partner, I caught the glint in her eyes, maybe it was the light, and saw what she was up to, midnight ruminator, stylish thought artist trailing a happiness as it ran away from her across the keys. At home she got up out of the bed to play. The noise some nights came crashing through the house, arpeggios and enfilades and sad, languorous breakdowns sweeping up the front stairs. But now not notes but flesh was what she wanted. Artesia—how could she have known—had gotten too close. The glint, spark, the burning cinder in Alice's eye—it had flown off the fire inside her and it made her wild. She dipped down and bit the back of Artesia's hand. Artesia snatched her hand back as if stung by a bee. *Yikes!* she cried, something like that. Her look of pain and anger, shrunk instantly by whatever look was in Alice's eye, screeched to a halt. Yes, now it's time to go, time to skedaddle. She jumped up and ran, brushing grimly by me without even a glance. Alice—you expected to see blood on her lips—looked up at me, at the room, at God or whoever tormented her, grinning. What could she be thinking?

"I loved that last piece," I said, sitting down. "How did it go?"

She glared at me, but my eyes—I knew, I had practiced this—were kindly, doused in tenderness.

"You don't really love me. You're not going to stay with me."

"I think it's my turn to talk like that."

"No, it's not. You were doing the whimpering last night."

"That wasn't whimpering. I didn't cry or anything."

"You were dry-crying. Sometimes that's even worse than whimpering."

"I like your perfume."

It was some Chanel I'd gotten her.

"It spilled in my bag. I put my hand in it and now I'm drenched. It made me swoon. Do you think I'm a reverent person?"

"Not just reverent—awestruck. That's your main thing."

I caught a glimpse of us in the window, two huddled in the lifeboat, digging at the floorboards. It was a wonder we were alive, that's how I thought of it. I said this, I had said it before. "You don't think we're having a good time," she said. "That's why you're going to leave me."

"No," I said. "It's impossible."

What was it, what was the allure? "We keep each other crippled," I said. "Sometimes I look at it like that."

"See," she said. "How could you stay?"

Plink . . . plink . . . plink. Do re me. The keys had a tinny cast, hollow, a metallic, grade school sound reminiscent of the lonely noises of after school days in West Miami, the two of us in detention, me stranded in a sunny classroom alone working on my confession as she in the next room played some lonely little tune she'd picked up in a dream. It was then—I couldn't say it this way at the time—that I began to think of human time, of past, present, future, and whatever unimagined other there might be, as one time. In her all three—and whatever else there was—went on at once. I said this now, or some version of it, some encapsulation as she dipped again to the keys and began to thrash out a little melody I had heard somewhere before—lying on the porch in my crib maybe looking up at the wind lifting the willow's long soft pinnulae—in a dream of my own. Some such thing. She didn't look up, but I could see the happiness in her eyes.

Scorchy came over and asked in a tensely pleasant way how we were doing.

"I don't know," I said. "I'm feeling a little strange. As if the whiskey's kicked in sideways or something. Did you hear about that wreck down in the Keys?"

"No," he said. "—oh, yeah, I did. You're talking about those cruisers. At Boca Chica."

"Yeah. They ran up on the reef."

"Preachers, weren't they?"

"A ministerial convention."

"I told you that joke about the preacher in the ditch."

"You told him that joke when he was eight," Alice said.

He rubbed his forearms hard, making the coppery hairs stand up. There was a photograph of Scorchy, in both the men's and the women's restrooms—same photo—brandishing his big hairy forearms above a dead shark, gutted on his dock. "Why don't you come play here again, Allie? Regular, I mean."

"I couldn't take the pressure."

Scorchy grinned, happy to say something generous, happy she turned him down, as he knew she would.

"You ought to anyway. I love listening to you."

"Okay."

His face screwed up as if it had been poked right in the middle. Alice laughed.

"Oh, that's right—I can't. We're going to the islands."

Scorchy hacked into his hand. "Well"—*agck, agck*—"if you change your mind, sweetie."

The night skipped from stone to stone.

Below Fifth Street the front doors of the little Caribe-style houses stood open to catch the breeze off the water. Old men in shorts sat on the curbs talking to other old men. Cubanos tinkered with cars that would never run again. Metal garden gates creaked like prison doors. A man on the corner buying shrimp, or maybe drugs, looked like someone I had known in prison in Italy, but he couldn't be because the man I knew was dead. Henry'd driven us back home to South Beach, talking all the way about Praxiteles. Then he started in about hate mongers, about how they didn't know how to love anybody and this scared them so much they flipped it all to the other side, and this got me to answering, in an offshore kind of way—the drugs drifting along like sunfish just under the surface—that most of us were too scared to love anything but what was easy.

Like what? he said.

And I said, Like cars or screwy women.

Screwy men, he said, open about his predilection these days.

Yeah, screwy men, Alice said.

Or tools, or procedures or money, he said. That it?

Fantastic acts, I said eventually. We were watching a Cubano woman—we'd reached the pier—who'd pulled down the top of her dress and sashayed about, letting everyone admire her. I thought I knew her, thought I'd seen her last week, or, no, the week before, when I was driving through the Sugar District feeling my way to some drugs, saw her standing on the corner of my father's old mission, closed now and boarded up, the verse from Proverbs stripped from the marquee of the old Grand Arts Theater it had occupied for twenty-five years, this woman, stout and handsome, mahogany-faced, swaying, shouting into the wind some violent words concerning her lord and governor, something I couldn't make out, but which reminded me of something else, of even older times when every corner had its preacher, lamenting and cajoling passersby, even little children like myself, to come along and roll in the arms of redemption. I'd loved listening to them, even as I scorned them. Now this dark-skinned woman, dark all the way down, wearing a spangled gold dress, basking in regard, doggedly joyous in this late night under the mercury lamps a hundred yards out into the Atlantic on a green pier. But what was wondrous, what was beyond wondrous since she herself in her bulging humanness was certainly wondrous, was—and I said something about this—she didn't bother to pull her top back up when the show was over. Her frontstage life became her backstage life—regality of the commonplace, someone said—Queen Desiree just a helpwoman, a good soul, pouring bait from one bucket to another and passing beer to her friends.

That's the amazing part, I said right on it

and Alice, who caught everything, agreed

Henry too.

As if, Alice said, you could take anything and celebrate it.

And that's the problem, I said, that's what kills us.

It's too much for us—that's what you mean, Henry said,

and I said, Yes, that's what I mean.

The woman's heavy breasts swayed against her body like dark monuments to plenty.

Three Delays

Later, in the park, we watched two boys fight. They boxed, as if trained for it, crouching, humpbacked, throwing punches. They were both slender, frail almost, and their brown bodies twirled in and out of the light. A freighter moved through the Cut, its high dark side like a wall passing. I was thinking, or maybe I wasn't thinking, only listening to Alice talk about how loneliness lived like a tapeworm inside the gut of happiness, or I was commenting on this, it was hard to tell, when another voice that seemed to come from far away so I thought it might be a voice from the dead maybe, or some memory just now returned, piped up, saying, Sure don't you know its the loneliness we can't live without, something like that, speaking out loud, so I was distracted. I had to break away, some personal imperative grabbed me, and I drifted over to the stage, where I climbed up and began to talk.

I was thinking about the jack-in-the-pulpits that sprouted every spring in my parents' backyard, in the low place where the dampness collected, and how these pale yellow slender plants frightened me in an obscure way, their grimy throats filled with dead bugs (as Willie J had pointed out), the way they came up in the mushy yard out of nowhere, the way, because they incited licentiousness with their wide-open throats and their thick stamens jammed down them, they were banned from altars in Christian churches—I knew this—thinking about Willie talking about them and how this made me go off into correspondences, the old saturated idea of how things were related—all things to all things—that business, and then I realized I had been talking all the time, drifting through the words into the old easy swing and rhythm of the preachifications of yore, and it began to come back to me, the euphoria of it—that's what it was—the way I would get lost inside a sermon, happily lost, and began to ride along in words like some Queen of Sheba riding in her golden car, easy and happy and given up to the ride, and how I guessed—spoke of this—this was my first real drug experience and how I must have needed one for some reason, and maybe we all did—that sappy bit—propelled—was this it?—by a recollection of a sweetness we had once known—which was probably why we went on and on about a lost paradise, all that, but which in reality was not a memory but only our tendency to enjoy sweetness wherever we found it. We were like bears, taking the honey wherever we came upon it. "But what I'm wondering," I said, "is about our tendency to criticize ourselves. What do we do about that?"

People were passing by, call them people, they looked from the stage like shapes of ex-people, like shadows in twilight, and it came to me I knew them, knew them as wanderers and seekers, those, like me, like us, who didn't want to go to bed because who knew what miraculous thing was about to happen, or maybe it was the other group, those others—like me, like us—who were frightened of what might climb into the bed with them, scared of their thoughts, of the feelings slinking up like battered children—all races and creeds, all examples of the American polity represented here—or maybe they were just too dumb for life, too bedeviled to catch the rhythm, bunglers who'd lost the pace and now stumbled along—*Honey, at least it's warm down here*—hoping they'd latch onto something.

"We look into the street," I said, "or the yard if we've got a yard, and we see something, some symbolic pitcher plant or some strange character carrying a blood-soaked package, and we get scared. What's up with that? Don't we believe in this world, in its rightness? We get scared for ourselves. It creeps over us, it jumps us in the night. So we have to get up and go outside, metaphorically speaking, we have to walk around. And for this we judge ourselves. Or we turn it around and judge others."

Off to the right there was a darkness, a black wing settled onto the grass, but this didn't bother me.

"Think about the blind man on the corner. Jesus touched his eyes and made him see. He didn't want him to stay blind—that wasn't good enough. Right there we have a judgment. All of us are blind—you know it, don't you—in one way or another. Call it blindness, or call it race, or ignorance, or that broken foot you drag through your love life. The government agencies say this is fine, we'll help you, train you to read Braille and all that, hold a real job, but we know the truth because our hearts tell us, our critical, judging, Christ-like hearts—we are inferior. You know it's true, don't you, you sad, crippled creeps."

"Sing it, brother." This was Henry. Alice lay with her head on his lap.

"Yeah," I said. "You know it. You sit on the side of the bed looking at the base of the wall, wondering how did this happen to you, how did your life get so fucked up. We all do it. You pan left, you pan right—it's the same thing. And then you're driving along and you see one of those little roped together lines of kids crossing the street up ahead and you just want to run them down. Splatter every one of them. Maybe you have to stop the car. Pull over to the curb and sit there a minute, to get your breath, to have a smoke, to quietly weep."

"That's good," Henry said. "You got it, Billy."

And I did, I had it for a second, the old eloquence, the words flowing. But it wasn't really there. I was older, heavier, slower, clumsy now. I veered away into an area, some aside about trees, their light-fingeredness, their life in the outdoors—"You never see trees coming to the back steps asking for anything"—and lost my place. I couldn't get it back. So I spoke of this, but even a talk on lostness got me lost. It was odd. I swayed on the concrete stage, behind me the scoop of bandshell upreared like a big mouth, and me leaning out of this orifice like the stamen of a jack-in-the-pulpit, the Sex Pistol for Christ, and then—that's what it was— I sensed something back there that was in fact a great mouth, a maw, about to devour me. But no, it wasn't that exactly. It was more like an emptiness. I began to sweat, to experience a dissolution, some insinuating, crusty sensation, a malarial, shambled fever in my blood that rose through my body to my face in a sweat and a shudder. I caught a glimpse of my bedraggled, useless self. Ah, man, I thought—get behind me, Satan. Then something unplugged—the drugs went into retro or some synapse flared, or maybe a vision of the old-time variety, a chip off the old phenomenological block, kicked in—and I saw us, Alice and me, that gracile woman lying with her head in Henry's lap, woman I pursued as a desperate suitor even though I already had her—I saw bad things coming for us. A switch flipped and I was back in the old days when I preached, the really old days when as a burning eight-year-old I had stalked the altar of some Holiness church out in far West Miami, some cramped one-roomer backed against a marsh, crying out the name of the Lord, seeing visions that flashed before my eyes like rainbow shapes, become human goblins and ghouls fleeing just ahead of the dogs of hell. Hellhounds on my trail! Sweet Jesus save me!

I pranced and kicked up on the stage, shouting. I cried out, whirling in a mire. The words were old, they were polished and finely wrought, they were the grand old tools of the trade, the imprecatory and rumbustious lyrics to the great profundo songs, but they choked me. I stopped. Out in the field, a baseball field, a concert ground, the grass needed mowing. The city wasn't really taking care of business. Not like it should. The lights of the town obscured the stars. Alice was asleep, she looked asleep. I stood there swaying, unable to say anything, paralyzed.

Charlie Smith

Chapter Two

As I said, I thought Senegol gave me a look, so I called her at her home in Key Biscayne and we met for a drink at the Royal Orange Hotel in the Grove, where I could not stop myself from touching her scar.

"It's become a means for me," she said. "A facilitator."

I hadn't questioned myself closely about the underthoughts accompanying my dealings with Senegol, but I began to experience the consequences of these thoughts as I sat with her.

The scar was smooth and ran like a rubbery worm for eight inches along her arm. It disappeared under her sleeve, so my fingers had to enter hidden territory to find its headwaters. It was at that instant, just as I touched the slightly bulbous terminus, that I remembered what I was doing there: I had come to apologize. To make amends for my behavior all those years ago. Anyone with sense could have told me this was not a good idea. Her fingers followed mine and she gripped my hand under her sleeve and I began to feel a little faint. I excused myself, went into the men's room and tried to climb out the rear window but it was too small; then I came back out. She said I looked better now. I didn't know if she meant right now or now in general. The mean, smart look was back in her eyes. I knew I was in over my head. Then I wanted to go upstairs with her, it was as if something in me gave way in a terrible and irresistible fashion—exactly what Henry had cautioned me about—and I couldn't stop anything. Her long blond hair was gathered at her neck. It made a heaped smoothness that fascinated me. What was happening? I hadn't moved, hadn't done anything more than touch her scar. But I was in trouble. I felt ashamed of myself even as I sat there. I got up.

"I have to go now," I said. How much time had passed?

"Why don't we feed the ducks?" she said.

I thought this was some kind of code, but she meant it in reality. We went out to the hotel pond, call it a pond, and fed the ducks. We had done this years ago on the night before she and Alice concocted the charges against me. That night came back to me like a whip cracking across my shoulders, a scene of the three of us in tears throwing chunks of wadded-up white bread at some—they weren't ducks, they were gulls. Down at their beach house in Islamorada.

"Why do you look so troubled?" she said. "Nothing's going to happen. I'm not going upstairs with you; I love my husband. I wouldn't do it. And you love Alice. I know that." She sighed. "Maybe that was part of what made me hate you so." She dusted bread crumbs off her hands and picked at the end of her left middle finger. Her nails were immaculate, bloody. "I never even liked you, Billy. You're so eager. It annoys me."

"Not as eager as I used to be."

Behind her eyes was the same implacable, witchy disdain. The same, in another, less interesting version, as in Alice's eyes. Something had put it there, some secret mishap or slur of blood, who knew. I sat down on a bench under two sisterly royal palms. She stood beside me and put her hand on my shoulder.

"You've become pretty pathetic," she said. "Do you know that?"

"Oh, I'm worse than that."

"You're becoming transparent. I used to like how substantial you were. You and Henry. You always seemed to know, even when you were at your most flighty and undependable, where you were going. There was something about you, some, I don't know, some attention you were giving to what you really wanted that you never let go of. But now it's gone. There's just this man-in-motion business. This pantomime."

I'd walked through a door—a door in myself—and there she was on the other side of it. One night years ago just before the rains came. I had thought it was only some craziness, some nutty lubricity in me I couldn't control, and this was true, but true only as far as it went. There was something else, something deeper and darker. I saw it now and I didn't want it near me any more than I had then. What would become of her? She'd live. Queen of a stronghold put together out of car dealerships, island properties, and hauteur, her body and mind weathering behind worked iron gates. Today she was a golden wand swaying beside me. Something impenetrable, oblivious in her tanned face, held armies at bay. A gush of feeling for her engulfed me. A tenderness, some missionary style sensation, some probably deluded altruism rose up—there it was—and I put my hand on her arm.

"You don't even remember it," I said, "do you?"

"What is that?"

"What happened back then."

"You mean after you raped me?"

"It wasn't really rape, Senegol. Not in the way you mean. There was no coercion."

And then I thought sure there was. Desperate soul, sure—who isn't—but totally awake, I'd flung myself into her as a man fleeing bandits might fling himself into a ditch. For a brief time I hid out inside her body. Pulled her up over me like a hood and squatted there in the sweet darkness of her being, letting the marauders ride by.

"You have a bleak look in your face," she said.

"I probably do."

"You've been misusing my sister for years."

"Do you remember what happened?"

"I don't."

"Not even what you felt when we were sitting on the beach there outside the house and we looked each other in the face. You don't remember?"

"Billy, I don't. You had brutalized me and we were about to make you pay. I expect I was disgusted and tired out."

She must have experienced what I did, I saw it in her face: for a moment—and I know this was true—I became her.

"There was something else—besides the calamity," I said.

"Maybe to you."

Elmer Huppert and a woman not his wife came out of the hotel and stood checking the fit of things, caught sight of us and stared. Two years ago Alice and I had taken a room up on the seventh floor above the upstairs pool and sat out on the balcony drinking vodka Collinses and pretending we lived here. We were drunk on money and love, purchasing interludes at hotels and resorts where we sat on cabana porches sipping mixed drinks and laughing. We had seen Elmer Huppert—once a law partner of her father's—then too, in one of the hotels, a resort in Palm Beach, clutching the arm of a woman he wasn't married to. He had stood—under a sea grape tree—looking at us with the same baleful, disengaged expression on his face.

"There's Mr. Huppert," Senegol said. "He'll think we're having an affair."

"We're having the opposite."

"An unaffair." She looked down at the ducks, a scruffy crew in dirty white uniforms. "Why do you still bring up this preaching stuff?"

"Who said I did that?"

"Alice was talking about it."

"I miss its influence over me, I guess."

"Aren't you glad to be free of it?"

"Sure. But I miss a set of standards that indicate something."

"Indicate what?"

"What's true and what's not."

"I couldn't find anything true in that folderol."

"It's hard to do."

"Look at old Elmer," she said. "Forty years I bet of running around on his wife. There's no way to stop him without shooting him. He makes me sick, but he also makes me laugh. There's a standard."

I think Elmer saved me just then. I might have thrown her into the pond if he wasn't standing there. A hot, electrified wind blew through me and I wanted to smash her. But Elmer, his lickerish, doughy face and his sad adulteries, stopped me. It wasn't only that

I was afraid he would turn me in. Senegol would have turned me in and I would have gone to jail again. It was something else. Some shame in me, some prideful unwillingness to let Elmer see who I was, the fear I was something that could be seen so easily, a small and shabby personality I wanted to conceal, sure. But something else too. It doesn't make sense maybe, but I think I saw him for what he really was: the portly, seersuckered, bamboozled, prevaricating gut-shot representative of life itself. A fuck-up and a fool, standing there lightly holding the arm of a woman young enough to be his daughter, some secretary he'd made promises to and was paying off with a trip to a grand hotel, but life's agent nonetheless. The one sent out to look for me. To give me, as he did now, a nod, just to let me know he was watching over me, taking care, the councilor reassuring me that something—animation, élan vital, soul, being, anxious orbital existence itself—knew where I was.

I leaned across the space that separated Senegol and me—a space suddenly transversible—leaned into the faint crisp smell of her, and before she had time to shy away, kissed her on her hard, thin lips.

Later when I explained this to Alice, she had her own take. It was at twilight time after a walk over to the wino apartment hotel across the street from Muncie's where we liked to sit in the old rank garden and discuss the flora. Among other things we were going through a nature period—it was one of the things that made us feel connected to life—our books of plants and Alice's sketches and our drunken discourses on the characteristics of tropical flora, native and the introduced variety, all forms, energizing us. We had long, elaborate conversations about gymnosperms and broadleafs and we carried specimens around in net bags, lying back in our drugstore loungers out on the beach studying hanks of grass and pine cones, all that, idiots really, passing time, but enjoying ourselves too.

The Ducat was one of the best spots for plant study. Its garden had years ago gotten out of control. White-frond traveler palms, capsize trees, gumbo-limbos, screw pines, ruddy mangoes, key limes, all these prospered among dozens of other articulations and equatorial preposterations. We wandered around, drinks in hand, exclaiming, loudly enumerating the blossoms we sank our noses into, throwing our heads back to check the fruit spread of coconut palms, the little white and yellow clustering of plumeria blooms, guava tenacity and such, taking a desperate, tricky delight in the otherworldly (yet approachable) rain-forest excess of it, untended, baroque and frail as it was, like the men, in fact, who inhabited the shabby stained apartments in the hotel, a besmuched biota of drunks and unemployed Sheetrock hangers, refugees from broken marriages, procrastinators and late night sobbers, all characters we knew well from our own homemade versions, nature boys like ourselves.

Twirling a hibiscus blossom between gin-reeking fingers, I leaned from the ripped chaise I lay in to let her in on the Senegol rendezvous. I experienced, I said, certain emotional epiphanies.

"Which ones?" she said.

"The tight-assed, squinched-up, nails along the chalkboard ones," I said.

"Be more specific."

"I almost gave her a karate chop."

"But which epiphanies—concerning what?"

Her pale eyes looked yellow in the shade of the buttonwood bush she lay under. I went blank.

"Which ones?" she said.

"The ones about being where I belong."

"You didn't know that?"

"That's not what I mean."

"What do you mean?"

She bent over her toes, the nails of which were painted an elegant gray pink. Her short yellow shirt lifted off her waist, revealing the muddy scar that rose like a fan of sea coral out of her hips. At night sometimes it bound her like a shrunken garment. I rubbed lotion into it and considered how it put me a layer or two closer to the center of her—looking at it that way, saying this to her.

"I saw how I can never get enough of you," I said.

"But what do you mean?"

"I wanted to apologize to her."

"You never apologized to me."

"That would have been an insult."

"No, it wouldn't've."

"I'm sorry."

"You are?"

"Desperately, abjectly, completely."

"Adverbially and totally, huh?"

"It's true."

"Ughm, ughm."

"What?"

"You'll say anything to get what you want."

"I already have what I want."

"No, you don't."

"What don't I have?"

Charlie Smith

She just looked at me, lying on her side by then, curled up like a baby in a bed, lying that way right out in the open, something animalistic, or no, something humanly primitive and exposed about her, this always central to her ethos, whatever you want to call it, her personal culture, this exposure, a little too much going on openly, a little too much revealed. She wouldn't say what was missing

We didn't talk anymore about Senegol, but that night in the kitchen she struck me again. Wearing jeans and a pale blue bra, her hands smelling of shrimp boil, she arched her back against the counter and as Hermione Gold, a little girl from next door, watched in surprise, she swung at me, catching me across the face with her open hand. Kapow! You could hear the slap out in the yard.

"Wow," Hermione cried. "Jesus, that's some whack."

The blow made me see stars, small ivory-tipped blue ones. As I staggered away the fury jumped into me, jumped into my face, into my eyes and hands, like some demonic subcutaneousness. I whirled around, launched myself across the kitchen and took her by the throat. She jerked away, snatched herself away, and spun around, swinging her arm wildly.

"Still a fucking hitter, huh," she said.

"Bash him with the pot," Hermione cried.

"Shut up, you," I said.

"Don't speak to me like that, you fruit butt," Hermione cried.

"You're doing the hitting," I said to Alice.

She unleashed a string of curses. Demon-eyed, spitting, her face rigid, mouth stony with poison, her execrations rang against the walls. There was no lead-in. We hadn't been arguing. But here was the curious thing: I reacted as if I knew exactly what was going on.

My fury surged like a wave breaking down a door. It wasn't Senegol, or not only. Whatever was going on had always been going on. We were, in a strange way, home. The room was bright yellow, our favorite color. Hermione, mean little smart-mouthed child, stared. Outside, the patio was lit; a gray cat bounded across it. I whirled, cursing, my body inhabited by a force larger than itself. I saw the utensils in the drying rack and in an instant inventoried them, selecting among them, judging the whitened bent tip of the carving knife, the gig points of the turning fork, weighing each, testing the balance and the tensile strength, rejecting the cheap ones, laying the table knives aside, excusing the dinner forks, discarding the spoons, rummaging to find one piece only: the big wedge of chef's knife jammed between the colander and the potato masher. Murder jumped in me. It tore like wallpaper ripped off. I lurched toward the rack, reached it . . . and stopped. The halt was so abrupt my brain hit the front of my skull, that's what it felt like. Something threw open the door, raced across and slammed out the other side. My mind was filled with skid marks. Alice still barking her curses. I crossed the room, shouted her name into her face and caught by return mail her look of fright, a startled, confused look, and she stopped too. Then, because it had been ringing since she slapped me, I picked up the phone.

"What the hell is it?"

It was Jonnie Devane, who wanted to know if we still wanted to help him out. I said yes sure, but I can't talk now. He called again later and I said yeah, okay, still wondering what exactly he had in mind—company? conversation? marital mayhem?—and then we drove over to the dock and helped him load his boxes of medical supplies and boarded the eighty-foot cargo vessel a little after noon two days later. We hadn't said a word to each other about the fight, we hadn't apologized, we hadn't talked it out, we hadn't even slurred and slinked around pretending it never happened. It really had never happened, no matter what the little shrimp from next door might think. Or if it happened—it was nothing to us. We came back into focus, that was what mattered. Yet an uneasiness, discomfiture, a hungry moment; a yodel from far back in the woods drifted out to me.

One night in the galley I tried to talk to Jonnie about some of this, about our fighting, but he was too straightforward for me.

"I wouldn't take that for a second," he said.

"You mean you wouldn't let a woman hit you?"

"Not twice."

"I could have killed her."

"See—that's what happens."

He went into his own story, snagging a point or two of celebration and triumph out of the misery of his love life. *Not a thing you can do about it,* he said finally, *but keep going with it—or get the hell out.*

The crew members drifted in and they too added their interpretations to the converse, their failures and misalliances outweighing the happiness, as usual in these matters, even the one who had been married for twenty years, but the happiness always of such startling purity and depth that none of the outrage and trouble really mattered. The Haitian, Dore, was the only one who claimed uninterrupted bliss.

"I receive it every night at my house," he said.

His happiness was based on what? I asked.

"On complete trust."

"Ah, that, yeah. That's great, but it doesn't cover everything."

"What about if one of you got a bad character?" one of the seamen, a tall red-haired man, said. "What about if both of you do?"

"Love will heal your character," the Haitian said.

"I don't know," I said. "I don't see any sign of that."

"Which the one with the bad character?" he said.

"I don't want to point fingers," I said.

"Ain't too many ways you can point them in a two person situation," the red-haired man said.

"Yeah, but I still don't want to."

"Maybe that's your trouble," Jonnie said.

"How so?"

"You're afraid to declare yourself. You got to set the pace in these things. You got to make it clear what the rules are."

"Aw, no with the rules," Dore said.

"You get in trouble with them rules," the red-haired seaman said.

"I don't mean rules like you think," Jonnie said. "I mean the covenant. You know? The guarantee. It means you got to act in a certain way because you made a covenant to do what you're doing. Like on this ship. You signed on and since you signed on you can't turn around and refuse to do your job. It's just like a ship. Look at us. Good or bad, we're trapped out here. I can't hire anybody else. I got to make do with what I got. You have to go along."

"Yeah, look at us," the red-haired man—Oscar—said. We all laughed.

"Right. So we made a covenant and we got to follow the rules of it," Jonnie said.

"Still, I don't know," the Haitian said. "—the rules."

"You just getting hung up on a word," Oscar said. "It's cause you don't speak the language so good."

"Don't importune my speaking the language. I speak the language very well."

"Yes, you do," Jonnie said.

The mate came in, a large blond perpetually scowling but equable man. A dutiful man who in a grim, peremptory way had made sure we were comfortable in our little cabin behind the wheelhouse.

"I could tell you stories about all that," he said.

"Speak, Chief," the red-haired Oscar said.

Passengers—out island farmers, fishermen, and their wives—moved in and out of the galley, getting cups of coffee, taking slices of salted green mango from the plate Alice had set out on the counter. Alice—where was Alice?—she was up in the bow watching the ship kick on through the low seas. The chief drew a cup of coffee and sat down.

"I don't know—all these miseries, love problems—the truth is, you got to prepare for your old age."

"Come on, Chief, you ain't old," Oscar said.

"Old enough. I see what's coming."

Dore nodded. He too saw. He was fixed up for it. "You listen to this man," he said.

"I learned about it in my period between wives," the mate said.

"You were a mess at that time," Jonnie said.

"Whoo, I remember that time, Chief," Oscar said.

"Not like I do. I was wrecked. I let everything go to pieces. I wouldn't clean up the house and I wouldn't go buy my food and I started spending all my time reading the newspaper at McDonald's."

"That's not cause of the love, is it, Chief?" Dore said.

"I call it that."

"I think that's something else," the Haitian said.

"Maybe that's just your nature," I said, addressing the chief.

"If it is, it's one I want protection from."

"What happened, Chief?" Oscar said.

"It got worse. I got in fights—with old folks. They all come to McDonald's. That's where they get their cheap breakfast every morning. I'd insult them and try to poison their good will. None of them looked too happy anyway. But all it was, was I was jealous. I was spite-filled and angry because of my losses."

"You mean your wife," Dore said.

"That's right. And hell, I didn't even like her. That's why I divorced her. I looked at her one day and I realized—in my heart, I mean—that I didn't like her and I never had."

"That's just a little thing," Dore said.

"No, it wasn't. It was a sterling silver truth. And once I came on it I couldn't avoid it. It was like a leak in a septic tank."

"I know that leak," Oscar said. Jonnie gave him a look.

"You can't avoid it," the mate said. "You got to do something about it."

"So you put her aside," Dore said.

"Yes, I did."

"And things got worse," Dore said. He nodded at the red-haired seaman. "This is what I am saying."

"They got worse—right," the mate said. "I uncoupled from myself. All my parts did. I was like a motor you dismantle and can't put back together. Christ almighty," he said, shaking his head. He got up, poured more coffee, took a slice of green mango and meditatively chewed it. He laughed. "I got rousted from McDonald's. Eighty-sixed."

"Like by the bouncer?" Oscar said.

"By the janitor."

"Whoo."

"It could have been the cops. I was all to pieces."

"What happened?" Dore said. There was a mixed look of sadness and chagrin in his face.

"I kept going down. I wound up living in my car, up around Kissimmee, out in the orange groves. I set up a camp out there, in the weeds."

"That's where you met Constance," Jonnie said.

"That's right. She was ministering to the workers. She came upon me."

"A church woman?" Oscar said.

"No, not a church woman. Private charity work. Someone giving out of the goodness of her heart."

"A ministering angel," Jonnie said.

"She fell for you?" Dore said. "A bum?"

"It took some time. We got to talking. I started helping her out. She had a plant nursery back in town and I helped her with it, watering the plants, all that. I pulled myself together, or she pulled me.

Her concern for me did. She gave me a room at the office, put up a cot in the storeroom, and I lived there. After a while we began to get close to each other. She was lonely too. It didn't look like it, but her life was rough on her."

"You married her?" Dore said.

"Yes, I did. She brought me back—marriage brought me back into life. But I almost didn't make it—I almost couldn't. I came this close"—he held up thumb and forefinger, slightly apart—"to letting it all slip away."

"Whoo, Chief, that's bad," the red-haired man said.

The mate looked at him. His face clouded and something that had come out in it as he talked, a wistfulness, a quiet, a sad child-likeness, faded. "Yeah," he said. "It's a bad story all right. But it has a happy ending. Or no," he said, "a happy ongoing."

"You still married to her?" Dore said.

"Thank God I am," the mate said.

I was becoming drowsy. Maybe it was the drugs, maybe it was the tale. Back in the cabin I had begun writing a story about our trip. About the fight, that is, and about the aftermath, about the quiet days when we approached each other with our rinsed and temperate attitudes of near sweetness, if we were ever sweet, of how she went out into the backyard and climbed into the little banyan tree and sat there all morning reading a book and watching the day fly. Of what she said to me when I climbed up with her. Of the look on her face, the quick birdlike movements of her head, the way her eyes were filled with fire while her voice was quiet and controlled, as if there were two separate versions of her, both operating simultaneously. I wrote about how I called Bobby Concannon and tried to talk to him about it. "I could have told you," he said and hung up the phone. What was it? She peddled up to the Cuban store and came back with a bucket of flan and that was what we had for dinner. Fine, I said, that's fine, and I meant it. Afterwards, drugged on sugar and complicity, we made love, quietly, abashed and mutely generous in the dark, stroking each other, like phantoms, touching each other for hours without saying a word. "Somehow," I wrote, "she doesn't really ask anything of me. And is grateful for whatever I give her." Could this be true? It wasn't exactly like that. She gave me small gifts. Something about them tentative, shy, fearful, like notes slipped under the door by a secret admirer. "We are each other's secret admirer," I wrote.

I went outside, followed by Jonnie. We leaned over the rail looking at the sea whispering its frothy kisses along the hull. "You're luckier than you realize," he said.

"I think I realize it."

"Yeah, I guess you do. I was out of line about what I said before."

"It didn't bother me."

We could have gone on all night about this, men attempting to understand women, bursting up out of the dark ocean of mystery like sea divers, all that, brutalizing our feelings, trembling, pontificating, but the evening slid away from us, the talk faded, the men went about their duties. Maybe Alice coming in, something wild in her face, as if she had come in not from the forecastle but from the ocean itself, windswept frigate bird crossing miles of emptiness to light here—maybe Alice had something to do with this. She was beautiful, sunburned, her dark hair swept back from her hawkish, unappeasable face, and she looked at us as if she knew what we were doing. We flinched like little boys. Maybe that was what drove Jonnie and me out to the rail. I asked him about our mission, which was still uncompleted. He said it was coming up late the next day.

I was getting more nervous about our part and I asked him about it. He still didn't want to say exactly.

"But you have to," I said. "It's making us jumpy—it's already made us."

"Company," he said.

"You're lonely?"

"Yeah, in a business way, I guess. Cornered maybe."

"Lonely and cornered? Shit, man. What is this?"

He was silent a moment. The ship throbbed on through the black, white-accented sea. "I got backed up moneywise," he said finally, "and I got to do this."

"But you said it wasn't any trouble. No trouble expected you said."

"Well, yeah. That's what they told me."

"Ah, crap."

He was taking over a run for somebody else. They'd put men in with him, the bosses back in Miami had; islanders, revolutionaries, flashfighters, he didn't have any power over them. I was there—we were on board—to make it look like he had backup too.

"I don't know who we could possibly fool," I said.

"Yeah," he said, and spit over the rail. He looked sideways at me, a knowing, sad, disappointed look, not the first one I'd received. "Yeah."

Through the open porthole I could see Alice sitting on the table, leaning over her knees talking to the red-haired Oscar. The man's eyes were fixed on her, wide-open, as if he was straining all the baffles to get everything she said in.

We coasted up the island in the dark to a small cove that was empty except for a fishing shack up under some melaleuca trees and waited. The moon was out, and behind the beach the country looked empty, half wooded with white coral rock protrusions everywhere, like the island's skeleton showing through. The white sand curving into bushes on both ends of the beach had a pale, ghostly shine to it. We lay out in the deep water for a couple of hours. Jonnie was scared. He talked about it and for a brief period got rushed and angry, but he calmed down. Alice sat in the bow looking at the shore. She wore shorts and a white T-shirt and she had gotten sun on the way over that made her face in the dark mysterious. I went out and sat with her. She had moments during the trip when she was talkative and others when she wouldn't speak to anyone. She liked the mate and the five crew members, but she didn't care much for Jonnie or me. She liked to lie in the bow reading. I sat beside her and we didn't talk. A breeze blew off the land, bringing the smell of vegetation and something else, cooking maybe.

After a while I asked her if she was hungry.

She said, "No, I ate a papaya a while ago."

I had seen her slicing it, squeezing lime onto it, watched her take it out to the rail and eat, picking each slice up delicately between her fingers and biting it from the end. But I just wanted to hear her speak.

"Do you want something?" she said.

"I think I'd like a hamburger."

"I'll fix you one."

"That's all right. I'll have one later, when this is done."

"You ought to eat."

I wanted to say I'd like to eat with you, but I didn't because I was nervous. I was nervous that she might start up. There was light enough to see each other's faces and I wondered if she could see what was in mine, but she didn't say anything if she did. "Jonnie's frightened," I said.

"I am too."

"This probably wasn't a good idea."

"Maybe we needed an adventure."

"What were you looking at?"

"The beach. These lonely island beaches always look like a haven. I always want to come out here and stay awhile, set up in a shack and live the beach life."

"Maybe we are already doing that."

"You know what I mean."

"Yes, I do."

I touched her arm, ran my fingers along it. Her skin was hard, it was not really as soft as you thought a woman's skin would be. It had been hard when she was a girl and it never softened up. It was one of those little things you thought about and got used to. Everything about her had become the standard for me. I'd told her what Jonnie said and she laughed and then her face had gotten serious and her brow clouded the way it did when she was scared. I'm sorry, I said. We're supposed to stand there looking tough? she had said. Confident I guess. She'd just looked away toward the horizon.

"He wants to impress Senegol," she said now.

"I know."

"That's why we're here."

Jonnie came out just then holding the radio phone. He was talking into it, telling the one on the other end everything was fine.

"Send the boat out," he said.

The mate came out carrying a rifle, a military gun. We came down from the bow. "This going to go all right?" I said.

"No trouble at all," Jonnie said. He conferred with the mate. A boat put out from the shore, running out from what must have been a small creek entering the cove. We could hear the noise of the motor, which was small, puny sounding, but normal, nothing strange about it. We watched the boat, a skiff, come on. It had a high prow like a shrimp boat. There were three men in it. Alice leaned over the rail watching it approach. I stood beside her, but I wanted to sink back into the shadows.

Jonnie came up to us. I said, "Did you want us to hold guns too?"

"I don't think you'll have to. We shouldn't have any trouble here."

"Good, because I was just joking."

The mate had moved back into the shadows on the far side of the boat. The winch started, a whining, coughing sound that made me flinch. They had the cargo already prepared. It was piled in a sling, a few wooden crates.

"This is all coming back to me," I said now.

Alice laughed, a friendly, tense laugh. I hugged her. Then I moved down the rail away from her. I thought two standing apart might seem more powerful. She looked at me, a fleeting scared expression in her face, something wan and assailable, but this vanished, her face hardened with concentration and she stayed where she was.

The boat snugged in and a man climbed the swing ladder. No one had said anything until he spoke. He shook hands with Jonnie and said he was happy to see him. "I can't tell you, my friend, how delighted I am."

"It's got my heart pounding," Jonnie said.

"Like a couple of lovers," the man said.

Another man came up the ladder and stood behind the first man.

He didn't say anything, but he didn't look particularly friendly. Jonnie directed the first man into the cabin, indicating I should come too. I glanced at Alice, who was still by the rail looking out toward shore as if she had decided to ignore everything. "Allie?" I said. She didn't answer. I wanted to drop all this and just talk to her. But I went on in with Jonnie.

The man was thin and tall, like me, and slightly stooped. He wore cheap pants and a cheap sport coat over a faded purple shirt. The ensemble looked like the clothes men wore at my father's old mission, clothes dumped onto a table from plastic bags and picked through. "Do you mind if I sit down?" he said.

"That's a good idea," Jonnie said.

They both pulled up chairs at the little work table fastened to the wall. There wasn't room for me so I sat on the bunk against the other wall. "This is my friend," Jonnie said. "He used to be with AID."

The man gave me a sharp look.

"It wasn't AID," I said. "It was a private charity."

"We don't ask for charity," the man said evenly.

"Of course not," I said.

I was very tense and wished I could go off somewhere and get high.

"Who do you work for now?" he said.

"I don't work. I'm just here helping Jonnie."

"This is Jonnie?"

"Mr. Updog," Jonnie said, giving I guess his code name.

"Yes. Mr. Updog."

"Do you have the money?" Jonnie said.

"I have it to the penny."

He was silent then, waiting. Neither of us said anything. Then the other man came in and whispered in the tall man's ear. "Thank you, Hans," the tall man said. He looked at Jonnie. "Everything is as it should be."

"Whoosh," Jonnie said. "I am so nervous. Are you nervous?"

"Yes, I am," the man said. He pulled two plastic sandwich bags from his coat pockets, one from each. The bags had currency in them, stacked bills bound with rubber bands. "We could have simply wired the funds to your account," he said.

"I like it better like this," Jonnie said.

"Old-fashioned."

"I like the actual feel of the paper."

"When you can taste it in your dinner, you will know the revolution is complete."

I'd heard something like this out in Timor, this freedom fighter phrasemaking. I took it as a bad sign.

Jonnie had opened the packets and was thumbing through the

money. He looked up with a blank expression on his face, his lips slightly taut.

"It's fine?" the man said.

"It's just right."

"Then we are concluded."

Outside, a moment later, after Jonnie ushered us out, the breezy, slightly muggy air seemed filled with life. I looked for Alice and saw her up in the bow, looking away from the action. I took a deep breath, experienced an easing in my shoulders. The man also breathed deeply. "It's good now," he said. He looked at me. "Are you taking notes of this, my friend?"

"I'm just the buddy," I said.

"Which agency do you work for now?"

"Let it drop, why don't you?"

"There is always someone filling your place in the affair."

"It's good to have a pal."

"Perhaps things are too easy for you."

I stuck my hand out. "Thank you for coming." An antic sense took me. I smiled at him, a broad smile, thinking of what we would do later, of how we would speak of this after the lights went out.

He looked toward the bow. "Is that your *novia*?"

"My wife."

"Perhaps your partner?"

"My wife."

The other man, a burly person, shorter, came up and said something to the tall man. The tall man excused himself and walked over to Jonnie, who was speaking to the man in the boat. They shook hands and the two revolutionaries went down the ladder. I moved to the rail beside Jonnie and we watched them get into the boat and move away. The motor made its small, cranky sound. The boxes were stacked in the center. The tall man rode standing up, his hand on the top box. He turned once and waved and then looked straight ahead toward the shore. A faint light had appeared on the beach at the point where the river entered the sea. The boat went past it and disappeared into the cut.

Jonnie swore under his breath. "Fucker," he said.

"What is it?"

"He shucked me on the money."

"How do you mean?"

"It's short."

I looked toward shore. The light had gone out. The island looked closed down, abandoned, as if nothing had ever taken place there, and never would, it was that dark and quiet.

"How short?"

"Several thousand. At least."

"Damn."

He hadn't said anything at the time.

"Ah, man. Fuck."

He threw a packet against the base of the cabin. Then he followed it, picked it up and banged it against the bulkhead. "Fuck, fuck, fuck."

"It could have been worse," I said.

"Yeah, sure, but Jeeze. Shit."

Alice had come down from the bow and stood behind him. Her face was grave. "What is it?"

"The rebel guy stiffed him," I said.

"He didn't pay him?"

"Not fully."

"Damn," Jonnie said.

The mate came up and Jonnie began to talk rapidly to him. "Wait a minute," he said to Alice and me, and the two of them went into the cabin.

"It's better than shooting," I said.

"I guess so," Alice said.

She had faded out when the action began, which was not unusual for her. There were times out in the world when, spoken directly to, she wouldn't respond. She was afraid to, but not afraid of the interlocutor, or of what he might do; she was afraid of herself, of the charge she might set off.

She glanced at the cabin porthole. "They're probably in there making excuses."

"I expect so."

"You don't have to look so distressed."

"Why not?"

"Maybe they won't do anything."

"It's not *our* fault."

"That squarish man looked angry. He didn't like being here."

"I didn't pay much attention to him."

We went into the galley and Alice fried me a burger. One of the seamen, the Haitian, came in, got a cup of coffee from the big urn and sat down just out of conversational range. We called him over. "Scary, huh?" Alice said.

"The other one had a gun under his coat. A little machine gun."

"I saw it," Alice said.

"You did?" I said. "I didn't."

"I don't like this work," the man, Dore, said.

"Pays pretty well though, doesn't it," Alice said.

"Yes, there is that. But it makes me too tense. I don't want any more tension."

"Now we can relax," I said.

"Not me. I won't relax until I am returned home to my house with my wife. Then I will relax."

I went outside and met Jonnie coming out of the cabin. "Jesus," he said, "What a trip, huh?"

"I think it's gone pretty well."

We went over to the rail and leaned over it, looking out. We were under way again. The island was a dark bulge off to starboard. Soon we would begin to see the lights of farmhouses. After that the settlement lights, little towns strung along the water, and lights up in the hills. But it was late. Maybe they had all gone to bed by now.

"What are you going to do about the money?" I said.

"Not much I can do. Unless I want to get a gun and go after it."

"It's not worth that, is it?"

"Is it to you?"

"It wouldn't be to me. Why?"

"We're going to be short on your end."

"My end?"

"My other expenses are set. There's nothing else I can do."

"So—what? You plan to owe it to me?"

"It was a risk. Sometimes this happens."

"It happened to you, Jonnie. It didn't happen to me."

"Yeah, it happened to you too."

I told Alice and she said not so fast mister, let me talk to him, which she did. She came out of the cabin furious, walked up to the bow, came back, went in the cabin again and shouted at Jonnie. Then she hit him. I came in after her to see the mate grabbing her arms from behind, so I hit the mate. Jonnie hit me and I went down and then for a few minutes there was a melee that Alice and I got the worst of. The Haitian came in and put a gun on us and that broke things up. They handcuffed Alice and me and left us in the cabin. After a while Jonnie came back.

"Look," he said, "I'm sorry about this, but you have to see how it is for me. I have to pay these men and I couldn't do this business at all if I didn't make my expenses. Besides, you didn't really do anything."

"Except come all the way out here so you wouldn't be so scared," Alice said. "You weakling."

"Yeah, okay. I'm not negotiating with you."

"There isn't anything to negotiate, shit hook," Alice said.

Jonnie looked at me, his eyes asking me to be on his side. "You should have said something to the guy," I said.

"Yeah," Alice said. "That's the point, isn't it? We have to pay for your damn cowardice."

"You wouldn't have done any better," Jonnie said.

They walked us back to our cabin, a small, square place with bunk beds and a tiny metal sink, and left us. "This is ridiculous," I said as Jonnie was leaving, meaning the cuffs, but he just shrugged. I sat in the one chair and a fright took me for a moment.

"You think I fucked things up?" Alice said.

"No. I think Jonnie fucked things up."

The deck vibrated faintly. We were running fast and steady. She got in the bottom bunk, first on top of the covers, then under them. "Why don't you slide in here," she said.

I didn't want to, but then I did. "Okay." I got in beside her and we snugged up together. Our hands were cuffed behind us and we had to help each other.

"They won't do anything," she said.

"No," I said. "They won't."

"What do you think will happen?"

"I don't know. I can't picture Jonnie harming us, not really,"

"Why not?"

"We went to high school together. It's hard for me to picture somebody from high school harming me."

"Jesus, Billy. Hitler went to high school. So did Ted Bundy."

"Neither of them were in my class."

"He would steal from you, beat you up and lock you in a cell, but he wouldn't really hurt you, not Jonnie from high school."

"You remember him too."

"I have to pee."

I helped her, undoing her shorts and working them down, and then I stood outside the head listening to her curse. My nose itched and I rubbed it against the door. I said, "We ought to move to the mountains."

"What for?"

"It's cool there. You can eat outside."

"Let's figure out what we're going to do about this first."

"Maybe," I said, "this is how they act before they give us what we want."

"What makes you think that."

"My faith in human nature."

"That's what makes me think the opposite."

"Jonnie had to make his display. In a minute he'll feel guilty about it."

"You certainly have a generous view of people."

"It's one of the things you love about me."

"Yes, it is, but I don't think it's always realistic."

"Let's go down to the Keys when we get back."

"That's a good idea. And see Munch and the baby."

I opened the door. Hunched over her knees, she looked at me wanly smiling up out of a universe of familiarity. I touched her face, just letting my hand rest on her lightly. She nuzzled my wrist and slid her lips along the edge of my hand. "I was thinking about your teeth," I said. "About how much I like them."

"You told me."

I had to pull the toilet paper for her. I wanted to get down on my knees and kiss her feet. I put the paper in her hands and held her body while she dabbed at herself. Then she helped me, pressing her ass against me as she undid my jeans, groping for me with a blindness that wasn't really blindness, careful even in tight quarters not to sprain anything, hooking me out and sliding aside. She was sweating, I saw it, a mist on her face, it was the old business, built of the shyness that left us only occasionally, like a good day in the middle of a corrosive illness, sunny day of peacefulness and bravery, not this day exactly. She turned her face away. "It's all right," I said. I don't really know why I said that because I was afraid then too, undrugged, rejailed, this time in the Caribbean, all that, at the mercy of people who were not the people I had once known, etc., but still I wanted some of what I had already begun to experience, how to put it—I thought, then and later—how to say that when she looked up at me I wanted to give her everything I had in the world.

Right then the door opened and the Haitian came in carrying a tray with food on it.

"Excuse me," he said and backed out.

We called him back and he returned and set the tray down on the little table in the corner.

"How about these handcuffs," Alice said, but he said there was nothing he could do. We looked at him, to see if he got the stupidity of it, which he did and made a gesture with his hands and went out.

"Hogs," she said, "dogs," bent down and bit up a mouthful of rice.

"Here," I said, turned, grasped a slice of mango and held it so she could bend down and take it in her mouth.

"Fuck this," she said, went back to the bunk and lay down. I noticed the backs of her legs were sunburned.

In the morning Jonnie came in with the mate and they led us out on deck. We were anchored off a small island, a rocky, sandy place with a few trees. Huge, pitted coral boulders were set at the edge of a cove like gates. "What are you doing?" I said.

"What we have to do right now," Jonnie said. The skin of his face had a plastic look.

"You're going to put us off on this place," Alice said.

"You'll be all right."

"This is crazy," I said.

"Come on," Jonnie said.

The island looked like a pocket desert poked up out of pale surf.

"Look," I said. "This isn't the eighteenth century. You don't maroon people . . . just because they disagree with you. Come on, man. Just because we argue with you."

"It's what I have to do."

"Why don't you try facing your responsibility, Jonnie," Alice said. "Why don't you try that?"

"There's a cachement tank," he said. "And Mick says there's fruit—papayas and melons and all that. You'll be all right."

I looked at Mick, the mate, and saw—I thought I saw this—that he wasn't thinking like Jonnie. It came to me they were going to kill us. But it didn't seem real. The next thought was there must be something to do. And then, I can live with this, I thought strangely, as if my ankle was just now sprained, as if it was some accident that wouldn't do me in. Then I started to feel depressed.

"The hell with this," Alice said, and headed up the deck. The mate stopped her.

"Listen," Jonnie said. "This is the only thing we can do right now."

"You could pay us our money," Alice said.

Jonnie frowned. His face was patchy with color and his forehead looked oiled. His left hand twitched against his pants.

I walked over to the rail and looked out at the island. Acacia bushes came down almost to the water. A few white birds jumped around in them. "Listen," I said. "Forget about the money. It'll be all right."

"What is that?" Alice said.

"Come on, sweetie. Jon," I said, tense and stiff in the face, "we don't need the money. The deal got fucked up slightly, but we're okay."

"You're just not dependable enough, Billy," he said, with maybe some sadness. "I shouldn't have brought you along."

"You didn't know I was undependable before? I mean, we hooked up in a courtroom, Jon."

"I don't know. I saw you with Alice. And Henry and all."

"It's not about Billy," Alice said, her voice harsh. "Billy's fine, you creep. It's about you. About your sorriness."

He made a gesture, faint, unoffended. "No. It's about the way things work out on the ocean. It's about this being my ship, and all that."

I laughed—a scared wiry little laugh with a squirt of hysteria in it.

"Funny, huh?" the mate said.

"Not yet." I felt like I did when I was a little boy over at my cousin Ike's house and I tried to ride his German shepherd. The dog wouldn't take it and everybody laughed at me. "Things are going to fall apart in a really bad way if we don't stop now."

"You need to make an effort," Alice said.

I could smell the island; it smelled dusty and vacantly sweet.

"Crazy things make sense," I said, "and you do them and then you hate yourself and it's too late."

"You sound like you're talking about you, Billy."

"I am. I know about this."

"You're pathetic," the mate said.

"It's a pathetic situation," Alice said.

"That's about to move on to tragic," I said.

"I don't know," Jonnie said.

Without moving his head, the mate gave him a split-second fixed look.

Alice came up close to Jonnie. Her face was calm, interested, a little sad, over it now. "It was our own fault," she said. "Entirely. We were mistaken about what went on. You were under terrible pressure." She continued like this until the mate put a stop to it. "Wait," she said, "wait," but the mate wasn't interested and the truth was Jonnie wasn't the one in charge.

They put us in the collapsible boat, ferried us over to the island, walked us up through the acacia bushes to a clearing where, as Jonnie said there would be, there was a concrete cachement tank, rigged with sloping wood panels to funnel the water in, a really ingenious contrivance that under other circumstances I would have liked to take a minute to study. We clustered up, Alice and me. I noticed the dark graininess in the white sand at our feet, noticed the streak of sunburn along Alice's forearm. The mate hadn't shaved for a couple of days. Then Jonnie, white in the face, choking on himself, raised his hand and started to say something and I felt the wail that had been down inside me all my life begin to lift off, to rise through my flesh and bones.

But it didn't get to the surface, not that day. As I turned to Alice, to let her in on everything I hadn't admitted so far, to cry into her face some fact or disputation or love, I couldn't tell, as she herself stared wildly at me, as if inside what she saw, some vast conniption, some impossible acrobatics, was taking place, just then, the Haitian raised his rifle and shot the mate in the face.

It wasn't like the time the young Fyodor Dostoevsky was put up before the firing squad for the czar's sport and kept there blindfolded until at the last second the reprieve came. This was much stranger. The mate had just opened his mouth to speak to Alice, probably to say he had loved her from the first moment he saw her, and his big blond face was turned away, just as he was about to speak to her, looking across us out over the island which was low and brush covered, maybe taking it all in, maybe admiring the rough beauty of it, when the Haitian, who had not spoken at all, raised the gun, and just as the mate noticed him, shot him straight on from six feet away.

"Enough of you," the Haitian said.

"Oh my God," Jonnie cried. "Oh my God." He went right up to the Haitian, who could have shot him too, and threw his arms around him. "Oh, Jesus, man," he said.

The Haitian still had the carbine ready, but he didn't raise it. He let Jonnie hug him. Then Jonnie stepped back and he began to cry. I was crying myself. I staggered over to Alice, who had dropped to her knees, and knelt down to her and placed my head on her chest and I was crying all the time. There was a lightness in me that was not freedom but frailty, and the tears blew through me like a rain blowing before a breeze. Alice cried too. Everybody—except the Haitian—cried. And there lay the mate, twisted onto his side under a jumbie bean bush, one hand sprawled out from the body, open, palm high, knees drawn up like a child's. The Haitian knelt and touched his face. Then he stood up and looked at us with a wild, sad, frightened look in his eyes, the look of a man who had just ruined everything.

Back at home, not long after this, I started out to see my mother, but then I turned around. I didn't want to talk to anybody I was related to, I never had. I met a man downtown at a bar—I was coming out of Bitsy's on Eighth Street, drunk slightly and slightly drugged, but still coherent, still able to experience myself as a real person in the midst of the stellar hum, when a man I didn't know came up to me and began to talk. He said he remembered me from when I was a boy preacher. We sat on a bench waiting for the bus and conversed. When the bus came I got on with him and rode out to Homewood, where he lived. He had a low-slung Florida house painted a beautiful muddy orange color, like a house in the islands, and he invited me in. I had supper with him and his wife and son, a little six-year-old deaf boy.

At some time during the evening, when I had stepped away to the bathroom to top up on the drugs, I ran into the little boy just coming out of his room. He had a book he wanted to show me. It was book of pictures of space travel, big color photographs. We sat on the bed in his room and looked at them. He had a wonderful voice, the words like driftwood bobbing up in a dark current of sound. Somewhere along the line I told him about the shooting, about how demolished we all were by it, and how sad it was, and what a mistake it had been, especially for the Haitian—especially for the mate—and about the burial up on the island and about coming home after Alice and I got off the ship in Freeport—we just didn't want to spend more time with any of them—and then about arriving on the short flight to Miami and driving home with Henry in the rain across the causeway just as one of the little pennant-flying island freighters was coming along in the Cut and both of us crying, so stupid and helpless.

Part IV

WE'RE PASSING THROUGH A PARADISE

Chapter One

"Why would you leave me now?" Alice said, speaking from her mental bomb crater, completely unrevulcanized by the shock treatments, which as I understood them were supposed to make a victim happy about her situation, or at least not as concerned. "I am so scared," she said.

Henry and I had to help her get dressed in the morning and then we wheeled her out in her grandfather's old wicker wheelchair to Henry's back dock patio and sat looking out across the canal at the swamp and drank coffee together. "Do I know you boys?" she said, and grinned. Did I say unchanged? She wasn't happified, you couldn't say that, but she had moments now of fleeting ebullience. Waking, she looked at her face, the beautiful square, chafed, Saxonette face I had loved all my life, and it surprised and delighted her. Just for a second. I saw it in her eyes, the delight, the monkey look of wonder and appeal, the old primitive entrancement, Eve catching a glimpse of her looks in the stream, some lost humanoid way back in Africa gazing at the reflection that would haunt all the rest us for time to come.

She looked, grinned, yes, and fell back into the welter of lostness that had overtaken her. A troubled expression came over her, and this was what she carried into the day. In the kitchen she'd ask us to stop the chair so she could look around. She was fascinated by the edges of things, by counters, table tops, and shelves. Drop-offs, she called them. "My mind's like an orange that's rolled off a table," she said. She looked at me and her eyes were yellow with forsakenness. "I've been squished by the fall," she said.

I half regretted not letting her stay in the hospital, which would have made the doctors happy, but I wasn't going to let them whack her another time with their treatments. I never could stop fiddling with her, with the situation, and this time, scared stiff by the look of dumbfounded desolation in her face, I had to act. Yet now, concussed, bewildered, reaching for a modus, for a mango, she seemed half formed, or half unformed, something being driven, like a therianthrope, back to its womb. No Mrs. Lazarus, but inchoate Baby Nell instead, half teased into the light, besotted and oddly vain, offering small presents to us such as pins and buttons she'd picked up on her journey in from outer space.

"Where will you go?" she said, looking at me from her cocoon of blankets.

"I'll be back in two days."

"But from where?"

"You see this canal?" Henry said. "This water out here?"

She looked at it.

"Billy's going to follow it down a ways to check on something. Then after a while he'll be back. All you have to do is watch the water and you'll stay connected to him. He's down on it, just a few miles away."

She cocked her head at Henry. "Do you think I'm an idiot? I would simply rather Billy stay here."

"Me too," I said. "But I have to go for a job."

No longer myself, but a reflection of the same misalignment, underdone too, something dribbling out of me, some soul evacuation going on despite everything I tried, I gazed at her, filled with longing. I didn't have what it took to take care of her—that's what the doctor said.

For various placatory and benumbing drugs, they had given her scrips, which I had filled. I tried each one; some did nothing and some slammed me against the bulkhead, picked me up and sat me down to a pleasant mental repast. These I split with her, but she at first wanted none of them. "I would stay off drugs myself," Henry said. "But that's just me."

"I don't know how to advise you, " I told her.

"Just leave them there on the table," she said. "And we'll see what happens."

There was a lot of screaming and crying on Rando. My part was to get this on paper, to listen and write a story about how it took you when your sixteen-year-old daughter was torn to pieces by a fish. (The old bridge, the one replaced after the hurricane but still used on the sly, had given way under some local *cocochitas* who were using it for a party, sending half a dozen automobiles into the channel. This really didn't at first faze most of the fallen, except for the ones hurt in the tumble, but it became a horror when they were attacked by sharks. Six died and nine others were ripped up by teeth. Ike wanted me to go down and interview the relatives of the dead and mutilated. Since he was the one got Alice released from the hospital I couldn't say no.)

There were quite a few crazed folks around. Some sat mute, staring into the back of the chair across the room. Others joked and cracked out an irrepressible and frightening laughter. Some argued about it as if they might come up with a line of reasoning that would reverse everything. Others raged. A few wept in darkened rooms, refusing food or comfort. Some huddled with lawyers. Others got busy, Florence Nightingale style, rushing from bed to bed. Still others were philosophical. A few were religious. A couple appeared unfazed. One man, a finish carpenter, seemed not to mind at all, right up until the moment he whipped out a case knife and slashed himself across the forearm.

The survivors I was most interested in were the ones who reminded me of Alice. A wild and murderous-tongued mother whose child had been eaten down to rib cage and pelvis, who screamed at the police and the minister, who with a hammer smashed the windshield of the patrol car and called the minister's wife a lying cunt—her I was drawn to. And the snappish, keen, rancorous father of another victim, who stood up at the memorial service and cursed everyone whose children were still living. I got into a brief, choppy fistfight with a man who stopped me in the street to berate me for feeding off corpses (human shark). He didn't mean anything by the punches, I could see that; I myself had no animosity toward him. I say I had none, but for a few seconds—the fight was interrupted by the photographer accompanying me—I was caught in it, half transformed by the physicality, by its proximateness to what I experienced with Alice. As I loomed above him, my fist drawn back, I wanted to drive my knuckles through his skull. I called her immediately afterwards and told her about it, but she was still snowed in by her ordeal.

"Have you taken any of the drugs?" I said.

She said she didn't know. "Maybe I have, but how can I be sure?"

"Do you notice an effect?"

Unable to remember much, she had begun to make things up. Her stepmother was trying to make amends, she said. "I wouldn't let her in the house." I knew this would never happen, and confirmed it with Henry. She told me she was about to take a trip. She wanted to see the blue waterfalls of Virginia, as she put it. "I feel as if a hurricane has soaked me," she said. "I'm looking for the bright spot." Even as she made things up, devised complicated, impossible scenarios that took her mind down twisting roads through a wildwood of importunity and confusion, she was troubled, like someone from an archaic country, by thoughts of the simple life she'd lost. The Land of Wooden Heads, she called the old world. "I haunt the borders of it," she said.

I pictured her halloing across the marshes of her degradation, all that.

"You've got to do something about this," she said.

I called Ike and told him I was getting nowhere.

"You're doing fine," he said. "The material is just great. The stuff from the morgue is so ghoulish and sensitive you'll probably win a prize."

"They're going to charge me for breaking and entering. I wasn't even looking for that crap."

"The part about being able to see all the way through the girl's chest, see her heart—what did you say?—still as a russet potato, yeah—that was striking. And the piece about the men going out in a boat hunting sharks with Uzzis—I loved that. Murdering fish, you said, extracting revenge from sea trout and mackerel, blasting the jellyfish—you got a touch, my friend."

"Touched—yeah. I'm lonesome, Ike."

"How can you be lonesome—you hadn't even left the state. Why didn't you bring Allie with you? How's she doing by the way?"

I hung up. When I turned around, the fellow who'd cut himself with a knife, the carpenter, was waiting for me.

He flashed his sling and said, "What's this about the morgue?"

"That was my editor. He wants some more hard news."

"You feed off this, don't you. People like you."

I was the complaint department, I knew that. One of them. "You want to get a drink?" I said.

"Yeah, sure."

We went over to Blinky's, a small fishing camp and barroom on the bay side, and drank a few. In the blue and red lights of the bar, composed by alcohol, the whole thing seemed to have a deep and familiar meaning, a meaning I could almost but not quite put my finger on. Beyond the big plate glass back window the lights of channel buoys swayed in the tide. A breeze skidded over the surface, turning up whitecaps as if it was sowing them. The moon was out, a scoured, flimsy thing. It was a crisp, cold night in the Keys, weather you would remember in the way one remembered things that only happened once, incisively, long ago. A way of being I had forgotten came back to me. I knew I fit in this set of circumstances, this weather and place, and even the situation, among these grieving folk and their sundered dead, knew it in the sad and confidential manner you knew someone you loved never really loved you the way she said she did, just something you brush against once in a while without engaging but never quite get used to.

Charlie Smith

"Yeah," the carpenter said (I mentioned this). "Me too. I don't know why I feel that way—and it scares me."

"Why'd you cut yourself?"

"There's a long explanation and a short one."

"Give me both of them."

"I couldn't prevent it—that's the short one."

"What's the long one?"

"Solace."

"That's shorter."

"What's behind it's not."

"Yeah?"

He tried to tell me, but he couldn't. There were a hundred reasons, motives, cul-de-sacs of the spirit stuffed with argumentia, sad insights and truths like carcasses beside the road, and every one fit, every little notion about how it took his mind off things, or even the one about how his daughter was a cutter too, or his wife, her look, the way she stared at him as if he was an idiot, but none of them put the cap on anything. Even here, down among the caskets, things weren't clear.

As we talked, people came and went, townspeople with their brains half murdered, mothers and fathers, close relatives, homefolk already striking at the snakeheads of bitterness, already set up now for a lifetime of the willies, inductees into the fraternity of those who slept with the light on, the midnight shiverers, tremblers, the chokers and those who yelled at the dark, the execrators and the cowed, the indifferent and the falsely gay, each with his or her take on the tragedy, each with some expressed or unexpressed conclusion or perception, some at last realized design scrawled on a napkin and stuffed into back pocket or purse, a meaning to pull out later in the privacy of one's own dereliction, to read over, like a poem composed under the influence of heavy drugs, a missive to truth and hope, perused in the yellow of bedside lamplight or sitting on the toilet at 3:00 A.M., the purity of it blurring even as the words stopped making sense. Just local folk, that is, wandering by, and strangers, and tourists caught in the wild fancy of frost in the Keys.

Tears, yes, the carpenter mentioned those, the noncathartic strain. Sweats. Shameful thoughts. Alice had showed up for a psychiatrist appointment, late in the workday, intake variety, and two hours later the doctor himself had driven her to the hospital. The carpenter's name was Burl, but he asked me to call him Allen. Alice had attempted to check in under a false name, but this not being the 1800s, it didn't work. The doctor said aside from that she was very docile. Abashed was the word he used, a word Alice and I sometimes employed. I could picture her, which I hated doing, false witnesser that I was, striding along, down a busy corridor, jaw trimly set, like a sail, fingers lightly poking at her own flesh, not quite stopping the leaks, the seeps of terror and chagrin, each step an erasure of hope and personality, each breath an irremediable loss, eyes snagging on nothing that could save her, one more fool confounded by a turn of phrase, a yes, a phone call, a spaz in the blood that made her wonder about something or recall it, a spot of discharge on her nightgown, a scent at the window, bird in the poinciana squeaking out her name, you couldn't tell, always something, a mistake made, unavoidable—I didn't want to talk about what was bugging her, which had caused another fight—now this hospital, redemption through diminishment, a rebushing of the spirit, restack, hope recused and replaced by a simplitude of affect, disaster converted into change for a Coke, a new design applied to the old matrix now so worn and crumbling, thoughts like smoke drifting in a stairwell, something else you can't remember, of no moment now, that was once so germane. In my mind, talking to the carpenter, I watched her stop and turn to ask for something, and give up on it.

"Exhausted—sad—calm," the fellow said, Burl, coming to the end of his story, "like what you get when you see what's really going on."

"What is that?"

"What's going on?"

"Yeah."

"There's no help for it."

"For what?"

"That's what's going on. This"—he lifted his cut arm in a vague, birdlike way—"all this. Dead children. There's no help for it."

"That's because you never found drugs," I said.

I ordered a plate of scrambled eggs, got up and went to the restroom, put a dollar's worth of quarters in the condom machine, pulled a random handle and pocketed what came out without looking at it. In the mirror a man with a haggard, alarmed face looked back at me. "Buck up, buster," he said. I opened the window and climbed out onto the deck—how many times in my life had I done this—went to the rail and looked down the channel. The bridge, the remains of it, a pulpy section of undigested roadway, slanted down, held by steel rods that looked like veins, shreds, a mass dark and without form, the whole confabulation nothing but the sea's upchuck. A chill sank in at my throat, the dead cold hand of a loved one—somebody's loved one—pressing against me. I shuddered and worked my fists, staring down channel, not really looking for anything, letting whatever was out there poke its head up if it wanted to, a little drama I tried to keep going at moments like this, as if to give the incident meaning. As always, once again, nothing appeared.

From the pay phone at a corner of the dock—skittering over to it—I called Henry for an Alice update. "She's maintaining the pace," he said.

"Ike's got me on a series," I said. "Which is why I'm still here."

"She has this tremor, that comes and goes."

"That's because they whanged her in the head."

"She says it gives her style."

"I like tremors well enough. But what if it's permanent?"

"She wonders about that too."

"Where is she right now?"

"Out on the dock."

"In this cold?"

"She likes it. She's wrapped in blankets, sitting in a beach chair with her feet propped on the rail. She wants to see if the canal will freeze."

"Now we're talking about her in this ridiculous, proprietary fashion."

"Pretty soon you'll be asking about her bowel movements."

"How're they holding, by the way?"

"Steady."

Off through the slant of plate glass the carpenter dipped a fork into my scrambled eggs and took a bite.

"What do you think's going on in her head?" I asked Henry.

"She's piecing things together."

"What things?"

"I expect most of it."

"I wake up brooding on the situation, in mid-brood. It infuriates me."

"She'll be all right I think."

She liked to sit in the shed while he worked on a sculpture, he said. She liked being in the stone dust and the sound of hammering. She liked the chisel work, the fine scraping, the whole process. "She falls asleep sometimes. She curls up in the big wheelbarrow and nods right off."

"She looks tormented when she sleeps."

"She always has."

"Really? I didn't notice it when we were children."

The carpenter finished the eggs and began working on the side of toast, in long strokes elaborately buttering a slice. Choose life, the Bible said, in Deuteronomy. I didn't guess it really mattered how you did that. In a minute the carpenter, Burl or Allen, looked up and saw me and then, convivially, he motioned for me to come in, like a host, indicating the tattered breakfast. I gave him a little wave, the copy of a wave Alice had used once, hand right up beside her head, from a ship railing, and left the premises.

Willie J and his wife Munch and the baby came up to keep me company, and then Munch and the baby drove up to Miami to stay with Alice. Willie walked around with me telling people to be calm. "I never saw so many folks so upset," he said, though to me, on the outside at least, it wasn't so much that they were upset, as the tragedy had thrown the rhythm off, in some harsh yet strangely subtle way. It made people leave a conversation a little early, or start talking too soon, or mention something they wouldn't usually or forget what they intended to say and have to come back for it, or they would buy things they didn't really want or refuse a courtesy and then overapologize, or someone would sit in his car in a parking space just a few minutes too long, so whoever was in the shop opposite might begin to wonder what was wrong, though truth was he already knew and had himself for a moment forgotten, and even policemen would lose their place temporarily in the tickets they were writing or employees go a little slower, or a little faster, women might stumble and catch themselves against the husband's sleeve, husbands who for the first time in their lives had begun to daydream about vacations in a foreign country, and children catch themselves yelling, or running faster than they were used to, small things usually, as if the invaders who'd taken over their bodies had nothing so much in mind as slight adjustments, little tinkering bits that only a native, returning maybe from a coma or a long distance trip, might notice. Otherwise life rolled on, it seemed. "God bless you," Willie said over and over, as if this were a password he had figured out and used to make a way for himself. "It's going to be all right," he'd tell a waiter or grocery clerk, or passerby, patting his hand if he could reach it, putting an arm around the fellow's shoulder.

"I'm just acting like this to keep from going to pieces," he said when I asked him about it.

I was in a vague area, pondering things, attempting to make up my mind about something that kept eluding me, and was unable to give him any useful suggestions.

Charlie Smith

"It's the way you put it that matters," he said when I tried to explain this, "not what you say."

I thought my state was a sympathetic reaction to Alice's predicament.

Maybe to life's, Willie said.

When I called Ike again he said he had expected me back at the end of last week. I couldn't remember. I was staying in a hotel above a restaurant off the Overseas Highway—a yellow building that caught the dawn light full in the face—and time had slipped away from me. I rolled out of bed—some morning: the next morning—and retired to a chair where I spent a few minutes gazing out to sea, watching a tanker crawl up the globe. A couple of slim boats skittered along, probably ferrying refugees up from Haiti or Cuba. The ocean was bright pale polished turquoise and untroubled by anything it had ever done. In the other bed Willie J snored away, riding the fumes of alcohol and disappointment. The couple next door, two women driven down from Detroit for the heat, began their early grousing. The cold had lingered, in itself an odd development. Cold down here usually evaporated like the dew and was lost to memory. It took a genius of empathy to get what people were talking about when they mentioned snow or ice or chilly gray days, even if you had only come from the blustery North last week.

I got out of the chair eventually, hungry and tired enough to need a little exercise, concerned about the noise of the surf rattling pebbles on the beach, about my soul, or something like that, touching my face as I descended the stairs, adjusting it, tapping my temple lightly to give warning to the rats inside, something terribly sad about the customers this morning, the battered wives and unctuous husbands, the proprietress Maureen yawning to reveal her blackened back teeth; I wanted some pancakes. There were none to be had so I ate something else, eggs or bacon, that I lost track of while I was still at the table. Maybe my mind was going. This didn't bother me at the moment, but I knew soon enough it'd scare me to death. I called again to the paper and Ike said I had turned a story in last night, flown like pixie dust over the wire. "What was it?"

"A feature about those guys who shot the fish."

I barely remembered it. "I think I'm coming down with something."

He told me to come home and I said I would, but first Willie and I took a taxi out to see friends and buy some oranges for Alice. Why would I buy oranges to take to Florida? Because it was only down here that you could get the special tiny Key orange, a compact nugget of sweetness that grew only in a small grove owned by Havermier Hughes, a fellow who had been a friend of my grandfather in the old days when they both conspired to make a killing from the new entrepreneurial paradise of South Florida. They were of course hornswoggled by much quicker and brighter men. Havermier had retreated to the Keys to take over the grove that had belonged to an old West Indian couple who had shepherded it out of the mists of time, and he and his wife now sold the oranges as well as a few Key limes from a stand out in front of their house on Pittance Road.

They were both sitting out on the porch when we got out of the taxi. I had forgotten my car, or for the moment forgotten I had one. They were wearing several layers of clothing as the TV said to do in cold weather, all of it summery: a pile of Aloha shirts and pairs of chinos for Mr. H and flowery frocks stacked one on another for

Mrs. H, that sort of thing. They looked like actors wearing fat suits. The oranges were ruined they said since two nights—nights I didn't exactly recall—since the thermometer, H said, had dipped into the freezing range just long enough to sear through the delicate skins of the famous fruit.

"They are already turning black on the trees," Havermier said. His wife, Mrs. Hughes, glared at me as if it was my fault, a squinty black-eyed look that carried with it the outrage of her people—as Havermier put it—ex-slaves from Trinidad. I felt as if it was my fault and suddenly, without intending to, began to weep. I passed this off as something in my eye, but Mrs. H caught it. "Sniveler," she said, got up and went back in the house.

"Don't worry about her," Havermier said. "She doesn't take setbacks well."

"What setbacks?" Willie said. He had missed the first exchange and was staring nervously down the road, as if he had left something in the taxi. "How are we going to get back?"

"Who is this?" H said, knocking his chest with both sets of knuckles. He was skinny and crusty-fleshed and had loosely shaped white hair hanging off his skull in long, disturbed comb-over remnants; he grinned straight at me.

"Jailbird," Mrs. H said from inside the house.

"How's your wife," H said.

"Another jailbird," came the ghostly interior voice.

"She's doing fine," I said loudly. "She may take another job playing piano."

"That's wonderful," H said, scratching at himself through his outfit. "I can barely move around in this regalia," he added.

"That some kind of bee suit?" Willie said.

"Bees? Not in this weather, son."

"Idiots," came the voice from inside.

H cast a glance back that way. "Would you shut up?" He slapped his hands together. "Let's go for a ride."

The door flung open and Mrs. H bounded out. "Don't you let him get in a car."

"Now, Mother. These boys don't even have a car."

"It's too cold to be out in the wilderness," Mrs. H said. She glanced around suspiciously, as if the cold lurked, some icier confederate of it, somewhere nearby.

"I need exercise," H said.

"Me too," Willie said, and took off running down the road. He ran to the intersection—about a block away—and sprinted back while we watched. He came up huffing, coughing and stumbling. "Whoo, that was good."

"He's as crazy as you are," Mrs. H said.

In the meantime Mr. H had given me a look, a conspiratorial look, and begun to edge out into the yard. "Let's walk," he said.

So we did, prying ourselves away from Mrs. H, who loudly complained and then stamped her foot and banged back into the house. We walked down to the intersection, the crossing of two blank and empty roads, beyond which on all sides, except for the grove, a scrubland of myrtle bushes, sea grape, cactus, and pinchweed stretched away past milky rain ponds and mounds of pocked gray coral; military land, all of it, of no use to anyone but developers and the Navy. Off to the right the road angled down through scrub pines to the beach.

We walked down the road toward the ocean, walked until we were out of sight of the house. H pulled himself up and stopped. "Let's have a smoke," he said. None of us smoked, but we stayed there anyway.

"We're not one mile from million dollar homes," Willie said, "and look at this. The true Keys."

H peered anxiously back up the road toward town. In a few minutes, minutes in which we talked aimlessly about boat traffic and cold in hot places, a car appeared, coming our way. H brightened considerably at the sight of it. The car went by us in a cloud of white coral dust. The old man peered after it and then looked at us out of a white-powdered face. "They never stop," he said mournfully. Since he didn't explain, there was no telling what he was talking about. But for some reason we understood. We hung there for a while with him in the roaring silence of ocean breeze and mewing gulls. Then we turned back for his home.

As we walked I focused on the emptiness before my eyes. It was easy to take like this, from this location, safe on a beach road. Yet no matter where I stood, the creep began, creep of insufferable thoughts, the serial blank spaces and shameful insights, the broken resolutions, all that. I sensed Alice slipping away and it was remarkable how this sensation opened a scary gap in my philosophy of life. Under my big poncho I was chilled. I imagined living on a cold, bleak coast. Maybe we should try Maine or the Maritime Provinces, get into weather, climate, let it take our minds off the spookiness of being alive. She'd been trying to read a biography of Charlotte Brontë, the same book she was reading before she was hospitalized. A cold and stony life on the north Yorkshire moors. Bleakness addressed by way of art, which did nothing to change the circumstances. Under *these* circumstances, she had asked me, is there anything that might help?

Alice would hate this place, this shabby keyscape. The cold would offend her, and these people would have to be corrected. Yet now, slapped around by modern medicine, there wasn't much she hated. The way out, for her, apparently was not through. This adage was something we quoted to each other, in bed. We believed it the way people who had never done a thing with their lives believed that soon they were going to get down to it. Shock treatment—that was just like her. I was glad I hadn't been in the car she drove through the flower shop window. They would have caught me too. The medical police were on the lookout for cutups like us. Yet ours was a common story, small-time miscreants, refuseniks of the minor variety, furtive delinquents slipping off the reservation, but only to the party store next door.

Chapter Two

When I got back home, after driving up with Willie J sick in the backseat, stopping regularly for him to almost but never quite throw up, after we sat for two hours at a picnic table outside Spurleen's Emporium in Key Largo while he took a nap and I began a story in my notebook about the day Alice and the other walkabout patients were transported in a van to the Celestial Lanes in Miami, a bowling alley we had gone to pieces in years ago and been tossed out of—*Stupid kids,* they said—where after she'd drifted through a game in which only the paid attendants kept score, I found her—tipped off by an orderly—and intending to gather her into my arms found myself hanging back, transfixed by her aplomb, by the serenity in her face, a serenity I'd not seen before but was happy now to see, I thought, and then realized I wasn't because what would come next: flight? divorce? what if now she decided to abandon our little composition at the Ducat, and how dispiriting this was, this thought, that I would be prey to such a huge and rapscallionly poverty—sick need, as the doctors might put it—and as I walked past her, unsure how to approach, and she glanced at me with recognition but no acclaim, her eyes assessing me, registering me—the disputatious husband and lover—without craving, needing nothing in particular from me, fixed now, if that was what I sensed among the litter of panic and outrage, the scurrying about, of—what?—some alternate or maybe even more factual and deeply embedded self, the one who was desperately trying, even as I passed into the refreshment area, to figure how to invoke the old clutch and grab; this was so crippling that after beginning the story and purposely miring it in details about Raisinettes and Pepsi without ice, about the light gleaming on the surface of the lanes, all that, all to stave off panic and shame, I closed the notebook and got down on my knees and embraced Willie—who was nothing like me—on the grass, hoping that some of his steadfastness and honesty, and love, I guess you'd call it, would enter me, and it didn't, and I thought, Man it's not going to stop until I suffer all of it, and this thought was like a dark message delivered to me despite everything I'd done not to receive it—what was there to do now?—I got up and we drove on deeper into traffic and into modern life that was only—it was clear—a puppy trying to lick somebody's hand—just like me, I thought—after getting something to eat—waffles for Willie J, pancakes with sugar syrup for me—and then back on the road, where eventually we passed the big white cruise ships moored like artificial dreams at the commercial docks, and crossed onto the island where I turned left and, six blocks up, rattled despite the heavy food, came to our viney and flower bestrewn house, and remembered we weren't living there anymore, that this had been part of the argument—what has happened to us?—that precipitated Alice's flight and her wreck (her detour through the flower shop on 48th Street), and for a moment, for a second which if I hadn't shouted out would have opened a gap that allowed all the ghoulishness of life to pour through, I was completely lost, until I remembered we were living now at the Ducat, or had been before her hospitalization, and still were if that was what Henry had in fact told me, or Alice was, in our old room still paid for by funds from her nearly depleted trust account, and drove there and discovered she'd checked out—a (new) woman—not to be found in South Beach, or in the Glades at Henry's, or at her sister Senegol's house on Key Biscayne, or even at her stepmother's in the Gables—just gone.

"Well—gone where, Henry?" I said.

"I don't know. She just eased away from the curb. Just started rolling."

Goggles up on his forehead, a streak of white dust on his cheek—he looked as if he had been caught in something.

"Yeah?"

"I think—don't take this the wrong way—I think she left with some fellow."

I let this information drift on the air a moment. "Where were you?"

"I was inside—we were at Joe's—Stone Crab—and she stepped out for a smoke."

"She doesn't smoke."

"Isn't that odd?" he said.

"A fellow?"

"From the ward."

"Somebody she knew?"

"I'm not clear on it."

A chisel of light, of pain, struck my head. I started across the studio, aimed somewhere specific, for a second sure of something, my hand raised—in my mind raised—to strike, but when I reached the door I stopped. Everywhere beyond the room, beyond the dustiness and the clay models draped in plastic sheeting, the stones stacked in the corner and the tools laid out on the long green bench, beyond this place, everything was formless and impossible to know. I stopped. An amazement, a wild, tearing sensation took me. Holes opened, gaps. Maybe this was a turning point. Maybe there were such, moments, crossroads, where it made a difference which way you went. I had never believed in these notions, not much, but maybe now, maybe then, as I looked out at the canal where a fish had just swirled back into the depths, leaving its mark, there had come a moment when I could choose another road. Maybe, but I don't think so. And how could I know?

"Which way did she go?"

Henry, despite himself, laughed. "Which way did she go?" he said, accenting each word evenly. "Man, we are a couple of sad sacks."

I caught it, the joke, turned all the way around, and as if reaching up through a hole filled with seeds, with husks, tried to laugh too. Partly I did. The western falling sunlight streamed through the panes of the big French doors. It reached to Henry's feet, clad in dusty sneakers. He was sitting in his blue wicker chair, wearing his white coveralls, holding the bit of a power chisel, turning it in his hands and looking at it, raising it to sight along.

"What is it?" I said.

"She wanted to be by herself, for a while."

"Then what's the guy for?"

It wasn't registering. The information had no substance. This was the only reason, I thought, why I wasn't screaming.

"I don't know—a chauffeur, a chaperone."

"Which guy was he?"

"I couldn't tell—a tall guy, black. I never saw him before."

Someone from the ward, a sufferer, someone for whom life had become too unyielding, too momentous or speedy, someone who'd needed a rest. Someone they'd gotten a rope on, for a while.

"Did you know she was going to do it?"

"No. She called."

"From where?"

"Downtown, the Rudnick Pharmacy—where we used to go."

"To say what?"

"Adios."

Now a reappropriation began taking place. The continent, the country, the floodplain of me began to be eaten up, eroded, subsumed. The woods gone swampy, the rivers over their banks, the fields submerged, the populace poling around in flat-bottomed boats. I swayed, hung up in the tree of myself like a raccoon, confounded by the deluge. This occurred almost immediately after, after I stepped outside onto the gallery, into the sunshine, the coolish remnants of it, winter day, a pellucidity in the air that was rainswept and fresh, a chilliness unlike anything you would think of, a displacement that promised in these environs not desolation or an icy lonely death but rejuvenation, alertness, a fresh awareness—how to put it, I thought, leaning over the rail looking at the far bank, which was tousled with reeds, and beyond the bank through the sawgrass and the little hammocks of pines and palms to the swamp, where the old life, unable to resist the encroach of progress, went on as if it didn't matter—how to say it was far too possible—probable—to see too much to get the facts straight. My mind always claimed to know what was up, but it was wrong.

"What's up?" I said. This later, at supper, after Henry had mentioned she told him she was off seeking inspiration, a lie I knew because the escapade had something to do not only with her but with me, with all of us, some gap she sought, some warning like a hankie left in a tree to inform the tracker it was too late, the pursued was not leaving a trail, but discarding, jettisoning whatever might slow her down, I was sure of this, ready to embrace despair—such a small step, you'd think it was panting on the doorstep, a dog, dog of despair, ready to lick your hand—and said this too.

Willie J, at the table out on the screen porch, eating crabmeat salad, looked at me with pity and love. "This always happens," he said. He held the baby on his lap. "I think he likes seafood." He grinned into the child's squinched-up, rapacious face.

"Where were you, Munch?"

Munch, she said, was off with the baby.

"Did you have anything to do with this?"

"I hate to say it"—she extended her hand to me, palm held flat, facing down—"but I'm afraid I did."

The hand was nothing—she'd never thought much of me. Her look now, of tolerance not compassion, of forbearance—it was an old look, worked up in grade school—was the best I could expect from her.

"How were you in on it?"

"Wait, Billy," Henry said. "I don't think it was like that."

"What do you know? What did you do, Munch?"

"She got sad about the baby."

"Because she doesn't have a baby? She doesn't want a baby, Munch."

"That's why she was sad. She said she couldn't think of anything she wanted. She said she'd discovered that she was lazy and indifferent, and what bothered her about it was that she didn't mind."

"Everybody in South Florida's like that," Willie put in.

"Come on, J," Henry said.

"How could you let her out of your sight, Munch?"

"You did, Billy."

Heat flashed in my face, in my body. Munch was making it up, every word. Or not that: she'd heard it this way, in some lubricious translation effected by light and longing, heard what Alice had said as these words, this ridiculous passage that had nothing to do with what was spoken or what was going on. *I'm dying,* Alice had said. *I'm feeling a little low,* is what Munch heard. *I'm drowning in a sea of corpses,* she'd said—*I need a little vacation,* is how it sounded. *Get out of my way before I kill you,* she said. *See you later,* is how Munch heard it.

I jumped up and ran out onto the dock. Stars were out all over, blurred and crinkly, little ragged white mishaps. The dock was like a chute: I ran to the end of it and plunged into the canal.

The black water closed over me with a snap, it was like that, and I was in the underworld, all alone. My breath went out of me, right out, as if vacuumed. A panic—the one I usually kept drugged—gripped me. No waters of the deep hid me from it.

I thrashed to the surface and broke through gasping, crying out like a man in a dream. Henry, who had followed, who jumped in right behind me, was close; he grabbed me. "Wait," I cried. "Fucking wait."

He stroked back. "It's just a passing thing," he said.

I swam away, a rickety crawl, at first nowhere and then down the canal. The water was bitter, tasting of root matter and desuetude. Henry followed, swimming along beside me. We kept our heads out of the water just as in the old photo from childhood, the two of us breaking the surface out in the swamp, eyes still closed, like creatures barely formed, just invented, unspent, flailing.

"It's really too cold to go swimming," he said.

"It's all right if you keep moving."

We swam around the long bend, staying with it, going on steadily without talking, making water time, until we got down among the cane fields. The cane rose up on both sides, tangled and pale in the starlight. The fields went on like this for miles. In the fall the smoke from their burning changed the world into a blue-swept ocherous landscape, in the old days it did. After a while we hove to at the bank, crawled up and sat in the grass at the edge of the field. Across the canal a dark place looked like a gator hole, something, a cave entrance, solid shape of black you could hide, or lose your life, in, these were my thoughts sitting there chilled almost immediately but not giving in to it, as if the cold were a form of death or loss it was possible to deny, to simply go on without surrendering to. I said, "There's more to it, isn't there?"

"Well, sure."

He pushed his long dark hair back with both hands. His wrists were fine, slender as a girl's, not the wrists you'd expect on a sculptor. *Sure*. He meant there was always more to it. But I didn't want to hear it. I preferred the clamors and stage fright of my own imagination. Real life, exposure, fact—receipts, pictures, mementos, charred campfires and gum wrappers—the evidence: I preferred making it up. But they wouldn't let you do that, not for long. They would come to your house with their notebooks and legal papers and they would make you look. They'd pull back the sheet: *Is this her?* Rather picture her, in a diner outside Bakersfield, dipping her finger into a café con leche, licking the coffee off, whiling away a lost afternoon. So what, the leathery companion beside her, grimacing at his reflection in the back mirror. So what? Such moments could go on forever, unchanged.

"No," I said, "don't tell me about it."

In this way my travels began.

Chapter Three

Three years later, as famous as I was ever going to get, I was back in Miami. Alice'd been back for a year, but we hadn't spoken to each other, not once. Henry called me when she got in, one afternoon in spring when all the poincianas in South Beach were blooming with fire in their hair; he called me at my house in Greenwich Village and told me he saw her, sitting in a red Cadillac convertible on Collins Avenue. He had gone up to her and she had gotten out of the car—leapt out of it, he said, like a gymnast—and grabbed him in her arms to hug him. "She's as strong as ever," he said.

"Unlike you and me," I said, and he laughed.

Just talking about her—the real life Alice—flooded me with electricity, but I didn't do anything about it.

"She's living with somebody," he said, "and she's got a little child."

He said that—child—and there was a click click click inside my skull, with no accompanying commentary, as if that was the natural noise your head made when this information appeared. But on questioning, Henry admitted that the child wasn't really hers, only a common law stepchild. I knew Henry would have been going out to see her, to see Alice and the child and her lawyer boyfriend and her new life, and I understood I wouldn't be allowed to do that; this was the curious way life worked: the world was filled with friends and acquaintances, passersby even whom I could see whenever I wanted to more or less, but she was not one of them; she was done with, gone, off the list. Since I was a little boy I had understood the world was set up this way, but I still couldn't believe it. No, I could believe it.

I was famous in my way because of another book I had written about her that had been made into a movie. When the movie came out, people I hadn't heard from since high school called me up. They wanted to get together for a drink when they came to New York and sometimes I would go, though I didn't drink (or do drugs) anymore. Sometimes they asked about Alice, but I didn't have anything to tell them. I could have found out something about her, maybe I could, but I didn't try to. The divorce papers came from California and I signed, but not where indicated, I signed somewhere else. So she was in California.

I moved into the Spenser Hotel in South Beach and spent my mornings writing and my afternoons at the beach. I bought a bicycle and pedaled it around town with my shirt off, getting tan and going slightly to fat from so much time spent at the desk, that and the flan I ate for breakfast every morning. I felt okay about life. I didn't see people much and I didn't want to. Henry I saw, but that was about all. I'd go out to the studio and sit with him while he worked. He'd branched out from funeral sculpture to the regular kind and now supplied galleries in several cities with his pieces. He had assistants now and a big stone yard I liked to sit out in where blocks of marble and granite and sandstone were piled up like the remains of old dismantled civilizations. The sun baked the blocks and I would climb up on one of them, some piece of red granite or a blue marble slab from Italy, and lie on it, getting what I saw as a treatment from the warmth and the mellow firmness of the stone.

Henry was living with Oscar Berman, an older man he had met through friends of his parents. Oscar was a former literary agent from New York, but not someone I knew. He was still a reader, however, and said he liked my books. We would sit out on the dock in the late afternoon waiting for Henry to finish up, Oscar drinking sidecars and me sipping a seltzer, and he would tell stories about his youth in the Israeli army when he fought against the Arabs in the Six Day War. I too had stories of war and gun battles, but they were not like his. Then he drove drunk into a telephone pole on Biscayne Boulevard and wound up in the emergency room at Miami Dade. He was badly hurt, and though his body would heal, they said his mind probably wouldn't. He lay in bed jabbering about his wife who had been dead for twenty years. He said he killed her. This was the kind of craziness that came after head blows like this. Henry and I staggered out of the hospital weeping, Henry staggering and weeping, me red in the face with emotion I was trying to keep in check. Oscar's state was only the catalyst for my emotions, which weren't related to his situation.

"The crazy thing," Henry said, "is he really did kill her."

"Not really."

"Yeah. He killed her with a shovel, carried her out into the Atlantic Ocean and dumped her body over the side of his Boston Whaler. Nobody found out."

"How could nobody find out?"

"I don't know. Probably he did it under cover of darkness."

"People are out in the dark too."

"Well, maybe he'll explain it when he's raving—Jesus, I don't care."

I liked accompanying Henry to the hospital. I hung around Oscar's room hoping he would go into the facts of his murder. But he didn't. "What did you do to her?" I asked him, but he was on his own track. I was through with alcohol and drugs, but I wasn't through running. Chemicals aren't the only form of anesthesiology. Here is another. One of his nurses was a young woman who was sister to a woman I had gone to school with and she said she remembered me. She had pale red almost blond hair and very fair skin she told me she could never let out in the sunlight—she said it like this: never let it out, like it was a special kind of pet—and I fell in love with her in a day. We had an affair that took me down to the Keys, where her brother lived. Her brother was involved in schemes for getting refugees out of Cuba and Haiti and wherever in the Caribbean refugees needed to get out of. He showed me something about the business. "You can write about it if you like," he said. "I know you know how to change the names and settings, and all that, so go ahead." He was a big burly man, also too fair to tan, but he looked nothing like his sister.

I said, "I don't think I'll write about it, but I'd like to find out more."

He said okay you can come with me sometime. The nurse, whose name was Emily, didn't care for her brother's business, but she liked me. We would drive out to little marshy cul-de-sacs, little inlets in the Keys, and make love in the car. She had a place and so did I, but we both liked being out in the car like that. She hated oral sex—going and coming—but I didn't mind that so much and she was tender and had a way about her that made everything she did seem familiar. She was not ambitious and not angry at anything. One day we were out at a little cut between the main island and one of the other small keys when she said, "This is one of the loading places."

"You mean for your brother?"

And she said, "Yes. He brings people in here sometimes."

We made love then in the fast furious obliterative way we liked, and afterwards I lay in the backseat with her, sweaty and feeling good, and then it came to me this was probably a drug too. I didn't mind, but I wanted to talk to someone about it. I thought of Alice. Whenever Henry mentioned her, something tremorous and electrical tunneled into me. I asked him not to speak of her, but then I asked him about her. We'd brought Oscar home in a wheelchair, but he was gone, distracted like someone with Alzheimer's, and Henry was so forlorn about it he could hardly drag himself out of bed. He was torn up about Oscar and about his own future, which he saw stretching away from him into dreary home care endlessness. I said, "It bugs me too."

"Why you?"

"Because I'm depending on you to run this hospice for me too, when I get old and incapacitated."

"Ha ha," he said. "You'll be cleaning up after me first."

I had to call before I went out there to make sure I didn't run into Alice. It made sense not to run into her. The electricity, the hollowness—these sensations were familiar to me, the old sick adrenaline charge. Connie, my temporary sponsor in NA, told me to stay away from whatever caused the adrenaline to surge. "I'll be dull as a toad," I said, and he said, "That'll do you good."

"What do you think?" I asked Emily. "Are you and I just getting a fix off each other?"

She didn't think so, but then they never do.

"I haven't even had an orgasm," she said. "If it was some kind of drug I would have had one, don't you think?"

"You haven't come?"

"No. I never have."

"You mean never, ever?"

"No."

It made me feel left out. I thought I ought to be angry about it, but I wasn't really. "Does not coming give you a relentless desire for sex?" I asked.

She looked at me with her small green eyes. Everything about her face was small, neatly and prettily arranged. "I get satisfaction just from doing it," she said.

"That's good."

But then it did start bothering me. It made me lonely, I thought it was that. I wondered if something was going on with her, something secret and unfathomable to anyone but therapists. I questioned her about this and she said she didn't know.

"You've never had an orgasm, at all?"

"Not that I know of. But tell me what they are like so I'll be sure."

I tried to do that, but she said what I described didn't sound familiar.

Then I found out she was married. Her husband was a painter living in the Grove, a man of some importance locally whom she never saw but had also never divorced.

"You're divorced, aren't you?" she said.

"Pretty much all the time," I said.

"What do you mean by that?"

"Nothing," I said. "Just every day I wake up and I'm still by myself."

"Like I'm married."

"Why didn't you mention it?"

"I didn't care to. I don't even like to think about it, much less talk about it."

Then I found out she did see him. Sometimes when I thought she was working she was actually at his house. "We never make love," she said when I confronted her with this. "Or not that often."

"It doesn't really bother me," I said.

"Why not?" she said, scowling.

"I don't know. I feel pretty easy about it."

"I don't think I want to be with somebody who doesn't get upset about me sleeping with another man. If you don't get upset, you don't really love me."

"That's probably right," I said.

She would have put me out of the car then except we were out in the Keys. Her brother was coming in with his boat. When he got in she made me ride with him. He was bringing in a couple of radicals from Barbados, that's what he said. They weren't anyone I recognized, but one was a rough customer who took offense at someone he didn't know being in the car.

"Look," her brother, whose name was Menile, said to me, "I'm going to have to put you out."

"Here?"

"I'll drop you off at Mile 28. The bus'll stop for you."

It was one of those things that couldn't be helped, I understood that, but still it made me angry. I walked up the highway to a burger stand and used the pay phone to call Henry.

Then I met a woman at a buffet downtown and went home with her. We made love out on her sun porch with her kittens running around mewing and climbing in the bougainvillea. Her name was Merit and she was a lawyer. She was Jewish and told me up front she was really only interested in Jewish men, but something about me had caused her to make an exception. "What was it?" I said. "You have monkey eyes," she said. I told her about my early preaching days and she said she was fascinated by this, though she never asked me about them. We saw each other regularly for about a month, then one night I simply couldn't get it up. "That's okay," she said, "I'll just rub myself against you."

There was something about it I didn't like. "I feel like a tool," I said. "An implement."

"Not you," she said. "Never."

But I did. When I left her house that night I decided not to go back. Then I met the wife of the publisher of a local magazine, Ariane, a writer herself and an editor, and we had an affair that lasted six months. We met at a Christmas party where I was taut with caffeine and talking ninety miles an hour. "You're not even making sense," she said, "but you just keep going." She had a sad, plain, sensual face that completely changed when she smiled. "Weren't you married to Alice Stephens?" she said.

"Boy, was I."

This flippancy was instantly followed by internal squirts of empty groping material I couldn't express. "Your face just turned white," she said.

"Okay," I said.

She liked it that Alice still had such an effect on me. "You have a lot of feeling in you," she said. "Most men I know are so blank."

She wrote all the time, all the time she wasn't working at the magazine. I'd wake up in the morning to the sound of her typewriter clattering, running at a tremendous pace, words pouring out of her. Her husband found out about the affair and canceled an article I had agreed to do for him. "I wish he hadn't done that," I said.

"What did you expect," she said. "You're fucking his wife."

"But you don't even live together."

"That's not what it's about."

One night I went home with a woman I met at a gallery, a young blond painter with a sad face and an apologetic manner. Ariane found out about it immediately, divined it, I thought.

"I smelled it on you," she said. "You are such a scamp."

"I couldn't help myself," I said.

"I know," she said. "I can tell."

I wasn't sure what she meant by this, but it was true the escapade didn't seem to bother her, not in any way I could figure. We liked to take night walks on the backsides of the South Beach neighborhoods, strolling alleys where old bougainvillea hedges draped over concrete walls and little roselike flowers poked out of cracks. We would admire the flowers and the light shining upon the sandy alleys, snagging in the leaves of loquat bushes and climbing halfway up the trunks of coconut palms. The light was yellow almost to orange and lay on everything like butter. Out there in the alley I'd feel safe between the houses, out in the back where people exposed their garbage and flowers got out of control; something would stir in me, some half order of feelings I couldn't quite grasp. It was then I would think of Alice, wondering what she was doing just now, if she was doing anything, if she was angry or feeling hopeless or drifting along to some music, and I'd think maybe soon nothing about her would disturb me anymore. "I can tell when you're thinking about your ex-wife," Ariane said.

"You mean Alice."

"It's okay. I don't mind."

I continued sleeping with the painter, with Mona, who lived in a ramshackle house in South Miami, a house stuffed with refuse and old unsalvageable furniture. Everything in the place looked misused, derelict, even the pots in the kitchen. Glass jars containing dead sweet potatoes were lined up on the windowsill above the kitchen sink. She had cleared a space in the living room where she kept her easel and the finished paintings she stored in a rack she built out of old lumber. Even her bed looked like something dredged up from the depths. We never spoke about any of this. Her mournfulness never left her; I asked her about it, but she acted as if she didn't know what I was talking about. "I'm sorry," she said in her distracted way and looked out the window. She reminded me of Alice after her treatments, but it was not that, it was something else. I started getting afraid one day she was going to go though a sudden personality change and pick up a knife, as if what she was in now was the chrysalis stage.

Then I met another woman, an editor at the paper, a friend of my cousin Ike's, and I began sleeping with her. We hooked up after a party at her house at which she asked me to stay and help clean up. She was just lonely, she said afterwards, that's why she went to bed with me.

"It's okay," I said. "I don't mind."

She wanted me to come around regularly, but I felt nervous about it.

"It's all right," she said. "I wouldn't depend on it."

I asked Connie, my NA sponsor, whether he thought I was in trouble.

"You mean with the women?"

"I'm sleeping with several at once."

"At the same time—in the same bed?"

"No—serially—it's a serial thing."

"Then don't worry about it."

But then I picked up a newcomer in NA, Stacy, a woman sober only a few weeks, and Connie got upset. His wife, also a junkie, invited her over to swim in their pool and I came too. We horsed around in the water and I could tell it was probably the first time in a long while she'd been able to loosen up without a drug. That was what drugs were good for, one thing, taking that relentless tension out of you and letting you step down into normal life. She started grinning and couldn't stop. Afterwards I drove her home and then went in and listened to tapes of her singing with her band. Her voice on the tapes was slightly flat, and she didn't seem to notice, but there was something gallant and tender about it, and something sad too; it made me think of everything we had to face up to in our lives and be good sports about. She asked me to stay over and I did, putting on the pajamas she gave me and getting into the big sofa bed with her. She was not as relaxed as a lover, but she was enthusiastic. When I told Connie about it he was angry. "You got to stop that," he said. "You know why? It's like shooting fish in a barrel. These puppies can't protect themselves."

I agreed. "Now do you see what I mean?"

"About what?"

"About using women—sex, whatever you want to say—as a drug."

"Well, cut it out."

"Okay," I said.

I went over to tell Stacy I couldn't come around anymore, but we went to bed again. Afterwards she said she understood. "I have trouble in this area," she said.

It's not you, I told her.

"Who else could it be?"

"Me. I'm using it for a drug."

"But what's wrong with that?"

"The same thing as any other drug, I guess. After the euphoria comes enslavement, degradation and despair."

"That's a pretty small price to pay."

Henry said more or less the same thing as Connie. "You know where I stand on all that," he said.

"I remember how you used to jump anything in pants."

"That was a long time ago. I've changed."

"Yes, you have."

Oscar in the sunroom drooled over his breakfast, keeping up a running conversation with his dead wife.

"What are you going to do?" I said.

Henry gave Oscar a long across the room look. "He's still a charmer."

"Probably not all the time."

"Sometimes I want to strangle him and dump him in the canal."

"So, why don't you?"

"I'd miss him."

Meanwhile Ariane was typing away. "I smell her on you," she said when I came in carrying a bag of grapefruit.

"No you don't."

"Where'd you get the fruit?"

"Emilio's."

"Let's take a walk."

We cruised up Pennsylvania and then over to Washington and went by the Cuban market where fruit was piled in heaps in big bins and the lights had that tallowy lubricity of the tropics at night and everyone working there spoke another language. The fruit was cheap and it was all of the tropical variety. Something about the setup was homey and exotic at the same time, the kind of arrangement that made me think life could be strange and colorful and completely familiar all at once. When I was getting off drugs I'd listen to Caribbean music and daydream of Little Havana, this mix comforting me. We walked around touching star apples and mangoes and big speckled papayas. Emilio's wife smiled at us and gave us a couple of tiny coconut cupcakes.

Back out on the street Ariane said, "I think you're going to have to run along."

"You mean right now?"

"Yes. I thought it wouldn't bother me how you live, but it does."

"It bothers me too."

"That's what they all say."

"But I want to stop."

"Men just think they can josh us along, throwing in an I'm sorry every once in a while, and we won't mind what they're up to."

"We're not all up to something."

"Yes you are—every one of you."

She sounded like Alice—there she was again. I wondered if this was the revelation of a pattern. Everything different on the surface, but underneath the same old ruckabuck. I might as well go over and look her up. But this was just a thought. Alice was living in the Grove in a big old tabby house that had a garden wall with red bougainvillea spilling over it like bloody teardrops and a Mercedes convertible parked in the drive and a maid in a black and white uniform who got off the bus every morning and walked up the drive carrying her lunch in a little brown wicker basket. That is to say on the second day I was back in Miami I had driven over there at dawn and sat in the car across the street from her house, tense with the crazy idea of settling up on our past, and then, so rattled and buzzing with interiority and desire, suddenly scared to death I would crash through the floor of my life, I drove away and hadn't been back. It took weeks to calm down.

Now I drove by Ariane's house. I could see her sitting in the window typing away, popping tangerine segments into her mouth. I sat out in front of her house two or three times and thought of going in too, of trying to argue her out of her decision, but I didn't. One night a woman walked by leading a three-legged dog. I got out of the car and talked to her, probably everybody did. The dog was a large long-haired speckled setter and she had owned him since he was a pup. His leg, she said—front right—had been cut off in a sawmill accident. I didn't believe this for a minute, but I went along with it.

"A country dog, I guess."

"I'm from Louisiana," she said.

"I had some dark nights over there once, in Louisiana."

"We all have."

I walked her home or at least to the corner. She wouldn't let me walk her all the way.

"I wouldn't be comfortable with that," she said.

But it would be all right she said to meet the next day for a drink. I didn't go into an explanation of how I didn't drink for now because going for a drink was how you had to put it in normal life. Nobody said let's go get some hard drugs, let's go shoot up, let's drop the spike, none of that in polite life, they all went on as if they never even thought of total immersion, and if you mentioned it they looked at you as if you were crazy, but they still wanted to go for a drink. "Is Forget's all right?" I said.

"That's spelled F-O-R-G-E-T, isn't it?"

"Yeah. They soften the G, like in France."

I went home and sat out on my seaside balcony watching the lights of the tankers move slowly across the dark. Then Mona called and I drove out to her house and spent the night. We ate beans and ham hocks from the pot and sat out on the porch watching the moths flutter and bang against the screen door. She always seemed confused by life, Mona did, but I didn't press her about it. She would stare off into space, thinking about something. She had been married twice and hadn't kept up with her ex-husbands. She didn't even know if they were still alive. It wasn't that she hated them or wasn't interested, it was that she couldn't sustain the effort of looking into things.

"I'm surprised you remember me," I said.

"Oh, I like you," she said. "You're easy to remember."

I enjoyed the quiet of the life we shared, the numbness of it. I liked how we stumbled around in the morning, confused about where we were and what was going on, smiling at each other in a sleepy and trusting way. She'd stand at the back door looking out at the weedy yard with a look on her face of someone who didn't know where she was but didn't really mind either. We were both going along with the gag as best we could, with life that is, but neither of us really believed in anything.

"You put my mind on things," Mona said, "which I like."

"Some things," I said.

A skittish breeze slipped along through the lemon trees in her backyard. The moon was out, a small, capsized moon, a tiny tear in the night wall, and I leaned out to look at it. She put her hand on my back and for a second the weight of it took me into a place where everything was strange. I didn't know who I was or where I was. Or who was touching me. The only life I ever believed in was the life with Alice, I knew this, and knew it had always been that way. And then the feeling or the knowledge of this, whatever it was, passed and I came back into the ordinary world we were in. Mona never asked me about my life.

"You can if you want," I told her, but she said she didn't like to intrude.

"I don't think of it as intruding."

"It's not good to pry into people," she said, her blond brows furrowing.

"I know what you mean. You might find out something scary."

"It's pretty much all scary to me."

The dog owning woman, Karen, told me she'd walked out of her marriage barefooted carrying a dollar bill in her hand.

I loved the sound of that, the picture of it.

"What else?" I asked.

"My ex-husband killed himself by drinking pine air freshener."

"When did that happen?"

"Four years ago."

"Do you mind if I write about it?" I said.

"What for?"

"That's what I like to do—make books about things women get into."

"Books to sell?"

"Yes."

She hadn't read anything I'd written or seen or even heard of the movie.

"Is it on tape?"

"No. Not yet."

She wanted to hold back on permission to use her in a story.

"I went to work at Burger King," she said. "I was so stunned and crazy that was all I could think to do."

Now she was a history instructor at Miami-Dade Community College.

At Forget's, where this conversation took place, she was drinking scotch and I was drinking coffee, both of us slightly buzzed. "You don't drink alcohol because you are an alcoholic," she said, "is that right?"

"That's close enough to it," I said.

"My father was an alcoholic. He didn't call it that, but that's what it was."

"What did he do?"

"He was a horse trainer."

"Racehorses?"

"For forty years."

She grimaced and looked away. "Pardon me," she said, "for asking so directly about the alcohol. It's not my business."

"It's okay. I'm not at ease with talking about it. But I would probably have to tell you anyway."

"Is that one of the rules—I'm sorry."

"Being honest, yeah."

"I fall short there."

"I hit it about once every ten tries."

We were out beyond ourselves a little, I could see that.

At her house once again I couldn't sexually perform. I went into the bathroom and tried to get something going, tried to imagine a stirring scenario, but it didn't work. It was the second time in six months, but this was different from the time before. "I really want to," I told her.

"I don't mind about it," she said with a sweetness in her voice. She said it in a believable way. The next night, after a walk through her neighborhood, I made it to the end, though it was difficult. "I'm scared," I said. "That's what it is."

"I'm scared too. But I like what we're doing."

"It's almost too real for me."

"Do you want to go slower?"

"Yes. I think I do."

"I'd like to snug up next to you. Do you mind that?"

"I don't know. Let me think about it."

We lay in the dark waiting. Soft rain blew in through the open window above our heads, but neither of us did anything about it. "What are you thinking about?" she said after a while.

"I was thinking about James Agee and then I started thinking about my ex-wife."

"I teach Agee's book in my class."

"I was thinking about his life. He was married four times I think."

"I like to think about the private lives of historical personages."

"That's probably all we would do if they let us."

"Good for me they don't."

We were silent again. The curtain sighed into the room, in slow motion, fluttering slightly as if trying to get itself to do something more but it couldn't.

"Your ex-wife?" she said.

"I think about her a lot."

"Sure. I would too."

"Sometimes I have to restrain myself from going out and waylaying her."

"To do what?"

"I don't know—bash her or beg her to come back—one of those."

"I used to follow my ex-husband around. Before we made the final break. I'd follow him to work and sneak up to his office and jump him."

"That would scare me to death."

"It did him too. I hated myself for doing it, but for a while I couldn't stop. I'd follow him after work too, even though he was only going from the office to the house."

"What were you after?"

"I wanted to surprise him, shake something in him loose."

"Was he seeing another woman?"

"No. I don't know. But it wasn't even that. It wasn't specific. It could have been that, but what it was really was some other lost missing thing. Some component that would explain what was happening. There had to be something there I didn't know about. I thought I could catch it if I jumped him."

"Could you?"

"In a way."

"What was it?"

"It wasn't what I thought. I don't know what it was. While I was doing that I suddenly got tired of looking at the back of his head."

"And that did it?"

"Yes. It was so blank. The back of his head was flat and the hair was brown, lighter than mine, and it lay on his head in this smooth way, like paint. There wasn't anything wrong with him really, with his head, it was fine, but I started to think of it as a blank. In bed I'd raise up and stare at his head. He always slept turned away from me and I'd stare at the back of his head. It was so distant and strange, like a basketball in a tree. I know I was crazy, but that was what was happening. I'd look at him, at his head, and I'd feel so lost, like love was never going to find me again. One morning I got up at dawn, pulled on a pair of jeans and a shirt, took a dollar off the dresser and left."

"Barefooted."

"That's right."

"I love that story."

"What happened with your ex-wife?"

"She drifted off too. It was probably like with you, in her mind."

"That's funny, isn't it? Maybe she set off looking for my ex-husband."

"Is he a lawyer?"

"No. He's not anything now."

We went quiet then, we lay there thinking about our lives and the strange turns they had taken. At that moment I felt immune to Alice Stephens. As if she could walk in the room right then and nothing in me would stir. I thought I knew this feeling for what it was; it was one of the main things I talked to Connie about. "These women drug me," I told him, "and I don't care about anything anymore."

"They don't give you any substances?"

"No, I don't mean that. Or maybe I do. Brain chemicals—they give me those. Endorphins and all that. A sexual rush in the head and body. I become a fair-weather friend to man."

"It's not their fault. You know that, right?"

"Yes. I don't mean it's their fault. They're not forcing anything on me."

"You sure you see it that way?"

"I wish I didn't."

But how did I see it? Sometimes I lay in the sun, out on the lawn behind the Spenser, and the light and the heat pouring onto me—I felt as if I was lying at the bottom of a bowl of melted gold. I wished there were a hundred hours in a day, all of them lit. And when I spent money, something clamorous inside me calmed down for a minute. And, conversely, when I went without things, didn't eat or walked around with my pockets empty, I felt admirable then. Some nights I'd eat all the ice cream in the refrigerator and then sit there, a slug on his balcony, stuporous and content. If I didn't do these things, if I didn't inject my brain with whatever was in these practices, some dark business would try to crawl into bed with me. Bed being wherever the hell I was. I wanted to cast blame for this. Clerks, ice cream impresarios, cash machines, America, girls—something.

"Well," Connie said. "You got to try to be optimistic. You're not the subject of the universe, you know."

"How do you know that?"

"Because I am."

It was a laugh line so I gave him one.

I thought things would be different with Karen. She rented the upstairs of a house in the Brightwood district. A young entrepreneurial woman owned the house and lived downstairs. The woman bought properties in the district, renovated them and resold them for a profit. Young professionals were moving into what had formerly been a neighborhood of derelict old residences and boardinghouses for winos and others living on the margins. It was a district I had thought I was headed to myself. But now the lawns were rich with watered grass and plantings and the houses wore fresh paint and there were expensive cars parked in the drives. I liked all this activity, but I also liked the old shabby houses and shabby people. For now there was still a mix, young couples getting out of a convertible as some bent fellow in a Salvation Army tuxedo jacket attempted to stay on his feet. The babies lolled in their carriages, casting wide-eyed looks at the winos conducting a wheelchair race down the middle of the street. Karen and I lay out in a hammock on the front porch, putting our hands on each other and laughing. I said, "I feel fulsome and content," and this was the truth.

I drove out to Mona's and told her I had to stop seeing her. We were out on the back steps and as she leaned out over her knees, two tears dropped onto the concrete walk, leaving large round splashes. "I'm sorry," I said.

"You don't have to be," she said.

"These things are a mystery to me."

"You don't have to try to explain it. I didn't think you would stay."

"I never know what I'm going to do."

"You probably had better go," she said.

Lemon leaves lay scattered on the back walk, some faceup, some facedown; you couldn't tell how things would fall. I drove out of her neighborhood thinking this is the last time you will see these houses, you son of a bitch, but then a week later I met a woman outside my lawyer's office, an art teacher, and went home with her and drank tea in the living room of her apartment a block behind Mona's. After a while the woman started crying about life's rough ways and her ex-husband's part in the disaster, and we went into the bedroom. I had no trouble with the sex. I figured her being a stranger, this being only an afternoon's dalliance, had something to do with it.

"I think I have solved the mystery," I told Karen.

"What mystery?" she said.

"The one about where I can't get it up," I said.

"You seem to be doing pretty well lately."

"But I think it happens because when someone I like—like very much—begins to get close, I get really nervous."

"I'm glad you've solved it, slugger," she said.

This conversation took place at her desk. She was very firm about me not disturbing her when she was working or disturbing her things when she wasn't there. Once she caught me looking at some photographs and without saying one word she took them out of my hand, put them back in the folder I had taken them from, and put the folder in a drawer. When I asked her about it, she said, "Don't touch my things." It was as if she was working something out, setting a mark for herself she wanted to adhere to. I liked this fine actually, and hoped it would rub off on me.

But Mona, Mona in her neighborhood. When I came out of the art teacher's house I saw Mona passing in her car. She glanced at me and the expression on her face—the familiar expression soaked in—was of such sadness I felt ashamed. I walked over to her house and met her getting out of the car. She was carrying groceries too. "Let me help you," I said.

"It's all right."

"No, let me."

But it wasn't the thing to do, I could see that. There was strain in her face, in her body, and she pulled away from me, leaning away as if I was holding her on a fine chain, the sadness in her eyes fraying into desperation. I wanted to say I have felt like that for years, but there was no way to. I had just to go. "I'm an idiot," I said and got in the car.

I drove to a phone and called Karen and she said I don't have to be in class until seven so why don't you come by, which is what I did, but then just before we got undressed I got angry about something, about her lack of attention, some form of this, and a fight swelled up and spilled out onto the porch where her landlady was reading a real estate document out loud to a couple about to purchase some reconstituted property, and it was clear the landlady thoroughly disapproved of us, but we were in flight by then and rolled on out onto the sidewalk and into the street itself, me shouting and waving my arms, hammering my point home, which I continued with maniacally until I noticed I was the only one doing the actual shouting and gesturing, in fact Karen wasn't really saying anything at all beyond an occasional yes or no, in fact she was simply standing there as if tied to me by a slack piece of rope, hanging her head as I rained down imprecations and calumny upon her.

"Jesus Christ what is the matter with you?" I yelled at her, a question actually better directed at me.

She looked at me out of eyes filled with pain. Pain and fear—I saw them both.

"Ah fuck this," I said and walked off.

The sun going down was blocked from view behind some mango trees, but I could tell it was a beautiful sunset. It made me think of the Glades, of the sun sinking into the grass prairies, turning them gold and red and pulling shadows up out of the woods like a dark rediscovered treasure. In my head the argument churned and slipped, and the argument—Mona and Karen and some thoughts of Alice in which she was explaining how she wanted to calm herself—I realized it wasn't an argument. We had headed in opposite directions around the block. But I didn't run into her. I thought I would see her on the back street, but she must have cut through one of the yards. I told myself this bit was nothing, nothing to what had already happened to me. I had been much worse than this and I probably would be much worse again. My body felt as if it was made out of wire, as if I was an outline of a person and wind was blowing through me. I remembered this feeling from the drug time, the pre-spike feeling, but I didn't want any drugs.

Down the street someone, a neighbor, was speaking from his front porch to people assembled in his yard. It was some kind of prayer service or business meeting, fellow workers or parishioners gathered for an evening cookout. I went over and joined them; it turned out they were salespeople for a door-to-door cosmetics outfit enjoying themselves at a company picnic. I knew a couple of them from my newspaper days. One, a photographer, remembered me too and I pulled him aside and tried to tell him what was going on. "Do you mind if I go over this?" I said.

He said, "Sure, okay."

I caught his signal to his wife.

I began to tell him about Mona and Karen and some about Alice as well, and as I spoke I seemed foolish to myself, some ridiculous person you wouldn't want to listen to, but I couldn't stop even as I became more distant from the words coming out of my mouth. His expression of concentration faded and he began to glance away across the yard. They were giving out awards of some sort, the man on the porch was. The photographer cleared his throat and began to rub his wrist. He had big scars on his wrist, burn scars they looked like, and then I remembered he had left the paper because he was burned in a fire. A bakery fire he had gone to take pictures of. "Are you sure you want to tell me this?" he said.

"I don't know," I said. "I'm pretty much off my rocker at the moment."

"Why don't you come get something to eat?"

"I think I need a whole lot more than food, but thank you anyway."

"Well, I guess I better go back to my wife."

As he trudged across the yard I saw below his shorts that his legs were burned too.

After that I went back to the house. The landlady had abandoned the porch and the place was dark and looked locked up, forlorn like one of the derelict houses she renovated, but it was open. I climbed the stairs and found Karen in the living room with the television on. She got off the couch and came into my arms crying. "I can't understand," she said, "how you could look at me with such hatred in your eyes." The early news was on the television. The Coast Guard was removing bales of marijuana from a rusty freighter. The drug agents were happy and the drug runners were sad. I watched the news over her shoulder as I comforted her.

Henry said, "Yeah, it's true we have long talks on the phone."

"What do you talk about?" I said.

"I'm not at liberty to discuss that."

"Give me the gist."

"Sadness, love, fear, enthusiasm."

"How's Oscar?"

"He suggested I dye my hair."

"It's good he's taking an interest, huh?"

"He wants me to remind him of his wife."

"Listen," I said, "how am I going to get her back?"

"I don't think you're going to do that, Billy."

"I don't think I can do anything else."

"Both of you have gone on past each other."

"I can't really believe that's true."

"She's got the little child."

"Bret, yeah, I know about him. But you said he's not her natural child, he belongs to the other guy. There's a world of difference between them, between her and Bret. Magellanic distances. Bret. That's pretty close to Brent, don't you think."

"Bret Brent—I don't believe that would work. And I think she really likes this fellow she's with."

"Shit. That doesn't matter."

"Bravado won't change it either."

"Let's go to the swamp."

"I haven't got time to do that. I got these commissions."

"Let's go out to the swamp and get Alice to come."

"None of us has any business at this time in our lives going out to the Everglades."

"Listen, I am making a mess of things up here."

"It'll be worse if you try to hook up with Alice."

"No, it'll be worse anyway."

People who know nothing about drugs think when you quit taking them you can then pull yourself together and go on with your life, like they are doing. But when you quit, everything you were taking them to keep buried comes to the surface. The everything is not some bank job you pulled that you didn't want to think about or some baby you slapped or some lover you betrayed, it's not so easy as that, though sometimes it seems these occurrences have something to do with it, and there is certainly plenty of work to do to correct the fuck-ups you have gotten yourself and others into during the low-down time. But what it really is is a deep faceless creature of terrible power and hatred that has been idling down at the bottom of your being; it is this monster that begins to rise to the surface. It eats everything in its way and it is going to eat you. You're sad, desperate, ashamed, scared, full of rage, and everything is futile, just like you knew it was. You can go off into blame—which is a whole career—if you like, but it doesn't change anything. You can start up a relay of substitute practices—money or religion or sex or power or deprivation or food or letters to the editor—but these are just more subterfuge. The monster stays the same. Almost everyone who gets free of drugs will tell you, to save yourself you have to get onto something larger than you are. Some idea or belief or practice, some involvement that sustains you, but doesn't have the downside of degradation and shame you found in the drugs. Many people come up with some kind of god, something they can call a god or use like a god; pray to, and depend on, and hang out with and serve. The monster, the rapacious relentlessness of it, the huge undeniability of it, the mean insistence of it, makes them. But then, sometimes, the thing they've found, the god, begins to wobble. It gets creaky and slow, but the monster hasn't lost a step. The monster begins to climb up over their back.

What do you do then? I never found but two things: you either sit on the bed and take it, or you go into wildness.

When I put the gun on Alice, she laughed at me, but when I put the gun on the baby she stopped.

"You damn shit," she said.

I had come around the side of the house a minute before. A breeze lifted the grapefruit leaves, turning their white undersides over. The baby sat in a small chair at a picnic table eating pieces of mango she fed to him.

She had looked up without saying a word to me. Her face showed no surprise at all. It was a blank, she was that quick. I said, "I have come on a special errand."

I took the gun out of the little net grocery sack I was carrying.

She still didn't say anything and her expression didn't change. I held the gun on her. And then she laughed.

Now I said, "Let's go in the house."

We went in and I made her pack a bag and get all her baby paraphernalia and then we went out to the car and drove off toward the Everglades. I made her drive. She said, "You could have just called me."

"And you would have said what?"

We passed my father's first church. It was rebricked now, and belonged to another denomination. When I broke away from preaching I had returned there to shout curses at the congregation, to revile and reproach them, but I was unable to. Mrs. Telfilio had come up to me and put her arms around me and I collapsed into tears. My father had called that afternoon to tell me how brave he thought I was. He was buried out back—God bless you, Daddy—under a eucalyptus tree.

She glanced at the baby asleep in the backseat. "I would have met you anywhere. Any time you wanted."

"How could I have known that?"

"How could you know anything else."

She looked out the window. "There's your house." A gray stucco edifice, half hidden behind oleanders and japonica bushes. "Do you ever see Frances?"

"Mother?"

"No, you don't, do you?" She adjusted herself in the seat, half turning to look at me. "Do you know how I know you don't go see her?"

I didn't answer.

"Because I go. I visit her every week. I take her cupcakes. She has an old lady's sweet tooth so I take her vanilla cupcakes with strawberry swirls on the top. Her mind is going. She makes up stories about you. Nutty little pathetic stories about what you are doing."

"Oh shut up, Alice."

I made her swing a right and we passed under the big mango trees lining her old street. "We're going on the tour?" she said.

"The brief one. Slow down."

The car slowed, slowed so much we were barely moving. Her house then: yellow with green shutters, the green bushes cropped up close to it under the windows like a fringe, a skirt bunched against a waist. Through the archway between the house and the garage light poured and I remembered everything.

"You married me the second time," she said, "—after the bigamy business—under that grapefruit tree."

"You wore a strange blue dress like a tablecloth."

"That's what it was."

"And you couldn't stop kissing me."

"I hadn't stopped yet."

She stopped the car a moment, in the middle of the street. We looked at the houses, the blank and unhelpful houses, the dumb trees. I felt just as I did all those years ago, just as I did yesterday, that I was in the middle of something I couldn't see the beginning or the end of.

"Nothing's ever over," she said, a sad and bitter note in her voice, but only a quiet note, no crescendo.

"Some parts are more over than others, I guess."

"Don't be philosophical, Billy."

We eased on along. I turned around and looked out the back window. There was a poinciana out front that I could always see from two blocks away, two limbs of it reaching into the street like a wing. I had forgotten that. "I just think how deep I was into it. How I was so committed to every part of it, even the bad parts."

"That's sounds nostalgic."

"Then you're not getting what I'm saying."

"I thought you would come driving up. Some days I sit out in my yard waiting for you. I did yesterday."

"Why didn't you call me?"

"I couldn't do that, Billy."

"I'm kidnapping you now—you and the baby."

"Is that what you want to do?"

"Yeah." The noise of my voice was a hollow noise, as if I was speaking from the belly of the whale. "It's a kind of testimonial."

"No, it's not."

"I'm just saying that."

"Preparing for the trial."

"Har har."

"He's not really a baby," she said, looking into the backseat where the tyke snored in his bundle of light wraps. "He's more a child."

We headed west, into the sun. The world had been built up since our childhood and youth. Now people lived out here, snugged into the swamp as if this country were really habitable. But you could get out past them. The road curved south, angling in deeper toward the swamp, which was a huge grassy field, unflooded at this time, a place that from a slight distance looked inviting, but when you got up close you saw was underlain with black mud pocked with little airholes, stinking in hot sun.

"They have dumped every kind of refuse into this wonderland," she said.

"We'll find a clear spot."

The child started crying. He was thick-bodied and had a big wad of carroty hair on top of his head like a wig. She pulled over, reached back and fiddled with him, spoke kindly words to him, kissed him a couple of times and gave him a bottle with some yellow liquid in it.

Mango juice, she said when she righted herself.

I thought this might be a good time to reveal to her that my pistol was a fake, a replica, but I decided not to, not yet. We drove down through the public areas of the swamp, along the road past the gator wallows and all that, past the tourist business and the canoe rental shops, on past where the road gave out into a lane and then into a track and there was a sign and a barrier. Beyond this, as I knew, the road kept going until you reached the old-time camps the original settlers were still allowed to maintain deep in the swamp. We swung around the post and board obstruction, almost getting stuck on the incline down into the watery, lily-pad-filled ditch, but made it, and continued on south through the grass. "Bret," she said, "honey, look at that eagle."

The bird swung in the west, drifting up high in a derelictous way, as if it was tired and didn't know what else to do. "Do you remember that time," she said, "when we saw the whole tree of them?"

"Let's don't go down memory lane. It makes my heart hurt."

"You'd rather speculate on the future."

"And, uh, delve into the present."

"Okay. Are you going to shoot one of us if we don't do what you want?"

"You aren't going to start criticizing me, are you?"

"No, I don't want to do that. I'm glad to see you."

"I've been putting it off—seeing you."

"You would. I was dying to get a look at you, but you were working on something."

"Well, I like to think things through. And besides, you're the one who got the divorce. That always makes the other one uneasy."

"There wasn't anything else for me to do."

"Well, of course not if you don't speak to me about it."

"If I could have spoken to you about it I wouldn't have gotten a divorce."

"You say that now."

She didn't mean it the way I was taking it, I saw that. But I couldn't change myself. A list, a tendency, something like a drug I took a bite of, was already entering my system, too late to countermand it, the byways and alleys all clogged with it, the desperate and fatal humors, all that, saturating me; I harshly grinned. She smiled back, without sweetness but with her full self in the smile. I saw that too. Her large even teeth were yellower than they used to be and there were lines in her face, vertical and cut for life, strange to me, something she'd put together on her own time and applied to herself. There were things I'd missed, I saw that. And the child was crying again, a stranger in the car, this sporting character, related to someone I didn't know at all, a boy who was sucking all this subliminally in, the violence and the dusty car ride and the swamp like a grand earthly coadunation, all its bugs fraternally singing, sprawling away just out the window. The whole world keeping up the pace. Cypress domes, like little kingdoms of the lost, rose from the grass in the blue distance.

We passed a couple of camps and then came to the Terrel place, where I had her drive in and park. Out back in a big shed they kept the airboat. "Is this where we were headed?" she said.

"Not particularly."

"It's pretty here. This is whose place?"

"Jimmy Terrel. We knew him in high school."

She put shoes on the boy, tiny soft blue sneakers with pictures of a funny rat on the sides. She kissed each shoe as she worked it onto his foot. "You can do that for me when you finish with him," I said.

"That's how it would be, I know."

"If we wanted peace."

"Which is why we are no longer married. It's why we should never have married in the first place."

"How can you say that?"

"There you are, sweetie pie," she said to the child and then looked up at me, smiling. "We could never keep the peace, Billy."

"That fact never really stopped us."

"But it slowed us down so much we were hardly moving."

"You don't know how it was for me."

"You're right. I thought I did, but I didn't. Still, people who live together have to be able to find a way to peaceableness between them. They can't always be snatching at things and throwing each other against the wall. We wouldn't face that. We needed to find a way to calm down. Both of us did." She shook a small blanket out of her bag. "I'm so glad you've started straightening yourself out."

I didn't like being approved of by her, not in this way. "I could get peace just by putting my hand on you."

"Not for long."

"I didn't bring you out here to convince you of anything."

"It's okay." She smiled again. "I'm already convinced."

"What about if we get in the Terrels' airboat and go over to Everglades City and get on a ship and head off to New Orleans?"

"I would love to do that if it were possible. But it's not."

"Why? We were headed that way when we got married the first time. That's what we were going to do when I came and rescued you."

"You didn't rescue me. We rescued each other. And anyway, we have traveled so far from that time."

"I haven't. I haven't traveled anywhere. I am right here where I always have been. Shit."

"Don't curse in front of Bret."

"He can't understand curse words."

"He can hear them. They penetrate."

"All right. But look—" I stopped. Even here, even now, even holding a (fake) gun you only got so much time. There was a limit and you couldn't go over it. This was one of the rules of the universe, I knew that. "Ah, Alice."

She had spread the blanket out on the ground and set the child on it. From her bag she took an array of small toys. The boy, a connoisseur, picked up first one then the other, setting each carefully—it looked like an act of care—back on the ground. The air, the February air of the swamp, was clean and bug free. There was a faint yellowing in the western sky. Around the unpainted board and batten house several trees had been cut back to stumps. Cabbage palms stood up in an isolated way, tousle-headed on their skinny poles.

She said, "When I first got back I would take trips on the bus—the city buses—by myself. I wanted to see the city that way. I've always loved how jumbled up Miami is. I rode all over it. Through all the neighborhoods and downtown and across to the beach and up to Hialeah—everywhere. I did it for weeks, one or two days a week."

"Did you ever think you would see me?"

"Yes, always. Once or twice I thought I did see you, but then I knew it wasn't you. You were always keeping out of sight."

"Not really."

"But I wasn't riding to find you. I knew I couldn't do that. I was just riding to look. I wanted to be a passenger. I wanted life, pictures, people—to see them, you know: a woman painting on a board or a barber sweeping off his sidewalk or a junkie shaking a radio; I wanted to see all the life tumbling around. And I wanted—I can't explain it—I wanted to see how one thing kept replacing another.

One thing coming after another—as if there was no end to it. I'd been so afraid there was an end. Everything the last thing. I got so tired waiting for it. That's why I had to go in the hospital—here and out in California."

"You were in the hospital in—"

"Let me say." She looked off at the prairie, at the flooded field of it and the grasses gold green and moving slightly, a breeze flowing across them. "Things didn't even have to be connected. They just had to come one after another. I wanted to be sure there would be one more."

"I know what you mean."

"Yes. You do. But me, I only figured it out later. Those days I just looked. One afternoon about sunset we were riding through one of the rough parts, down below Calle Ocho where it's so grubby and defeated and the buildings have weeds growing from the cracks in the walls. The sun was going down—it was right near your father's old mission—and everybody on the bus was either sleeping or daydreaming about something—nobody was looking out the window but me, and the thought came to me, this one thought, that we are passing through a paradise. It was the ugliest neighborhood in town, I guess, but just then it looked like a paradise. It didn't just look like it, it was a paradise. Everything was."

"That's fine, Allie," I said. It was clear she believed every word.

I got up and walked to the boathouse, went in and looked at the airboat. Spidery and delicate, backed by a rocket, like something from a dream, this boat, ready to go. The Terrels kept it gassed up and I knew where they hid the keys. I reached around behind the little panel and there they were. I took them out and went over and got in the boat. It rocked slightly, and I felt the press of its flat bottom against the water, the tension, the resiliency of it. There were two keys, one for the lockup chain and one for the engine. I climbed up on the seat. Out the front doors open water stretched away a hundred yards to the dark channel cutting through the prairie.

Here's what happens: you cross the open water and enter the channel and you follow it as it winds through the grass past the hammocks and woodland domes, the swampy islands upon which various animals live their animal lives; you go on through the buggy days and the long buzzing nights and you don't let mischance or false pathways deter you, you keep right on with your goodwill about life and your stubbornness, leaving each lived day behind you, the husk of it drifting in the shallows of the past; you stay with the trail, pushing on and riding the slow current of boggy water draining down the sleeve of the continent—keep on no matter what—until one day, some sunny day, you come to the blue blue waters of the Gulf.

Six days after this day, in a little town on the eastern shore of Virginia, Henry, who'd driven up he said crying most of the way, collected the child and took him back to his father.

Part V

YOU ARE WELCOME HERE

Chapter One

After breakfast, after Alice drove off to school—after apple season when I had no more work in the trees—I'd trudge up the hill and at the head of the neighbors' driveway call the dog, try to get him to come to me. After a while he might appear on the porch and look at me, balefully, as if I was some tramp who better not get any closer. "Come on, Delite," I'd say, but he wouldn't come. It was the late nights, the drunken rages, that got to him, put him off. Sometimes I'd bring a toy, a twist of rawhide or a ball. He was a retriever, but he wouldn't retrieve. You could throw a steak across the yard and he wouldn't run after it, not when I was looking. After a while it would get to me. He was like some woman—some Alice—I couldn't make forgive me. "Okay dammit," I'd shout. "Be like that. See if I damn care."

I'd report this to Alice, around three-thirty when she drove the car up the drive, coming slowly, barely moving, a car at a creep, as if she couldn't bear to come home, as if the car itself was tired, worn down and hardly capable of locomotion—I'd be waiting, hanging around the yard on sentry duty. There'd be an interval then. Instead of getting right out she'd sit in the car and take up her knitting, which was something new. Her knitting—a foamy substance, linen suds, exuviating out of her fists like a white protoplasm. She'd sit in the car knitting while I careened around the yard hacking at trees with my ax or shaking my fist at the cows. The cows moaning, cow love calls, sad-faced desolate women, only one thing on their mind. One pass or another I'd intersect with Alice, snag the window, lean in and say, "The damn dog has been brainwashed. She doesn't know us anymore."

Alice acted as if she didn't even notice the dog. "What's that?" she'd say, and under a furrowed brow go right back to her knitting.

I decided to drug him, the dog, snatch him, bring him home and retrain him.

"You have to love them," Alice said.

"I already know that."

"But can you do it?"

"You're living proof."

"That what you call this?"

I ground up a couple of Quaaludes, sprinkled them over hamburger, and set this at the edge of the yard under a bush cherry. One of the neighbor kids found it, noticed the white powder, and because I had put the meat in a dish the neighbors said came from our house, we were suspected, suspected of trying to poison the dog. The sheriff came out and talked to me, but he couldn't prove anything.

Later I wrote off for a dog whistle, and when it came I sat on the front steps blowing into it. The dog didn't come.

"Just because they can hear it doesn't mean they are going to answer to it," Alice said.

"I thought with this I was supposed to be irresistible."

"That's only to me."

I said, "What about the other guys you married. You never talk about them."

"They were an open and shut case."

"How so?"

"They opened the door and I got shut of them."

"You are so funny."

"I was in a zombified state."

"That's how I remember it too."

I wasn't really trying to use it against her, I was just interested. Sometimes I ran my thumb over the snag of her past, and then I would go out on the porch and light up a reefer and yesteryear would fade into the blue trees. I had never really doubted we belonged to each other.

"Love is the answer to this problem," she said, out on the porch.

"The dog?"

"Us too."

"How could you ever have gotten the idea I didn't love you? I went to prison for you."

"You mean Jacksonville?"

"No, I mean the first time. When I was a juvenile. That fight? You remember that fight?"

"It was your idea to cut the boy, not mine."

"That was the only way I could get him off you."

"You already had a record."

"Record. You mean those phone calls? I was just trying to get you to talk to me."

"And then those women."

"Ahn ah. Those were low points I'd prefer not to talk about. I live in shame over them and you know it."

"I'm sorry I mentioned them. Still, you're avoiding the subject."

"Which is what?" I blew hard on the whistle. Nothing but silence. "Damn this thing."

"Love. Same as always."

"What was the name of the first one?"

"I've never loved anybody but you."

"You've been married four times."

"Only once for love. Or twice."

"Which?"

"Both times I married you."

"You bigamist."

Beyond the pond, the road to town, an old hog trail, seemed to hang in the air among young lime-leafy elms. The day had just toppled into summer, surprised by bounty. At the pond, the landlord's wife, Lardy Bundle, in bright red boots, bent to lift a bucket of mud from the feeder stream. She poured the mud into a small wheel cart. Her daughter slapped at bugs. My arms felt hollow, weak from lifting my life, like a man who'd just made love hanging from a tree. I lay back on the seat, dreaming for a moment of a place much farther away than this. A blankness came into my mind, a quiet, that faded, and I reentered the world.

"I know," Alice said—it was later, nighttime now, "lie down on top of him."

"The dog? Smother it?"

"No. Just lie on him. That's what you have to do."

"Is this something you recall, or are you making it up?"

"I read it. Your weight—your body on top of the dog—makes him realize you're the master. He'll stay with you then."

"I should have tried that with you."

Charlie Smith

"It's not too late."

Next day, to the boy up the hill, a boy with skin as yellow as cream, I said, "If I give you a dollar will you bring my dog down to the house for me? You can have him back, but we have to take him to get some shots."

The boy looked at me as if he knew I was lying, just as others did. "I'll do it for ten."

"Ten? You're a real entrepreneur, aren't you?"

"He likes where he is."

"Okay, ten."

"You got the money?"

"Sure. I got it right in my pocket. You want to go get the dog now?"

He made me show him the cash and then he went up the hill and got Delite, whose new name was Jessie. "Come on, Jessie," the boy said. He didn't even have to put a rope on him. The dog growled and shied when he got near me. "Come on, Jessie," the boy said. "This man won't hurt you." To me he said, "He doesn't like strangers."

"I'm not a stranger," I said, a little sourly.

He squatted down and took the dog's head between his hands. I slipped my hand onto the collar and the dog twisted in the grip, tried to bite me and yelped. "Delite, come on, it's okay." My face went red with embarrassment. "Come on, dog," I said.

"Don't you hurt him."

"I'm not going to hurt him. Help me get him in the house."

Together we walked him up the steps and I put him in the house, shutting him up in the kitchen.

"You sure got Jessie spooked," the boy said, looking around at the books stacked in columns on the floor, at the soot smears reaching from the fireplace deep into the living room rug. In the kitchen Delite barked and whined, and began to scratch the door.

"Don't worry about it," I said. "I know dogs and he'll be quiet soon."

"Ten dollars isn't enough for this," the boy said.

"It's enough for me."

"I thought you were going to take him to the vet."

"I have to wait for the car. Why aren't you in school?"

"I don't like it."

"I see."

We eyed each other, an understanding approaching. He was a mental desperado too.

"You don't have to worry about the dog now," I said.

"I don't worry. 'Bye, Jessie," he called, and went out.

I waited until Alice got home, got home wearing a long multicolored, Joseph coat-colored scarf her kids had given her. They'd sewn it themselves, she said, taking turns, a patchwork. It was her birthday, a day neither of us ever forgot. I'd bought her a pair of binoculars for watching the lightning bugs at night as they wobbled and careened above the valley, and a hammock, come all the way from Mexico. "I want to try both at once," she said, her eyes alight, a look in them of glee that was the look I remembered most fondly from our youth. It came and went, that look, like a dream in her eyes, and it was a look that would make someone get up out of a sickbed and follow.

"I'll hang it up out on the porch," I said, stroking the long red rope of the hammock, "but would you show me how to do with the dog first?"

Charlie Smith

The dog didn't like her much either, but we got him to the bedroom. "Now put him on the bed," she said.

"Come on, Delite," I said. The dog wouldn't get on the bed. "Jessie," I said, "come on."

"You have to take charge."

"I can do that."

I lifted the dog and got onto the bed. The creature squirmed and whined, jerking his head. He nearly broke loose, twisting around so I had him upside down. From my knees—following Alice's directions—I leaned forward and went down on top of him, trapping him under my body. He kicked and thrashed, whining, making a little surprised, heartbroken noise, like something one of us could make under the same circumstances. I reached under me, to touch him, to let him know I was only pretending, unable to go through with it really, a sucker, ready to apologize, but he writhed around, digging under my body, and bit me right through my jeans, bit my genitals, my cock. It felt as if he'd torn it off. I leapt off the bed yelling. The dog dashed away.

"What is it?"

"Agh—God." I went down on my knees—for the pain and for the prayer in that position. Horror flashed in my head.

"Oh, Billy. What did she do?"

"He fucking bit me." I just managed to squeeze this out.

"Where?"

"In the cock."

"Let me see."

"I think he bit it off."

He didn't, but the device was bruised, red, purpling. The skin was slightly torn. It ached deep inside. A panic began to overhaul me.

"You're white."

"I think I'm going to faint."

"You better lie down."

"We have to get to the doctor."

"It doesn't look that bad."

I was standing in the bedroom with my pants around my knees. The dog was out in the living room barking. "First I'm going to kill that fucking dog. And then I'm going to the doctor."

She ran out ahead of me and let the dog out. I came behind, crouched over, seared, tears in my eyes. At the door I felt nauseous, lurched out on the porch and vomited off it. The pain sliced into my stomach, popped into my legs. Sweat sprang out on my face. I dropped, slipped onto my side, but I got up, pushing on the chair. The cows rushed toward the fence, moaning, my ladies, worried that I wouldn't get up to feed them. Alice helped me to my feet and we shambled to the car. The dog was back up the hill, standing in the yard, barking fiercely.

This was how we met Dr. Morton, who became our supplier of drugs. My cock was only bruised. It didn't need anything, the doctor said, but time. He was gentle, unhurried, careful with me, reassuring to both of us that nothing was really wrong. "I had a little boy in here last month," he said, "who came down hard on one of those backyard trampolines and crushed his penis. He thought he was going to die, but he healed perfectly. You will too."

"What about the pain?" I said.

"I'll give you something for that."

He was a small, neat man with a closely cropped bald head, his residual hair like a nap, his face smooth and thin skinned, the skin buff, as if soaked in an expensive faint dye, a quiet smile on his lips, only a few tension creases around his tidy mouth. He gave me a shot.

"What's in the needle?"

"Percocil."

Artificial morphine, a substance I was familiar with.

After that I felt fine. He wrote me a scrip. He had hands as small as a child's and unmarked, pale and soft as a child's, but the writing was cramped, aged looking. We got the scrip filled first thing—driving on into town and getting the pills and then sitting in the shade of a big oak in front of the sandy brick courthouse drinking a soda and dropping a couple of the pills on top of the shot so I went past the feeling of well-being the shot gave me, the feeling not of drunkenness but of humanness, into a feeling in which small packets of light danced in my fingers and crackled in my hair.

The next day I didn't feel like going into the dining room, where I did my writing. I wasn't interested in the novel I was working on, another homage to Alice, so after an early walk I took a pill, drove Alice to work, and then I went by the orchard and said hello to Randle Reed, the orchard owner, and my former boss, and sat in the kitchen with his wife Sammie and had a slice of apple pie for breakfast. The trees out the window were pale druidical green, filled with young apples, and the sky above them was a resonant blue with some fancy cloudwork off to the left. I sat in the chair feeling the sweetness of being alive, the sweet cinnamon taste of the pie in my mouth, listening to Randle and his wife tell about the photographers who came by last week to take pictures for a magazine article and how they made them all dress up in the magazine's idea of farm clothes, which was a little embarrassing to everyone, except they liked the clothes and got to keep them and now wanted more outfits.

"Is that one of them?" I said, indicating Randle's ensemble.

"Yeah. What do you think?"

Randle got up and turned around holding the sides of his long soft blue denim jacket out. Under it he wore soft gray coveralls. Sammie, who got up too, was wearing denim as well, but puffy, voluminous denim, jacket and pants, a farm suit for rich ladies.

I said, "Those cows are driving me nuts."

"Still?"

"Every time I come out on the porch they're either waiting for me or they lumber up crying like they can't live without me."

"What do you think of the suit?"

"You look ridiculous."

"I don't think I'm ridiculous, I think I look good."

"You're not ridiculous—the outfit is. Farmers don't dress like that."

"I'm starting something new. We both are."

"Feel this cloth," Sammie said. "It's soft as duck down."

I touched the cloth, rubbed it between my fingers and for a second wanted to go past this and take her wrist in my hand, run my hand up the skin of her, rummage the flesh of her to the center. "You're right—it is soft."

"You ought to like it," Randle said, "being from Miami and all."

"In Miami we don't wear that much. Shorts and flip-flops—that's us."

"You got style, though."

I didn't try to explain my point of view to them, it didn't matter. I didn't mind their new outfits.

"What's difficult," Randle said—this a little later as we dumped apples into the cider press, "is to match colors. I'm okay with the actual styles, but the colors baffle me."

"My dog bit me on the cock."

"I heard about you trying to poison him."

"That was a lie told by the law."

"Who set out that bait?"

"Man, you know it all, don't you?"

"Why would you want to poison your dog? You afraid to confront him directly?"

"I couldn't get close to him. And I wasn't trying to poison him, I was trying to drug him. Slip him a mickey."

"What for?"

"Get him back to my house."

"You can't make your dog stay?"

"I don't really want to talk about it."

"I wouldn't either. It sounds pretty embarrassing."

Outside, behind the apple house, beyond the big back window I stopped to look through, the mountain fell away in green stages. A couple of months ago a field down there, just visible now through the trees, was filled with daffodils, March flowers, so-called in the mountains, a bright yellow range of color like the gold at the bottom of rainbows. Far down there, past all that, far to the south, the new superhighway was going through in a cloud of dust. If we waited we could hear them blasting, the crump bang of the dynamite traveling up the valley like thunder, pushing its dark cloud. The raised yellow eyebrows of the cuts, fresh scars in the mountainside, showed through the trees. I went back into the house for a glass of water and there was Sammie on the couch, changed into a dress with her leg cocked up on the ottoman. She didn't take her leg down while we talked, letting me look if I wanted to, her voice bright and engaging and notating nothing but the time passing. "I haven't seen your place," she said. "Not since Calvert fixed it up."

"He didn't do anything special to it."

"It's pretty out that way."

"We've just got the garden in."

"I'd like to see it. Maybe I'll drive out some morning."

"Um."

Yes, so she did, some morning later that week—drove out in her yellow car and parked behind the house and came in wearing shorts that cut up into her ass, finding me unshaven and drugged, wearing a poncho at my desk as I stared into the typewriter at a phrase that wouldn't untangle, some moment I was describing in which Alice came out from behind a waterfall with a look on her face like a monkey surprised, an extraordinary look.

"What you doing?"

"Working. I'm working."

I went out to the living room and turned the music up, Berlioz it was this week, mournful and unashamed, the big fist of the piece opening cramped and muscular fingers, all that, and then I went out to the porch and sat in one of the armchairs. She followed me out eating a doughnut. "You want one?"

"Sure," I said.

She opened the bag and held it out to me. When I reached in she snapped it shut on my hand. "You," she said.

"You too."

Little wrestle then to get my hand out.

"I wanted to come before." She had short red hair, a pixie face, upturned.

The drugs built calm lions in the Africa of my spirit.

I said, "So, is this some kind of Madame Bovary kind of thing, run around after the local gentry . . . kind of thing?"

"I don't know her."

"Maybe she's from Winchester."

"I'm entirely my own person."

"That's where we're different."

"I take long walks in the woods. Sometimes I think I'll just keep walking, and not stop."

"If you ever try it, that's not as much fun as you might think."

She looked off at the pasture that was coming up in pokeweed, slender purple stalks with long lancing leaves, nodding in an early breeze. "I want to travel," she said in a small, wispy voice, a voice unbeguiled and humble. "I want to fly away."

"Sure."

"I know what they say, about you take your troubles with you. But what they don't say is how there's always a little lag time before they catch up. That's the time I want. I don't care if it's only fifteen minutes."

I offered her some drugs, but she didn't want any. "You shouldn't take them either. I think they're getting to you. You don't look very good."

"I have to take them for my wound."

"Which one is that?"

I told her about the dog bite.

In the other chair now, she pushed forward on her elbows and stared at my crotch. "I can't see anything from here."

"I feel better, though. Morton worked wonders."

"That molester."

"Who?"

"Morton. That doctor. He's from Richmond. He's a child molester."

"How do you know?"

"Everybody knows. He's takes those boys on camping trips and he makes them undress in front of him and everything else. He plays around with them."

"Why doesn't he get arrested?"

"None of the boys'll say anything. Nobody else either. He's a good doctor, I guess, and people need him. He'll come to your house and he won't even charge if you can't pay. That's how he buys everybody off. Like he does with you."

"The drugs, you mean?'

"Exactamento, cutie."

For a moment the light, the sunlight filtered by haze, streaked her legs white, left streaks like zebra stripes on the long, exposed flesh of her legs so I was caught a second daydreaming of flesh, of her flesh and then of Alice's, of the darkness of Alice's skin, which was a phenomenon that had happened as time passed, an oddity, unexplainable we guessed and never spoken about except between ourselves, wondering what this was, some aging or mellowing risen from the inside—mellowing, she said, let's hope—and then the sun shifted or Sammie did and the streaks faded and I was staring at her pudgy white flesh. She stretched, coming up off the chair. "Don't you want to?" she said.

"No," I said. "I can't."

"Won't or can't?"

"Both."

"Oh, dog." She grinned. "You know somebody?"

We laughed and then she trotted down the steps and drove off and I went back inside and tried to work, but I was unsettled, amazed, and disturbed slightly—not too much—wondering not about Sammie but about Randle, and about myself, realizing I liked to be in this position, liked the confidentiality of it and the confidence it gave me, the serious sense of purpose, it was almost this, and then I leaned back in the chair and watched as a coyote slunk along the far edge of the garden, out in daylight, this mournful wolf reject I guess you'd say, spiteful and jealous, which was something I identified with, the scruff up on the back of the neck, the gray, yellowish fur patchy, torn; and then he stopped and looked across the tops of the young bean plants at me and stared, maybe he could see me, maybe not, some creature not too different from him in application and design, I might think this if I wanted to, but you couldn't explain this to a canine, not in any meaningful way, which, I thought as I sat there staying quiet, was part of the loneliness of being on earth, the familiarity of everything combined with the way you still couldn't talk about it, get it across to anyone, unless some miracle happened.

"Well, I'm spent," Alice said first thing, rushing up the drive that afternoon, up the front steps with her arms filled with dried grass, and flung the grass down on the porch, went back, got another load and flung that down too.

"What's going on?" I said, and she said she'd decided to make a grass quilt, get into the native crafts, which was the sort of idea we were coming up with at that time, on occasions when we weren't spending all our time wondering what in the world we were doing in the mountains, wondering why we'd left the subtropics at all. "Let me help you," I said, and she said, "There's no more to do except make the quilt." In the car she also had a bag of fabric scraps, which I brought up to the porch for her. "I need an I don't know what you call it—a stretcher—a loom," she said, "whatever it is."

"Maybe somebody could make that."

I told her what Sammie had said about the doctor. I didn't tell her about Sammie. But she was psychic, Alice.

"Our doctor?" she said.

"Yep."

She whirled and rushed out down the driveway to the car, flung the door open and stood, one foot in, waiting. "Well, you coming?"

"Where?"

"To that doctor's."

"You going to punish him?"

"Worse."

I didn't comment, but I got into the car.

And then later, after we didn't do anything, after we drove to the doctor's office that was in a white cottage in his front yard and Alice stormed in and demanded to see him and he came out and took her into the back and I followed and he talked to us—how can I explain it?—in such a way that we were not convinced but quieted, and then he gave us a prescription for more drugs, and released us, after this sometimes I'd see him pass on the road in his black Lincoln Town Car and wonder if he'd just come from disturbing the peace of a child, some child who now knew what sadness was all about—and rage and bedevilment too—but would have to go on anyway, no matter what, some boy entering the house alone and going out to the pump room for his fishing rod and going on out to the garden to dig a few worms and going on then by himself down to the creek and throwing his line in and standing there in the dim coolness of the creekside watching the line slant down into the dark water and disappear into it.

Chapter Two

I got drunk at Alice's class picnic and they fired Alice for it and then we couldn't get jobs because the rumor started that we weren't married—someone told lies about us—and my publisher vetoed the novel—*Why don't you go back to the old stuff*, the editor, no longer Minx, said—and we didn't qualify for welfare or even food stamps, and Randle found out about Sammie, and blamed me, which was natural, I did have a part in it, so there was no orchard work, and I was seen punching a cow in the face and this got back to Calvert, who didn't exactly fire me, but got someone else to look after the herd—we didn't discuss any of it, but now we had to pay rent—and the ex-army drug supplier friend of Edouardo's was on me about receiving drugs on the cuff, and then winter came.

For a while we enjoyed the reductions. Being poor was a romance, a story. You could catch sight of us in the basement at Dillon's rummaging through the wire baskets of cheap sneakers. We bought dried beans by the ten pound sack and soaked them overnight and boiled them with ham hocks and ate pokeweed gathered from our own fields and ramps collected in the woods and there was food from the garden, a little bit, and then my friend Wayford shot a deer and gave us a haunch that I hacked up with an ax and packed in the freezer. Alice sewed patches into the crotch of my jeans. We sat out on the porch bundled in ponchos, drinking birch-root tea cupped in gloves with the fingers cut off, like Russians, talking of enormities. But by March poverty had lost its charm. The money ran out and the car broke down, so until Calvert came by to ferry us to town to Crump's Local Loan, where we pawned Alice's grandmother's silver bowl, we were stuck in the house, which was too small for full days of the two of us.

One evening I took a gun up into the orchard on the hill and tried to waylay a bear, but there were no bears in winter, I remembered. Then I got scared because it seemed the coyotes were tracking me, following me through the denuded trees, some of which had the gnarled hysterical branch schemes of trees in bad dreams, and it was getting dark, the sky synthesizing blue and red into a glowing otherworldly purple that at first delighted me then gave me the willies. I started to run. The grass, uncut and bent over like lank hair, grabbed at my cheap sneakers. Behind me a noise in the undergrowth could only be coyotes, become bold, sensing weakness. The hill slanted sharply down. I gave the dark world behind a quick over the shoulder and as I did lost my footing and went sprawling, pushing the gun out ahead of me. It went off, slapping buckshot into the trunk of a large tree. The muzzle blast was six feet long. Defenseless now, a buffoon on my own property, jittering, muttering phrases from my reading, I sprang to my feet and careened into the dragging branches of another tree. Something—it seemed to me—something alive, creaturely, grabbed at me, and I reeled back and fell again. The slick wet grass smeared itself upon me. Snakes, I thought, forgetting they were underground by now. I leapt up and raced for the house, for the lights, for Alice whose shape I could see in the living room window—if I could just get back to her—quilting away. "Hey!" I cried. "Hey!" or "Help!" or "Christ Jesus save me!" one of those imploratives, and ran full tilt into the fence, which caught me across the face, flipping me onto my back. I lay there stunned. After a while one of the beasts, some monstrous animal, snuffled up and licked me in the face. I struck out at it, hitting it across the nose, sending it yelping into the darkness. Delite, it turned out, come finally to forgive me.

The next morning I couldn't find the gun, and suspecting conspiracy, treachery, I hiked up the hill and confronted the neighbor, attempting as I stood on his porch to call the dog to me, the now once more unforgiving dog, and when he came out, the neighbor, a thickset man wearing a pajama top under his overalls, I accused him, or some member of his family, of stealing my weapon, which I had borrowed from Wayford, and he ordered me off his property. "I'll show you a damn weapon," he said.

"Yeah, okay, fine," I said. "But where could it have gone? Bears took it?"

"I don't know nothing about your gun. 'Cept I heard you shooting in the middle of the night. I was about to call the sheriff on you—again."

"It wasn't the middle of the night. It was hardly dark."

"I'm not going to quibble with you. You just spin your ass around and head on down that hill." The little boy in the doorway behind him snickered.

Yes, we were fodder, I was fodder, for local comedians.

Wayford, who'd loaned it to me, forgave me for the gun, which never showed up, carried off I guessed by some beast in the night, or child next door; he told me, his form of forgiveness, that I could work it off. This meant take part in a still run, which we accomplished some days later. I waked that morning from a dream in which Alice mercilessly mocked me. She slept long hours now, the sleep of the depressed and unemployed. The hood of unhappiness had settled over her once again. I raised myself and stared into her sleep face in which battles took place, deeply secret battles I had watched all my life, dream fights she never fully remembered but carried the residue, the outcome, of, into the day. She was becoming gaunt, worked at by fear and failure, a sunkenness in her cheeks; the bones themselves seemed to curve more profoundly, sinking more deeply into the interior of her face. Her mouth, her thin, rounded, delicate lips, moved as she whispered, uttering cries so faint I couldn't tell what she was saying. Somewhere back in the mists of her spirit she called for help. I took it this way. Yet I didn't rouse her. If I could, I would have entered her dream, stepped forth onto the scumbled plain of it to fight for her, to save her, but, unable to, I did nothing to break her free of it. Her eyelids fluttered, a current moved up through the depths, passed through her, and then she was looking at me. "Where were you?" I said.

"All over."

She smiled, her top lip catching on her teeth. Her face, which in sleep was hard, tight, softened. Then she said something harsh. Something thoughtless, I can't remember now what it was. Little sparrow of ugliness flicking by. A door opened on a torrent of rage—and slammed shut. There was another world beneath this one, a world in which we crouched in a hotel room naked and smeared with feces, drugged, terrified, screeching at each other. In this room

I grabbed her by the throat and flung her across the putrid bed. Now, in this present, I said something, something hard, which I refused to consider hard, but which in her eyes I could see was. Something in her cowered, disappeared, and came back angry. "You prick," she said. Yes, yes, how true. "Prickette," I said. She cursed me. I cursed her back. She slapped me across the eyes. From there we went straight to hell.

We clambered down into the ravine through a rhododendron slick—rose tree, I said, to myself, thinking of my father speaking about the Rose of Sharon—and discovered the still had been found and smashed. Wayford thought he knew who did it. Not government agents this time but Solomon Dulac, an enemy and still runner who had haunted his operation for years. The boiler was upended and stove in with an ax, and the copper stolen; the ground stank with mash that lay drifted like rotted sawdust against the trunk of an oak, and the shed had been broken into and the sugar and the corn scattered on the ground. Even the wooden tripod-hoist up on the ravine edge had been toppled and lay cracked and splayed against a tree. Broken glass was everywhere. Wayford went down to the creek and washed his hands and then he squatted there looking at the rushing water. I came up behind him and stood awhile without speaking. "We used to catch salamanders in this creek," he said finally. "Little red speckled ones. They were so bright looking."

"What do you want to do?"

"Straighten this out, I reckon."

Go to war—no, he didn't mean that. Would I come with him?

Sure, I said, as long as there's no shooting. These days, on the usual evidence, I felt always only an inch from being arrested.

"It's not that kind of straightening," he said.

The bleak, battered winter landscape streamed by, snow-streaked in the open places. In a field, far off near some black trees, a flock of Canadian geese poked about, nosing among cornstalks. The trees on the mountainsides looked shorn, cut back, so lifeless they seemed dead. Alice had made a hoop to contain her quilt and finished a cover that was simple and beautiful, made of scraps and tatters of different colors. "Like we'd do in prison," she said when I complimented her on the work. Vivid colors, she meant, mostly absent from prison life.

My jaw hurt where she'd socked me. I'd hurled her into the closet and locked the door. From inside there'd come silence, nothing. I could hear the clock ticking, hear the call of a thrush out among the pines. I stood there an hour waiting for her to ask me to let her out, but she didn't say a thing. Damp closet, cramp, blackness—they were just fine. Eventually I got lonely. "You okay?" She didn't answer. "Alice. Do you want out?" Breeze faintly rattled the window pane, but she said nothing. "Come on, honey." I pressed my ear against the door. "If you want I'll open it. I'll even apologize." Nothing. "I'm sorry," I said, "I was way off base. Won't you come out?" Two beats of silence and then her voice: "Get down on your knees and beg me." I did that, dropped as if the string was cut, and banged my knee on the hardwood floor. "Ah, damn." She offered no comfort. "Please," I said, "please open the door and come out. This whole place out here, everything—it's got no life in it without you.

Come on, please. You're my face card, honey, come out." All that. I said, "I'd be out here all by myself if it wasn't for you."

"It probably wouldn't be any different."

"That's where you are wrong."

I started in about prison, talking about it, about how some men just let everything go—wailed or cried or masturbated while they talked on the pay phone—gave it all up sometimes and fell in love with dereliction and hurtfulness, but this didn't ring true so I stopped.

It was quiet in the room, in the closet. I noticed a book I had been reading—it lay beside the chamber pot I used as a midnight bathroom—a book about waking up old, and I thought about all the people I'd planned to visit—the living and the dying and, by now, the dead—and hadn't got around to. My mind started to wander and I wanted a drug in my veins, something sweet, a cupcake of a drug, with butter icing, and then I wanted to lie on the floor playing with the dog.

"Let's take the day off," I said.

"You mean like we always do?"

"No. Let's go somewhere."

"Okay."

Wayford slipped the truck down a gear and we turned up a rising gray dirt road. The country looked like some kind of sweetener needed to be sprinkled over it. Some new dream injected into it. The apple trees we passed, entering a stretch of gravel pavement, looked wasted, misused, water sprouts drooping like worn-out antennae off the branches. A gully, red and eroded, cleaved away down a steep hillside that a few bony cattle clung to like stranded mountaineers. A shack here, a shack there. Tufts of animal hair in the fences. Someone had nailed the body of a coyote to a telephone pole.

The road jogged steeply left and then at the top of a rise plunged downhill into gloom. Brown pines stood in a field, half their needles at their feet.

Beyond a blank grassless hill face a house appeared, a languishing board house with two stories and galleries all around and one side sagging slightly, the kind of house in summer I'd love to come upon, and speculate on, a house wearing in its hair all the nests of yesteryear, a house not falling into the future but rising from the past. I thought of bringing Alice here; this was the kind of place we were headed to. We turned into the driveway, which was paved in what looked like crushed bone, and trundled up to the front porch. All the shades were drawn. We got out and knocked and then the silence fell back onto us, a silence all around the house and out in the yard, beyond which a two strand fence gave in to a steep fallaway pasture that opened into air that stretched away to brown vague distant mountains.

"Solomon," Wayford called. "Woo, Solomon."

Silence again, like two ends rejoined, then a voice from inside the house said, "Woo, Solomon what?"

"Solomon, it's Scooty."

Scooty? I looked at him. He smiled.

"What you want?"

"To talk to you."

"I can shoot through this door just as easy as I can open it."

I took a quick step back.

"I don't have a gun," Wayford said.

"That's good for me. What do you want?"

"I need to speak to you." He said this in a gentle voice, the voice a man would use speaking to his scared child, if the child was grown and shaking a gun on the other side of a door. My mind drifted and I thought about the drugs I received from my (back in Miami) good friend Edouardo's Norfolk buddy in wadded-up plastic bags stuffed in a Prince Albert tobacco tin, and how Alice laughed at this, warning me not to get into smoking, that was what I had to watch out for, and I looked away across the landscape that was beautiful at that moment in its play of browns and grays and the softened wintry blacks seeped out from under the pines, and it didn't seem to matter that I was not going to live forever, that everything I loved was going to disappear from the earth. Wayford knocked softly on the faded white door. It opened and a large man in overalls stood there. He held a gun propped against his leg. "What is it you want, Scooty?"

Wayford opened his hands, one of them extended to the man. "I want to apologize to you. Those things I said back at the meeting were wrong. It was small and mean of me to say them."

"It's too late for that now."

"You've been good to me in ways you probably don't even realize. I am sorry for my ingratitude. I know it's put a burden on you."

The man stared at him, stared a long moment. His face was wide and colorless and built of folds and pockets and shadows. His eyes were small and bright and pale blue. He was still and then his mouth moved, a long, pliable mouth, rubbing against his teeth. "Yeah?" he said.

"I transgressed against you and I'm sorry for it."

"Yes you did."

"You didn't deserve it."

"No, I didn't."

"I am as sorry as I can be."

"You ought to be even sorrier."

"I just needed to come over here and tell you."

"Now you done that."

He looked at me and all the hardness, and unforgivingness, was in the look, as if it was being passed to me, as if that was how you did it, shifted the weight to someone else, except I was simply a stranger, a nobody in this affair, but maybe that was how you did it too, hand the craziness and desolation off to some stranger who would simply take it out of the room and set it down somewhere and go on about his business, because right after this look, another appeared that was a look not of easefulness but of attention shifting, as if, just by way of this, it would soon be all right to go on to other things. That was how I saw it, standing there in the fading light on a late winter day. Solomon made a small gesture, flicking his hand away from his thigh. Just that. He stepped back and closed the door, closing it slowly and smoothly, stepping back into the gloom of the hallway that seemed filled with dust motes floating on an insular breeze. We stood on the porch as the house sank back into its quiet. Wayford pressed his open hand calmly against the door, and then he patted the wood.

What happened after this was that one of Solomon Dulac's sons ambushed Wayford outside his house one evening just at dusk and shot him dead. Wayford's wife was off at her sister's house helping with the new baby and didn't get home until late. When she couldn't find Wayford, she called her brother-in-law, who came out to look for him, but they didn't find him either. The next day the sheriff came out and he and a deputy tramped around in the backyard and discovered the body in some bushes just where the woods began. Something, some animal it looked like, had disturbed the remains, but they could tell it was Wayford.

That same night somebody fired a shot into our house. The shot came in the window, slapped through the living room wall into the bedroom and tore a hole in Alice's party jacket hanging in the bedroom closet. I was sitting in my chair in front of the fireplace, leaning in to put another piece of green wood on the fire, when the window broke and the wall thumped and there was a cracking noise. I didn't know what it was at first. Something in me—I knew this something well—didn't want it to be anything awful. But it was. I hit the floor just as Alice came to the bedroom door. I made a harsh pushing gesture and crawled at her and a look appeared in her face of surprise and humor and chagrin, and then fright, and she dropped down.

"That was a gunshot," I said.

We lay on the floor a long time, afraid to move. We were afraid even to raise up to turn off the light. We lay there listening for somebody coming. There wasn't any sound outside, nothing unusual. Then Delite, up the hill, began to bark. His bark was strident and excessive, unlike his usual disagreeable yapping. There was something panicked about it. "Thank God for that dog," Alice said.

We stayed down awhile longer then we got cautiously up. The phone had been cut off for lack of payment or we would have called the sheriff, but now there was only one thing left: hightail it. So we got into the (repaired) car and—to throw any trackers off; this was our idea—drove to Philadelphia to see the Duchamps in the Philadelphia Museum of Art. We got sidetracked by a bitter, frightened argument at a wayside picnic area in Delaware and arrived just at dawn, crossing the river from Camden like a couple of addled Walt Whitmans coming into the old city for an early diner breakfast. From our booth we could see the bridge soaring away into fog and hear the sounds of ships out on the river, the cry of ships' horns, that is. This made us nostalgic for the South, for tropical weather, and we decided we would head that way, to Mexico. "You want to go right now?" Alice said, and I said, "Sure, don't you?"

"What about the Duchamps?"

"Okay, we better get them out of the way."

It was like a ritual, a numb postulation we had to go on with. Neither of us cared about Duchamp or knew anything about him, we had simply seen his name in a book, but we went over there anyway. We were the first customers in the door. Afterwards we bought postcards we signed with fake names and addressed to ourselves (Rural Route 6, Highland Meadows, VA) and mailed at a box on the corner. Then we walked by the river and watched the early morning rowers. The fragile, skittish boats, the dark trees, the massive icicles hanging from the bridges, the spidery oars reaching into the smooth surface to pick up nothing—these frightened us, and a man shouting a curse from the far bank added to this, and something Alice said, so we returned to the car and drove back to the diner and had another breakfast. Then we drove south as far as the northern tip of the Chesapeake Bay, where in a little water town we put up in a motel that had small white windmills attached to it, next door to a state mental hospital, and took a room where we got on the floor and did exercises, like demented people, drunk, counting cadence and glaring at each other, until we were exhausted and fell asleep across the beds in our clothes.

I waked the next morning to the sound of big ugly motors and went out to see heavy yachts, as big as train engines, lumbering by, leaving wakes like furrows in the earth. We had breakfast in a pink dining room and then faltered between the restaurant and the car and fell back to the motel and began to delay. "You idiot," she said, but I knew she didn't mean it. Later we caressed each other's bodies, apologetically almost, hardly looking at each other, making our distant, overwhelmed, earnest love, and we felt better, felt familiar to ourselves. In the afternoon we took a walk on the grounds of the mental hospital and sat awhile with some patients who were fishing in a group. Every once in a while one would break into tears, another into wild, independent laughter. The big robotic boats churned by. The disturbed people never gave the boats a glance. Alice got the willies, but she didn't take the situation personally. We walked around the grounds awhile through a parklike place under big leafless beech trees. We had one of those lonely two person dinners and then got drunk with our waitress out back watching the lights across the bay. We ate leftover crab cakes and drank a Riesling wine that tasted like mineral oil and shared some drugs with the waitress and her boyfriend, who came by later on his way home from his job as an armored car guard. He was hugely fat and I wondered out loud if there was some rule about that, if the company minded. "Everything's tough for a fat man," he said, smiling sourly. The waitress took offense, misunderstanding, and accused us of insulting her boyfriend. After that we left.

Chapter Three

Seventy-eight hours later we were in Mexico, driving through a pecan orchard. This was after going through customs twice. Discomposed, arguing, in confusion, we'd passed through the first time without stopping, and when nobody hailed us, simply headed south. What a convivial, easygoing country, we said. Only later, ten miles down the road, we discovered, by way of a police checkpoint, that we needed permits. It's so typical of us, Alice said. "We just want to get into the swing of things," I told the officer. He pointed north. We made a U-turn and headed back to town.

Back at the border, the river feculent and gray beyond us, America a whitened dimness, receding, nobody in Mexico surprised or outraged to see us again, we slipped into the line. For a time Alice was unreachable, mired in a sullen silence. An oppressed silence. Her head turned away, her eyes like windows in a slot machine, clicking and spinning, at the mercy of her internal machinery. An inspector glanced at her with attention, but he wasn't our inspector and passed on to others. She growled when I spoke to her. "Actually," I said as we stood at a long yellow counter, "now's the time when you might want to perk up." For a second she came out of it, bringing with her a smile, a faded radiance. "You have to have me, don't you—even if you kill me," she said. In the grainy, bleak light of the customs shed the arm she raised to touch the inspector's sleeve looked stringy, wasted, and I saw—I hadn't noticed this before—deep hollows in her cheeks, shadows at her temples, the paleness of her skin. Maybe it was only the light. "We're fine now," I said, half to the official and half to the air. The man gave me a look, unstartled, complacent, as if he had already seen through me.

On the other side of the pecan orchard we stopped at a monastery. "I'm tired," she said, "aren't you tired?" I was. Still, I had to choke something down to stop the car. "Let's pretend we're nonchalant," Alice said. "Let's act like we don't need anything." Yet when they let us right in—"Its against our rules to refuse," a monk said, sighing—we hurried through the compound and out the back in a rush until we reached a dry riverbed rippling away under sand. There we fetched up, winded, gasping actually. The desert on the other side had a futile, ransacked look and this stopped us. A cold wind carried the scent of snow. We looked each other in the face and she said, "You bring out the beast, I mean the rabid dog, in me." It was that kind of vacation, so far. She looked away, like a shy one, and we turned back.

In the garden the monks had planted flowers they brought from the old country, but these were mostly dried out and winter dead. A few cactuses kept the life force going. Alice went into the church while I lay on a bench outside. It was cold, but still I took my sneakers off. Philadelphia ice salt streaked the canvas uppers. For some reason this seemed particularly poignant. Last year, about noon on a spring day, Alice had told me she was pregnant. Then the next day she'd come in, wearing a crown of daisies, and said no, it was a false alarm. Then the next day she'd said the false alarm was false. And then the next day again no pregnancy. I had taken her into my arms, some stupid trick of hope and despair revolving in me, and lain with her on the bed until whatever was jammed up in her came loose and she began to cry. "I keep thinking," she said, "that the animals are going to come out of the woods and comfort us."

Alice came out of the church, touched my hair and said she had been praying for ugly possibilities. "Hard—ninety miles an hour." In her prayers she named scenarios—natural disaster, crime, loss of a limb in a highway accident—that might come, stockpiling prayers for these occasions in case at the moment of crisis she was unable to pray, or forgot. I'd written about this. Now, she said—this was the way things went in Mexico—she had prayed for our unborn child.

"What?"

"Unconceived," she said. "Our unconceived, unborn child." The sun behind her head gave her a halo I deeply admired.

"I am particularly grateful it's you," I said, "and not some phantasm down here in Mexico with me."

"We hadn't been here that long."

She held a small round medallion in her palm. "The priest gave it to me."

"That's idolatry, you know."

"Yes, thank God."

"Do you think our love is just idol worship?"

"Sometimes I wish it was."

"It's tough isn't it when you see right to the mystical core of a human being."

"You mean like dogs do?"

It was morning in Mexico and everywhere we looked there were vast incomprehensibilities. The desert, for one, stretched away on the other side of the road like an unclaimed country. And the little washed-out homesteads tucked away in the bushes. A child chasing another child with a radio antenna, switching him across the back with it. Someone—so we discovered when we went out front—had stolen the rear tires off the car, this was another. "It couldn't be personal," I said, "could it?" "Not yet," Alice said. The road looked like a strip of tape measuring something all the way to the mountains. A woman in an office looking onto the parking lot said two men in a truck took the wheels. "Didn't it seem odd to you?" I said. She said no, it didn't really seem that odd. I shook with tension and morbidity, as they say. To Alice who was working her way up to a fit, I said, "You think it's going to be like this all the way through Mexico?"

"Not if we don't get more tires."

The woman phoned a gas station, staring out the window as she did so, intent on something that had nothing to do with us—only ocotillo and other bedraggled choya out there, not even any other visitors, somewhere behind us the monks pressing an ear against God's door, leaving little notes—and came back smiling a distant smile, her wide face almost blank. It took two hours for help to arrive and it turned out to be two boys in a pickup truck. A quick check and let us run back to the station, *por favor,* which they did, returning with two retreads. "Sure, retreads are fine—*bueno,*" I said. The stolen tires were retreads, quite a bit like the ones they sold us. The boys were friendly and competent, one maybe fifteen and the other about ten, and we liked this, child labor, something throwaway and human about it, knowledge fallen off a truck into the world, picked up by children. I didn't want to argue about whose tires they really were. We thanked them and gave each a dollar extra—we hadn't changed any money—and then we drove off through the pecan trees onto the highway and made Monterey that evening.

I crossed the street to a bar and got drunk on mescal and entered a long tedious discussion with an old man whose pants were held up by a rope. For a good part of the conversation he didn't even know I was talking to him. After a while both of us—him first then me—began to accompany the discussion with signs, big scooping hand and arm signals that, as far as I could tell, signified nothing. We just liked doing this. Then it was dawn in Mexico and I walked out arm in arm with the old fellow and we stood at the top of the steps watching the light struggle to its feet out in the street. "Yeah, daylight in Chihuahua," I said, getting the state wrong, but saying something with feeling, impressed with life, impressed to be out of the icy Blue Ridge. Then I thought of all the things that never came to fruition, the projects and attempts at reconciliation that fell short, just the material for après barroom contemplation, and this felt so familiar to me, so complex and insufferable, so like life in every place I'd lived in, that hope began to hiss and deflate, the old hope for sweetness and tenderness and all the lovely nesses you get into in the drug life, all deflated, all losing air. For a second it got scary there in the street where a pale yellow light illuminated a trash barrel turned on its side and a blue chair leaned against a house wall, the emptiest chair in the world, I realized, and so I said adios to the old gentleman, walked down the street to our hotel and tossed pebbles at Alice's window. For a second the chain of being almost came clear, but this passed. The pebbles sounded like bits of metal hitting the wall. Then one went through the window and the police came and I was taken to jail.

Alice—whose window it hadn't been—flagged a lawyer down in the street and I got out two days later with a fine. We had to give the lawyer my suitcase—an old expensive leather one that had belonged to my father—because we didn't have the money to pay him, or said we didn't. After the fine we had fifty-seven dollars in small bills that we changed at the bank into pesos. We spent twelve pesos on reefer and went out to a long stone wall overlooking an arroyo and smoked and talked about how our lives had gone so far. She was queasy most of the time now, and thought this odd. "I feel carsick," she said. It was cool in the evening and someone had given her a pomegranate—despicable, useless fruit—and we opened this and chomped gobs of seeds and squeezed them with our tongues. She bent over me—I lay in her lap—and let the juice fall into my mouth. "My grandmother—" I started to say, and stopped because I didn't want to think about the old life. "Mine too," she said, and stopped. "Maybe we can get jobs," I said. She didn't say anything. The moon was up, capsized in the east above dark mountains. Even in the dark you could make out the rocks everywhere, in the street, in the hills, piled along the crest of the closest mountain. An odd lonely sensation came over me, some reduction in the flame of life, all that, and I began to tell her a story about New York, about exhausting myself one afternoon and having to sit down on the curb on Seventh Avenue to catch my breath and someone, an old woman, coming up to me and asking how I was. It was a long story with no real meaning beyond the telling, beyond the sound of my voice there in Mexico. "We have to do something to save ourselves," she said.

"That's what we're doing every minute," I said.

"No. Something different."

"Let's come up with a marvelous plan. I am all for that."

Two children went by leading a small dog on a rope.

"Do we have enough drugs?"

It was the first time she had asked a question like that.

"Yeah."

"How much?"

Two Prince Alberts, I told her.

"That'll be enough?"

"This is Mexico—they make it down here."

"But they don't sell it to you unless you have money."

"When we begin to run low we'll head for the surface."

"Like in frogman movies."

"Exactly."

"Do you think when we get low—when we run out—we'll bitterly accuse one another?"

"Oh, yeah, sure."

"You think we'll betray each other?"

"In a New York minute."

"Good. I don't want to be surprised by that." She was silent. A siren distantly began, sputtered and faded. "Will I have to sell my body?"

"Of course. Constantly."

"How about you?"

"I'll probably start robbing."

"You won't have to sell your body?"

"I will if somebody wants it."

"You should have to sell your body too."

"You're right. I'll sell my body to anyone who fronts the drugs. I'll do that first thing. They'll have to stand in line to get to my body."

"Good. I would be lonely if I was the only one."

"You won't be the only one."

"It doesn't mean you get out of robbing, though."

"I don't want to get out of robbing. I want to rob too."

Leaning over her knees, she brusquely massaged her ankles. "We're probably only going to do this for a while longer, isn't that so?"

"Do what?"

"Live like this."

"I don't know. I don't want to think about that."

"I think we ought to start thinking about it."

"All right."

We were silent for a time.

"Are you thinking?" she said.

"Hard as I can go."

"I'm not kidding, Billy. We're in trouble and it's the kind of trouble that always gets worse."

"You are just noticing that?"

"No. But I'm scared."

"Oh, honey, this is only Mexico. What can happen here?"

"You've already been in jail."

"Not for long. And it was not at all intolerable. It was a better jail, in fact, than several I have been in in Florida."

"All this is going to kill us—don't you understand that?" She got up, walked a few steps along the wall and looked down from it at the trees and the flat-roofed houses. From there she spoke again, turning to me, showing her hard face to me. "You block off all the love I have for you," she said, "just by acting like an idiot. You've always done that. It amazes me. You're like a millionaire—a trillionaire—tossing his money in the river. You think you've got all the money there is, but you don't." She flung an arm out, tossing the nothing in her hand away. "Christ. Sometimes I want to murder you. Sometimes at night I think about going out to the kitchen, getting a knife and coming back and stabbing you."

"Haven't you already tried that?"

"No. Whatever I've tried up to now wasn't that."

I pulled my legs up and wrapped my arms around my knees. "I don't understand why it is still cold. This is the fucking tropics."

"Billy."

"Al! Al! Don't ask me what the fuck to do. I don't have any idea."

She didn't come over and wrap her arms around me as I wanted her to. She would do that. She would come up to me, anywhere, and put her arms around me and raise her face and kiss me. I could tell she couldn't help it. Neither of us could. But she didn't do that now.

She said, "We have to do something optimistic. We have to begin a project of some kind. Some wholesome bit of work."

"You mean like build a dam?"

"Sure. Like that."

I was impressed by this talk, impressed by the way she still seemed to have authority in her life, and I wanted to do what she suggested. We went down the hill to a pizzeria where I got drunk on beer and sat reading fotonovelas until late. In these books love and truth were eventually rewarded. When luck ebbed there was always fate. According to the fotonovelas, if your love was true, you could count on fate. What I didn't count on was her telling me she was pregnant. "Was that what you were praying about?" I said.

She leaned her torso onto the table, lay across it, her hand touching the last pizza slice, and her face then in profile looked alarmingly sad.

"I will probably be able to go on for a little while as if it's not happening," she said, "but not forever."

"It's time to head home."

"Is that a depressing thought to you?"

"You mean, having tried to make it out in the world, our hero, forced to return to his sordid local beginnings, sinks into depression and suicidal thoughts?"

"Yes."

"I don't think so. When is the baby coming?"

"In the fall. And it doesn't mean you have to start lying to me."

"It aggravates me that you held out on me. Held back this information."

"I just admitted it to myself."

"When?"

"When we got out of the car at the monastery. That's why I started running."

"I thought that was something the two of us were onto—running away from everything through a monastery. It seemed poetic to me."

"I knew I was pregnant. All at once."

"I have to lie down."

"Let's go then."

Which we did, exiting, turning left when we should have turned right, crossing streets we'd never seen before, winding up not at our hotel but at a small park like an ex-dump by a watercourse, a walled place looking across a stony riverbed at houses whose lights were all off, like an adjunct abandoned city over there. I was never ahead of the panic, not for one minute, and when we got to this place and stood under a straggly tree I didn't know the name of, I fell to my knees and began to weep. She knelt behind me and draped her body over me. The weight of her, the pressure, the now fertile substance of her pushing me down into the earth—as if that was the proper procedure to refasten, reenter maybe, the earth we had risen out of—calmed me. I wished I was in a black hole with her as the lid. Her breath, smelling of hot peppers, blew past my face. As children we would sink into the water—out in the swamp—and hold each other, falling through the black. "Oh, honey," I said finally, "I have to draw a breath."

She peeled off and lay beside me on the ground looking up at the whitened sky. "I am so amazed," she said.

"I am too."

"If you had to get a license to do this—"

"They'd be hunting us for forgery."

"I am so scared."

"Was this the project you had in mind?"

"I guess it's why I brought it up."

She turned her head and grinned at me and there was something crazy in the grin, something crazily brave and out of touch in her whole face just then, yet this did not startle or frighten me. It was a look that went all the way back to childhood. I had probably seen it when we were six standing at the altar just before I broke up her first wedding, but I don't remember. If not then it was soon after. As if there was another part of her, an extra part that was not more than human but another kind of human, the rattled, demented, wily, scared to death kind they usually kept locked up. It was coming out of every part of her now, not just her eyes, not just her face. It was in her hands and her shoulders and her breasts and her pelvis and every other part, and it overwhelmed me. I shivered and the shiver was from terror. I never could deal with her. I put my hand out and my fingers seemed to cross into a space that was part of another universe, a universe just inches away from this one, all the time, set there permanently, in reach if you were in the right set of circumstances. She lived over there. The look on her face, that was their look.

Then this was none of it. It was just Alice, scared and bristling with the wild surmise of birth, her face rinsed not with alien waters but with the incredible happenstance of this moment. She cried out, a small perfectly unique cry, and came into my arms.

Then for a day and a half I wouldn't speak to her. The pregnancy panicked me and I was angry and looking for the exit. Every street was a potential way out and I stayed alert, scrutinizing avenues and the open doors of bus stations and highway signs, memorizing mileage, preparing myself for the moment when I would fling the car door open and roll out onto the shoulder, spring to my feet and run away. She caught this and called me on it and we had a vicious argument that people on the street in San Luis Potosi turned their faces from, embarrassed for us both. Nobody around us could explain anything, so we didn't bother to ask. They only wanted us to vamoose.

We wandered off and found a bench near a strip of greenery, a few big camphor trees ensconced on a small grass sward. The leaves of the camphor trees were dusty, and among them small clouds of fuzz, like hair balls, floated. The bench too was dusty, but we swept it clean and sat down on it. She looked across the street and then her eyes seemed to lock—her old trick—on nothing, or on something internal, some constellation of thoughts she studied, attempting to discover—what? Maybe the design of. Or the road through to paradise. I stroked her arm and she came back.

"You aren't jealous, are you?" she said.

"No, it's not that."

"You've no reason to be."

"You don't have to tell me that. It's just that I am so unprepared for this."

"Honey, you're unprepared for lunch."

"And you—what? You're all of sudden Mrs. Fertile Life of the Earth?"

"I could be."

"We'll never be more than scarecrows in the garden. That's our fate."

"Oh you are so negative."

"Shut up."

A quiet came upon us. Across the street a man took down a rusty red sign and put up another, also red. They both advertised men's clothes, *Apropriado y Elegante*. He himself wore a dark suit and a red tie. The sleeves of the suit were pushed up his forearms and he wore a white handkerchief around his head. The new sign looked exactly like the old one.

"How angry are you?" she said.

"You mean in percentage points or gallons?"

"You're really angry."

"I am really scared."

"It's smaller than a tadpole. You don't have to be scared of it."

"I wish I wasn't, but I am."

"And I guess all its kin."

The man went inside and came out again with a woman. The woman looked at the sign and then she pointed at one corner. The man untied his handkerchief and wiped the corner. The woman broadly smiled. They embraced and went back inside.

Because the car broke down and we didn't have money to fix it, we sold it for three hundred dollars and bought train tickets to Tampico, where we could catch a ship for Miami. We spent the night before we left in the Comodoro Hotel, ate a bistec dinner and then took some soft drugs and lay down in a big bed that looked down on a plaza where young people—people whose lives we would never be part of—sat out at café tables after midnight. On the other side of the plaza floodlights cast a bony, exculpatory radiance upon the front of a large church. "You have an extraordinary look," I told Alice.

"Dazed?" she said.

"*Contemplativo.*"

It was a rainy night in San Luis Potosi, a cool night, but not too cool to leave the windows open. We lay on our backs, just touching, our thoughts cradled by drugs, nowhere to get to just now, nobody to please, nothing to defend or accomplish. The baby swung in an other land of harmony and distance, a place where congenial servant folk paid attention to such matters. "We will have to get down from here after a while," she said. I agreed. But not now, not yet.

It was a stirring night. I woke to look at her. Her face a white road through the wilderness. Her body a mountain range, her body the moraine, the high mesa on a winter's day, wind blowing through the creosote and the sage. We had kept stopping the car to get out and look at the desert. So this is what it's like, we said, meaning *everything*. We'd had years of wild love. You could come around to our back door and ask for lessons, but we wouldn't give them to you. We weren't stingy, we were just busy. Her face—was too much for me. Love leeching my heart to pulp. The rind never had time to grow back. Each day like the first day in the fucking Garden of Eden, each a day where you started over from the top with a different woman always the same woman, named Alice, wife of Billy. We'd had years of what everybody else was dying to get. Every day I had enough of her. Every day I had to get some more. Now she sleeps, resting on her side, her face angled into eternity. I liked to wake her up just enough to bring her back to the world. I liked to do it more than once. "I'm not your toy," she said, but she was, toy and dream and rest, as the poet says—golem, rapid transit device, Checkpoint Charlie, mistral, my day at the beach. *In the Blue Ridge we used to get high sitting at the kitchen table in our bungalow*—that was how the last story started. *In the afternoons we got high and took walks through the woods down to the creek where we stripped naked and bathed in the cold water, sometimes arguing, sometimes sullen, shocked by each other still, rageous, terribly frightened, an inch away from a fit sometimes, an attack of fury and hatred that would cover over our terror, our powerlessness, the fear we had of arriving nowhere holding nothing. The hemlocks dripped their secret elixirs upon us, the moss was damp like secret hair and the rocks blackly glistened. We were never at home on the earth. Not for a minute. Love—call it love—made us forget this, dragged this knowledge down, put it under the ground awhile.*

So we got on the train and rode through the mountains where the pines were scrawny and we saw a vista opening under a cloud bank—above which was a sky shimmering turquoise—upon a valley with maize fields marching straight up the mountainside without terraces or contour plowing and shacks from which ribbons of smoke curled. The train seats were blue plastic. A woman wearing no shoes knelt before a small child, covering him with a flood of sweet-tempered language. An old man told me a story about his days as a traveling salesman for Porto Rico Coffee. Out the window refinery fires burned at the tops of small slender stacks. We got out in Quexirio and ate sandwiches from a basket a young woman carried on her arm. The air smelled of petrol, but under this smell was something astringent, and clean. The stacks of the local cathedral were serrated and along the roof-line buzzards perched. A teenage boy in expensive yellow clothes sat at the wheel of a Jaguar looking scornfully at the train. Some rich man's son.

We reboarded and I got high in the restroom and then Alice got high and we went out to the vestibule where a few people were smoking and taking the air and conversation lagged and then swelled again. We stood at the Dutch door looking out on the property, the vast half completed estate of Mexico, a landscape that whatever god fashioned it had quit work on and gone away—as she put it to a man leaning against the bulkhead smoking a thin cigar. *"Que?"* he said, insulted, and glared, but you had to allow for that in a foreign country, the usual secret grievances complicated by culture and language, it put extra stress on any situation. *"Imbécil!"* he said. I tried to soothe him, to appease the curl of scornful lip, but he would have none of it and pursued us back into the car shouting insults. *"Es loco,"* I said loudly with a stupid grin, making the nutcase sign next to my temple, but the people gave me the blank stare treatment, regulation so far in this country. We entered the next vestibule with this character trooping along behind, raving. I would have introduced him to the group out there, but he was on us so fast I didn't have time. A conductor was smoking in this place. *"Su excelencia,"* I said, "can you do something about this *asesino?* He is threatening us."

Not possible, his shrug said.

Alice said, "This must be that fatalistic, dark side of the Mexican character we hear so much about."

"The old Castilian/Aztec strain that embraces death like a lost brother. That the one you mean?"

"*Exactemente.*"

The man, standing right beside us, a little generator, chugged away at his insults. "That's good, " I said. "Keep it up, Chico."

"Puss face," Alice said, leaning across me.

"*Narcotizios,*" our pal said.

We were at that moment beyond shame, but not wholly beyond alarm. To Alice, I said, "Drugs."

"You're out of your mind," Alice said to him.

In the end he chased us off the train. A city, industrial hub, where manufacturing gates opened on men standing around heavily used automobiles. Factories faceless behind cream colored bricks. Roughed-up mountain backdrop and a gaseous atmosphere and streets paved with black, glassy asphalt. These replaced the railroad cars. It had started raining again.

"I thought this was supposed to be a desert country," Alice said.

"Estacion de camion?" I said to passersby.

Someone directed us, pointing with his cap.

We trudged through the rain carrying what was left of our luggage, our duffel bag and paper sacks. At a taco stand with outdoor stools we had supper. It was night, we just noticed. Fog or smoke swirled just above our heads. There was the heavy sound of traffic and the even heavier sound of deep-lunged machinery. The man behind the taco counter had gaps between his teeth. A small thing, but this had meaning to Alice, who suddenly began to spy her future. The one where she was snaggle-toothed and raving on a greasy couch, mother of a stillborn child. "Keep eating," I said.

"If I do, I'll vomit."

I don't know why, I was ravenous. Even if she was about to fall off a cliff I was going to keep eating. That's how it goes in the drug life, you're always betraying, for a *taco de jambon,* your real love. Nothing happened, she just walked off across the street. Somebody came up to her over there, a man, he was quick, like a hawk. What was it about her? I thought. She's not that beautiful. How close did you have to be to pick up on wit and dander? Watch out, I might say, to whomever approached, but the truth is some prefer sauce picante. The man, tall, leaned down to speak to her. Then recoiled, an appalled look on his face. Alice had probably offered to eviscerate his mother. Shown him, metaphorically speaking, a mouth full of roaches. Or maybe, and this was also true, she had scared him with her impuissance, her self-evisceration, maybe opened the sack and shown him the traduction and defenselessness at the bottom of her. This what you're looking for, bud? My heart in a bag?

So what next? The man moved off, was replaced by another man, some guy who with one finger—she was looking at a sign—tickled the back of her neck. She whirled and slugged him in the face. The man staggered back, clutching his nose.

"*Gracias,*" I said to the counterman and hurried across the street, stumbling, smelling in my nostrils the tomatillo sauce off my taco, wondering at that instant what I was doing in Mexico, no, what I was doing in life, what was this—life—what was going on?—and grabbed her by the arm. "You too?" she said. So, Alice: her hair rained on, cheeks wet, plasticky, the spite not really obscuring the despair in her face (no, the bafflement), the sharpness of her features under the yellow streetlight; she looked like a rat, bound for rat jail. The look she gave me in the midst of a string of curses, the underglance so familiar from the whole of our lives together, was frightened—it too so familiar—yet still assessing, checking the weather in my face, this look snapped out like a tongue of sparks, call it that, or was simply a window thrown open, some gallery window at the top of the house where the mistress, overwhelmed by grief, peered out for the thousandth time to see if her beloved had hove into sight.

"Oh, come on," I said. "Come off it and come on."

"You know the way?"

"To the bus station, yeah."

As it turned out I didn't know the way, so we wandered wet and gracelessly up and down streets into vertiginous districts and byways of humiliation and scorn, past little tin bodegas from which jukeboxes like singing neon elephants blared the broken-hearted sugary music we realized now had long ago become our theme song, all such music, calling to us in its sloppy, relentless way to come in and join up, drink among the *borrachos*, the Lowry characters and *perdicionistas* stranded a thousand feet down in the cave-ins of their lives, all that; so we did; and passed the night into day. Later we found ourselves asleep and then waking inside a large clay water pipe left at the edge of a hillside—"Like the woman," she said, cackling as she waked, "in that Steinbeck book (who was she?) who made a home in an abandoned boiler (who was she?)"—and returned to our journey after a wash at a spigot in an empty square, empty but for a young woman leading by the hand a small child who was oddly and wildly red-haired, and so onward, and reached the station at last where we boarded the early Tampico bus.

I caught glimpses of us in plate-glass windows as we passed through half-dressed villages where no new enterprise had started up in a generation. It was my favorite picture so far in Mexico: me in white shirtsleeves, sunburned, hair wild, my eyes unfathomable behind my shades peering out like a turtle *tranquilo,* beside me just visible a dark-haired woman statue brooding on its chisel scars. Bare plots of ground by little square houses, men on horseback, a chain gang in white leisure suits sinking picks into rocky earth, the men all linked together—these a few of the sights. We slept and fitfully waked and at a stop in a little town I didn't catch the name of I shot up in the antediluvian restroom of a café and got caught by an entering fellow passenger who gave me a look of disgust that frightened me.

"We have to go," I said, and she said, "That's what we are doing," and I said, "I mean hightail it," and she said, "You mean leave the bus?" and I said, "That's exactly what I mean, let's go." She looked at me with such disappointment, such sorrow, it was as if all the misfortune of our lives together was gathered in the look, but what could I do, I had been eviscerated myself. "Right now," I said. The drugs and the few crumpled bucks were in her purse, but everything else we simply left on board and walked off down a street that looked promising.

"You got a plan?" she said.

We'll disappear into the landscape, same plan as always, my heaven on earth, we'll integrate, merge, mingle, synthesize, coaxiate, mix, unite—that plan.

"Us?"

"I simply want to get quiet a little while."

"I see. You want to position yourself properly."

"Yes. Get the right run-up for the next trick."

She shook a bandanna out and tied it around her hair. "Is Mexico part of South America or North America?"

"Central America. Why?"

"But officially—there's no Central American continent—which is it?"

"North America, I guess."

"Good."

"Why?"

"I wouldn't want you to have been in jail on three continents, that's all."

"You are such a funny girl."

Under some trees—I didn't catch their names—the pavement ended; there was a line, an asphalt lip in the dust, and then there was pale cream-colored dirt and we came out from under the trees into an area of shack houses and bitter little poisoned yards and children in clothes made out of cornmeal sacks, all that, poverty, and kept walking until somebody's dog, or maybe a freelance dog, some friend probably of Delite's, some relative maybe, dashed out from behind a little adobe mansion and bit me in the back of the leg. I went down crying out—shocked, scared—and bounced back onto my feet, not quickly, without athleticism, but as fast as possible. "Fucking dog." I felt outraged, ridiculous, bereft. It's always too late to do anything. The dog, the cur, the coward, scurried away, a look on his face of abjectness, sullen resentment and some other curious thing—duress I guess it was, an oddly familiar abashed look.

I trudged on, limping, giving the limp some play, the surprise of the attack engrossing me, the shock. I stopped. "I think I have to sit down."

"Okay."

She helped me to a tree and I sat down on a buckled root.

"Did he hurt you?"

"It's emotional—spiritual."

"It would be for me too. I would take it personally, and everything else. It would panic me."

"Am I panicked?"

"Going by your face, I'd say a little, not much."

"I'm not stoic?"

"No, not that."

"That's good, I think."

"It's what we all hope for—straight up feeling."

"Would you find me a stick?"

"Of course."

She came up with one pretty quickly, a crooked piece of branch. With a weapon in hand I felt better and was able to continue the journey. That was what I was calling it. The journey. I didn't want to have to go into it, the meaning, the purpose, the destination. I was grateful she didn't press the issue. The houses, while there were still houses, made of tin—front, back, sides, and roof—slanted toward the western light. From windows peeled up on sticks people we would never know peered mutely out at us. They were all stoics, I could see that. "But you," Alice said, "you'll never be a stoic."

"Not with you in the world."

"I think it's natural with you—emotionalism."

"My ecumenical emotionalism."

The road curved around a hill and then the houses disappeared. It was sunny, but there were wet patches from the rain. Off in a field burros tethered to stakes stood waiting for whatever came next.

"Poor little strangled road," she said. A two tracker by now, dry grass in the center strip. We rounded another hill and beyond it a valley opened out, piney and scrubby, layered rocks, streaks of red clay, the ground under the bushes crumbling, slant gullies and rock faces, a path or two, a real wilderness configuration. A couple of Indians in their uniforms of loose white cloth passed, heading to town. They carried gray bundles swung over their backs, hobo Indians. We greeted them, but they didn't acknowledge us, didn't look our way. I was slightly hurt by this. "This the path to New Orleans?" I yelled to their retreating backs.

"Billy."

"Well, we're friendly."

"They have a different style."

Me standing in the track staring at their reserve that would be so easy to break down—they were small men—seeing it for what it was, taking it personally anyway. "I'm feeling a little choked up." Suddenly I was. It wasn't just the drugs or the location, the circumstances, it was the timing, the accumulation. I said this.

"In what way?"

I bent over, stared down at the path. The grass was dusty, the small white pebbles were dusty. "I wish I got along better with animals."

"I wish there were more of them around."

She went off on that for a while. A fantasy she had of kindly animals coming into the house at night, joining us in the bed, comforting us.

"They're not nobodies," I said.

"Who? The animals?"

"The Indians. It's not that."

"Of course not."

"No matter what they pretend." All around us one of those landscapes that looked empty unless you were born in it. "And I don't think it's a style."

"What do you think it is?"

"It's more like a desperate trick."

"Silence in the face of the unknown."

"Yeah, that trick."

The sky was vast, cloud decorated, not appalled by anything.

"What they don't realize is we're shy too. It's not really a cultural problem."

"No, it's not."

"Ah me. Rejected by animals and Indians. What's next?"

"Sophisticates?"

"We weren't a hit in the city either."

"Weren't we?"

The Indians were long gone; just like in America, we had the country to ourselves. To the right the view was clipped by the mountains, but to the left, rumpled and striding away, the landscape unrolled, prostrate all the way to the border. I smiled.

"What?"

There was a wonderful cleanliness about her at this moment. Her face was smooth and her brow clear and her deep-set eyes, peering out over the landscape, were bright, and her body was erect. Even her feet, in new sandals with a crisscross of tan straps, were clean, as if she'd walked not in mud or dust but in water.

"Stop a minute."

She did a little vaudeville halt, arms still churning. "Erk."

I sat down in grass beside the road, making a space for her in the weeds that smelled of chicory and lemons, drawing her down too. Pat, pat—right here beside me. "You are such a beautiful woman." She smiled, a slim smile, *retrouvée,* as they say, still the only, just the woman for me. I rose on my knees and began to massage her shoulders. She loved that. I haven't even mentioned how much she loved that. "Oh, goosey," she said, sweetly shuddering. I moved both hands up, pressing into the groove just under the neck cords, pushing up to the hollow where the cervical vertebrae entered the skull, pushing up into the skull, feeling the shape of it that always surprised me with its smallness, its neat delicacy and abrupt otherness, probing, rising onto the skull itself, the big lockout of the head, feeling the same old embarrassment I first experienced at age ten when I did this, embarrassed to be touching her head like this, feeling the hair and the scalp and the slippage of skin over the bony plates, somehow this a verboten area no one addressed in this way, even her maybe, so I felt the same old odd offending nature of it, the trapped little child feeling of it, as if she could surprise me in a forbidden, awe-struck act. She made her little animal noises of appreciation. "That is the best feeling."

I moved forthrightly down her back—she was less defenseless there—gripping my way along her shoulders and down her spine, troughing the muscle on either side of the backbone, its little spirules and starbursts, getting the re-hang of her body, reclaiming it for her, tilling the muddled soil, aerating it, reseeding. I was so interested in her.

"I know," she said.

"Did I speak?"

"Yes."

"I can't hold back with you around."

"No."

My hands ached so I stopped.

"That was perfect," she said.

I asked for the drugs and then I fixed us a little picker upper. We lay back in the grass and went to sleep. When we waked it was dark again. The stars were out, little minty bursts in the black.

"Well, what now?" she said.

I laughed. "I thought—when you opened your mouth—you were going to say something forceful. You really have changed."

"I'm not so decisive."

"Well, me either."

"So—which way?"

"Only the oneward—I mean the onward."

Hours later we stumbled into a village. Again the dogs took after us, yapping with those craven, stupid, resentful barks you get out in the country. Nobody came out of the houses, though. With the stick, I kept the hounds at bay, the spiral-tailed curs, there weren't many of them. Up at the cantina a light was on so we headed that way. They were serving—the kitchen was still open—hominy soup and beans and tortillas, just right for us. This was in the living room of a house converted to a café and bar. Behind the counter the other life of the family went on. Through an open door I could see children sleeping on pallets on the floor. In the front room a couple of cowboys drank beer. The place was smoky, as if some larger gathering had just ended. We wolfed the food, in the way you do sometimes in the trekking life, coming out of a stupor where you remember, as if it was a triumph in the distant extraordinary past, about food, about eating, and here it is again. "Delicious," I said. Smack, smack. Big puffs of hominy sunk like tombstones in the gray broth. I dredged them up and gobbled them down. "I love it in Mexico," she said. Now shadows like dark caterpillars had begun to work themselves out of her cheeks. Her neck was segmented and plasticky, like a neck that came in a box. A moment of rage then, my way of staving off terror. A flare snapped out and was gone. And then some quiet, ministerial work, her hand touching mine, the touch like a fire I had to bear up under, or like an acid, burning me. Tears came to my eyes. We looked at each other and then we were both crying, the tears unimpeded by anything we could bring to bear, trickling down our faces. The cowboys gave us covert glances, but this country's huge tenderness expressed itself in circumspection; nobody asked about our trouble.

Then a little girl, a twelve-year-old maybe, in a simple village outfit, brought over a couple of beers. "*No mas,*" I said, but she smiled and pushed on with the transaction, a gift. "*Gracias,*" said my wife, a sharp girl.

I said, "You know, all this is especially beautiful because if you saw us at this time you would not say look at that interesting couple, those swells, trekking in Old Mexico, you'd say oh look at those losers, or you'd say there but for fortune go I, or my my, or why don't they get jobs or what is this world coming to, or get away from me creeps, but you wouldn't say what a feat of artistry, of gallantry even, you wouldn't pick up on that at all probably, but that is what it is, not only our predicament but our lives, every stacked up minute come to this, this suffering and trouble, yet here we are, two artists in costume, staying in character to the end, bearing up under the whirlwind, under the flood, under pestilence and famine, all that, and still pushing on, like the Israelites fleeing Egypt, fleeing all the Egypts—which is what every one of us is doing in his or her own way don't you know? fleeing, leaving old Pharaoh behind and pushing on into the wilderness, where despite trial and trouble, the manna still falls from heaven and sweet water springs forth from the rock."

Charlie Smith

I didn't say this or anything close to it, but for a moment it seemed as if I did. Some beautiful way of putting things that flashed through my brain. I got up and went to the window and peered out, expecting an ambulance or a vision, something, expecting nothing, simply moving on the nerve, but it was too dark to make anything out. She started talking about a Humphrey Bogart movie, his breakthrough, *Petrified Forest,* where he played Duke Mantee the unrecoverable killer, and Leslie Howard played the poet, the type of man women love, a man like me maybe, but it wasn't this, not these similarities really that engaged her, but the setting, which was her way, she loved settings, the roadhouse in the desert, the people stranded without a vehicle, all that, what then.

"Trapped in a roadhouse at the end of time," she said. "It's like that for you and me every day."

That was certainly a way of looking at it, I agreed.

She called to the waitress, the daughter of the man who, fat and wearing an I Love New York T-shirt, sat with his skinny wife behind the plank that served as a counter, her hand up, a moment of intensity she wanted to celebrate. The girl scurried out carrying two more beers. "Oh, I didn't mean that. What is the word? *Gracias,*" she said again, "*lo suficiente, senorita.*" Said with a Mexican accent, a woman who spoke only Cuban Spanish. But what did she want? She couldn't remember.

And then for a time we were scared to go on, it looked that way, unsettled, aspiring to something we couldn't name, the old story, which included a replay on the beer call, getting drunk now, chatting into the night, the proprietor *dejo de hablar,* standing by, even after the cowboys left, the girl sleeping on a box in the corner and the wife scolding from deep in the house, ordering the husband to close up, but him not doing it. That was how it went. And Alice and I somniloquizing into the narrow hours, the compressed and evacuated time of darkest night, telling each other improbable stories about who we were. There was a list, a text, proofs of tender ministries in the harrowment of our experience, gestures of kindness and generosity on beaches and in gala house warmings among people who had never thought of us as friends, who didn't like us, flimsy proofs of our being well received, respected in the face of all the evidence to the contrary. The jokes at our expense, we agreed, were sometimes well meant. The ridicule was in fun. They were friends, all of them.

"Amigos." It was the proprietor. Indicating the situation, closing time hours past, the need for sleep, all that.

I made my hand gesture of acquiescence. "You *betamento*."

"Muy simpatico," Alice said, coming out with the Spanish as if it was her native tongue.

"You are really something," I said.

"Gracias por los cervezas," she said.

It turned out the beers weren't free. I had known this, somewhere in myself I had. Yet it was disappointing. The girl had mentioned it.

"No, no, it's all right," I said. Tears almost in my eyes. "Don't worry about it. We know you have to make a living." The proprietor indifferent to this chatter. Waiting for his money, which Alice fished from her purse.

"Our luggage," she said. "Our stake."

The man smiled a grim and heartless smile.

I nodded at him. "We have depths. And facets that would blind you."

He rubbed the bills between thumb and forefinger, probably a habitual gesture.

"You think we printed that money ourselves?" Alice said. "You think it's counterfeit?"

The man behind his mirthless smile said nothing.

Alice grinned her sly and merciless grin. "I could get it out of you if I wanted to. The truth, I mean. You would have to tell me. You think we're crooks?"

"*Gracias, campaneros,*" he said.

"Ah, yeah, well, sweet talk won't help."

Dawn, this day's version of it, had caught my eye. The bottom of the night sliced off, a quick diagonal cut left to right, leaving an opening through which a daffodil-colored sky poured. Just the other side of the screen door. I walked through this door into a day smelling of citrus and frying lard and garbage and some deep country odor, a wilderness effusion of cracked twigs, herbs, and such, that knocked me over. "Alice," I said. She had to tear herself away from the cantina owner who was about to take one in the face for the Better Business Bureau.

"Oh, what now?" she said. Life a non sequitur, a blank card.

She exited, stumbling a little, but holding herself with the estimable grace of one who had overcome a crippling mental and physical handicap through sheer willpower. "Oh, this place," she said. Straggle of little houses tiny as the circus cars containing a thousand clowns. The street winding among them, a few jacaranda trees blossoming, and—now we were walking—through gaps we could see other flowers—we hadn't noticed these yesterday—flowers triumphant you might say, little purple blossoms on bushes scattered everywhere. The dogs up and on duty. But me with my stick.

"Let's get out among them," she said, meaning the flowers.

"Then let's feel around for a place to sleep."

She cocked a look at me. Despite fatigue and continuous failure, drunkenness, still a zest in such a look. "How about a hug?"

I gave her one, deep dish hug, raised from the depths.

"Oh my soul," she said, and laughed as her backbone cracked. "Oof, oof." This one of her regular noises—of happiness—me drawing huge wages off the act, wages I'd never know what happened to. "Oh," she said, "I can't breathe."

"Me either."

Both of us in a dirt street bent over panting, the dogs yapping.

We came to a dip, a brushy patch, other bushes, willowy and bunched together, a dry streambed or sluiceway. "Okay?" I said.

She agreed, staggering by now.

Up the streambed and then a left into an opening among the bushes, a small clearing, sandy and sprinkled with seed husks, a place the wind wouldn't get to. We lay down and slept there.

Later we lost track of time and then found it again, but it was a stranger we didn't recognize. I was the one who gave out. I'd been concentrating on the path, the one track of it, its fringe of grass, the way it moved, each little sidestep somebody's idea, kicking off to the left to avoid a couple of boulders or to the right to draw closer to sandy ground, thinking of this, of some Indian pioneer deciding to send the path downhill at this particular angle, and then I thought maybe it wasn't his decision at all, maybe the path was only a deer track or a pig track and the humans were just following along. This thought was so dispiriting I had to sit down.

Then came a hiatus in which I concentrated on the extraordinary sight of a leaf print in the clean white sand at my feet—like a protofossil—and then Alice was speaking to me. "Yeah, I see," she said.

Collapse comes like this: first there's an internal staggerama, and then there's the zombie walk, and after that you're in the morgue poking a corpse with an electrical cord. Except the corpse is you. It is for a second blindingly urgent and then you simply don't give a shit. "Yeah," she said, "I see." She laughed, and in the laugh I heard her weariness.

"Get up," she said. "Let's go."

"I thought I just explained to you."

"You did. Get up."

I looked her in the face and I didn't care what she thought of me. It was a special moment. Fatigue had eliminated emotional involvement. She looked back and there was something sullen, squat, froglike in the look. A throwback look, fibrillated down to the simple vertebrates. Nothing personal in it at all. I could have said Save yourself or something else gallant, but only if this was a movie. In life I didn't say anything. "Okay," she said. She was that far ahead of me, still.

She shoved me, nudged me, getting down beside me to do it like a woman setting her back to the wheel, and then she got up and without preparing the victim, slapped me in the face.

"That didn't really hurt," I said.

This after a period of silence in which I pictured condors rising on heat threads into the blue.

She dragged at my clothes, trying to haul me back into the river of time. "Come on!"

I fell over into some shrubbery, only a foot or two. "I am appalled at you," I said. "I can't tell you how disappointed I am."

She sat down beside me. "I'm sorry."

"It's okay. You'd probably do different if you could."

"I'm not so sure about that." Then, "I'm afraid we won't get out of here."

"In a minute I'll try."

"You want something?'

She had a plastic water bottle slung by a piece of cord around her neck. She opened this and gave me a swig. The water was warm and had bits of leaf matter in it. "Crunchy," I said. There was a pause. We had been together twenty-five years at this point—since we were six—a fact that just then truly amazed me.

"Man," she said, "what a mess this all is."

I had a desire to take some drugs, but I didn't want to give in to it. It was amazing how whatever happened you still wanted a kicker. "This isn't as bad as it could get," I said.

"Let's not go into that."

"I can see you're determined to save yourself."

"I'm not really thinking on a large scale."

"You just want to go the next step. You're like that, I know."

"You're talkative for somebody who can't get going."

"I can get going. I just need a rest."

"I'm scared you're giving up."

"Well, that's a possibility."

"See? Get up."

"I'm just kidding. I gave up years ago." She took a long pull on the water bottle. "You want to go easy on that stuff," I said.

"The desert has touched your brain."

"Mauled it you mean. No touch about it."

"I think we should stop joking."

"It's my way. Joke or scream, one or the other."

"Why don't you squeeze that scream and get the hell onto your feet."

"That's certainly a suggestion I will take under advisement."

"Do you want a nap?"

"I can always use a nap."

She sat down, snugged against me. We were backed by frilly bushes, like scrubby poincianas, but they weren't that. The place smelled of urine.

"Somebody else has been here," she said.

"It's the highway of life."

"No, I mean you smell that?"

"Didn't I already mention it?"

We slept, a sleep in which I was open-eyed much of the time, as we both were, like the apocryphal babies parents' talk about who stay awake for years preparing revenge. Our baby. Our crippled, brain-damaged, blind baby we would spend the rest of our lives blaming ourselves for. I felt as if I was floating above the situation and then with sorrow found myself down in the grubbiness of it, the ditch of fucked-upness, the dyspeptic sense of myself as unprepared for this or anything else. Yet I couldn't move. I couldn't shake myself out of the sleep or lethargy even though my eyes were wide-open. I couldn't even turn my head. Slowly the sky revealed itself to my consciousness, or my dream, if that was what I was having. It was a soft, tender blue, a curved sheet of blue, wholly ministerial. A small propeller airplane chugged across it. The sound was faint, almost not there. I imagined this was the Messiah returning to earth, by way of a Cessna. I gave a faint, welcoming wave. Then Alice was shaking me, almost gently, telling me to get up and come on.

"There're people up here," she said.

"That's obvious."

"No, I mean actual people."

"Police?"

"No. Campers."

"Can we go around them?"

"No. Let's talk to them."

It was a two-man outfit with motorcycle and sidecar, camped under an awning strung from the branches of a big thorny tree. We came around the bend in the trail and there they were, sitting on the ground eating a snack. A big man in a vest and a smaller, thin man in a white shirt cutting slices of cheese off a big sweaty wheel. "Why, welcome, friends," the big man said, getting up. His belly was vast atop spindly legs. He also had a huge head and crinkly brassy hair mashed up under a captain's hat. He threw his arm out as if throwing open the gate to a great estate and invited us to join them. We had been on light rations for some time, though with the drugs we didn't notice that much, but now I realized how hungry I was. The thin man, who smiled a thin but chipper smile, slid pie slices of cheese onto paper plates and passed them to us. The big man, sinking like a house to his knees, said, "No matter where you are in the world—wilderness or Third World country—you have to keep up the good life."

"Salsa?" the thin man said, offering a bottle.

"I am Sir Wiloughby Creech and this is Garesh," the big man said.

The man didn't have any kind of English accent, but he had a manner that was all noblesse oblige and a certain remoteness I had always associated in my mind with the aristocracy. They said they had been traveling through Mexico, looking at ruins. "We are on the trail now of one of the Seven Lost Cities," he said.

"This is the road to it?" Alice said.

"According to our sources," Sir Wiloughby said. He glanced at his companion. "Bread, Mr. G?"

Garesh rooted through a pack and pulled out a plastic bag of tortillas.

"We are fans of the native cuisine," Wiloughby said.

"Us too," Alice said.

"We have no refried beans, however," he said.

"We're not picky," I said.

"Pooty," Garesh snickered.

"That either."

While we ate, Sir Wiloughby questioned us on our history, background, all that, a touch of questioning, skimming lightly. We had no story prepared, it was typical of us, we hadn't even thought of one.

"Something told us to get off the train," Alice said.

"Federales?" Garesh said.

"Not exactly."

"It's all right," Wiloughby said. "We understand. These pestilential police down here. Even a saint would not be able to help running afoul of them."

"We decided to head cross-country," I said.

"Much the better plan. No other way really to get to know the place. I detest all those tourists fortified in their steel-ribbed hotels and resorts. Frightened of the people who have spent hundreds of years building up a culture in this place. It's idiotic."

Alice said, "How far away is your lost city?"

"One day, two maybe," Garesh said, scratching his head with the butt of the fork he was using to cut off chunks of cheese.

"We can't actually be sure," Sir W said. "Our map isn't accurate as to mileage. But we're close."

"How long have you been looking?'

"Months. We've been on the trail for months."

"Out here?" Alice said. It was the same tan-colored landscape, nothing new about it, maybe snow off on the crest of a distant mountain, it was hard to tell, snow or a patch of diamonds spilled out of heaven.

"We have a questing spirit," Garesh said fastidiously.

"We arrived at Salina Cruz by ship from Mozambique—a long tedious journey," Sir W said. "After several years in Africa. There too we searched for treasure."

"And found it," Garesh said.

"Yes. Only to be hornswoggled out it of by rebel forces. Africa is not a stable place," he said.

"We had to flee for our lives," Garesh said. "Through the jungle. You ever have to flee through a jungle?"

"Not yet."

"It's like that dream where you're running through glue."

"Cement," Sir Wiloughby said.

"What is that?"

"Cement. In the dream you run through cement."

"I run through glue. I don't know about you, but I run through glue."

"Have it your way." He scowled at Garesh.

"Yeah, fine. As I was saying. We had to flee through the jungle. You can't imagine what it was like. Roots, vines, bugs." He shuddered. "You come to a town and everything's shut down. I mean a big town, a city. Everything's shut down."

"There's ruin for you," Sir W said.

"Yeah. A ruin. That the people have just gone on living in. No electricity, holes in the road, all the stores closed, no kids going to school, nothing working, like some ghost town with the ghosts still in it, everybody throwing the slops out in the street. Their idea of commerce is some old woman by the road selling three peppers. Three peppers. Jesus."

"We barely got out with our lives."

"Yeah. And it wasn't the first—or the last—time either."

"I used to live in Indonesia," I said.

"There's another wreck of a country," Sir W said.

"You have to stay away from those islands," Garesh said. "There's just not enough room to maneuver on an island."

"We had to run for it too."

"And where is there to flee to? On an island?" Garesh said.

"Except the open sea," Sir W put in.

"Yeah," said Garesh. "And that's where the real trouble starts."

"Then it all depends on the speed of your craft," Sir W said.

"Not enough variables for my taste," Garesh concluded, smacking his lips.

Alice then, back on her feet, patting the seat of the big Indian bike, said, "Does this motorcycle run?"

"It's in perfect shape, my dear," Sir W said. "We are however suffering—at the moment—from a lack of—petrol."

"Someone didn't keep his eye on the situation," Garesh said.

"This is an equal partnership," Sir W said without looking at his companion. He got smoothly to his feet, graceful for a big man, up in a flow of flesh. It was a pleasure to watch. "I'm feeling fully human," he said, patting his chest with both hands. "Filled out to the limits of my faculties."

Alice said, "I wonder how many people this motorcycle could carry?"

"This motorcycle?" Garesh said.

"You think it could carry four?" The sidecar was like a big black teardrop.

"This motorcycle," Sir W said, "could carry a football team."

"European football—soccer," Garesh said.

"But first we have to get it to a petrol station."

"That will take a little doing," Garesh explained.

"Will it roll?" I said.

"Certainly," Sir W said. "As I said, this machine is in perfect shape. It will roll from here to kingdom come."

"That's where we're headed," Alice said.

"Har, har," Sir W said. He pulled a large compass from one of the side pockets of his fatigue pants and studied it. He looked up with a foolish, over-expressive grin, as if in the compass's face he had discovered a photograph of someone he longed to see. "We're right on the true line of our quest," he said. "We're not one degree off."

"Time to break camp," Garesh said.

We pitched right in helping, in our way, stumbling around, picking up items and setting them back down. They had a couple of laundry bags they put things into, food in one, the camping gear in another. These bags they attached to the rear sides of the motorcycle. "This where it goes?" I said, pushing the packet of paper plates into the food bag.

"Either one," Garesh said.

"Woof," I said. "This is exhausting work."

He looked at me. "You don't look as healthy as you might."

"Foot travel's worn me down."

"We could tell you stories about hiking," Sir W said. "We have spent many a day on foot, my friend."

"Months," Garesh said.

"What happened to your African treasure?" Alice said.

"Exactly what always happens, my dear," Sir W said. "Squandered on safe passage."

"When you have to buy your way out," Garesh said, "they will really charge you."

"Look at the Congo," Sir W said, touching the side of his nose.

"And Uganda," said Garesh. "And the C.A.R."

"And don't forget Liberia."

"Who could forget Liberia?" Garesh shuddered so hard his hands shook. Then he grinned, a monkeyish, fetching grin of delight. He patted the rump of the loaded conveyance. "Off we go."

We had to push the vehicle. The four of us struggled with it, keeping it on its way down the trail, which was not built for motorcycles with sidecars. If they had petrol, Sir W said, they could travel cross-country, but without it they were restricted to the trail. There were smooth, easy passages and then others like construction projects, hazards such as you find in a narrow river where logs and boulders blocked the stream. We became mired in sand, we had to trek far out of the way to get around some leviathanic outcrop, we had to shove the contraption uphill. There was something ennobling about it, I thought, some semblance to it of honest labor that appealed to me, but only for a short while.

"Look," I said, "we need to step off over here to do some business."

Alice glanced up from her shoes, which she was staring at as if instructions were written on them.

"What's that?" Sir W said. "Oh yes, of course."

We headed off into a welter of bushes, picking our way into a little safety zone off there in the wilderness, and split a charge. We were in a rooty, leafy place where sunlight entered as if through a web made of gold coins. Once the drug got into us, we experienced all the qualities that made life a little bit of heaven. Our dreams merged with Mexico and converted everything in it to paradise. Things went on that way for some time, softly, without complaints from any inhabitants. Then slowly we roused, came gradually up as one would come up on a good day out of fields of golden wheat. The child? Yes, yes. In the mornings Alice vomited, but that wasn't unusual in the drug life.

Strange, she said, how deeply she felt the child. How deeply in her.

We have to do something about it, I said.

Like what? she said, testily.

I don't mean that. Get shelter—something.

That is my plan, she said.

Okay, I said.

We walked awhile and came to a clearing where some rocks scattered on the ground reminded us of the skulls Alice had collected in the house on Meridien Street in South Beach. It amazed us how far we had come from that time and place. "Anything you do," she said, "—any first step—begins the chain of obligation and trouble." I could have said exactly the same thing, and told her so. "But then," I said, "the opposite is also true." We didn't get carried away by this recantation, or any other. Our predicament—fundless, witless, pregnant in the wilderness—had our attention. If we had been geniuses we could have gone on then calmly with the tasks of genius. Our task was to get back to the path, eventually. We accomplished this to find the treasure hunters gone.

After that we pushed on along the trail and soon enough came up on them. They were struggling with the motorcycle, but things were going slightly better since they were headed downhill.

"We thought you might have found another route," Sir W said.

"Not us," Alice said.

We wrestled through the afternoon with the bike and camped that night by a small stream that wound away under some creosote bushes.

Three Delays

"It is amazing," Sir W said, "how the desert is actually a Garden of Eden. There's more growing here than in some gardens in Kent."

"Is that where you're from?" I said.

He smiled. "That's a question one need not answer in the questing life. Nothing personal."

"We're actually from Miami," Alice said. "In case you were wondering."

We settled in under the stars again, on a blanket the treasure hunters gave us, and it was cold, as it had been on the other nights, and it was difficult to sleep, as it had been on the other nights too. "What are we doing?" Alice said.

This question was charged with strange forebodings. "I'd prefer not to answer that."

"Well, how are we going to get out of this?"

"That too I'd prefer not to comment on."

"Is there any point or subject you're willing to address?"

"Astronomy. I'm willing to talk about astronomy."

"Okay. What do the stars say about our chances of coming out of this alive?"

"That's astrology."

"Why don't we talk about how it could have been different," she said almost brightly.

"What could?"

"Everything. Why don't we talk about that?"

"I wish we knew sign language," I said, touching her.

"I do too."

"That's something I always wished for."

"Is it possible to shout in sign language?"

"Sure." I sat up and began to make large swooping gestures.

"What are you doing?"

"I'm shouting in sign language."

She said, "You know the problem with finding your true love at such a young age and sticking to him—you know what it is?"

"I know several problems."

"But the one I'm thinking of?"

"What?"

"That there won't be other lovers to talk about it to."

"That's important to you?"

"No, it's just something that came into my mind. You won't talk about the big questions, so I thought of it."

"You got your eye out for a change?"

"No."

"Actually, I know what you mean."

"People tell their later lovers about the earlier lovers. Those stories. About my manic-depressive boyfriend. Or my boyfriend the alfalfa farmer. Or my one-armed manslaughterer boyfriend. They make their lives into a special adventure."

"You want a manslaughterer ex-boyfriend?"

"No. I already have the boyfriend I want."

"Well, you're on an adventure."

"I want more than just the one."

I looked straight up. The stars were a trail of dust across the sky, dust that might someday form itself into something, some way of expressing things. Or maybe only dust that had already been used up, dust from the pulverization of worlds no one remembered anything about. I wished I was more careful in my life, more respectful, got more the hang of things. There were a hundred areas I could go into, at any time, areas where I fell short of expectations. Somehow there always seemed to be a great deal of information I didn't possess.

I put my hand on Alice's skin, the skin of her arm that was smooth and nearly hairless. She moved slightly, acknowledging me, and then her hand touched mine, rubbed the back of it for just a second. It was a harmonious, loving touch, something simple, like a prayer. I wasn't going to get away with anything, I didn't have any nutty ideas about that. I said, "We've got a lot of adventures going."

"Hmm."

"Don't you think?"

She was nearly asleep, but she hauled herself back into the world for questioning. "I'm way on past that."

"Where are you?"

"With my troubles."

"Which ones?"

"My obsessive thoughts."

"Ah, sweetie."

"I was thinking about those bug-eyed goldfish you see in pet shops. I saw one fish once—it was down at Stancy's, on 27th Street—he had eyes like big bulging marbles. And one of them was hanging by a string—"

"I thought you were thinking about the baby."

Silence, starlight. "Maybe I have that wrong."

I pushed up on an elbow. "What do you mean by that?"

"Maybe I misapprehended the situation."

"Did you do something?"

"No."

"Has your period started?"

"No. It's still delayed."

"So what have you misapprehended?"

"I was thinking about the baby. I picture him at the railroad station. He's got a ticket, but he doesn't want to get on the train."

"The baby?"

"I see him at the newsstand and then at the restaurant, our baby, sitting in a booth drinking coffee."

"That's a precocious baby."

"It's a picture."

"Sure."

"I don't want him to have to get on the train until you and I are living right."

"Honey, I'm afraid we'll be too old for babies by then."

"I've had enough of your joking."

"I'm sorry."

"If we had a baby now you'd just stand around and mock him."

"I'd only do it to keep from crying."

"Well, that's not good enough for me."

She said this sadly, without any fever in the reproach. Her hand lifted and she waved it slowly into and out of the shadow of a leafy tree between us and part of the sky, her hand crossing into the black and out again into brightness.

"I'm sorry."

Her hand made smooth erasing motions across the sky. "When you mock somebody it's a kind of stealing. It's hard enough to believe in yourself. And if you mock, you take that away from them."

"Didn't we already meet at the party, honey?"

"What?"

"You sound like you're talking to somebody you just got introduced to."

"It's the little things that make a marriage, Billy."

"Yes, I know."

"We should try to be more kindly toward each other. This can't always be some fiery love affair, you know. Not forever."

"*Tene mal genio.*"

"What is that?"

"Having a hot temper."

"I'm tired of the fireworks."

I leaned over so I could see her. "I don't know what I'm tired of. Maybe what I'm tired of doesn't have anything to do with that. Maybe fireworks are the small potatoes of tiredness accelerators."

A momentary silence. "You mean there are other things we don't even think of, don't you?"

"Yes."

"You're always like that."

"Life's always like that."

"Life's however you think it is."

"That's just some strategic comment, right?"

"Well, I have moments when things are very simple for me. I cherish those moments."

"How do you want to begin—in our life of quietude?"

"By living proper lives."

"You mean with jobs?"

"If it comes to that. But more I mean living with kindness. I want us to be kind, responsible people. Drug free too."

"I knew you'd mention that."

"I've never mentioned that before in my life."

"But I knew you'd get to it. They always do."

"Who's they?"

"The reformers."

"I'm no reformer. I'd like us to lie in bed together reading. Something like that."

"With the baby between us."

"I'd love it."

"That baby, we could probably send him out for a six pack."

"He'll be a quiet, generous spirited baby."

"He'll be jumpy—like us."

The wave recedes and you feel the sand being pulled out from under your feet. This was what I was thinking. I thought: This is where the story's supposed to start, at this point. What you do after this. Not this, but what you do after.

"It's like the title of a song I've been trying to remember," she said.

"What is?"

"The baby."

Despite everything, she saw herself as a fortunate person. Someone born under a lucky star. You wouldn't think a person angry all the time would think of herself that way, but she did. I saw myself that way too. *Yeah,* we'd say, sweating and scared and shaking after a fight, breathing hard, maybe this time gone too far, maybe only one more step between us and the knives we'd picked up, but we'd stand there, in the house we'd lost to debt or out on Meridien Street under a gumbo-limbo tree or outside her stepmother's house with the silverware in a bag, and we'd say it to each other, a couple of nutcases: *We're really lucky*—and the nuttiest thing, the nuttiest thing we kept coming back to no matter what, was we meant it. It was one of the fundamental sure things that bound us together.

"I can't even hear myself talking," I said.

"You remember Oscar Juarez?"

"Sure. Oscar *Suarez*. From high school."

"I saw Oscar the day before we left for the mountains, when we were so beat down, just before you kidnapped me and that poor little big-headed child. He's a shoe salesman in one of those discount stores on Valencia Street. I went in there for some reason, some confusion I thought at the time, some scared, muddled thing making me, like this was my future I had to get used to—bewilderment in discount shoe stores—something that had me, made me go in, and there he was. He was so glad to see me."

"I remember how sweet Oscar was. He brought empanadas to school, that his mother made."

"He was working in the store. I saw him—I was so rattled—and all at once I thought, I am all right. Because Oscar is here. He showed me around and helped me, he was so kind. And I thought, maybe I will always be all right—because Oscar is here. Not just here, but everywhere. Maybe Oscar will be in all the discount shoe stores of my future. And then I knew he was, I knew he always would be. I was so happy."

"And then you got in the car and a year later wound up lying pregnant on the floor of a desert in Mexico."

Charlie Smith

"Well, Billy, something always happens."

Something old and worn to a shine began to rise from the darkness of myself. It had risen before and I had always put a hand out to stop it. I did that now too. I said, "If you left me, I would fade out like a dying Indian tribe. I'd disappear like the ivory-billed woodpecker. They'd see me, near the end, standing down on Calle Cinquo wearing one of your nightgowns, explaining things to the traffic."

It was true. When she had slipped away I was so demoralized I began believing in astrology and fortune-telling. I took to the small comforts of confoundment. The stargazers and the fortune-tellers all said she loved me. They said we would find our happiness. I had them write it down, I paid them to. At night, in my alien motel in some town in Louisiana, or California or Illinois—later even in New York—I would put on her peach-colored nightgown—the one she left hanging in the closet at home—and sit at the table behind the closed curtains, and I would take out these slips of paper upon which some soothsayer had written her guarantee that we would find each other again, that we would find each other and reassemble our love and everything would be all right, and I would read these promises over, read them as if they were my Bible or the sacred constitution of my country.

I said, "I think I am going to be a longer time getting to the new life than you." The words didn't matter—I didn't know what I was saying—just the sound of them carried the truth between us.

But she was asleep by then.

We pushed and pulled the bike down the trail that descended through stubby pine trees to a shallow valley that ran several miles along a damp, trickling river. The riverbed had pools in it the color of sand. The air was cool and then warm and it smelled of the herbaceous world. There was one place, a flat area near some willows by the river where the air smelled of honeysuckle, maybe a vine nearby, some familiar, recrudescent presence, and we took a break there, Alice and I did, to sniff the air. The smell was faint, drifting, unstable, but we both got some of it in our nostrils. An old half fallen in adobe was tucked in among the willows. She ran her fingers over the sheared-off top of a wall, picking at the clay, getting it under her fingernails, showing me the orange rims, and then we went into the main room, a clay-floored room with nothing in it but sand. We gave each other one of our looks, of complicity and fortune. Her crazy, misconceived, so-called lucky life was in her face. “Hey,” she said, as if she had just come back from somewhere. “Hey,” I said. We danced around in the house, stumbling and calling it dancing, rocking in our tracks, lurching one way or another, catching each other’s hands, grinning and losing the grins, scuffing in the sand. Probably we would come back there and live, we said, fix the place up, raise a family of new Mexicans in Old Mexico.

After a time the trail widened again into a road and then split or was joined by another road, both of them double tracks, faint but with that look of threadbare permanence human scrawls have out in the desert. The *busquedoros* paused to take their bearings and then continued along the track we were on.

“I sense a breakthrough,” Sir Will said.

“Break through your ass,” Garesh said smirking.

At mid-afternoon we came to a village. Straggled cluster of houses, with cantina and this time a church. The thatch-roofed church was made of wood poles raised in front to form the outline of a wall topped by a steeple. The cantina was a grocery store with a bar off on one side and, through a large opening behind it, a filling station. The filling station part consisted of a hydraulic tire jack, a few patched tires, some cans of oil stacked against the wall, and a table upon which were gallon glass jars of gasoline. "Eureka," said Sir Will, softly rubbing his hands together.

"It's evaporate," Garesh said, sniffing the jars. We had followed them into the shop and stood blinking in the dimness.

"Far better than nothing," Sir Will said.

"We'll see."

We wandered around the village in a slightly muddled way, stopping in the middle of the dirt street to peer into darkened houses where women in full length dresses slapped tortillas down on grill plates. A child scraped at a bone with a knife blade wrapped in a rag. An old man sitting in a kitchen chair out in the yard ate green olives from a can. It was a regular place, the village, behind the harmony the usual bitterness and fear, you could tell that, but it looked good to us. We were passing under a camphor tree when Alice began cramping up. "I knew this was going to happen," she said.

I ushered her over to a chair somebody had left out in their little clay yard and sat her down in it. Well, here comes the Mexico rejection, I thought, the *disenteria,* and said this, but she claimed that wasn't it.

"So what's going on? You have any idea?"

"Sure," she said, "I do."

I got down on my knees and held her around the waist.

"Not so tight," she said.

Down the street Sir Will and Garesh stood by the motorcycle as a young man in jeans squatted down looking at the motor. He reached in, his dark fingers sinking deep, as into a body, and then he looked up at Sir Will. "This one is a mystery to me," he said, and Garesh squatted down and looked into the innards and then he probed with a finger. I was talking to Alice all the time, completely aware of her, but also aware of the village around us and of the sweep of mountains stretching away on the other side of the valley, the pale colors of the hills and the rocks like abstract sculptures and the faint green shadowing in the hollows where the rain had brought life to the country, all that, the mechanic too, who went away and came back carrying something in a teacup, which he poured carefully into the engine. Alice leaned down over her knees. "Oh, Billy," she said. "I have to lie down." The mechanic stood up, smiled sweetly and indicated Garesh should go ahead. Garesh got on the bike and kicked it, but the bike didn't fire. He did this a couple of times. The bike coughed and spat and hacked and fell silent. The sound of it brought the other world back.

"Oh, Billy." I lifted her off the chair and lay her on the ground. "Take me somewhere," she said.

I picked her up and crossed the street with her to the church and lay her down on a bench. She curled up on her side, clenching her body around herself like a little child refusing to do its business, determined, moaning, I thought she moaned. "Yes, yes," she said. "I'm moaning." Then, "Jesus, Billy." Then louder: "JESUS, BILLY." Inside her body the baby had turned to fire, that's what she meant.

The pit, the seed, the tiny duplication suddenly conflagrated. "AH JESUS GOD." Little on fire god, ready to eject.

I saw the blood on her jeans. A streak, just red enough to be red, in the crease of her ass—and turned her on her back to get the jeans off her, but she wouldn't let me. She pressed her hands hard between her legs and gripped them with her thighs.

"Al," I said, "you've got to relax."

It seemed really important to get her jeans off. I fought her for them. She cried out, moaning and crying, and held onto the waist, but the pain was too great for her and she couldn't stop me. I could see she wanted to press everything against herself, hold it tight to keep what was inside from getting out. It was all instinct and pain. "Help us," I cried. "Somebody come here and help us! *Socorro!*"

Her panties, torn and dirty, were soaked in the crotch. I pulled these off too as she wailed at me, grasping them with one hand as she pushed against herself with the other. "Oh fucking God," she said.

I caught some of the blood in my hands and for a second I thought I could just shove it back up into her. It was slimy and dark and had a yellowish tinge, a gray tinge, and I thought *Somewhere in this mess is our little baby*—a nub swirling around, little sad heart beating—and I was struck with grief like a blow. I was crying trying to find him, find her, rubbing the slickness between my fingers crazily, trying to feel the piece of grit that was our child, but I couldn't locate it.

I pressed her wadded panties up against her. The blood kept coming. It was hard to keep her on the bench so I picked her up and laid her on the packed earth floor, the bloody floor of abnegation and obedience. "Not on the ground," she cried. I took my shirt off and put it under her. Mice scurried in the thatch above our heads, vermin as usual between us and heaven. She began to speak then, in an angry, sarcastic voice, her eyes staring up into the roof. "Sure, sure, sure," she said.

Then, in a way that seemed vague and completely random, totally purposeless, people began to appear, not rushing in, no emergency squad, but drifting, stopping by, the strangers we traveled with, and villagers, *viejas*, amigos we hadn't met yet, who knew who else. The women figured out what was going on. Two of them approached and as I raised my bloody hands to strike them, they knelt beside Alice and began to minister to her. Things telescoped in, and then out. Someone produced a poultice made of tobacco—it smelled like tobacco—and pressed this against her. "You have to stop the leak," I said. The women pushed me away, impersonally and firmly.

I got to my feet and it felt as if I was leaving my flooded home. There was blood on me, all over my arms and my pants and speckling my chest. I dropped back to my knees and I would have shoved in between the women, but something stopped me. I lay down on the floor so I could see her from there. Her face was turned up to the ceiling and her eyes were closed. She was pale and there was a crinkling around her eyelids, as if the substance had drained out of them. I broke into sobs, big explosive sobs I couldn't control. One of the women reached behind her and without looking shoved me, hit me. I crawled a step away and crouched on my knees crying. Then I thought, *We have to get out of here*. This was an important idea. I jumped up and went straight to the treasure hunters. "Does the bike work?"

Yes, it did.

"We have to get to a real town."

"Yes, of course you do," Sir Will said.

But the bike wouldn't carry a football team, nor four, only three. "Garesh, you drive them," Sir W said. "I will remain here."

There was no other working vehicle in the town, none expected before tomorrow.

Garesh said, "You think we ought to move her?"

Sir Will looked at me. "Now, what do you think?"

"I don't know. I want Alice to get some help."

"Of course. But then these women—they must have quite a bit of experience with this sort of thing."

"This isn't 'this sort of thing.' This is some different thing."

"You're exactly right. Fire up the conveyance, Mr. G."

"You want to go right now?" Garesh said.

"Yes. Now."

"Maybe they can get the bleeding stopped."

I ran back to the church, waded in among the women, thinking of Jesus in the temple tossing money changers behind him like curs, but I didn't have the moral grit for that and there was no way to tell what the right thing to do was. She lay on her back, quiet now, white in the face, her eyes closed. Something scary was in her face, something lost and vacant, and I saw she was going to die. Then a woman, a round-faced young woman in a blue dress, looked up at me and smiled. She was probably the Indian Virgin Mary, and I thought, *What is she doing here*, a woman as busy as she must be, but her smile was sweet and reassuring. I sat down on a bench. Then Alice unsqueezed her eyes and looked around, looking for me, and then she found me. "I'm here," I said. A feral unfamiliar spooky tenderness was in her eyes, a ridiculous, wasted, pure tenderness, probably what she was born with—miscarriage like a spiritual archaeology—and she touched me with this and extended her hand. I got up and took her hand and it was like taking a hand offered through the door of a train that is leaving the country you have known all your life. *I never had you at all*, I thought, *not one part of you, not for a minute*. Then the light ghosted out of her eyes.

Other women were all around me; I shoved back against them, physically, hitting someone; then others, men close by, hauled me out by my arms. "I just want to be straight with you," I said. They sat me down on a bench outside the door and someone brought some homemade liquor to drink, mescal I think, in a speckled gourd. I took a sip. "This is what got us in trouble before," I said, and laughed a maniacal laugh that made sense to me but put detached looks in the faces of the men. The motorcycle outside the door was running. Garesh sat astride it. I got up and entered the afternoon, the open-ended and evacuated Mexican afternoon, patted Garesh on the shoulder and crossed the street into the cantina where I ordered tequila. I came to the door and said, "I'll be back in a minute."

"Probably that's a better idea," Sir Will said.

Later several of us were out in the desert in a little adobe compound that may have been the farmstead Alice and I had come on earlier. There was a bar, and some dusty women in loose clothes sat at it, and there were a few cowboys hanging around and everyone seemed amazed to be alive. I mentioned this to the man next to me and he grunted out words of a false bonhomie. Fiends grumbled in the corners, re-evaluating their lives. Nobody in the place knew anything about what was going on outside their own heads, this was clear to me. A woman took off her shirt and danced on the bar, but later I decided this had only been in my mind. I stepped out back and swayed above a gulch in which dark leafy trees surged in the wind. Whatever was out in space looking this way could still see me, I knew that. Then I got in a fight with a small square man, Mr. Solid Block, and was beaten to the punch. I didn't mind anything that happened to me. I rode in the back of a pickup truck to a ranchero far out in the night, some outpost set against the dark, and lay in a barn buried under horse blankets. Someone came out and ministered to me, a woman I didn't recognize. I made vague and transparently self-justifying remarks about the whole situation. Later I got up, insulted someone and took a beating. I wandered down to the river and lay by a pool waiting for elemental business to come upon me, but nothing happened.

When Alice's ghost found me I was asleep on a couch in a room behind the kitchen of a house I didn't recognize. She was much better, she said, though sad.

"I think I'm going to change how I do things," she said.

"Yeah, well, honey," I said. "It's just one more fantasy."

She looked steadily at me for a minute. Her face was pale and her eyes were lighter than I remembered. She said, "I think we ought to split up for a while."

"Okay," I said.

Then she went away.

Three Delays

This occurred in a back room in a village or town, one of the dribble of settlements outside Tampico, which had been close by all the time. The police apprehended me there, choking on stupid thoughts, and they took me to a hospital. For a while I lay in a bed thrashing my legs as if I was running. I remembered this clearly later on the plane home to Miami.

Charlie Smith